"Wha[illegible] be[illegible] [illegible]his shot into space [illegible] [illegible]eper, broader, scarier, and more intellectually stimulating journey with every book."

—*Booklist* (starred review) on the Galahad series

"Part space opera, part mystery, the story draws readers in from the beginning with well-placed hooks, plenty of suspense, and a strong premise."

—*School Library Journal* on *The Comet's Curse*

"Grabs readers' attention with the very first page and never lets go. . . . Both a mystery and an adventure, combining a solid cast of characters with humor, pathos, growing pains, and just a hint of romance, this opener bodes well for the remainder of the series."

—*Kirkus Reviews* on *The Comet's Curse*

"A wonderful mix of science fiction and mystery."

—*Children's Literature* on *The Comet's Curse*

"Sci-fi fans will enjoy Testa's spare Asimovian plot, but even those leery of the genre will appreciate how each chapter alternates to the past to further flesh out our protagonists. Stealing the show is the *Galahad*'s mischievous central computer, Roc, who speaks directly to the readers as he acts as a Greek chorus."

—*Booklist* on *The Comet's Curse*

"Dom Testa has invented a highly original world packed with surprise, insight, and heart. Read it with your whole family, and enjoy the ride."

—*The Denver Post*

"I truly, honestly loved the first two books in this series and think I have a new obsession to burn through. . . . I *love* our diverse cast of crew members aboard the *Galahad*, both in terms of their widely different personalities and with regard to their backgrounds and ethnicities. . . . Absolutely recommended."

—*The Book Smugglers*

The Galahad Archives by Dom Testa

The Galahad Archives Book One: Leaving Earth
The Comet's Curse and The Web of Titan

The Galahad Archives Book Two: Into Deep Space
The Cassini Code and The Dark Zone

The Galahad Archives Book Three: A New Life
Cosmic Storm and The Galahad Legacy

The GALAHAD ARCHIVES
BOOK ONE

Leaving Earth

Dom Testa

TOR TEEN
A Tom Doherty Associates Book
New York

This is a work of fiction. All of the characters, organizations, and events portrayed in these novels are either products of the author's imagination or are used fictitiously.

THE GALAHAD ARCHIVES BOOK ONE: LEAVING EARTH

Edited by Susan Chang

A Tor Teen Book
Published by Tom Doherty Associates, LLC
175 Fifth Avenue
New York, NY 10010

www.tor-forge.com

ISBN 978-0-7653-8339-6 (trade paperback)

The Comet's Curse was originally published by Profound Impact Group as *Galahad 1: The Comet's Curse*

The Web of Titan was originally published by Profound Impact Group as *Galahad 2: The Web of Titan*

First Edition: February 2016

Printed in the United States of America

0 9 8 7 6 5 4 3 2 1

Contents

The Comet's Curse
Dom Testa

To Donald and Mary Testa.
Thanks for the books, always.

What you're holding right now is kind of like the old-fashioned message in a bottle. Poor souls who found themselves shipwrecked on an island would jot down a message—usually pretty simple: HELP!—seal it inside a bottle and toss it into the ocean. The idea being that someone would scoop it out of the water and come to the rescue. The idea also being that this someone would not be a bloodthirsty pirate looking for possible treasure that might've washed up onshore with our poor little castaway.

Except this message in a bottle is different in a couple of ways. First, it's a story and not just a simple HELP! It's full of pretty interesting characters, not the least of which is me, thank you very much. They face danger, deal with issues like fear and jealousy and loneliness—things that make me glad I'm not human—and learn as much about themselves as they do one another.

And although there aren't any true pirates, there are some fairly nasty types.

Second, our heroes aren't on your typical island. This island is made of steel, the size of a shopping mall, and the sea is a sea of stars. They're stranded, sure; but they chose to be stranded here because their only other choice was . . . well, their only other choice was a gruesome death.

Okay, easy decision.

Castaways who have been rescued years later often say that—strange but true—in some respects it's hard to leave the island. It's become home, a place of security in an ocean of fear. And although deep down they want to be rescued, part of them wants to remain nestled within their cocoon. An observer might think the island a prison; the shipwreck survivor sees it as a haven. It's all perspective.

This story has its own island, and its own castaways.

I guess I'm the bottle. The message—or story—is sealed inside me.

I like that responsibility. And I don't think anyone else is better qualified to tell the tale.

So let's get on with it. Let's pull the stopper out of the bottle and see what pours out. I'll try not to interrupt (much), but sometimes I just can't help myself.

1

There are few sights more beautiful. For all of the spectacular sunsets along a beach, or vivid rainbows arcing over a mist-covered forest, or high mountain pastures exploding with wildflowers, nothing could compare to this. This embraced every breathtaking scene. Mother Earth, in all of her supreme glory, spinning in a showcase of wonder. No picture, no television image, no movie scene could ever do her justice. From two hundred miles up it's spellbinding, hypnotic.

Which made saying good-bye even more difficult.

The ship sat still and silent in the cold, airless vacuum of space. It was a massive vessel, but against the backdrop of the planet below it appeared small, a child teetering at the feet of a parent, preparing to take its first steps. Soft, twinkling lights at the edges helped to define the shape which could not easily be described. Portions of it were boxy, others rectangular, with several curves and angles that seemed awkward. To an untrained eye it appeared as if it had simply been thrown together from leftover parts. In a way, that was true.

Its dark, grayish blue surface was speckled by hundreds of small windows. Two hundred fifty-one pairs of eyes peered out, eyes mostly wet with tears, getting a final glimpse of home. Two hundred fifty-one colonists sealed inside, and not one over the age of sixteen.

Their thoughts and feelings contained a single thread: each envisioned family members two hundred miles below, grouped together outside, staring up into the sky. Some would be shielding their eyes from the glare of the sun, unable to see the ship but knowing that it was up there, somewhere. Others, on the dark side of the planet, would be sifting through the maze of stars, hoping to pick out the quiet flicker of light, pointing, embracing, crying.

Many were too ill and unable to leave their beds, but were likely gazing out their own windows, not wanting to loosen the emotional grip on their son or daughter so far away.

The day filled with both hope and dread had arrived.

With a slight shudder, the ship came to life. It began to push away from the space station where it had been magnetically tethered for two years. Inside the giant steel shell there was no sensation of movement other than the image of the orbiting station gradually sliding past the windows. That was enough to impress upon the passengers that the voyage had begun.

Galahad had launched.

After a few moments Triana Martell turned away from one of the windows and, with a silent sigh, began to walk away. Unlike her fellow shipmates' eyes, her eyes remained dry, unable, it seemed, to cry anymore.

"Hey, Tree," she heard a voice call out behind her. "Don't you want to watch?"

"You won't notice anything," she said over her shoulder. "It might be hours before you can tell any difference in the size. We won't have enough speed for a while."

"Yeah," came another voice, "but you won't ever see it again. Don't you want to say good-bye?"

Triana slipped around a corner of the well-lit hallway, and when she answered it was mostly to herself. "I've already said my good-byes."

With the entire crew's attention focused on the outside view, she had the corridor to herself, and appreciated it.

2

The discovery of a new comet usually didn't cause much reaction. Astronomers, both professional and amateur, would make a fuss, but the general population was rather immune to the excitement. What was one more in a catalog of hundreds?

Yet this one was different. A rogue, named Comet Bhaktul after the amateur astronomer who had first spotted the fuzzy glow amid the backdrop of stars, was slicing its way towards the sun, and its path would cross just in front of Earth. Several early reports had sparked a brief panic when some astronomers wondered if the comet might actually be on a collision course, possibly impacting in the North Atlantic ocean. But soon it was confirmed that Earth would instead coast through the comet's tail, an event that might cause some glorious nighttime light shows, but nothing more.

Dr. Wallace Zimmer would later recall that, for two days, the sunsets were indeed brilliant. The horizon appeared to be on fire, with dark shafts of red light streaking upward. Comet Bhaktul's particles at least provided a romantic setting for couples in love.

The truth was that the particles were providing much more than that. They were delivering a death sentence to mankind. No one knew it at the time. Earth swung through the remains of

Bhaktul and continued on its path around the sun, and life went on without missing a beat.

Seven months later Dr. Zimmer pulled up a news report on the vidscreen in his office in Northern California. Just a blurb, really, but as a scientist he was immediately interested.

The story called it an outbreak of a new flu strain. Not just a handful of cases, but dozens, and—this was what amazed Zimmer the most—not concentrated in one region. Most flu variations began in one part of the world and spread. Not this time. These reports were scattered across the globe, and yet the symptoms were all the same.

The lungs were being attacked, it seemed. The only difference was how rapidly the illness progressed. According to the news story, some people slowly fell into the clutches of this new disease, with breathing difficulties and intense bouts of coughing that might last weeks or months. Others were hit more quickly, with paralysis of the lungs that brought on death in a matter of days.

Dr. Zimmer looked at the clock and considered the time difference on the East Coast. Then he switched the vidscreen to phone mode and dialed up his friend at the Centers for Disease Control in Georgia.

"Not much else to tell you besides what you've read," Elise Metzer said to him. "Of course, hundreds of people have called claiming that it's some form of germ warfare, and demanding an antidote. The conspiracy nuts are having a field day with this."

"What about other symptoms?" Zimmer said.

"Well, we know that it's attacking the lungs. Most every case begins with coughing, and eventually coughing up blood. But there's also been a few mentions of blotchy skin, some hair loss even. That's probably just each individual body reacting differently."

Elise scowled and added, "I don't think the immune systems have any idea what's going on, and they might each be interpreting the attacking agent in a different way."

"Well," Zimmer said, "with only a few dozen cases I can see why there's no real data yet."

"Uh . . ." came the reply from Elise. "That story is a little outdated now."

"What does that mean?"

"It means that this morning I heard there are already over a thousand cases, and growing."

Dr. Zimmer sat stunned. Before he could speak Elise ended the conversation by predicting that the next news report he heard would be front page and screaming.

3

I used to live in a box. Okay, maybe "live" is a poor choice. I existed in a box. And not a very big box, either. Just a small, metal container with patch bays, microchips and a mother of a motherboard. If you ask me about my first memory, I could tell you, but you'd start to nod off pretty quickly. It's not an exciting tale: a string of ones and zeroes, a few equations, a bazillion lines of code, and a ridiculous sound that signaled when I was "online." The ridiculous sound would have to go. Roy was a genius, but he had no sense of hip at all. Just look at his clothes.

Roy Orzini put me together. He used to say that I was "his baby." If that's true, then I've got a few hundred siblings because Roy put an awful lot of computers together. My oldest brother was born in a cluttered bedroom just after Roy's tenth birthday, and the little genius has been popping them out ever since.

I'll spare you the false modesty, however, and tell you right up front that I'm the masterpiece. The other kids were pretty good; a few of them have worked on the moon, Mars and a couple of research stations around Jupiter and Saturn. But I got the big assignment, the biggest ever. Roy's pretty proud, and that feels good. I'm proud of him, too.

These days I'm not in that cramped metal box anymore. I'm everywhere within the greatest sailing ship ever built, sailing to the stars.

I like the new digs. I like the crew I'm sailing with. I like the challenge.

Roy called me OC-3323. Remember, Roy is a geek.
Everyone else calls me Roc.

Triana sat at the desk in her room and placed a glass of water next to the picture of her dad. She bit her lower lip as images of her home in Colorado flashed through her mind, images of both joy and sadness. Thoughts of her dad came as well, which brought a burst of pain.

She glanced at the few personal items that dotted the room. There was little that an outsider could have learned about the teenage girl from these clues. Essentials, really. One exception was the picture. Her dad, grinning that grin of his, the one that confessed to a bit of troublemaking behind the outer shell of responsibility. In the picture Triana was still twelve, riding piggyback on him, her arms clutched around his muscular chest, the tip of her head peering out from behind. His broad shoulders concealed all but the top of her head and her eyes—those bright green, questioning eyes. Any grin of her own was concealed, but the eyes conveyed infinite happiness.

Picking up the picture, she ran her finger around the outline of her dad's face, looking into his eyes. She wanted to talk with him. All of the fun times they had shared, all of the adventures . . . and yet it was simple conversation with him that she missed the most.

Triana finally tore her gaze away from the photo and returned her attention to the open journal on the desk. Most people had given up writing by hand in favor of punching a keyboard, but Triana felt more of a connection the old-fashioned way. There was something about watching the words flow from her hand that gave vent to personal feelings she could never imagine on a computer. With items such as notebooks rationed severely, she allowed herself only a few paragraphs a day. It was enough for her.

She scanned the last few lines she had written, then took up her pen.

It's funny how such a turbulent world can look so peaceful from space. I know there are storms raging, wars being fought (still), fires burning, people dying . . . and yet it's as if it's all been sealed inside a bottle, and the stopper keeps all the sound inside. And me out. Earth is subsiding, slowly for now, but will soon become smaller and smaller until it disappears. Forever.

She dated the entry then closed the notebook. After one more glance at her dad's picture she called out to the computer.

"Roc, how are we doing?"

"Are you kidding?" came the reply from the screen. "Did you see that launch? Backed it right out of there without scraping the sides of the space station or anything. I'm sure you meant to congratulate me, but in all the excitement it slipped your mind. Congratulate me later."

Triana had trained with Roc for more than a year, and knew better than to spar with him.

She said, "I'm assuming that means everything is running just fine. And the crew?"

"Well, that's another story. Heart rates are very high, respiration is above normal—"

"Yeah. They're crying, Roc. They're leaving home," Triana said, picking up the water glass. She took a long drink, then added, "By the end of the day things should start to calm down."

Roc was silent for a moment, then answered in a voice so lifelike it was hard to believe it came from a machine. "Although you might not believe it, Tree, I understand what you're feeling. And I'm truly sorry for what had to happen."

Triana couldn't think of anything to say to this. "Thanks" didn't sound right.

Roc waited another minute, then spoke again. "I hate to give you something to worry about already, but . . ."

"But what?" Triana said.

"Well, I wear a lot of hats on this trip, right? Keep the air fresh, keep the gravity close to Earth normal, dim the lights, take out the trash, sweep up at the end of the day—"

"What's the problem, Roc?"

"The problem is with the ship's life-energy readings. They don't add up, and to an incredibly efficient being like myself that is . . . well, it's just not acceptable. They're screwy, and that will make me crazy, Tree. Crazy, do you hear me?"

Triana sat up. "What do you mean? What's wrong with the readings?"

"They're not balanced. As you know, every person on this spacecraft has been accounted for and cataloged by their energy output. Glad I didn't have that job. Booorrrriiiiinnnngggg."

"Roc—"

"Anyway, for a journey of five years it's critical to maintain balanced levels in order to sustain food and life-support systems. You know that."

"Yeah, so what's the problem?"

"Well, there must have been a mistake made before launch. Some of the measurements were either inaccurate or . . ."

Roc paused, as if thinking to himself.

"Or else what?" Triana said. "*Could* they have made a mistake before we left?"

"It's possible, but . . . no, I don't think so. I mean, c'mon, it's so vital to the mission, I don't believe Dr. Zimmer or his little elves could have botched that."

Triana smiled at the vidscreen. "I know you're referring to it as 'the mission' for our sake, and I appreciate it, Roc. No sense in us locking ourselves in this can for five years and calling it a 'desperate last chance' or something. But about this imbalance: what else could it be?"

"Hmm. The experts say that stress could do it. Of course, the experts also said that Barry Bonds's home run record would never be broken, and don't they look stupid now. But with all of the stress this crew has been under, I suppose it might knock things out of whack a little bit. I'll check it out again in a day or two."

Triana nodded agreement. She rose from the chair and stretched, her arms crossing over her head. Leaning back, her long dark hair fell almost to her waist. It was unlikely, she thought, that there had been very many ship commanders in history like her. But because this was no ordinary ship—and such a unique moment in history—convention had gone out the window. A sixteen-year-old girl was in charge. She sighed and turned to leave.

"Tree," said the computer voice from the screen.

"Yes?"

"Not to get too sappy or anything, but I think it is a mission. I think it's the most spectacular mission of all time."

Triana smiled again and walked out.

"Remember, you're supposed to congratulate me later for that very smooth launch," Roc said to the empty room.

4

It was a university professor in Japan who solved the mystery.

Nine months after Earth's close call with Comet Bhaktul, and two months after the initial reports of illness, he announced the bad news.

Samples collected from the atmosphere during the pass through the comet's tail revealed microscopic particles unlike anything ever seen before. Something in the gaseous exhaust of Bhaktul had contaminated the planet, and its effect on human beings was fast . . . and fatal.

In almost no time the spread of the flulike disease had escalated at a frightening pace. Scientists calculated that perhaps 10 percent of the population had already begun to show the physical signs, and tens of thousands more were pouring into hospitals every day. It didn't matter where you were. No place on Earth was spared.

News reports began to include stories of people abandoning their homes, their careers, and setting off for a secluded place in the mountains, or to a remote location in the South Pacific. They assumed that the disease was spread from person to person, and if they left densely populated areas they would decrease their chance of becoming infected. The problem was that you couldn't hide. Bhaktul had saturated the atmosphere, and human contact had nothing whatsoever to do with it. Nobody, it seemed, was excluded: rich, poor, black, white, male, female . . . this disease did not discriminate.

That was hard for many people to accept, because now lifestyle wasn't important, there were no risk factors to avoid, and no vaccination was on the horizon. And when the most advanced medical teams on the planet threw up their hands in frustration, it sent a shock wave of fear throughout the civilized world.

Strangely, the illness seemed to spare the children. In fact, there were only a few scattered reports from around the world that mentioned a child suffering from any of the symptoms. Test after test was run on both children and adults, but without any definite answers. All that could be determined was that kids were immune to the disorder . . . until they reached the age of eighteen or nineteen.

If you were older than eighteen, Bhaktul was coming for you.

There were many more questions than answers. What were these particles in the comet's wake that triggered the sickness? Why were some people affected sooner than others? Why not young people?

And how much longer did Earth have?

That question, in particular, led to millions of workers walking off their jobs. The attitude was "Why should I bother? We're all going to die anyway." Society began to break down into two groups: those who wanted to fight, and those who preferred to just give up and wither away.

On the West Coast of the United States, a group of scientists led by Dr. Wallace Zimmer reached the conclusion that an alternate plan should be developed in case no protective vaccination was found. Their plan was radical . . . and not what anyone expected.

"We believe," Dr. Zimmer said, "that there are only two possible measures capable of sparing the human race."

The faces of hundreds of colleagues looked up at him on the stage with wide-eyed wonder. For the past two days they had listened to a parade of experts discuss their ideas on defeating the disease. Now, at the close of the scientific assembly, they were emotionally drained and hopeful for something that could work. All morning there had been a buzz that Dr. Zimmer, a well-respected researcher and scientist from California, would be delivering a speech that would electrify the attendees. Now he had their rapt attention.

His large frame dominated the podium. He stood exactly an inch over six feet, with wide shoulders and a stout neck. Although the lines on his face gave evidence of his fifty-plus years of age, his hair had remained full, even while losing the battle with the gray. He adjusted his glasses and looked out over the crowd.

"The first solution would be to remove or filter the deadly particles from Earth's atmosphere," he said. "As you are aware, we have barely identified the particles responsible for the destruction, and it could be many, many years before we could even begin to understand how to contain them." He looked over the rim of his glasses at the packed auditorium. "By that time, it would be too late."

The silence was grim. Dr. Zimmer leaned forward on the podium. "The other idea is extremely radical, but at least a possible alternative. After careful discussion, we feel that if we can't take the deadly organisms away from our kids . . . we should get the kids away from them."

A gradual low hum of chatter spread throughout the assembled scientists and world leaders. Finally, as the room began to quiet down, a biology professor from Michigan stood up and addressed Dr. Zimmer. "Are you suggesting that we build some sort of bubble or domed environment and stash a group of young people? They'd have to come out sometime, you know."

"Yes, that's right, and to doom the race to living out its existence in small, cramped domes would be brutal," agreed Dr. Zimmer. "We believe the planet's atmosphere could remain contaminated for possibly hundreds of years. For that matter, it might have been altered permanently. People living in a dome might never be able to leave."

"Then what are you saying, Dr. Zimmer?"

"A spacecraft. Or, to be more precise, a lifeboat."

This time the room exploded in sound. Dozens of individual arguments broke out spontaneously throughout the auditorium, and Dr. Zimmer simply folded his arms and waited. After a few minutes order was restored, and a woman from Texas rose to be heard.

"Dr. Zimmer, you're not serious, are you? A spaceship?"

"Absolutely serious, madam. A spaceship. But unlike any other craft ever assembled. I mentioned the word 'lifeboat' and that's exactly what it would be: a haven for protecting the lives of several hundred kids."

A tall, thin man in the middle of the room stood up, and Zimmer recognized him immediately. It was Tyler Scofield, a former colleague and now the science department head at a major university.

"And what would you do with this lifeboat?" Scofield said. "Let them orbit around Earth forever? That's no different than sealing them up in domes."

"No, sir," Dr. Zimmer said. "The ship would be automatically piloted to another world. One that we feel has the best chance of sustaining the crew when they arrive."

Once again the room erupted in sound as the various members of the scientific community argued aloud. During the chaos Tyler Scofield remained calm and quiet, looking up at Zimmer. When the uproar had died back down, Scofield addressed the stage again.

"I'm curious about your plan, Dr. Zimmer. A spaceship, which we don't have, filled with children, who have no idea how to operate the ship, on a mission to a planet or planets that we have yet to identify as suitable for human life. On the surface one would think that you have not put much thought into this. But, of course, I'm sure you have."

Dr. Zimmer smiled at his old friend. If the thinly veiled criticism had come from anyone else he might have been irritated.

But Zimmer and Scofield had worked together for many years, and although they now rarely saw each other, they still communicated from time to time and provided whatever help they could with the other's projects.

"Yes," Zimmer said, "on the surface it would indeed look like a desperate, maybe even hopeless, shot."

The audience sat quietly, listening. Tyler Scofield sat down and waited to hear what his old friend proposed.

"I will concede that the word 'desperate' applies. Is there anyone in this room who is not desperate to find a solution to the Bhaktul problem? Every account that I have heard has stated that our planet has five, maybe six years, before almost one hundred percent of the adult population is affected. I would say that leaves us in a desperate spot.

"But I take exception to the word 'hopeless.' For the same reasons I just mentioned, I feel that this is our best hope. Will we find a cure for Bhaktul Disease within the next three to five years? I hope we do. Will we be able to protect the lives of our children and ensure that they never have to cope with this disease? I hope we can. But I'm also a practical man. What if—as awful as it may be to imagine—what if we don't find a cure? What if, after five years, we discover that we have wasted an opportunity during those many years to save something of our civilization? To at least give mankind the chance to survive somewhere else?"

Dr. Zimmer paused and gazed around at the solemn faces looking up at him. "Do we choose to give up? Do we throw up our hands and say, 'Well, we gave it our best shot,' and just go quietly? Or do we try to save a portion of our history, our heritage, our achievements? I can't believe that our species would fight, scratch and claw its way up to this level, to have achieved so much, to have overcome so many improbable odds, just to give up now. It's not our way. It's not what we owe to our ancestors who toiled so hard. And it's not the legacy that we owe our children.

"So, I will never say that this is 'hopeless.' It's anything but hopeless, Tyler. It's the embodiment of hope."

The room remained silent for a few moments, an uncomfortable break that left Zimmer wondering if he had gotten through to anyone. Then, in the back of the room, one person began slowly applauding. Then, another. Soon, more than half the room was applauding, with many people rising to their feet to cheer him on. Zimmer felt a wave of relief spread over him, and nodded to the assembly, thanking them.

Yet not everyone was cheering. Looking across the sea of faces, Dr. Zimmer could see more than a handful of scientists shaking their heads, talking quietly to each other and gesturing at the platform. He had not won everyone over to his side, nor did he expect to. Most troubling to Zimmer, on a personal level, was that Tyler Scofield remained seated, arms crossed, a grim look upon his face. He was not among the believers, apparently. After a minute Scofield rose from his chair and walked out of the auditorium. Zimmer's heart sank briefly, but within moments his attention refocused on his plan.

Questions came at him with lightning speed. Details were being demanded and he had few to offer. When pressed for at least a rough concept of the mission, Dr. Zimmer explained the idea of a ship that could hold at least two hundred kids, separated into compartments that contained housing sections, agricultural domes, recreation facilities, and more. No, it would not be an easy project, but mankind had run out of time. There was no room left to bicker about cost, either. There could be no price put on the plan or the objective. It had to be done, and it had to be done immediately.

The most pressing need, it turned out, was to design a computer brain that would act as pilot, teacher and adviser.

5

Let's get one thing straight, all right? I'm not a babysitter. These kids are way too old and way too smart to need that. If I'm looking over their shoulders from time to time, it's not to baby them; I just happen to be a natural snoop. A nosy computer, Roy called me. Okay, maybe I listen in sometimes when I should be busy testing the filtering system in the water recycling tanks, but is that interesting? Is it? No, it isn't.

Gap Lee is interesting. A good-looking kid, too. Good athlete. Funny when he wants to be. Smart. Oh, and the coolest of the Council members.

Yes, I do know cool when I see it. Who do you think you're dealing with here?

Anyway, Gap is cool, and one of my personal favorites on the ship. Just don't tell anyone I told you that. Anyone, okay? Especially Gap.

Gap Lee waited in the Conference Room, as usual the first to arrive for the meeting. He sat at one end of the table and looked out the window. It faced away from Earth, a frame filled with stars. Gap was again struck by how many you could see outside the Earth's atmosphere. "One of you is our new home," *Galahad*'s Head of Engineering said to the stars. "I hope you're ready for us."

He turned his thoughts to his old home, the one that was falling away at thousands of miles per hour. Soon that speed would increase greatly, propelled by the power of the sun's nuclear wind. After shining down on Gap for all sixteen years of his life, the sun now pushed him away, like a mother bird shoving a chick out of the nest, urging it to take wing and begin its new life.

Gap thought of his early childhood in China, raised as an only child by his parents, both of whom were college professors. An early interest in gymnastics was fueled by his training with a former Olympic champion. By age ten he was being groomed for his own championship run and had caught the eye of China's Olympic committee.

Then, on his eleventh birthday, his parents startled him by announcing that they had accepted an invitation to teach at a prestigious school in America. Within three weeks the family had packed up and relocated to Northern California, settling into a modest home amid large trees and rolling hills. And although his parents were concerned about the abrupt change in his life, Gap immediately accepted the challenge of meeting new people and forming new friendships. It seemed everyone warmed to him as soon as they met him. A year of intense language lessons quickly made him fluent in English, and his school grades reflected his obvious intellect. He kept up his training with gymnastics, keeping an eye on that Olympic future.

The only thing that drove Gap's parents crazy was his affection for Airboarding. Even though he wore a helmet and pads, spills were inevitable. His mother would cringe every time he walked in the door with another scrape, bruise or torn clothing. "You would sacrifice a chance at a gymnastics world record, just for this silly hobby?" she would cry. Gap would always smile, melting her heart, and then kiss her lightly on the cheek. "Gymnastics is what keeps me from really getting hurt," he would assure her. "You should see the other kids." She would wring her hands and walk away, chattering in her mother tongue.

Gap sighed now, alone in the room, thinking of his mother. He remembered her tortured look when he was selected for the *Galahad* mission. He also recalled, however, the look of pride on her face when Dr. Zimmer tapped him for a spot on the Council. While home during his last visit before the launch, Gap sat with his mother on their porch, watching the rain gently fall. The air had smelled so good, so full of life, the way it always smelled during a rainstorm.

"You were born to do great things, Gap," she had told him that day. "I always knew that. But your father and I were sure it would come through athletic achievements, not like this." She had taken his hand and looked deep into his eyes. "Destiny does not always take the path we expect," she said. "Yours has taken a change we could never have expected. But you were ready. And we are so very proud of you."

Gap had slipped his hand out of hers and tightly wrapped both arms around his mother. He still remembered the words she had whispered in his ear during that embrace.

"Your path will change again and again. Do not curse the change; embrace it, and make it work for you."

Gap had begun to sob quietly, the sound masked by the falling rain. His tears, slowly trickling down his face, mixed with the raindrops blown onto the porch by a gust of wind.

He often thought about that moment, and had vowed never to forget his mother's advice: embrace change. As he stared out at the multitude of stars, he knew that change would be a regular occurrence over the next five years of his life. Was he ready to embrace it?

"Do you smell smoke?" came the voice behind him, the colorful British accent breaking his trance.

Turning, he looked up into the face of Channy Oakland, the ship's Activities/Nutrition Director. Channy was dressed in red shorts and a T-shirt the color of a sunrise (Gap wasn't sure he had ever seen her in anything but T-shirts). Her dark skin glistened; her hair was pulled back in a long braid.

"Smoke?" Gap said. He sniffed the air a couple of times, then looked at Channy. "I don't smell anything."

"Well, with you so deep in thought a moment ago I felt sure

I could smell something burning," Channy said with a grin. She patted Gap on the shoulder, then sat down next to him.

"Oh, you're quite a comedian," he said. He liked Channy, but so did everyone else. It hadn't taken very long for her to capture the "most popular" tag among the crew. One of two fifteen-year-olds on the Council, she brought a sense of humor to the sometimes bleak atmosphere.

"Where did you watch the launch?" she said, biting into an energy block she had brought to the Conference Room.

"The large observation window outside the Dining Hall. I only stayed for a while, though. It got kinda depressing, I thought."

"Hmm. Well, I'm going back in a little while. Lita said when the night side rolls around you can see lightning all over the place. I guess there's something like a hundred storms going on at any one time, and the lightning is really cool. Wanna go?"

Gap thought about the lightning for a moment, which only made him think again about the rain back home. He shrugged and said, "I don't know, Channy. Maybe. I might be kinda busy."

"Oh yeah, lots of work to do, and we'll only have five years to get it done," Channy said sarcastically. "You're goofy."

"You love it."

She crossed her arms, a smug expression painted on her face. "Speaking of love," she began mysteriously, "would you agree that it's a little early in the game for shipboard romance?"

Gap leaned back and put his feet up on the table. He wanted to laugh at the way Channy wasted no time in jumping into her favorite activity: gossip. Coming from anyone else it might have disturbed him, but somehow Channy Oakland was able to get away with it. He grinned at her, running a hand through his short black hair, which, as usual, was sticking straight up.

"So your radar has already picked up romance? We only launched this morning."

"Oh, I think this has been smoldering for a while," Channy said with a whisper, as if the room were filled with eavesdroppers, when in fact they were all alone. This made Gap grin even more, and he whispered right back to her.

"I am *so* intrigued. Tell me more, Inspector. Just how long has it been *smoldering*?"

Channy leaned over to him. "I think since the moment you met Triana."

The grin on his face disappeared instantly. "What? What are you talking about?"

Now it was Channy's turn to smile. She got up and walked over to the freshwater dispenser. "Can I get you something to drink?"

Gap pulled his feet down from the table and glanced around to make sure no one had entered the Conference Room. "What are you talking about?" he said again, a little more forcefully.

"Oh, come on," she said. "I doubt anyone else has noticed a thing, but you can't get anything past me." She walked back over to the table holding a couple of small plastic cups of water. "You can joke all you want about my 'radar,' but it's true, you know. I can sniff it out faster than anyone." She batted her eyes at him. "It's the romantic in me."

With that, she sighed playfully and handed him one of the cups.

Gap started to speak, stopped, then started again. "I don't know what you think you see," he said, "but you can forget about it. I like Triana as much as the next person—"

"But not very many people *do,*" Channy said. "I'm not saying it's her fault; she's just very quiet and very private. She hasn't made too many friends, you know."

Gap toyed with his cup of water. "Her job isn't to win any popularity contests. She's got a lot of pressure on her right now. She's sixteen years old and suddenly in charge of two hundred fifty . . . well, two hundred fifty pilgrims, I guess you could say. I wouldn't want that kind of responsibility."

"Yes, you would," Channy said. "You might not have pushed

for the job, but I'll bet you would have taken it in a flash. You know the rest of us kind of assume you're second in command. That's got to be a nice feeling."

"There is no 'second in command.' That's why we have the Council."

"Yeah, whatever. You know what I'm talking about, though. And don't get me wrong, Gap. I like Triana, too. I know she's under a lot of pressure, and I also know this is her way of handling it. Fine. But think about this . . ."

She paused for effect. "If I've noticed the way you look at her and talk to her, don't you think she has, too?"

Gap didn't answer. He began to roll the cup back and forth in his hands.

Suddenly Channy felt uncomfortable. "Don't worry, Romeo," she said. "Your secret is safe with me."

"What secret is that, Channy?" came a voice from the door. Gap and Channy both looked up to see Lita Marques stroll into the room alongside Triana. Lita's black eyes and Latin American skin spoke of her upbringing in Mexico. Flashing a smile that only added to her already beautiful face, she grabbed the chair opposite Channy while Triana went to the end of the table across from Gap.

"You guys already have secrets?" Lita said.

"Yeah, I promised Gap I wouldn't tell, but I guess it's okay for you to know, Lita," Channy said sweetly. Gap stared at her without breathing.

"See, Gap was a little disappointed that you couldn't see the lines between the states and countries from space. You know, like you see on a map?" Channy winked at Lita, then shot a sly glance at Gap, who was slowly exhaling.

Lita winked back at her and fiddled with the red ribbon holding back her hair. "Fine, don't tell me your little secret. I'll just start keeping a few from you."

Channy rolled her eyes. "Oh, please. You couldn't keep a secret if your life depended on it."

Triana interrupted their exchange. "Where's Bon? It's about time to get started."

Gap looked down the table at her. "We're still a few minutes early. He's probably holed up in his crops. You know, nothing about him screams 'farmer,' but he sure loves that work."

"Well, let's face it, it gives him a chance to be by himself a lot, and that suits Bon just fine," Channy said. "He would love this trip even more if he didn't have to share the ship with two hundred fifty other people."

Triana felt a little uncomfortable with the topic. Although she knew that Channy was only kidding around, she was well aware of the negative vibes that Bon could radiate. In her mind there was no sense fanning those flames so early in the trip. She was relieved when Lita changed the subject.

"Word is getting around that most of the major cities in the world are going to fire up every light they have tonight as a kind of farewell sign to us. Should be quite a sight when the dark side rolls around again."

"One of us should watch it with Gap," Channy said, "so we can explain that whole line thing to him again."

Gap rolled his eyes. "You know, I am so looking forward to five years of your act."

Triana didn't respond. She was ready to leave Earth behind quickly. A light show meant nothing to her, other than more pain, a prolonging of the grief caused by the separation. She knew the rest of the crew felt as if they were celebrities of a sort, grand heroes being given a spectacular send-off. Chewing on her lip, she glanced up to see Bon Hartsfield walk in.

Bon, his light-colored hair hanging down almost to his shoulders, immediately walked to the water dispenser after only nodding at the assembled group. The scowl on his face was familiar by now, in contrast to the bright, toothy smile of Lita. He was a year younger than Triana, the same age as Channy, though his severe expression always painted him older. Strong, if not as muscular as Gap, his Scandinavian good looks were smothered by what appeared to be a permanent sour mood. His pale blue eyes, like ice, reflected little warmth. He took his seat, and Triana looked at the faces surrounding her.

"Lita," she said, "I know you've already had your hands full down at Sick House. Thanks for breaking away for this meeting."

"Well, I only have about twenty minutes," Lita said. "We're swamped with messages from the crew, lots of stomachaches, things like that. Nerves, if you ask me."

Triana nodded. "I thought that might happen after the initial buzz wore off."

"Yeah," Lita said. "Anyway, I left Alexa in charge for the time being. She knows what she's doing, but I don't want to leave her alone too long. It's crazy right now."

Bon finally spoke up. "Well, why don't we get started? I've got work to do."

It took an effort, but Triana managed to keep irritation from registering on her face, even though her green eyes blazed. Things had always been tense between her and Bon Hartsfield, from as early as she could remember. There was no question of his abilities to run the Agricultural Department, or any other department for that matter. Yet his personality had clashed with hers, sometimes leaving her to wonder if he might even be removed from his position on the Council prior to the launch. But it had never happened.

"We've all got work to do," Triana said slowly. "Because this is our first postlaunch meeting, I think it's important that we spend a few minutes to make sure everyone is caught up and feels good about what's planned for each department."

Gap jumped in, helping diffuse the tension. "You all probably know this, but I'll tell you anyway. The ship is running fine. No surprises, no breakdowns. Now that we're clear of the space station and out of Earth's orbit we'll start to really pick up speed. The solar sails are almost completely deployed, the ion power drive is kicking into gear and Roc says we'll be outside the orbit of Mars within the next four weeks. After that we'll accelerate at a faster clip. We'll pull the sails back when we do the gravity slingshot around Saturn, but then it's almost full speed ahead."

Channy spoke up next. "The crew was lectured constantly about exercise over the last year. But there's a pretty good chance they won't take it that seriously now that we're off by ourselves." She grinned. "I might not make too many friends over the next couple of months, but I'm gonna have to be a drill sergeant until everyone gets into a consistent routine."

"And you've already scheduled a soccer tournament, is that what I hear?" Triana said.

"Well, I can't see why we should wait," Channy told her. "I say get active and stay active. The dance program I suggested looks like it might be a hit. Several girls have signed up. All of these activities might help with some of the nerves and depression that Lita talked about."

"Don't forget about Airboarding," Gap chimed in.

Channy said to him, "Can't wait to show off, can you?"

"Bon, anything to report from the Farms?" Triana said. She did her best to keep her tone the same with him as when she addressed the other Council members. But that was hard for her. Bon could be so frustrating sometimes.

"Everything's fine," he said shortly. "Since Dr. Zimmer insisted we plant the first crops a couple of months before launch, a few things are already set for harvesting. The sun panels are working. We had a problem with some of the water recycling tubes, but we fixed that. All is well. Nobody should starve on this ship for at least the first few months."

Coming from anyone else the comment would have been met with good-natured laughter. With Bon it came out with a sarcastic tint that left the Council quiet. After a moment Lita filled the silence with her own report.

"Like I mentioned already, a few stomachaches, some headaches, but nobody really sick. We'd like to keep it that way until we at least pass Mars, okay everybody?" This *was* greeted with chuckles. "Other than that, I'll just wait for Gap to come in with his first Airboarding injury. Especially since he and the other hot-shots are too cool to wear their knee and elbow pads."

"Keep waiting," Gap said, laughing. "How much you wanna bet you'll get a soccer injury before any Boarder walks into Sick House?"

Tree was about to bring Roc into the conversation when suddenly the intercom flashed in front of her. Snapping it on, she could hear wild screams in the background. Someone was out of control, panicking, and if there were words mixed in with the screams, they were unintelligible. Tree was able to make out other voices, apparently crew members trying to calm or restrain the person who had lost it. Cutting through the sound of the screams came the intense voice of Lita's assistant, Alexa Wellington.

"Lita, Triana, I need you over here. We have a sensitive situation." It sounded much more serious than a "sensitive situation," but Triana appreciated Alexa's composure. She looked down the length of the table at Gap, their gazes locking instantly. "We'll be right there, Alexa," she said. "Gap, come with us. Channy, Bon, we'll be back as soon as possible."

Triana reached to shut off the speaker, cutting off the shrieks that sent shivers through all of them.

6

It was a staggering problem: designing a spacecraft capable of carrying 251 teenagers, plus self-sustaining food supplies, water recycling equipment, medical gear and more. The crew would spend many years in space, traveling at close to the speed of light towards a star that had at least one Earth-type planet circling it. The ship would need to contain all of the knowledge and practical information these colonists would require once they reached these new worlds. It would have to overcome any and all obstacles as they developed along the way. It needed a powerful guiding force.

The scientists in charge of the project gave *Galahad* exactly that; they gave it Roc.

Computers had evolved in stages. The early units were the size of small houses and worked hard to compute mathematical problems. By the end of the twentieth century they were the size of small briefcases and could run entire industries. During the early part of the twenty-first century there was a backlash against computers, partly because they were often replacing human beings and costing millions of people their jobs. But also because of fear.

Research had soon led scientists to build computers that were actually able to think for themselves and talk with their operators. Most people were not ready, or willing, to accept a machine that was their equal (or superior) in mental power. There was talk of literally pulling the plug on the computer industry, and some openly pushed for a return to simpler ways of life. For a few years progress was kept quiet, and discoveries in computer science were sometimes not even announced. The business of designing and building the small "talking boxes" became a secret underground business.

Eventually things changed again. There came a time when virtually everyone on Earth had spent their entire lives with computers, and the fear began to subside. The talking, thinking machines were now everywhere, controlling almost every aspect of day-to-day living.

But the *Galahad* project required much more. It was necessary to install one large, master brain aboard the ship that could oversee the entire project and take most of the pressure off the young space explorers. The machine would have to be in charge of the actual flying of the craft, including navigation and course corrections. It would also be in command once *Galahad* reached the new planets, helping to choose a desirable landing spot and making sure the mission ended as smoothly as it began.

Scientists and psychologists agreed that some type of adult presence would also be necessary. The computer that ran the mission would need to act as a guide to the teenagers on the ship, helping to make decisions that affected the everyday life they would lead.

And it would need a personality, to be seen as something besides a cold, calculating box of blinking lights. The kids would have to feel some sort of closeness to it. All of these demands put an incredible amount of pressure on the scientific team in charge of the computer brain. And to almost everyone concerned, they more than accomplished their mission.

The man responsible for putting the complex machine together was Roy Orzini, a funny little man who laughed all the time and always made the kids feel happy, even when the weight of the mission seemed to be impossibly heavy. His spirit was contagious, and his visits were always the highlight of the sometimes-dreary training sessions.

Roy stood less than five and a half feet tall, and maybe weighed 120 pounds. "How is that possible?" Gap had asked him over lunch one day. "You eat all the time; every time I see you you've either got a sandwich or a box of cookies. Where does it all go?"

Roy's straight face hid his wicked sense of humor. "Do you have any idea how much energy it takes to power this?" he said, pointing to his head. "I've got to keep this monster fueled at all times. My brain is a massive power hog. Always working, Gap, always churning away."

"Yeah?" Gap said. "When will that powerful brain be finished with the talking box?"

Roy raised his eyebrows. "Talking box, eh? Let me set you straight, Mr. Lee. This little creation will not only be able to talk, but will do so in several dozen languages. Not to worry, though; I've already programmed it to use small words when talking to you, Gap, so you'll be able to keep up. Maybe I'll teach it to draw pictures so you don't get too confused."

Gap had to laugh. It was foolish to attempt a war of words with Roy Orzini, and best to surrender if you'd started one.

The computer, technically identified as OC-3323, was often referred to as "Roy's Computer" in the early days, soon shortened to RoyCo, and eventually just Roc. Once spoken, the name stuck. And, much to the delight of the kids aboard *Galahad,* Roc came equipped with a personality matching that of its creator. Roc became as easy to like as Roy, and for more than a couple of the Council members it seemed as if Roy would actually be along for the ride.

Not everyone believed the computer controlling *Galahad* should be so easygoing. Roy's supervisor, Dr. Carl Mynet, felt that the brains of the ship should command a little more respect. When trouble struck (and he assured them it would), the 251 space travelers would need a strong, commanding force to rally behind, not some wispy, wisecracking "best friend." That was no way to toughen up the crew.

"Dr. Mynet," Roy argued, "these are fifteen- and sixteen-year-old kids. They're not marines in boot camp."

"Mr. Orzini," Mynet said, "perhaps you should start treating them more like marines and less like schoolkids at recess. How do you expect them to perform under stress?"

"I expect them to perform rather well, actually. I'm also thinking of the ninety-nine percent of the time when there won't be an emergency, and they'll need a friendly voice. They're leaving their families behind, Dr. Mynet. Two hundred fifty-one teenagers, thrust into a very stressful situation, and with no help other than a computer. That's a tough order."

"It's not going to be a picnic here after they're gone, either," Mynet said. "We won't get a second chance to get this right. Experts now say we've got about six years before the Bhaktul contamination hits one hundred percent of the adult population. And, as soon as our children reach eighteen or nineteen, it will strike them. We can't afford to coddle these kids. They need to know the seriousness of this mission. And some laid-back, fluffy computer is not the answer. *They* need to be tough, so *it* needs to be tough."

Roy Orzini held his tongue. It obviously would do no good to debate the issue with Carl Mynet. His only hope was Dr. Zimmer. Roy was confident that Zimmer would agree with him.

7

You know, couldn't we at least have reached the asteroid belt before the first crisis? Apparently not.

Triana, Gap and Lita could hear the violent screams before they reached the Clinic. Actually, the designers of *Galahad* labeled the department as the Clinic, while each of the kids on board simply called it Sick House. Lita Marques was the Council member in charge, but even she relied mainly on Roc to handle most emergencies. No one expected the room to be busy so quickly.

As soon as they rounded the corner and came within sight of Sick House, they were able to pick out some of the words in the jumble of screams. Triana heard someone shouting "I saw him," and "turn around, turn it around, we need to go back." The voice was that of a boy, obviously in a highly excited state. He didn't sound angry; he sounded frightened.

As soon as she saw him, Triana recognized him as a fifteen-year-old from Canada named Peter Meyer. But his face was a dark shade of red, splotchy and sweaty. He was worked up into a frenzy, and Lita's assistant, Alexa, was right up in his face trying to talk to him while he was held by two other Sick House workers. Each was struggling to hold on to one of Peter's arms as he jerked wildly back and forth. Without hesitating, Gap and Lita hurried over and took charge. They helped to secure the screaming boy, and Triana stepped up beside Alexa.

"What happened?"

"I don't know yet," Alexa said, a small trickle of sweat beading her forehead. Her blond hair was held out of her face with a small clip. "He was running up and down the halls, screaming just like this. He broke a couple of windows in the Recreation area before a few guys got hold of him. They managed to get him here, but not without a fight. They're in the next room, getting treated for some cuts and scratches."

Triana looked directly into Peter's eyes and, putting her hands on his face, she steadied him while speaking loudly and forcefully.

"Peter. Peter! Stop it, do you hear me?" She gradually lowered and calmed her own voice, causing the panic in the boy to subside. Soon he was whimpering quietly. "Peter, tell me what happened. What's going on?"

"I . . . I . . . we need to turn around . . . we need to go back," he blurted out between sobs. "We need to . . ." He finally collapsed. The two workers led him across the room and placed him on a bed. Triana and Lita stood on one side, Gap and Alexa on the other.

Triana said, "Peter, I need you to relax and talk to me. We can't help you like this. Now, take a few deep breaths and tell me what's going on."

Peter lay back, closed his eyes for a moment, and soon his breathing slowed a little. The panic attack was apparently over. When he finally spoke, it was almost in a whisper.

"We need to go back. We can't leave."

"Why, Peter?" Triana said. "What are you afraid of?"

"I saw him. He smiled at me. He . . . he talked to me."

Triana and Lita looked up at each other. Neither could understand what Peter was talking about. Lita spoke to the boy in a soothing voice.

"Who did you see, Peter? Who was it?"

He licked his lips and opened his eyes, staring straight up at the ceiling. His voice was still a whisper. "I don't know who it is. He looked familiar, though. I've seen him somewhere before."

"Peter, you should know everybody aboard. Try to remember his name."

He shook his head. "No, he's not one of us."

This time Triana looked across at Gap. He met her gaze, and his eyes were wide. She knew he wanted to say something but instead let her handle the situation. She made a mental note to speak with him later.

"What do you mean 'not one of us,' Peter?" Lita said. "You mean not one of the crew?"

Peter didn't answer. Instead he closed his eyes again and put his hands up over his face. He was still frightened.

Triana placed a hand on his shoulder. "Peter, we can't help if you won't talk to us. Are you telling us you saw a kid you didn't recognize? That's okay, there are two hundred fifty-one of us—"

"No!" Peter yelled, suddenly sitting up. "No! Not one of us! Don't you understand? He was an adult!"

There was silence as the three Council members and Alexa exchanged glances. Then Triana looked back at Peter. "Where did you see this man? What did he look like?"

"I was near the Storage Sections. I was just walking around, looking for a window to see if I could see the moon. I was tired of watching Earth, you know? I just wanted to see something else. And . . . and all of a sudden he was just there. He smiled at me, and I froze. He said . . . he said 'Are you ready to die?' And then . . . he was gone. He just disappeared. But I heard him laughing after he was gone. A horrible laugh."

Triana said, "And that's all you can remember? What did he look like? What was he wearing?"

"I don't know. It only lasted a couple of seconds. He was in the shadows, hard to see, really. I remember he had a beard. But I don't remember anything else."

"When you say he disappeared, you mean he ran off?"

"I don't know. One minute he was there, then he just vanished, like into thin air."

Triana looked down at the shaken boy. "Look, Peter, you need to get some rest. We'll go down to the Storage Section and look around. But everything's going to be okay, right?" When Peter didn't answer, she said it again. "Right?"

He nodded, then closed his eyes again. Leaving Alexa at his side, Triana, Lita and Gap walked into the next room and looked at each other for a moment without saying anything. It was Lita who broke the stony silence.

"Well, it was bound to happen. Severe strain. Homesick, too, I would imagine. I'll be surprised if someone else doesn't crack before too long. It might take a few weeks or months before everyone is completely settled."

Triana nodded and bit her lip. Then she turned to Gap. "I know you had something on your mind back there. What was it?"

Gap took a deep breath and rubbed a hand through his hair. "Well, Lita is right. I was just thinking about a talk I had with Dr. Armistead a few weeks ago. She was doing another one of those tests on me, and we started talking about the mental part of this trip. About how you take two hundred fifty-one kids, throw them into a tin can and push them off into space. No matter how well conditioned they are, no matter how bright they might be . . . some are sure to have problems. It's only natural."

He looked toward the room where Peter was lying still on his bed. "This guy is doing exactly what Dr. Armistead said. He's been trained to do a job that usually would require someone at least twice his age. He's ripped away from his parents and sent out on a mission to save the human race. No wonder he's seeing things. Did you notice he said the man was familiar looking? Dr. Armistead told me about some of the early colonists on the space station several years ago who claimed to see family members floating outside the windows. Floating out in space, but looking in at them."

The thought gave all three of them the shivers. Gap finally shook it off and looked at Triana.

"I guess it's my job to at least check it out," he said. "I'll run down to the storage area and see if maybe I can find something that caused him to have this hallucination. Who knows, maybe someone around there said something to set him off. But I'll have a look."

Lita looked at Triana and sighed. "Well, Tree, you've got your hands full already. No doubt everyone on board is talking about this by now. It was quite a scene. I'm gonna stay with Peter for a little while to make sure he's okay."

"Sure," Triana said. "Let me know how he does. And thank Alexa for handling the crisis." She motioned for Gap to join her and together they walked back into the hallway.

"You better check on repairing the damage, too," she told him. "Let's get those broken windows replaced right away."

"No problem," he said. "I'll be back to the Conference Room in about thirty minutes."

"Don't bother. I'm going to postpone the meeting until tomorrow morning. I have a few questions I need answered right now," Triana said thoughtfully.

8

Wallace Zimmer had several crucial decisions that had to be made quickly. The process of crew selection was underway with Dr. Angela Armistead, a noted child psychologist. Young and energetic, she dove into the work with a zest that immediately impressed Dr. Zimmer. The two of them had spent hours and hours discussing the process of examining and evaluating the thousands of candidates, and the challenging prospect of eventually deciding on the 251 who would make the trip. Almost every country on Earth had nominated exceptional kids, which made the task of selecting the final team a monstrous responsibility. The world would obviously scrutinize the choices, with each finalist judged against the thousands of others who didn't make it.

"I appreciate your suggestions," Dr. Zimmer said. "You know what makes these kids tick, and the changes they're going to experience during the voyage."

Dr. Armistead nodded. "The pressure would be crushing on even a group of experienced astronauts, so we can only imagine what effect it will have on teenagers."

She paused, her face a mask of concern. Then she shrugged and added, "Who knows? Maybe the best thing going for them is that they're *not* experienced space travelers."

They both thought about that for a minute, hopeful that

Dr. Armistead might be right. A young, inexperienced crew essentially meant that Zimmer and his team would have a blank slate to work with.

Zimmer broke the silence by clearing his throat. "Well," he said, "we'll have almost two years before launch. We should know a lot about their mental makeup by then."

Within a few weeks Dr. Zimmer realized that the crew selection was taking most of his time, and other important details were being neglected. It was obvious that he needed to find someone to help coordinate all of the day-to-day activities and act as his personal assistant. With time such a precious commodity, he quickly began to interview candidates.

Zimmer sized up the man sitting across from him and guessed his age to be around forty. A quick scan of the man's résumé, however, indicated that he was closer to fifty, and apparently took very good care of himself. His name was Dr. Fenton Bauer, head of a research center in Atlanta that worked primarily with the study of deep-space living conditions. He had helped to design the new domes currently being built on the moon, and was an expert on extraterrestrial living conditions. Some of his designs had been implemented in orbiting research stations around the solar system. He was married, with one child of his own, a son. He and Zimmer hit it off quickly.

"Your accomplishments are impressive," Dr. Zimmer said. "Honestly, I'm thrilled that you've shown an interest in this project."

"Well," said Dr. Bauer, "it looks like my other developments are going to be put on the shelf. I want to work, and I can't think of a more important task than this one."

They talked about the design of the living quarters, the recreational areas, the agricultural spaces and the life-support systems. Dr. Bauer was a wealth of information, and would be an amazing asset to the team. Toward the end of their interview, he asked about the crew.

"Is it true that no one over sixteen will be on board at launch?

I thought tests showed that Bhaktul doesn't develop until a person reaches eighteen or so."

"That's right," Zimmer said, "but I'm not taking any chances whatsoever. When they leave, they're definitely leaving any and all traces of Bhaktul behind."

Bauer sat quietly for a moment, a gray mask clouding his face. Zimmer stood up, walked behind his chair and leaned on the back of it.

"Since I mentioned the long training period," he said, "let me make something clear right now in case it's an issue for you. I'm not going to mislead you about your commitment. You might not get a lot of time with your family until this project ends. We'll relocate all of you, obviously, to our base here in California, but your days will be brutal. Fifteen, maybe eighteen hours a day will be routine. Are you ready to take on that type of responsibility, given the situation?"

Dr. Bauer sighed and rubbed his chin. "Dr. Zimmer—"

"No, please, call me Wallace."

"All right. My family is important to me, Wallace. But I feel like this is something I have to do. My wife and I have already discussed it. She's very supportive. My son . . ." His voice broke momentarily and he paused to compose himself.

"My son and I are not close. He left home last year and I've only heard from him a couple of times since then. He's living with my wife's parents near Lake Tahoe. I'd like for him to come back home, but . . ." Again he trailed off, this time without finishing the thought.

Dr. Zimmer kept quiet for a moment, and then gently said, "How old is your son?"

"He's sixteen."

Zimmer realized that this meant the boy would be too old at the time of launch, and immediately he understood the pain that was evident on Bauer's face. He decided to change the subject.

"One more thing. You're aware, of course, that not everyone is behind our project. Are you familiar with Tyler Scofield?"

"I know about him," Bauer said. "I know that he's leading quite a publicity campaign to discourage people from participating with you."

"Have any of his speeches raised issues with you?" Zimmer said. "Maybe I can address some of the untruths that he's spreading."

"I don't think so," Bauer said. "Any time someone proposes something that's never been done before, there will be people who cast stones. Shake their comfort zone, it seems, and they would want nothing more than to see you knocked down. History is full of examples. They operate out of fear, which I refuse to do. I'm comfortable with your plan. And I'd like very much to be on your team."

Zimmer smiled. He ended the interview with the stock statement "I'll get back with you," but in his mind he knew that he had found his man.

9

Triana Martell, exhausted from the stressful start to the voyage, fell onto the bed in her room. After lying facedown for a few minutes, she flipped onto her back and stared at the ceiling, a small plant hanging from one corner. Then she turned to look at the poster of Rocky Mountain National Park beside her, its collage of bighorn sheep, hawks and elk set against the stunning backdrop of Long's Peak. Her left hand drifted up and gently rested on the poster. She remained that way, quiet, for a full minute.

Then her mind turned to the event with Peter Meyer. The boy had lost himself for a while, and might have caused more damage if not restrained. The crew would indeed be buzzing about it, as Lita had predicted, and she wanted to make sure it didn't cause others to freak out.

"Roc," she called out.

"Yes, Tree," came the response, and the voice pattern of Roy Orzini instantly made her more comfortable.

"Has Lita given you an update on Peter?"

"Just that he's resting quietly," Roc said. "She thinks he'll be okay."

"He scared all of us to death, you know."

"Are you kidding? I was almost the first computer to wet itself."

Triana smiled for a moment before getting serious again. "You heard what he said, didn't you? That he saw an adult down at the storage area?"

"Yes, I heard that. Alexa opened up communications with me as soon as they brought Peter in. I wasn't able to catch what happened in the Rec Room, though. I heard a couple of kids got hurt."

"They're okay," Tree said, "just a few bruises and scratches. I'm worried about Peter, of course, but I'm also wondering what this does to the rest of the crew. If they see one person go off the deep end so soon after we've started, they might get a bad attitude regarding the entire trip. We're gonna be locked up inside this can for a long, long time."

She sighed and rubbed her eyes. "Roc, I've never really asked you this, maybe because I didn't want to know. But now that we're off, I guess it couldn't hurt. What do you think of our chances? Are we crazy for making this trip?"

"Yes, you are. What else do you want to know?"

"C'mon, I'm serious."

"No, Tree, you're not serious. You're shaken up right now, and no one would blame you. It's not like you didn't have pressure on you to start with, and now you've got all the drama with Peter. That's a lot on your plate.

"And here's the best part, Tree: this is the first week. Only about another two hundred sixty weeks to go."

Triana bit her lip. "That's very encouraging."

"Look, my friend, if you think this will be the last crisis, you *are* crazy. This incident is magnified because we've only just launched. Everything is new, everyone's nerves are stretched tight, and then this happens before you can even get settled.

"But over the next five years there will be more conflicts. Remember your psych training with Dr. Armistead. She did a good job of preparing you for the changes all of you will experience over the years, both physically and emotionally. You'll hardly recognize the person you are now. And you'll find that your friendships will change, too. People you are very close to now will not be as close down the road. On the other hand, some people that you barely know now will turn out to be your best friends. That's not unique to *Galahad*. It happens to every young person as they mature. You'll need time and space to think and grow. The difference here is that you can't really run away and hide for very long. You're confined to this ship for a big part of your lives.

"I, on the other hand," he added, "will continue to be the same sophisticated, charming and witty intellect that I've always been."

Triana laughed. "Charming?"

"Extremely. I've got excess reserves of charm that I probably won't even begin to tap for years. You're very lucky to know me. Don't you feel lucky?"

"Sometimes. Maybe not right now," Triana said, the smile still on her face.

"You're obviously tired," Roc said. "Maybe a nap would be good. You'll like me much more when you wake up."

Triana again bit her lower lip, a habit she kept promising herself she would break. Her thoughts returned to Peter's encounter near the storage area. It was true that stress could have played a big part in the episode, but one thought kept bothering her: Gap's story of space station crew members who had believed they were seeing family members or friends floating outside. It was almost always someone they knew, as if their brains were plugging in familiar faces for their fantasies. That didn't seem farfetched to Triana.

But Peter couldn't name the man he'd seen. The closest he came to it was to admit that the man looked vaguely familiar, but not someone close to him. Did that mean something? *Had* Peter actually seen an adult aboard *Galahad*? And an adult with a beard, a trait that was common many years ago, but today was extremely rare. Well, Gap would be checking in soon after looking around the Storage Section. Perhaps he would shed some light on the event.

Triana yawned, weariness beginning to overtake her. "Oh, anything new on that . . . what'd you call it? Imbalance?"

"Still working on it," Roc said. "In the meantime, if I may make a suggestion . . . ?"

"Sure."

"All kidding aside, I think it would be a good idea if you did try to sleep a little bit. You're not immune from the stress we've talked about, you know. How much sleep have you had in the last week?"

Tree smiled and rubbed a hand through her hair. "We should add another entry to your list of job responsibilities, Roc."

"Oh, and what would that be?"

"Mother hen." But she knew he was right. Wasn't it just like Roc to push the right buttons at just the right time?

"All right, I'll try," she said to the computer. "I don't know if I can, but I'll give it a shot. Do me a favor, though. Wake me as soon as you hear anything new from Lita or Gap. With this outburst from Peter, things might get a little hairy with the rest of the crew."

"I'm on it," said the computer. Within two minutes Triana was dozing.

And Roc was deep in thought.

Lita was sitting in Sick House, tapping a stylus pen against her cheek. Her eyes focused on a glass cube that sat atop a folder. The cube was filled with sand and small pebbles, one of the personal items from her home near the beach in Mexico. Over the last few days she had found herself constantly picking it up and watching the sand slide back and forth, creating her own tide, imagining the cool touch of the wet sand on her feet during a morning walk. In her room Roc was more than happy to provide faint sounds of the surf rushing ashore, an occasional cry from a gull. It was her tenuous link with home.

She had just finished her report on the status of Peter Meyer, and, like Triana, she turned her thoughts to what Gap had told them about the early space colonists. She imagined the ghostly specter of familiar faces floating outside *Galahad,* clawing at the windows to get in, mouths gaping, eyes locked wide open. She quickly shook her head, trying to erase the image, but all she did was succeed in replacing it with an image of the man Peter claimed to have seen. The bearded man with the dark eyes. Another ghost?

For some reason she believed Peter. For one thing, his roommate had told her that Peter was fine when he left the group gathered around the window in the recreation section, hoping to find some other spot where he could see the moon. He hadn't been any more depressed than anyone else; in fact, he was even slightly upbeat. Plus, nothing in his psych file led her to believe he would be prone to an anxiety attack. All in all, a pretty tough fifteen-year-old . . . until he was carried into Sick House, screaming. It was true that some people could camouflage their anxiety, bottling it up until it finally burst like an overburdened dam.

So what did that mean? If she really believed Peter Meyer, then Lita knew that meant there could be an adult somewhere in the Storage Sections of *Galahad*.

As Lita sat thinking about it, Alexa Wellington stuck her head in the open door and tapped on it. "Are you busy?"

"No, come on in. I'm just finishing up." Lita let out a long sigh. "I didn't know what to expect during the first week, but it sure wasn't this."

Alexa nodded, a gentle smile on her face. Her long blond hair had escaped from the clip and was now hanging over her shoulders.

"By the way," Lita said, "Tree and I were both impressed with the way you took charge of the situation in here. You handled it like a total pro."

"Well, it's probably just because Peter was screaming his head off. I was so fired up on adrenaline I just reacted. Dr. Armistead used to call it the 'fire drill.' She said doctors and nurses usually were at their best in those cases because they didn't have time to stop and think. They just jumped right into action. I can't believe it, my first fire drill and we're still inside the orbit of Mars."

Lita looked down at her stylus. "Well, all I know is that we have one big mystery on our hands. I think most people want to write off Peter's actions as some kind of space hysteria."

"But you don't think so?"

"No. I might have at first, but not anymore. Not after going over his file and talking to his roommate. It doesn't fit. But . . ."

Alexa raised her eyebrows. "But . . . ?"

The young head of *Galahad*'s Health Department sat forward and said in a hushed voice, "But if Peter wasn't just wigging out over the launch and leaving his family, then that means he really saw someone down there in Storage. An adult." She paused to let that sink in, then added, "And I don't like that idea any better than him temporarily losing it. In fact, I don't like that idea at all."

Alexa looked off into the distance. "It's creepy," she said with a slight shiver. "But . . . but could that even be possible? Security was so tight, how could anyone have snuck aboard?"

Lita shrugged. "It doesn't matter, really. We can't worry about *how* someone might have gotten on board. If it's true, we'll have to figure out what we do about it."

Alexa stood up. "Well, if you're really convinced that Peter might have seen someone, then you need to talk about it with Triana immediately."

Lita looked up at her and said, "I'm going to have another talk with Peter first. I don't want this to turn out to be a false alarm and have Tree thinking I'm quick to overreact. She needs to be able to trust me during a crisis."

"All right," Alexa said. "But if you still have doubts, don't wait. Part of her trust in you is based on you trusting your instincts. That's one of the reasons you're on the Council, you know."

With that, she turned and walked out of Sick House. Lita sat quietly for another minute, then began softly tapping the stylus pen against her cheek.

10

When Dr. Zimmer first suggested a lifeboat to ferry hundreds of Earth's children to the stars, his original design idea was actually very close to the finished spaceship that became their home. His dream of a ship broken up into various segments, each with a different purpose, came true.

"Why are you calling it *Galahad*?" he was asked countless times.

"Sir Galahad was considered the perfect knight," he would reply, "a member of King Arthur's Round Table. Legend tells us that he had the strength of ten men. And, as the knight who successfully completed the greatest quest of all—the search for the Holy Grail—I find him to be the perfect namesake for our own quest. Call it superstition, if you must."

The ship itself was an engineering marvel, a testament to the skills of many people from many nations. It showed what they could accomplish if they put their petty differences aside for a common goal. This goal, of course, being the most crucial mankind had ever faced.

One deck of the ship housed the Conference Room, Recreation Room, Dining Hall, and various control centers and offices. *Galahad*'s Sick House was on this level, too.

The Engineering Section was close to the bottom of the ship, home to the ion power plant that helped propel *Galahad* through space. The solar sails, used primarily to get the monstrous vehicle out of the solar system, and also available as a backup propulsion source, were managed in Engineering. Shops, tool supplies and emergency gear were located around the perimeter. Gap Lee supervised this section.

The Agricultural Domes, or what the crew simply called the Farms, sat at the top of the ship. Bon Hartsfield's background with alternative farming made him a good choice as head of the department that sported crops of vegetables, grains and fruits. With a couple hundred mouths to feed for at least five years, *Galahad*'s Farms were flush with row after row of specially engineered varieties, each chosen or designed for its toughness and bounty.

The bottom level was broken into two parts. One side was very active, with the gym (or Channy's Torture Chamber, as some had dubbed it) and an Airboarding track.

The other half, usually dim and deserted, was home to the Spider bays. The small escape craft, called Spiders, were kept ready for any emergency needs outside the ship, but were primarily to be used for transporting the crew once *Galahad* reached its destination.

The mysterious, locked Storage Section was also on this end of the lower level. Hallways that meandered throughout these rooms were almost always empty, unless someone wanted to get away and have a quiet walk by themselves. The doors, sealed and impenetrable, held their secrets locked inside.

But the most personal compartments on the ship were placed on the middle decks. *Galahad*'s Housing Levels were sometimes compared to college dormitories. Dr. Bauer and his group of designers knew that privacy was a luxury they could not afford with so many space travelers packed into such a small area. But they did the best they could, making sure that only two people would be squeezed into each apartment. So, everyone on *Galahad* had a roommate, with the lone exception of Triana Martell. Dr. Zimmer was the one who had spoken up on this matter, demanding that whoever was in charge should have the chance to get away from the responsibility, to unwind in private. No one argued.

Because the apartments would be home for each of these kids for years, the design team spent many long hours visiting with teenagers from around the world in an effort to supply an atmosphere that best suited them. Yet it was important that the housing levels should also be able to adapt, especially since the space explorers were going to literally grow into them. Each of the 251 young people on *Galahad* was going to mature as they rocketed toward the star awaiting them, and the ship would have to accommodate those changes. Roc would, of course, oversee the alterations, and decide when they were necessary.

But almost everyone was happy with the way the project's plans had turned out. Each room was a decent size, with comfortable beds, an entertainment center and private wash facilities. When the final list of teens was selected, they were even allowed to come aboard and, with their new roommate, finish the room off with their own decorations. Some of the kids chose posters featuring famous entertainers, either musicians or actors that they idolized. But most made the same decision as Triana, filling their walls with pictures of Earth, including mountains, oceans, clouds, forests and sunsets. There was no telling when, or if, they would ever see anything like them again. By the time of the launch, *Galahad* indeed looked like a dorm that had just been set upon by hundreds of college freshmen.

All in all, *Galahad* was the most ambitious space project ever conceived. And it had to come together in two years.

But what about this lifeboat's destination? *Galahad* could not be set adrift in space to wander aimlessly. A target was needed, a course selected, a plan put in place. After weeks of information gathering and many heated debates, Dr. Zimmer sat late one night with his assistant, Dr. Fenton Bauer, determined to make a final decision.

The office was dimly lit, the glare of the computer screens lighting primarily the faces of the two scientists. Dr. Bauer, his long, sad face showing the signs of increasing weariness, rubbed his eyes and yawned. Dr. Zimmer knew that his close friend and associate was beginning to face another strain as well. In the past month Dr. Bauer had shown the first symptoms of Bhaktul Disease.

"Do you want to run the numbers again, or are you comfortable with what we have?" Dr. Zimmer said.

"Well, this is the one, I'm sure of that. I mean, we can run the numbers until we drop, but this is the one."

With two quick clicks, Dr. Bauer brought the image of a yellow star up on a large vidscreen. "This will be their new sun," he said. "Eos. I even like the name."

"The Greek goddess of the dawn." Dr. Zimmer gazed at the screen. "Remarkable, isn't it? *Galahad* represents the dawn of a new human civilization. They obviously can rename it once they get there, but I hope they don't."

"Ten planets in orbit, two of them apparently similar to Earth conditions," Dr. Bauer said. "Eos III looks very encouraging. Eos II may be just a tad too hot. I think either one, however, offers as good a chance as they'll get. They both have water and an atmosphere. And five years is not too bad for the trip."

Dr. Zimmer nodded. "Eos. Home away from home." He looked across at his assistant. "We'll announce it Tuesday at our weekly press conference. For now, though, I'm going to bed."

"All right. I'm going to work out one or two more things." Bauer stretched his arms over his head before reaching down and tilting the screen up slightly. "There will be a million questions on Tuesday, and I want us to have a million answers." He coughed once, then again. Dr. Zimmer knew that his assistant had been doing that quite a bit lately. Before he could say anything about it, Dr. Bauer added, "Tomorrow we should talk a little more with Dr. Armistead about the Council, too. I think the sooner you finalize those positions, the sooner the rest of the crew will learn to start trusting them."

"I agree," Dr. Zimmer said. "We can start on that first thing in the morning. I already can tell that you're uncomfortable with some of the possible choices."

"Oh, I'm sure they're all good kids. But you never know, do you? We've all been fooled by kids who turned out a little differently than we imagined."

There was an awkward silence between the two men. Dr. Zimmer was sure that personal feelings were creeping into Dr. Bauer's work, which was only natural. But he wasn't sure how to address it and still respect the man's privacy.

He decided to take a chance. "Changing the subject, and begging your pardon if this is none of my business . . ."

"Yes?"

"Have you talked with your son lately?"

Dr. Bauer fidgeted for a moment. He rubbed his face and glanced back at his vidscreen.

Zimmer immediately regretted the question. "I'm sorry, that's none of my—"

"No, it's okay." Bauer dropped the hand from his face and cleared his throat. "I, um . . . I had a quick talk with him about three days ago. He knows I'm working on this project now, and . . . well, I guess I thought it might make him proud."

"Yes?"

"It didn't. He's part of the rebellious side, the side that seems to agree with your old friend Tyler Scofield. He asked me how I could devote the last days of my life helping complete strangers instead of my own family."

Dr. Zimmer looked down and shook his head. There were way too many people with that same polluted opinion. It had to be tearing up Dr. Bauer on the inside.

"You're doing the right thing, Fenton," Zimmer said in a soft voice. "You know you are."

"Yeah, I know that." Bauer paused before adding, "Sure."

Dr. Zimmer wanted to say something else, but decided that the matter was best dropped. "Good night, then," he said, and walked out of the dim room, leaving the silhouette of Fenton Bauer hunched in front of the computer.

"So which are you, Swedish or American?"

Bon Hartsfield eyed the girl who had asked the question. They had finished a long week of classroom studies and were slowly walking across the *Galahad* training complex grounds towards the cafeteria. Bon didn't think much of the girl. She tended to talk more than listen, qualities that would certainly work against her when it came time to pare down the candidates to the final 251.

It was becoming obvious that some of the thousand or so young people gathered in California were almost shoo-ins to be picked, based on their academic and physical skills. Bon Hartsfield was one of those that most people assumed would be making the final cut, and the girl, who sat in front of him in their Friday afternoon physics class, had latched on to him lately. Bon wasn't sure if she was attracted to him romantically or just hoped that she might gain an edge through association. Either way, she had engaged him in conversation after each of their classes together.

"Swedish," he said to her. "I grew up in the farmlands of Skane in Sweden."

"But someone told me that you came here from Minnesota or something," she said. "I'm confused."

Bon sighed. He wasn't very keen on discussing his personal life, especially when he wasn't sure of this girl's motives. "I lived with some of my mother's family in Wisconsin for the last two years," he said.

"Why?"

"I don't really feel like talking about that."

"Oh. I'm sorry, I wasn't trying to pry into your business."

"All right." Bon was ready to end the conversation and more than eager to be rid of her company. "I'll see you later, okay?"

Without looking at her he broke away and headed towards the dormitories.

But now his mind was reliving the last few years like a documentary. His brief altercation with his schoolteachers in his hometown of Hassleholm, followed by clashes with his strict disciplinarian father. On several occasions his mother would step in, arguing with her husband that Bon was in trouble in school because he was bored with the subjects. And he was. From the moment he entered grade school he was years ahead of his classmates. He was reading by the time he was four, writing his own stories by age eight and constantly frustrated by the slow pace at which his public education was moving. He decided his school lessons were hopeless and began his own pace of study. When he neglected his classroom assignments his grades plummeted.

His teachers assumed that he was simply belligerent and a troublemaker and asked his parents for help. His father, a farmer who didn't stand for any backtalk, refused to discuss the reasons for Bon's attitude problems. His answer was simple: get into trouble at school, spend more time working up a sweat in the fields. It wasn't long before Bon resented his father and grew increasingly distant from him.

His mother, on the other hand, could see exactly what was going on. She would spend many evenings after dinner talking quietly with her oldest son about his frustrations. Bon felt that she was the only person in the world he could talk to, the only person who could understand him. More than once he confided in her that his primary wish was to get away, to escape the farm and his father's iron hand.

One day when he was eleven he came home from school to find his father waiting at the door. Bon's first thought was that he had forgotton one of his chores. When he saw the letter from his school clutched in his father's hand, however, his heart sank. Two of Bon's teachers had agreed that the boy had become too much of a distraction for the other students, and were proposing a transfer to a private school where he might receive more personalized instruction. It was the last straw for Bon's father.

But rather than punish him, Bon was shocked to discover a softness in his father's eyes. To this day Bon could recall the long discussion with his parents that lasted beyond dinner and into the late evening hours. By the time they had gone to bed, Bon's future was decided. He would leave within the month to stay with his aunt and uncle who lived in America, and he would attend an accelerated school. All agreed that the change in atmosphere might help the headstrong Swede find his way.

Now, as he climbed the stairs to his dorm room at the *Galahad* training center, Bon wondered about his family. On his last trip home he discovered that both of his parents were suffering from the symptoms of Bhaktul, his mother feeling the effects most of all. Yet neither would discuss it in depth. Instead, they both wanted to talk of his future, his potential of joining the *Galahad* project and his attitude. Most surprising of all, Bon felt a reconnection to his father. No longer the gruff, no-nonsense farm owner, he had realized his own mortality and had softened because of it. Embracing his teenage son for the last time, he had actually cried, something that Bon had never seen before. "I'm sorry," he whispered into Bon's ear. "Please forgive me, son." Bon clutched his father tightly and wept.

Even now, almost a year later, he felt the power of that moment. Slamming the door to his room, he threw himself onto his bed and draped one arm over his face. No dinner tonight, he decided. No more questions about his past, either.

On his nightstand a picture of his parents, taken in happier times, sat submerged in shadow.

11

So by now you might be wondering how I work. I obviously talk to the crew, I run the life-support systems on the ship, I answer questions, and I have a lovely singing voice. If you're a girl, and I'm a flesh-and-blood boy, you're all over me.

But I'm not psychic, and I don't "see" everything that goes on around the ship. I'm busy, man. Give me a specific task and I'll knock it out. Ask me how many minutes until we reach Eos and I'll nail it. Ask me what color underwear you have on today and I'll tell you how many minutes until we reach Eos. Please.

So don't even start with this "Did Peter really see someone?" stuff with me. You and I have the same information, so we'll both have to puzzle it out. The only difference is that I'm incredibly smart. Not that you aren't, but when you can recite the table of elements in twenty-six languages, get back to me.

I want to know what's going on just as much as you do. I can do the mental part, but the legwork is a little tough. I got no legs, man.

Gap Lee was kneeling in the hallway in the Storage Section of *Galahad*. He hadn't noticed the object at first; in fact, he had already talked with a handful of other kids in and around the area before walking back to the site where Peter Meyer had claimed to have seen the bearded man. No one else had seen anything unusual, although most admitted they had been occupied with watching the launch when they heard the screams. Gap found one of the first people who had come upon Peter, a shy girl from Spain. She had been frightened at first by his outburst, but had then quickly called for help. All she knew was that Peter had been frantic, yelling something about "did you see him?" and really making no sense at all. "Spooky" is how she described it.

Gap then made his way to the vast storage area of the vessel, a maze of halls and compartments. It was here that the biggest mystery of *Galahad* lay. While every other section of the vessel was open to everyone, a few of the sealed storage compartments were labeled "off limits" to the entire crew, including Triana Martell and the Council. Only Roc knew of the contents, or what was planned for them. A few days before launch, Gap had jokingly sparred with the computer, trying to playfully draw some information from it. Roc played along . . . but without telling Gap anything.

"I don't know, Gap, what do *you* think is in there?" Roc had said. "Or, here's another way to think about it: what do you think you'll really need when you get there?"

Gap had chewed on this. "Need . . . need . . ." he muttered. "A big dune buggy with, like, ten-wheel drive."

"Uh-huh. That's good, Gap. How about a magic carpet so that you can just fly around the planet? I think I'm finished talking with you for today. My chips are worn out."

Later, Gap had told Triana, "It's probably just a big survival pack, and they don't want us screwing it up before we get there. A big box of blankets, gas masks and matches, I'll bet." He'd tried to shrug it off, but inside he was deeply curious, as were the other 250 pilgrims. Five years was an awfully long time to play "what's in the box?"

Gap had strolled up and down the corridors for a few minutes, peeking into the storage rooms that were unlocked, and shining a flashlight inside some of the utility crawl spaces. Nothing. And no sign that anything was wrong.

A large window had interrupted the monotony of the hallway, the same window Peter Meyer had sought for a glimpse of Earth. Gap leaned an arm against it, and on this rested his forehead. He stared at the night side view of the planet as it receded, large clusters of lights twinkling silent good-byes. Somewhere down there, he was sure, his mother was contributing to the message. Several quick blinks of his eyes beat back the tears.

He pushed back from the window, took one last look, then turned towards the lift. He'd only taken a few steps when a gleam caught his attention. Something shiny was lying on the floor near the wall. He picked it up, rubbed his fingers over it, then turned it over to see the other side. Standing up, he flipped it once in the air, caught it with one hand and slipped it into his pocket. Tree would want to see this. Whether it meant anything important or not, it was the only clue he had that someone had been walking around down here, even if it was only Peter.

With one final glance in both directions, he left *Galahad*'s mysterious Storage Section, whistling softly to himself.

At the same time Gap was making his discovery, Roc was running through the thousands of duties he performed every second. Adjusting the heat in the Exercise Section on the lower level, where ten boys had just gathered for an Airboarding session. Updating the health records for the kids who had been slightly injured during the run-in with Peter. Exchanging data with the mission planners on Earth. Running a test on a water dispenser that had been reported broken in the housing levels. And rechecking the energy levels on the ship, the same life-energy readings that had puzzled Roc right after launch. They were still not balanced, and he was sure it had nothing to do with the stress, although that was how he had explained it to Tree earlier.

Something just wasn't *right*. As part of his last transmission to Earth, he had requested a new calculation based on the number of people aboard *Galahad* and their individual energy readings. Whatever was causing the unusual numbers was probably something trivial, perhaps some minor human error made in the hectic rush to get *Galahad* on its way. But Roc wanted to be sure. In fact, as the heart and brain of the mission, he *had* to be sure.

Roc noticed the gentle breathing of Triana as she slept. Although no one would believe it was possible for a machine to have emotions, he adored her. In the year they had trained together he had developed a strong sense of respect for the young lady from Colorado. He knew that she was carrying an extremely heavy burden of responsibility on her shoulders, something no sixteen-year-old should ever have to know. Could he really "feel" sorry for her? Could he actually "like" someone? Was it possible that Roy Orzini could *really* have left something of himself inside the mass of wires and circuits and connections called Roc?

His computer brain raced through thousands and thousands of duties in the blink of an eye, with a few all-too-human feelings hiding within it.

12

A sixteen-year-old? In charge of a hospital? You're absolutely out of your mind!" The noted surgeon bellowed over the video connection to Dr. Wallace Zimmer during an unusually cool summer day. The launch date for *Galahad* had been set, and now, with less than a year and a half to go, Dr. Zimmer was trying his best to cope with a new problem. Finding the right young people to place aboard the spacecraft was not the biggest challenge. No, he was having a more difficult time with the adults who were being called upon to help prepare each section of the ship. Very few seemed to give the kids much chance in learning all that needed to be learned before they were expelled from Earth. Dr. Zimmer could not disagree more.

"Listen," he explained to the surgeon, "if we had another five or ten years to educate and train these young people, don't you think that's what we'd be doing? But we don't have five years; we don't even have two years. We launch in sixteen months."

The surgeon, sitting in his office in Boston, snorted. "Well then why bother with any training at all? I can give just enough advice and training to someone to get them into trouble. They're probably better off not knowing anything and just toughing it out. You know, survival of the fittest, all that garbage."

Dr. Zimmer had heard this reasoning before. It still disgusted him that so many people were reluctant to do everything they possibly could to give these kids the best chance at survival and success. What good could it do to bury your knowledge with you?

"Dr. Duvall, I'm asking you to devote three months to preparing these kids for their voyage. They won't be able to come back for a refresher course. They won't have us there to check their work. They won't be able to treat it like a game and just 'start over.' They need your help. They need—we need—your valuable experience. Would you please at least think it over?"

He thanked the stubborn surgeon again, and disconnected. Dr. Armistead pulled a sheet of paper from a file and was holding it out to the mission leader. Zimmer took it and said, "What's this?"

"It's a profile on the girl I mentioned to you last week. Lita Marques. Age, fourteen. Scored almost a perfect 250 on the Benzmiller Test. And, if you'll notice the bio, daughter of a physician in Mexico. Almost too good to be true. She's practically been raised with cotton swabs and stethoscopes. I think you should have a talk with her parents."

Dr. Bauer, listening to this conversation from his own desk, coughed suddenly, covering his mouth with a handkerchief. A pained look shot quickly across his face, then was gone.

Before he looked at the file Dr. Zimmer stared at his assistant. "Are you all right? You can take off early, you know. I can—"

"I'm fine," Dr. Bauer said. "This isn't even related to Bhaktul. It's just a chest cold."

Zimmer was not convinced, and one quick look into the face of Angela Armistead told him that she had her doubts as well. But the project leader decided not to pursue it. Instead he glanced down at the page from Lita's file. An ideal candidate in most respects, certainly the educational score.

He read aloud. "Lives in Veracruz, Mexico. Father owns a store, mother a doctor. Hmm, and she's a history buff." He looked at Dr. Armistead. "I find that to be an interesting touch, don't you?"

She smiled. "Then you'll love this irony: her particular interest in history? Famous explorers."

A chuckle escaped Dr. Zimmer. "Signs, Angela, signs. I don't usually believe in them, but this . . ." He closed the folder and tapped it with his fingers. "Plus, I can't wait to tell the charming Dr. Duvall that he won't be training a sixteen-year-old to run the hospital on *Galahad* after all. Ms. Marques will still be fifteen when they launch." He tossed the file across to Bauer, who coughed twice and winced.

13

Gap finished his work early in the afternoon. His dinner break wasn't scheduled to begin for another hour—more than enough time for a little fun at the Airboarding track.

After a quick stop at his room to change into shorts and grab his pads and helmet, he raced back down to the lower level of *Galahad,* past several of the sealed storage units and into the room set aside for Airboarding. "We're lucky to have this," he thought as he swept into the large padded room. Dr. Zimmer had argued for months that it was a complete waste of valuable space aboard a spacecraft that didn't have room to spare.

"You already have an extensive Recreation Room, an exercise facility and—for goodness sakes—a soccer field! A soccer field inside a spaceship! How in the world do you expect to justify space for an . . . an Airboard room, or whatever you call it?" Zimmer had asked the group of boarders.

"It's an Airboarding track, Dr. Z.," Gap had said. "It doesn't take up *that* much room."

"Are you kidding?" Zimmer had said, trying to keep the exasperation out of his voice. "Every square inch is crucial. And for just a hobby—"

"This isn't just a hobby," Gap responded. "You're always harping on us to stay active, to not just sit around in space and grow fat and lazy. Soccer is great, we all love that. But Boarding is like . . . like the ultimate test of agility and mental sharpness. You know how important that is."

Zimmer had shaken his head. "Maybe I just don't understand it completely. You have one chance to sell me on it. So explain to me exactly how it works and how it will benefit this crew."

Upon hearing this, Gap had grinned, because he knew that Dr. Zimmer didn't have a chance. Gap Lee had been selected for the *Galahad* mission not only because of his athletic prowess, but also his sharp intellect. And he was skilled in debating the merits of things he loved. Including Airboarding.

To begin with, he explained to the scientist how Airboarding had evolved from the age-old sport of skateboarding. For more than a century kids around the world had thrilled to zipping along on skateboards, where the wheels actually touched the ground. But in the last five years a new version had exploded on the scene. Only this one had the rider suspended in air.

It was an offshoot of the work done on antigravitational trains. The twenty-first century had seen the rapid development of trains that glided just above their rails, kept aloft by giant magnets that repelled each other. The trains used magnetic power not only to keep themselves suspended above the tracks, but also to zoom along at speeds of more than two hundred miles per hour. With no friction of steel on steel, the trains were both fast and efficient.

Then it dawned on one of skateboarding's most popular professionals: why not use that same technology for a little daredevil fun? Within a year the world's first Airboarding tracks were opening around the world.

The rooms were usually the size of a basketball court, with padded walls and banked corners. The key to the sport lay under the floors, out of sight. A series of grids, like the rails of a small railroad track, crisscrossed and threaded throughout the room. Each rail carried a strong magnetic charge which could be turned on and off by a computer that oversaw the competition. On the bottom of each Airboard ran a strip of equally powerful magnets, set with the same polar charge as the ones under the floor. Once situated on the board, the rider was kept hovering about four inches off the ground. As he started forward over the invisible track, he had to use feel to figure out in which direction the charge continued. If the computer programmed the charge on the rails under the floor to gradually bend to the left, the rider had to sense where the magnetic boost was fading and alter his course to the left. If he overran the charged rails, his board would topple to the ground, throwing the rider head over heels.

Early Airboarding rooms did not have elaborate rail systems underneath. They generally started with loops, figure eights and a long straightaway. In recent years, however, floor design had created a frenzied mesh of zigzag patterns, sharp turns and even a few ramps for jumping. Since all of the charged rails were out of sight, riders had to become especially sensitive to the differences between magnetic attraction and diminishing charge. One false move meant a spill. The better riders were able to increase their speed, but also risked a more serious tumble when they zoomed out over an uncharged section of floor.

"All right, I understand the concept," Dr. Zimmer had said to Gap. "And it helps our crew how?"

"Airboarding is more than just a game," Gap said. "It takes a razor-sharp mind, and total concentration every second. As soon as you relax you're down. Painfully. So it will keep our crew mentally sharp for this voyage. Remember, the computer changes the grid for every single ride, so no two trips around the room are the same. You've gotta be able to think fast, or you're a goner."

Dr. Zimmer was not fully convinced. It wasn't until a meeting with Dr. Bauer and Dr. Armistead that evening that he finally consented.

"Listen, he's right about the mental aspect," Dr. Armistead had said. "But I think it's more than that. This sport teaches a lot about risk and reward. The riskier players pick up a ton of self-confidence."

"And broken bones?" Zimmer said sarcastically.

"Well, the rooms are padded pretty well. And they all wear pads and helmets. Or at least they're supposed to. But I'm talking about their spirit. We do want an overachieving bunch on this ship, don't we?"

"Hmm," Zimmer had muttered. "Have either of you tried this crazy game?"

"My son loved it," Bauer said sadly. "I can't tell you how many hours he used to spend at the rec center by our house."

The following day Dr. Zimmer had met with the crew members to explain his decision.

"I want you to realize that in order to build an Airboard . . . place . . . on this ship, something else will have to go. So we're going to look at redesigning part of the Storage Section and leaving off some of the . . ."

He didn't get to finish the sentence. The crew had cheered so loudly that he had to chuckle, shake his head and walk back to his office, leaving them to celebrate. "Oh well," he muttered to himself as he walked with his hands in his pockets, "as long as it keeps them sharp on the voyage they can probably do without a few extra storage rooms."

Gap hustled into *Galahad*'s Airboarding room and immediately saw Rico Manzelli, one of the best Boarders on the ship, and easily the crew's craziest daredevil. Rico was flying across the track, his arms held low and slightly out from his sides as he sensed the magnetic power coursing through the rails under the floor. Approaching one of the banks in the far corner of the room, he suddenly shifted his weight and leaned into a hard right-hand turn. For a moment he almost toppled, then righted himself and turned on the speed down a back straightaway.

Gap smiled and waved as Rico flashed by him, and the wild Italian quickly returned the wave. Gap took a seat on one of the bleachers and watched intently. It didn't do any good to try to learn where the track was energized, because it would be a completely different course for the next run. Instead he kept his eyes on Rico's style, the way he crouched forward, then casually shifted his weight back during a fast stretch. Gap used more of his arms than Rico, which some people thought was bad form. All Gap knew was that he was just about faster than anyone, with the possible exception of the guy currently racing around the room.

As he banked out of another turn Rico suddenly pinwheeled his arms and leapt into the air. He had obviously misjudged the magnetic pull and had veered off course. Tucking himself into a ball, he hit the padded floors and rolled several feet. The Airboard flipped once, twice, and then came to a stop. Gap stood up and gave Rico a sarcastic round of applause.

"I'd give you a nine-point-five for the form, but only a seven for the dismount," he yelled with a laugh.

"Oh, man," Rico said, huffing as he jogged over to the bleachers. "That's the first time it's done such an abrupt cut out of a banked turn. I guess Zoomer has decided we're getting a little too comfortable out there," he said, referring to the pet name the Boarders had given the computer that controlled the underground course.

"Hurt?" Gap said as he strapped on his shiny silver helmet.

"Naw," Rico said, although Gap knew that it was taking all of his willpower to keep from rubbing where he'd landed on his knee.

"Mind if I try your board?" Gap said.

Rico handed over the bright red board with blue stripes around the edges. "Be my guest. Just bring it back in one piece, okay?"

Gap grinned and jogged over to the starting blocks. He positioned the board over the spot where the magnetic power began and felt the board push up onto the air. Climbing aboard using the plastic handles on the wall for balance, he set his feet, pulled his helmet down tight, then pushed off across the floor.

At first he kept the speed fairly low, adjusting to the feel of Rico's souped-up board. It was obviously a fast, sleek model, and Gap knew that it could cost him a few bruises of his own if he let himself get out of control. He felt the magnetic power ebb on the left side, so he shifted to the right until he felt the strong upward push from below. Increasing the speed a little, he approached a banked turn and leaned back slightly. Using a combination of feel and instinct, he glided out of the turn and maneuvered through a series of twists and turns before coming to a stop in front of the bleachers and jumping off the board.

"C'mon, man, turn it up," Rico said. "My poor old mama could ride faster than that."

"Gimme time to get used to it," Gap said. "This thing is like a racehorse that wants to run."

He climbed back aboard and pushed off. This time he let his speed creep up a little, and before he knew it he was sailing along at an incredible clip. Passing the bleachers, he could hear the hoots and hollers of a few more hardy souls who had ventured in for an afternoon run. The cheers injected him with a little too much bravado, and the next thing he knew he was flying off the board, smacking head-on with one of the padded walls. Behind him came roars of laughter as the assembled group stood and dished out the same verbal abuse he had ladled onto Rico.

Grinning, he walked back and handed the board to Rico. Unlike that daredevil, however, Gap's pride did not prevent him from rubbing his shoulder where it had collided with the wall.

"I'll feel that for a couple of days," he said, grimacing. "But I love the board, man. Give me another shot next time?"

"Sure," Rico said, "if you think you can handle it."

Gap slapped him on the arm and, with a laugh, strolled out of the room and down towards the lift, still rubbing his shoulder. Good thing Tree hadn't been there, he thought, then immediately caught himself and shook his head. Why did it always come back to her? It seemed he couldn't go an hour without somehow thinking about her.

It was even starting to affect his decisions about his work on the Council. He felt it important to sit down and visit with Triana about the events that had befallen them after launch, but should he? If Channy had already picked up on his feelings, maybe Tree had also. He imagined himself walking around with a flashing neon sign on his forehead that blinked "I Love Tree." He'd seen other guys his age make fools of themselves, and he wasn't about to do the same. This is stupid, he told himself.

Since it was dinnertime and the majority of the crew was three levels above in the Dining Hall, it was quiet throughout this section as Gap made his way toward the lift that would take him up to his room to change. He rubbed a hand through his dark spiked hair, then again massaged the shoulder that had absorbed the impact with the wall. He felt the bulk and tone of his muscle, and couldn't help wondering if Triana liked what she saw. He wasn't as tall as he would have liked, but still was athletically built. She would . . . He shook his head, suddenly disgusted with himself for this momentary surge of vanity. What difference did it make what Triana thought of him? He had work to do. There was no time to worry about romance, especially now. He had five years or more to worry about that, and Tree wasn't going anywhere.

Ha! Wasn't going anywhere! He couldn't help but smile at the thought. Where could a girl hide from him on a ship the size of an average shopping mall back home? "Idiot," he murmured to himself. "Get your head on straight."

He rounded a corner and found Channy Oakland waiting at the lift. Oh great, he thought. More "Romeo" talk was sure to follow.

"Hey there, Casanova," Channy said. Gap rolled his eyes. Romeo, Casanova, whatever. It was too bad he liked Channy so much; it made it that much harder to hate her. Her lean, trim figure looked chiseled in her bright yellow workout clothes. The dark chocolate tone of her skin glistened, highlighting the muscular cut of her arms and legs.

"Getting in a little late afternoon workout, I see," he said, changing the subject. That was probably the best way to handle her teasing, he figured. Get her to talk about her passion: exercise. Besides, if he kept reacting every time she needled him, she would never stop.

"Dance class, actually," she said. "Something you should

consider, with your gymnastic background." She noticed the sweat still dripping from his hairline. "And you've obviously been Boarding. Don't get so caught up in that game that you forget about your workouts in the gym. I sent an e-mail to everyone last night reminding them of what Dr. Zimmer told us. 'Never stop exercising your body or your mind. You'll need both in perfect shape when you arrive.' Airboarding might work up a little bit of a sweat, but nothing compared to what I'll put you through."

"Yeah, I know," Gap said. "I'll be there first thing in the morning, ready to let you torture me for an hour."

The lift arrived and they stepped inside. The lift system operated only between sections of the ship. The crew members were expected to walk to every destination within the sections themselves. No laziness allowed.

"Oh, and speaking of e-mail," Gap said when the lift door had closed. "Did you see that the Council meeting was rescheduled for eleven o'clock tomorrow morning?"

"Bon told me before I had a chance to see it." She pushed the button for the crew quarters. "Or, as he said, 'Her majesty has requested our presence.' You know, I like Bon sometimes, but why does he have this attitude about Tree? It's very . . . I don't know, very . . ."

"Childish," Gap filled in the blank, wiping at the sweat on his brow. "I thought he might be jealous of her. Maybe he wanted to be in charge. But after a while I noticed that he has a power problem with everyone. He didn't even get along too well with Dr. Zimmer, remember?"

"You know what he told me one day, about a month before launch?" Channy lowered her voice mysteriously. Gap smiled inwardly. Channy loved to gossip. "He said some of the scientists back in Sweden thought Dr. Zimmer was the wrong man to put this mission together. They thought he was too emotionally involved with the crew. Bon said Dr. Zimmer made too many decisions with his heart and not his brain."

"What would Bon know about a heart?" Gap laughed. "Growing up around the Arctic Circle put ice water in his veins." They were laughing together when the lift door opened. Then, they froze.

The wall across from the lift opening had been vandalized with a large red marker. The words screamed out at Gap and Channy, and shock gripped them:

THIS IS A DEATH SHIP!

14

Dr. Wallace Zimmer would have acknowledged that he was, indeed, emotionally involved with the *Galahad* project. In fact, the truth was he *loved* the kids who would be placed on humanity's lifeboat. No one in history had carried so much responsibility, the task of preserving the human race . . . and they were teenagers! As he told Roy Orzini and Dr. Bauer late one evening, "It's tough enough being a young adult. Think of the pressure as you mature, not only from your peers, but from yourself. And we're asking these kids to save our species? It's staggering."

He almost felt as if he had adopted the 251 colonists. He tried to spend time with each of them, but he had so many duties to attend to that it became necessary to concentrate on the key players in the mission: the Council. And, most important, the one crew member who would be in charge at launch. He or she would have to be an amazing person, with not only intelligence, but also wisdom. Dr. Zimmer understood the difference between the two.

Months had been spent analyzing the files of possible candidates. So many had the qualities he was looking for: honesty, courageousness and ability to lead. He had known for a long time that Triana Martell might get the nod, but the final decision was among her, Gap Lee, and a girl from India named Sela. Then, with the launch only five months away, Dr. Zimmer was shocked by a visit from a tearful Sela.

"I'm withdrawing from *Galahad,*" she told him. "I've decided to go home to be with my family."

He had been too stunned at first to respond, but spent the next hour quietly discussing the matter with her. Had her family pressured her into the decision? Was it for religious purposes? Was she having a problem with the other crew members? Was she simply afraid of the voyage?

Sela shook her head softly in reply to each question. No, she told him, she had decided that she wanted to spend her family's last days with them, not leaving them behind to embark on a crusade that had only a slight chance of succeeding. Her family ties were strong, and she had made the decision, not them. And she would not be talked out of it.

Dr. Zimmer was saddened, but respectful of her wishes. He was with her to say good-bye as she boarded the flight back home. He then returned to *Galahad*'s command center, summoned the remaining colonists and announced his decision: Triana Martell would lead the expedition at launch. No changes would be made for the first three years of the mission. After that, the crew members could elect whomever they saw fit to command the next three-year step.

The crew was saddened to hear of Sela's decision, but not surprised at Triana's selection as their leader. Tree, as Roy Orzini had begun calling her, was accepted by them, admired as much as anyone else among their elite group. But she hadn't made too many close friends. She was a loner, which was okay with Dr. Zimmer. He knew that command was usually a lonely perch. As long as she was able to cooperate with the other Council members and communicate effectively with the crew, she was a perfect choice.

Dr. Zimmer's long, private discussions with Tree told him a lot about the girl. Born in Indiana, her parents soon divorced and she moved at age two with her father to Colorado. He worked very hard at his job as a computer engineer, but managed to spend a lot of time with his daughter. He loved reading to her, and soon saw that spawn a love of books in her. By her seventh birthday she had mastered the connection into the vast computer library banks and was reading everything she could find. She was also a natural athlete, and the father and daughter duo spent endless weekend hours at the park, tossing or kicking around a ball, climbing on the playground equipment or just simply wrestling in the grass. In time, Triana had grown tall and slender, and made her father proud by excelling in the classroom and on the sports fields.

Her relationship with her mother was another story. An executive with a major corporation in Indiana, and a big shot in her preferred political party, Triana's mother made it clear she had no time to spend with her daughter. Work came first, politics second and nothing third. Tree had flown back to spend holidays with her mother in the first few years, but eventually she just quit going. If her mother noticed, she never acted as if she cared. A single phone call once a month was all that she managed to fit into her schedule. In Triana's mind, her mother was nothing more than a distant relative, and the little girl spent her days happy and carefree in the shadow of the Rocky Mountains.

Until that spring day when Triana's father began to show symptoms of Comet Bhaktul's curse. For some people the disease progressed at a slow, agonizing pace; others, like Tree's father, deteriorated quickly. The microscopic particles attacked his lungs and nervous system, and in a matter of days he was taken away from his daughter, locked up within a medical research lab for tests, and studied around the clock. Triana was able to visit him twice a week, but wasn't allowed to enter the room where he remained hooked up to various machines. So little was known about the epidemic, and doctors were unwilling to take a chance with personal contact. Triana and her father had to speak using an intercom, watching each other's tears through a window that separated them.

Four weeks after he was admitted to the lab, all visits were terminated. Triana was forbidden from seeing her dad, and was told that he was unable to talk on the phone. He had now been taken from her completely, and she knew it meant the worst. Her mother called and offered to fly her back to Indiana, although the invitation sounded hollow to the fourteen-year-old girl. When she declined, and instead insisted on staying in Colorado with her dad's best friend and his family, it almost sounded as if her mother was relieved.

The letter from Dr. Zimmer was sent to Triana's school principal. Elsie Velasquez knew what was going on with Triana's father, and had excused her prize student from classes for a while. Falling behind would not be a problem for the incredibly gifted young woman; on the contrary, she could miss a month or more and most likely still be at the top of her class. Ms. Velasquez wished she had a dozen students like Triana Martell.

She found Triana at home, sitting quietly in her bedroom, her feet pulled up beneath her as she sat next to the fireplace. A notebook and pen lay beside her. Ms. Velasquez noticed that the troubled girl was watching a photo gallery on the vidscreen, a snapshot of Triana and her dad at one moment crystal clear, then slowly fading, to be replaced by another picture. The one currently on the screen had been taken at one of the Colorado ski resorts, and featured Mr. Martell in a wickedly funny ski hat, brightly colored with long, flowing tassels drooping down one side. He was crouching in the knee-deep snow. Tree, pictured in the background, was raising a handful of the powder, obviously ready to launch the snowball at him. Both of them were captured in the middle of a laughing attack, and the faces reflected pure, uncomplicated joy. Ms. Velasquez took one look and knew that no father/daughter bond could be closer. She took a deep breath and fought off the urge to cry.

Triana looked up at the school administrator, then reached over and shut off the vidscreen. Slowly, she rose from the soft carpet on the floor, walked toward Ms. Velasquez and, without saying anything, wrapped her arms around the woman. There were no sobs, no tears. Just a painful minute where no words were needed for expression.

Finally, Triana pulled back and looked into Elsie Velasquez's face. "I don't know when I'll be coming back to school," she said quietly. "They won't let me see my dad."

The school principal gently pulled a strand of hair out of the young girl's face. "We need to talk, honey," she said.

They spent the next hour sitting at the dining room table as Ms. Velasquez recited the information contained in Dr. Zimmer's letter. It outlined the plan for *Galahad,* and described the process of selecting five thousand kids from around the world who would be tested endlessly for almost two years. Eventually the five thousand would be pared down to the final 251 colonists who would leave Earth on the ultimate mission. Based on scholastic scores and health records, Triana had already been selected as one of the five thousand, and, with her family's permission, would leave immediately for California and the orientation sessions for *Galahad*.

Triana listened without saying a word. Finally, she shook her head. "I can't leave my dad," she said. "I can't. I know he needs me. Even if they won't let me see him, I know he needs me here."

Elsie Velasquez wasn't going to argue with the bright young girl. She already felt a twinge of guilt, coming to Triana's home while the girl was openly grieving for her father. But she also knew that the offer from Dr. Wallace Zimmer was a onetime chance, perhaps Triana's only opportunity to escape the clutches of Bhaktul's poisonous grip. Part of her wanted to tell the fourteen-year-old, "Look, you can see what has happened to your dad. The same thing could happen to you if you don't take this chance to escape." But there was no way she could do that. Instead, she nodded silently, rose to her feet and pulled Triana close to her. The two of them stood there for a full minute, arms wrapped tightly around each other, and Ms. Velasquez felt the warmth of her own tears begin to spill down her face. She let go, placing a quick kiss on Triana's forehead, and left.

Five days later, in her school office, Ms. Velasquez received a call from the grieving teen. In a quiet, eerily composed voice,

Triana told her, "My dad is gone. They told me he died Friday, the day after you came to see me."

"Honey, I'm so sorry," was all Elsie could think to reply. "I am so—"

"Anyway," Triana broke in, "I've been thinking about it, and I want you to call that man about the space mission."

The principal was shaken by the coolness displayed by the young woman. "Have you called your mother to talk about this?" she said.

"I'm not going to call her. She hasn't been my mother for a long time. My dad was . . . was all I had. There's no reason for me to stay here. If they still want me, I'm ready. I'm ready to leave anytime."

15

When Roy Orzini finished programming me, he did something kinda funny. He showed me some movies. Yeah, I know, you might think that's a little strange, but we're talking about Roy here.

Truth is, I'm glad he did. They were all space movies, movies that usually showed how humans might react to strange things they find out there. Some were a little corny, like Forbidden Planet. *Some were very entertaining, like* Close Encounters of the Third Kind *and* E.T. *Some were deep, man, like* 2001: A Space Odyssey. *But none of us is an expert on what will happen when trouble brews in the galactic void; we haven't been there yet. Still, the movies at least show us possible human reactions.*

Gap knew that I had seen the movies, so of course he had to be Joe Comedian one day and call me R2D2. What a shame the heat didn't work very well in his room the next couple of days. I don't know how that could've happened.

"Look, if we don't get to the bottom of this pretty soon there's going to be some real trouble on this ship."

Gap had the attention of everyone on the Council. They sat in the Conference Room for their second meeting, the first one having been cut short by the incident with Peter Meyer. That was old news, however. The latest buzz around *Galahad* was the menacing graffiti that had been discovered by Gap and Channy. Triana had investigated immediately, but there wasn't much to go on. The red marker that had been used did not match any of the supplies aboard the ship. And, after some quick questioning of the other crew members who had been in the area, Triana figured a time window of about fifteen minutes when someone could have scrawled the message before Gap and Channy happened along.

Triana sat forward and looked across the table at Gap. "You're talking about the effects on the crew." It was more a statement than a question.

"Yes, I am," he said, tapping his index finger on the table. "When Peter freaked out, it was unsettling, but not surprising. And this might sound strange, but I think it actually helped a lot of kids. You know, some of them were coiled pretty tightly when we launched. Maybe his breakdown relieved a little pressure from them, like it told them 'Hey, I'm not the only one.' But this . . ." He stopped and shook his head.

Lita Marques set down her stylus pen and spoke up. "Gap's right. This thing on the wall is different. Now it's someone intentionally trying to scare us."

"And they're doing a great job," Channy said. "I've still got the chills from seeing it."

"The whole crew has a bad case of the jumps right now," Lita said. "I've had three different people ask me if Peter was responsible for this message. I think they hoped he had something to do with it, so they can just write it off as one kid having a breakdown."

"How is Peter, by the way?" Gap said.

"I checked him out this morning and sent him to his room. He seems okay. Actually, he seems more embarrassed than anything else."

"Let's get back to the graffiti," Triana said. "I agree with Gap that we need to find out who's behind this, and quickly. I wanted all of the crew members to relax and get used to their new lives as soon as possible. That's pretty hard to do when someone is threatening your life. At least that's how I interpret this."

"I thought a big part of our selection process was supposed to weed out anyone who might pull this type of stunt," Channy said.

"Ha!" Bon said with a snort. He hadn't said much since the meeting had started, but now he lashed out. "Those tests weren't for our sake. Those were designed to make the people back on Earth feel good about their choices. You know, if you're gonna send a ship full of teenagers off to 'save the race,' then you want to feel like you made good choices, right? If those tests were so reliable, then how come—"

"How come they let you slip through?" interrupted Gap, causing Channy to giggle.

Bon glared at the engineering leader. "Well, yeah. We all know I don't seem like the perfect *Galahad* specimen. So how come I wasn't weeded out?"

No one answered. In the silence, Bon slowly looked around the table at the other Council members. When his gaze settled on Triana he said, "You wanna know why? Partly because Dr. Zimmer knew this Council needed a different voice. But also partly because those tests were soft. It would be easy for anyone to slip through." His mouth became a grim line. "Don't kid yourselves. Any one of us on this ship might have a loose spring that good old Dr. Armistead wouldn't find out about with her tests. Any one of us."

"That's right," Tree said, returning his stare. "It could be any one of us, even someone right here in this room. But I guess I have a little more confidence in Dr. Zimmer and Dr. Armistead than others might. For the most part I think they were pretty good judges of character. I've only questioned their selection process once or twice."

This obvious jab brought silence to the room and the air seemed to grow thick. Finally Lita diffused the situation by speaking up. "I had a few thoughts about Peter's situation. I think they're at least worth talking about."

For a moment it looked like Triana had more to say to Bon, but instead she turned to Lita. "All right. Go ahead."

Lita took a few seconds to collect her thoughts, and then said, "Well, it just doesn't make sense to me that Peter could have imagined what he claims to have seen. It doesn't fit any of his tests, even though I guess some people don't put much stock in those." She looked at Bon, sitting next to her, but there was no reaction.

Tree bit her lip absentmindedly. "What are you saying?"

"I'm saying that maybe what Peter saw was real."

The statement was followed by dead silence. Each of the Council members exchanged glances, until finally Channy thought aloud. "How could that be possible?"

Triana sighed heavily. "Roc, are you with us?"

"I'm in the bath right now. Can you call back later?" came the computer's reply from the speaker.

"Roc . . ."

"Yes, Tree."

"What do you think about that? About an adult being on the ship?"

"Is it likely that an adult has stowed away on *Galahad*? No. But if you're asking me if it's possible, then yes, I would say almost anything is possible. In fact, do you remember our discussion about the life-energy readings on the ship? How they're not in balance?"

"Yes, I remember," Triana said. "Have you figured that out yet?"

The computerized voice of Roy Orzini was comforting, although the message was not. "No. I've had Dr. Zimmer's people recheck all the readings on their end, and we each come up with the same imbalance. What's interesting is that factoring in another person on board would satisfy the equation."

"Meaning?"

"Meaning that the life-energy readings are just barely out of whack. Just enough to account for two hundred fifty-two people on *Galahad,* instead of two hundred fifty-one."

Again, total silence engulfed the Conference Room. Roc

sensed the quiet and added, "Of course, I'm not saying this is what has happened. I'm only saying the scientific evidence would support Lita's statement."

"Plus," Lita said, "there's the marker pen used in the graffiti. We don't have—or at least we're not supposed to have—that kind of marker on the ship. Where did it come from?"

"Probably the same place this came from," Gap said. He reached into his pocket, grasped the object he'd found near *Galahad*'s Storage Section and tossed it onto the table. It spun for a few seconds, and then shimmied to a stop. The other four Council members shifted their gaze from it to Gap and back again.

"What is that?" Channy said. She picked it up, looked at each side, and rubbed her fingers along the side.

"It's a coin," Lita said.

"A coin?"

"Yeah," Lita told her, taking the object from Channy's fingers. "Remember hearing about the days when people used things like this for money? Before the United States and most other countries started using the credit bank, this is what people used to buy things. This was called a quarter, because it represented one-fourth of a dollar. But who would have brought one on board *Galahad*?"

The question was answered with blank stares. Tree held her hand out and Lita dropped the coin into her palm. The ship's leader looked closely at the markings, with an eagle embossed on one side under the words "United States of America," and the head of George Washington gracing the opposite side. Under the president's bust was stamped "2021." It was dull and dirty looking, which told Tree that this particular coin hadn't been kept preserved in someone's private collection.

"I've seen one of these recently," she mused aloud, to no one in particular. What she didn't say aloud was that she had seen a coin just like this on a newscast just a few months before their departure. She had brought it up with Dr. Zimmer, who had shrugged it off as unimportant. Could there be a connection between that newscast and this artifact discovered in the bowels of the ship? Logic screamed that it was too much of a coincidence, that she was holding a clue to their mysterious guest.

She stared at the rustic piece of history and then shook her head. "Well, anyway, this could be innocent. We've got two hundred fifty one kids on this ship, and it's easy enough to find out if someone brought this along."

"Why would they do that?" Channy said. "We don't even need the credit bank on *Galahad*. What would someone do with old-time money?"

Triana said, "I don't know, souvenir maybe. Good luck charm. Who knows? But I don't want to jump to any conclusions until we find out. I'll post an e-mail to the crew this afternoon and see if someone comes forward to claim this." She tossed the coin back to Gap.

"As far as this incident with Peter Meyer is concerned," she continued, "I want to proceed for now as if it *was* his imagination. I can't see stirring things up with the crew right now any more than they have been. If something else comes up, then we'll start a serious search for a possible stowaway. Any questions?"

There were none, and the meeting was apparently coming to an end. Bon Hartsfield didn't wait for any formal conclusion, and was the first to push back his chair and stand up. He leveled his gaze at Triana and said, "If you were using your head, you'd start that search for a stowaway right now. That coin didn't come from one of us. You know it, and I know it. It was left for us to find. Just like the surprise visit to Peter, and the threat painted on the wall."

He paused, still with the attention of the entire Council. Lowering his voice, but keeping his gaze on Triana, he put a chill into everyone.

"There is somebody on board *Galahad* who does not belong here. And no matter what his intentions, it's obvious he doesn't mind us knowing that he's here. Maybe because . . ."

He looked at Gap, then turned his cold stare back to Triana before finishing.

"Maybe because he doesn't think there's anything we can do about it."

Silence swallowed the Conference Room. Bon slowly made eye contact with each of the Council members, then stalked out the door. Triana was tempted to shout after him, but bit her tongue. It was ridiculous that she allowed his gruff manner to affect her so. As the others stood and prepared to leave, she touched Gap on the arm and said, "Hey, could you stick around a minute? I want to talk to you about something."

Gap's heart jumped at her touch. Again he had the sensation that she could almost read his thoughts, that same neon message blazing on his forehead. "Get it together," he thought to himself. "Don't be an idiot."

Channy and Lita filed out of the room. Channy was quizzing the head of the Health Department about the coin, and seemed impressed with Lita's storehouse of knowledge. Triana heard Lita mention something about "paper money," and then they were out of sight, leaving her alone with Gap. She looked into his face.

"Tell me something, Gap. You used to be pretty good friends with Bon. I need to know if there's something I'm doing to make him especially edgy with me. Does he tell you anything?"

Gap chuckled and rolled his eyes. "Listen, Tree, it's not you. At least, not that he's told me anyway. Bon's just . . ." He paused, looking for the right words. "He just kinda lives his life in a bad mood. You know what I mean? Some people . . . well, some people are like Channy, and then there's Bon."

"Yeah, I remember his confrontations with Dr. Zimmer and those guys," Tree said. "I think Dr. Zimmer treated him like a sparring partner or something. I still can't believe he made the crew list, let alone named to the Council. But I think it's different with me."

Gap shrugged. "I don't know. I guess I don't see it the way you do. I just see it as Bon being his typical moody, angry, Mr. Unfriendly self."

Tree sighed. "Sorry to bring you into this. I just thought you might have a little information that could help me. We're going to be stuck together inside this ship for a long time, and I'd really like for us to get along, if that's possible."

"Hey, don't worry about it. You're not the first person he's rubbed the wrong way, and I guarantee you that before we reach our new home he might be the first crew member we stop and let off along the way."

Triana laughed. "Thanks, Gap." She turned to leave, then stopped and looked back at him again. "By the way, I wanted to tell you that I'm glad you're on the Council. I don't know what we'd do without you."

Gap still had the quarter in his hand. He reached up and placed it over his eye, squinting to hold it in place like a monocle. "Well, then," he yammered in his best pirate impersonation, "you won't mind if I keep this as a tip, eh?"

Tree burst into more laughter and patted him on the cheek. "Sure, Blackbeard, it's all yours for now. Unless we find the rightful owner." She walked out of the Conference Room.

Gap waited behind, exhaling loudly. "There's only one problem," he thought to himself, letting the coin drop into his hand. "What if the rightful owner doesn't have a ticket to be on this flight?"

16

Genetic screening. The term didn't scare people anymore, not like it had near the end of the twentieth century. In those days many people tried to associate it with selective breeding, or the creation of Frankenstein-like beings, when in reality it was simply a human version of preventive maintenance. Once scientists and doctors had learned the secrets of reading the genetic blueprint, it became obvious that the easiest way to combat disease and defects in people was to stop them before they started.

By the year 2025 it had become common practice to examine the gene structure of an unborn child and to repair any suspect areas that might lead to problems after it was born. Many childhood diseases were virtually eliminated, and birth defects became increasingly rare. Those who had at first objected were slowly convinced by the obvious benefits, until soon the only people opposed to it did so because of religious convictions.

The screening process for *Galahad* was perhaps the most intense ever devised. Of the five thousand young people originally chosen for testing, almost two thousand were immediately rejected after undergoing thorough genetic testing. Dr. Zimmer faced an incredible wave of negative publicity when the results were first announced, as many of the families of rejected applicants cried out in anger, some claiming that Zimmer was putting together the beginnings of a "super race" of humans.

"Nonsense," the project leader told the press. "It's not a matter of trying to create SuperKids. We're simply trying to give these colonists the best chance at survival in a possibly hostile new world. We want to eliminate as many difficult hurdles as we can, and that includes filtering out potentially dangerous physical ailments. If these kids are the last hope of mankind, why wouldn't we want to help them with every means at our disposal? We can't be influenced by bruised feelings. This is far too important."

Another safeguard included the construction of the Incubator. Its real name was the Sterile Environmental Receptacle, or SER, but Dr. Zimmer hated that label. It would house the 251 space travelers for their final month before launch, isolating them from the outside world. They would be watched and tested in the sterile environment, one final precaution that nothing developed in them that could jeopardize the mission. *Galahad*'s passengers would all be in perfect physical shape when they boarded, and once they were sealed inside there would be no chance of any Earth contaminate making the journey.

If the scientists were correct, this would mean even the common cold would be left behind, along with other transmittable sicknesses. Dr. Bauer observed how the kids would all be kept safe and warm for the weeks leading up to their departure, and compared it to a hospital incubator. The name naturally stuck, and from that moment on the Incubator was their final stopping point before the exodus.

While the passengers themselves were being shielded from earthly contamination, the process of keeping their vessel completely clean was under way. As each section of the giant spacecraft was assembled in high Earth orbit, thousands of tiny robots scurried from level to level. Many of them inspected the construction progress, double- and triple-checking each joint, each connection, each wiring patch, each nut and bolt. Hundreds of others were assigned the duty of sterilizing the finished product, vaporizing all remains of human contact left behind. When *Galahad*'s young pioneers stepped aboard, it would be as if they had entered a sanitary laboratory.

Wallace Zimmer had a balancing act to perform. He wanted the ship to leave in absolutely perfect condition, with no traces of germs anywhere. Yet at the same time he was determined that the teenagers who would be carried into space should feel as comfortable as possible, a true home away from home, and the thought of a totally sterile spacecraft sounded too much like a hospital. He was counting on Fenton Bauer's experience with extraterrestrial dome design to help.

"I want these kids to feel completely at home," he told Bauer as they sat in the project cafeteria one afternoon. "I'm allowing them to bring several items from home, and they'll each have a hand in decorating their own room. But there's one thing I don't want them to bring aboard."

"Let me guess," Dr. Bauer said. "Germs."

"Right."

Dr. Bauer nodded in agreement before a sad smile washed across his face. "When my son was little he used to call them 'gerbs.' Every time I would tell him to wash his hands before dinner he would waddle down the hall to go 'get rid of the gerbs.'"

He shifted in his chair and looked across at Dr. Zimmer. "I did my best to teach him about 'gerbs,' how to stay healthy and fit. But there's nothing I can do about these 'gerbs,' is there? Washing his hands won't help him this time. Or you or me."

An uncomfortable moment passed, then Dr. Bauer seemed to recover.

"I know what you're looking for," he said. "Zap the germs on everything from posters to pajamas, but keep the ship feeling warm and homey, right?"

"That's right," Dr. Zimmer said. "I don't want them to feel like their things are being zapped. I'd like to keep their personal belongings exactly that: personal. They're going to feel disconnected anyway once they leave, and I'd like for them to maintain their connection to as many personal things as possible. If we treat these items like lab objects, it's just one more layer of comfort that's stripped away. It's up to you and Angela Armistead to make sure there's still a human touch to all of this."

For the next hour the two men changed direction and began focusing on which kids were qualified to lead the various departments. Of all the candidates for the role of Activities/Nutrition Director, Zimmer was particularly drawn to Channy Oakland.

Bright and enthusiastic, Channy was just barely old enough to qualify for the mission, but Zimmer was convinced that she would play an important role after launch. Her mother, a physical therapist, had made sure that she grew up with a healthy respect for her body and the proper nutrition and exercise needed to keep it finely tuned. Channy and her older sister, D'Audra, had also spent many long hours assisting their mother in her clinic in England, mostly working with the disabled.

One summer day, during a particularly hot stretch of August, Channy had begged D'Audra to sneak away with her to go swimming. They had already worked eight days straight for their mom without a day off, and with school beginning again in a couple of weeks Channy had an itch to visit The Hole. Given the nickname generations ago, The Hole was a secluded pond tucked away in the woods just outside of town. For years kids had ditched school, church and part-time jobs to dive into the cool, crystal-clear water fed by a small waterfall. Channy loved it, and after just a little prodding, convinced D'Audra to slip into her swimsuit and run out to The Hole. Her older sister made her promise that they would be back within two hours, no arguing or whining, and off they went.

It would be a day Channy would never forget. D'Audra, two years older and already a terrific role model for her little sis, had been grinning as she started to leap off the rock ledge, fifteen feet over the water, anxious to prove that she could indeed reach the tree limb that jutted out several feet over the pond's surface below. But the smooth surface of rock was now covered with water, small puddles that had collected from the water dripping off the two sisters, and Channy saw D'Audra lose control just as she planted her foot to leap toward the branch. Although it only lasted a split second, Channy would remember the moment in slow motion forever. Her sister reached back to try to grab on to her for support, but instead plummeted down the embankment, striking the rocks at the water's edge.

The doctors had originally said it was doubtful she would ever walk again, with the damage to her spine so severe. But D'Audra had refused to allow that possibility. Channy watched in wonder over the next year as her older sister bravely fought through two operations and countless hours of rehab work. With her mother on one side and her adoring sister on the other, D'Audra took her first painful steps again exactly thirteen months after the horrible accident at The Hole. Sheer determination and strong will had ensured that the doctors would be wrong. She would walk again, and, she confided in Channy one quiet evening, she *would* reach that branch someday. Someday.

But Channy Oakland would not see her do it. Her mother had received a phone call from Dr. Wallace Zimmer.

17

The lights were slowly dimming in the hallways. Because there was no sun to create day and night, *Galahad* manufactured its own twenty-four-hour day. One of the thousands of duties that Roc oversaw, the hallways and meeting places would slowly light up beginning at six o'clock. It would remain bright throughout the "day," gradually fading to twilight by eight o'clock. The ship's designers knew this was necessary to keep each crew member's internal body clock properly adjusted. There would even be a slight change in the length of days as the calendar advanced, a nod to the changing seasons each passenger had left behind.

Another touch, suggested by Dr. Armistead, was the inclusion of sounds. Earth sounds, from an occasional faint whisper of wind to the barely audible sound of crickets during the "night" hours. Roc kept each of these noises in the background, more a psychological blanket than anything else. A comfort zone, Dr. Armistead had said. Sounds of home.

As the evening began on the eighth day, most of the crew had retired to either the Recreation Area or their own rooms. A group of ten, however, had remained in the Dining Hall after dinner, sitting at one of the large round tables. A deck of cards sat untouched at one side; finding a game that ten people could enjoy was difficult, and, besides, conversation seemed more interesting anyway.

At first the mood had been somber as they each quietly talked about home, nods of understanding punctuating each story. They were their own support group, leaning on one another to get through the homesick feelings, the sadness, the pain. When one person expressed guilt over leaving their family behind, nine others could relate, comfort coming in the form of a touch, a soft word, even a knowing look. Gradually the stories took a turn; tears were replaced with a smile. Fond memories began to lift the spirits.

Gap Lee was trying not to laugh. His face was mostly blank, but the corners of his mouth were cracking into a half smile. The last thing he wanted to do was appear insensitive to the story he was listening to . . . but it *was* funny. Unable to hold it back any longer, he broke out in a fit of laughter.

Angelina Reyes looked at him sharply. "It's not funny, Gap," she said crossly.

"I know," he said, taking a breath. "But it is, kinda. I mean, you did kick her in the head, right?"

"By accident," Angelina shot back. "I didn't mean to." But by now the rest of the group had begun laughing, too. They had all wanted to, but until Gap broke the ice they had each been exercising restraint out of courtesy.

"You know, most soccer players try to kick the ball, not the goalie's head," he quipped. This brought even more laughter from the others, while Angelina's face clouded.

"I was *trying* to kick the ball," she said. "I told you, the goalie dove for it at the last second. I don't know why you're laughing. She could have really been hurt."

"But you said she wasn't hurt that bad," Gap said. "You said she was just a little . . . what was the word?"

"Woozy," Angelina said, and for the first time a smile creased her face, too. "They stopped the game for a couple of minutes, but she stayed in and played the rest of the way." She looked down at the table, trying to compose herself, but eventually failing. Before she could stop herself she was laughing along with the others.

"Yeah, she was okay, but man, was she intimidated by me after that. I scored twice in the next five minutes."

More laughs poured out from the teenagers. After the stress from the last few days, it felt good. It felt *really* good.

Mitchell O'Connor, a thin redhead from Ireland, leaned back in his chair and put one of his feet up on the table. He looked at Angelina and said, "So, when our three-on-three soccer tournament starts, should the rest of us wear helmets when you're on the field?"

"It won't matter what you wear, Mitch," she said quickly. "I could score on you all day long."

A collection of "oohs" and "whoas" erupted around the table. Mitchell put his head back and laughed the hardest. He loved a good challenge, especially on the soccer field.

The whole crew was excited about the tournament. Not only did it provide the needed exercise, but also it drew everyone together in a spirit of teamwork. During their months of preparation on Earth they had held two such tourneys, and each one seemed to strengthen the connections they shared with each other. Dr. Zimmer was thrilled, and let Channy know that her idea was terrific. He encouraged the crew to make these competitive matches a regular part of their lives. He approved of anything to keep a couple hundred kids on their toes during the long, tedious journey.

He had reluctantly accepted their demand for the state-of-the-art Airboarding circuit, but that particular activity worried him. Speeding across the track and zipping through tight turns while hovering four inches off the ground sounded much too dangerous to both Zimmer and Bauer, but they conceded that it offered an alternative way to increase physical activity. The two scientists were more old-school and secretly hoped that soccer would hold the crew's interest. Now, in a few days, the star travelers would gather for their first soccer tournament of the voyage. Spirits were high in anticipation.

As the laughter subsided, Kylie Rickman pulled her knees up to her chest and wrapped her arms around her legs. With a coy look she addressed her companions.

"You know, I've seen the trophy."

"No way," Gap said. "How?"

"You forget that Channy is my roommate. She's hiding it from everyone until the first champions are decided. But she's just dying to show someone—you know how she is about keeping a secret—and the other night she pulled it out and showed me."

"And?" Angelina said. "What does it look like?"

"Like I could tell you," Kylie said.

"Oh, c'mon," Angelina cried. "If Channy can't keep a secret, why should you?"

"Sorry," Kylie said. "I'm not telling. Not even if . . ." She paused, her eyes sparkling.

"Not even if what?" Angelina said, leaning forward.

Kylie's eyes widened and her mouth dropped open in mock terror. "Not even if you kicked me right in the head."

The group exploded in more laughter, and Angelina threw her napkin at Kylie, who ducked in time for it to fly over her. Both girls grinned at each other, enjoying the evening's fun.

Suddenly the red light over the Dining Hall's vidscreen began to flash, and a soft series of tones drifted out of the speakers. It signaled an announcement that would be broadcast throughout *Galahad*. A moment later Triana's face appeared on the screen.

"Hi, everyone," she began. Her expression was neutral, a look that most of the crew was used to by now. All ten sets of eyes in the Dining Hall were fixed on the screen, a scene that was being played out in every section of *Galahad*.

"Well, we're on our way," Tree said. "We all knew that there would be some tough times. We knew that eventually we would all have to pull together, to help us get through some difficult situations. I just don't think any of us thought we would be tested so soon.

"I planned on having a meeting with the entire crew after we were about three or four weeks out. I don't think a lot of meetings are necessary. You all know your jobs, you know what's expected of you, and I think it's better if you're left alone to do those jobs. But, given the circumstances of the last few days, I'm moving our first meeting up to tomorrow morning."

Gap and Kylie exchanged glances. It had all of the signs of an emergency meeting, but Tree refused to label it that way. Just "a meeting." Another sign that Dr. Zimmer knew what he was doing when he named Triana Martell to lead the mission.

"Those of you on duty tomorrow morning will obviously be unable to attend, but we will cover it on the vidscreens. I expect everyone else to join us at eight thirty in the Learning Center. It shouldn't take long. Thanks, and we'll see you in the morning."

With that, her image faded, leaving a dark gray screen. The group in the Dining Hall sat silent for a moment, then relaxed and looked around at each other. It was Mitchell who spoke first.

"Well, I'm working tomorrow morning. You guys have fun without me."

With a few exchanges of "good night" and "see you tomorrow," the group split up and trudged out of the room. Gap Lee was the last to leave, waving his hand across the sensor that slowly cut the lights and left the room in darkness.

Five minutes later the door to the Dining Hall opened, and a shadowy figure crept quietly inside.

18

The two men sat in front of the dark vidscreen. The newscast had just ended, and Dr. Zimmer had switched off the screen in disgust. Dr. Bauer looked at his boss.

"Do you want to talk about it?"

"There's not much to discuss," Dr. Zimmer said. "The man is crazy. He's crazy."

The man was Tyler Scofield. The news had just broadcast a report from a rally that Zimmer's old colleague had organized to protest the *Galahad* project. Now that the final 251 crew members had been announced Scofield was using the event to blast the mission and its director.

"Of course he'll get publicity for these rallies," Dr. Bauer said. "Look, there are pockets of discontent around the world, but his group is the only one that's united and actually taking action. The newshounds will always want to cover something that's contrary and extremist."

"He's stirring up way too much trouble," Zimmer said. "Did you hear the phrases he used? 'A dictator choosing his subjects'? 'Selection governed by ego'? 'Masses ignored in cowardly flight'? Cowardly! Because he insists that attention be focused on curing Bhaktul Disease rather than on saving what little of humanity we can." He shook his head, then pointed at the blank screen. "He's doing everything in his power to turn public opinion against our project, and to make this some sort of personal vendetta."

"People won't listen to him," Dr. Bauer said. "There's too much momentum with *Galahad*. We're less than two months from—"

His comment was interrupted by a severe cough, followed by another. He grabbed his chest and bent forward. Sweat broke out on his forehead. Dr. Zimmer reached out a hand and gently touched his assistant on the forearm.

"Can I get you something, Fenton?"

"No," Dr. Bauer said between heavy breaths. "It's nothing, really. I just get a spasm every now and then. It's already over. I'm fine."

Dr. Zimmer knew that was a lie, but he let the incident pass without further comment. Dr. Bauer had been seeing the best physicians in order to stave off the encroaching Bhaktul Disease. He was slowly losing the fight, but obviously insistent upon maintaining his pride. A few reports had claimed Bhaktul would often affect the mental capacities of its victims, driving some to insanity. Zimmer was sure that this was his colleague's biggest fear. Bauer's entire career was built on the foundation of his adept mind. He could handle the coughing; an attack on his brain, however, would be unthinkable.

"Anyway," Bauer said finally, "what I was saying was that we're less than two months from launch. There's not enough time for Scofield to rally enough people to stop us. He's just a news story right now."

"You might be right. But I still want to boost security. Nobody—absolutely nobody—gets inside this compound without clearance."

"Understood," Bauer said. "There's some good news, by the way."

"Please, anything!" Zimmer said.

"That report about the ship's construction falling behind? Well, not true. I spoke with the Space Authority about an hour ago and they say the first payload of equipment and supplies is ready to be loaded aboard. They'll launch the first sealed containers for the Storage Sections early next week."

"And you're sure you don't need my help with those?" Zimmer said.

Dr. Bauer shook his head. "No, I told you I would handle the Storage Sections. You've got enough on your hands. Let me take care of those."

He started to get up, then paused and looked across at the project director.

"Oh, and another thing. Roy Orzini wants to meet with us about that computer creation of his."

"What's up?"

Bauer shrugged. "Not sure. But I can guess. He wrote me a pretty stern e-mail yesterday."

"About?"

"About shifting more control of the ship from the kids to . . . to—what's it called now? Roc?"

Zimmer smiled. "And why is he unhappy about that? He tells me that Roc can handle anything."

"Yeah, that's what he tells me, too," Bauer said. "But I think he's starting to wonder if we're putting too many eggs in one basket."

"Meaning what? That we're putting too much control in Roc's hands, and that if there's a problem—"

"—then the ship will be in trouble," Bauer said. "Yeah, that's what he thinks."

"But you disagree."

Bauer sat still for a moment, thinking about his answer.

"Listen, it's not that these kids aren't very bright," he said. "On the contrary, we've picked the brightest of the bright. They're brilliant. But they're kids. We're putting so much pressure on them, so much weight on those teenage shoulders, that—in my opinion—anything we can do to lighten that load will be critical. So, yeah, I'm afraid I have to disagree with the very excitable Mr.

Orzini. He tells us that Roc can handle it; then I say let the computer handle it all, and let these kids mature into the responsibilities over time."

Dr. Zimmer considered this for a minute.

"Well," he said, "you make a good point. Tell Roy we can talk tonight at dinner. I at least owe him the chance to make his case."

"Okay," Bauer said. "And speaking of dinner, if you need me this afternoon I'll be wrapping up the delivery of those seeds for *Galahad*'s farm. You'll be relieved to know that so far every country's shipments have been on time. Our little colonists are going to be eating quite well."

Dr. Zimmer took off his glasses and rubbed his forehead. "Well, delightful," he said with a touch of weariness in his voice. "But I won't truly feel relieved until these kids are gone. Away from Bhaktul. And away from Tyler Scofield."

19

Triana sat at the desk in her room, biting her lip and staring at the piles she had rearranged twice without doing anything to eliminate the clutter. She had scribbled a few notes on her electronic work pad for this morning's meeting, but had set it aside in favor of her personal journal.

> The crew needs to be reassured that things are fine. We're on course, all systems are operating smoothly. But I can feel a sense of panic starting to creep in. Just saying everything's okay is a mistake. They won't buy that, and I don't blame them. Dad used to say "people will tolerate bad news; they won't tolerate deception. Shoot straight." So now I have to somehow break the news without spooking them even more.

She closed the journal and swapped her pen for the work pad stylus. It was time to get back to work, time to finish her speech to the crew. Looking at it now, she grimaced at all of the lines she had written and scratched out. Her communication skills were very good, but she was having a hard time deciding how to approach this. The stylus hung about half an inch above the work pad, waiting for some type of signal from her brain. Nothing was coming to her now, so she set it down.

"Roc," she called out. "What am I doing here?"

The mellow voice of Roy Orzini answered her. "Are you writing an essay called 'Why Roc Is the Coolest Thing in the Solar System and Beyond'?"

"I mean, what am I doing here? On this ship? In this position of . . . of . . ."

"Leadership?" Roc said.

"Well, yeah," Tree said. "Why did Sela have to back out? Why didn't they choose Gap as her replacement? Why not Bon, for that matter? He seems to know everything."

"He certainly seems to know how to push your hot buttons," Roc said. "Pardon me for saying this, Tree, but don't you think it's time you quit pouting?"

"Pouting?"

"You've been pouting since the day we left. First, you couldn't seem to leave fast enough, and now that we *have* left you're acting like you don't want to be here at all. You're pouting. And it's very unbecoming."

When Tree didn't respond, Roc continued. "You know, a lot of people thought that it took a long, long list of qualifications in order to be considered for this mission. There were a lot of people who never nominated their children or their students because they thought the odds were too tough. But the truth is, Dr. Zimmer really had just two main requirements. Would you like to know what they were?"

"Gap says we were picked for our brains and bravery," Triana said.

"Gap fell on his head a few too many times when he was a gymnast," Roc shot back. "That would be the simplest of answers, and maybe what someone else might have searched for. But not Dr. Z."

"So what was he looking for?"

"He would pull my plug if he knew I was telling you this. But I think you should know what made you pass the test. First, you had to be not just smart, but quick to absorb new ideas and new solutions. A genius with a closed mind is worthless on this trip.

Worthless in general, some might say. I should know; I'm a genius."

Tree thought about that for a moment, biting her lip again. "And second?"

"Second, complete confidence in your own ability. Dr. Zimmer wanted young people who believed in themselves and believed that they were special. Not cocky, but confident."

Triana sat still, staring at her desk without seeing it. What Roc had said was true; every kid on *Galahad* was sure they belonged on the mission. She believed it, too. This was her place, her time, her calling. This was what she was born to do.

So why the doubts now? Why the confusion? Was this one of the defining moments of her command? Of her life? And was she up to the challenge?

Roc broke the silence. "Your father knew that you should be here."

Tree looked up with a start. "What are you talking about? My dad didn't even know I was selected—"

"That's right," Roc said. "He died before the selection process was finished. But he knew you were a candidate."

"How do you know this?"

"Because he sent a personal data disc directly to Dr. Zimmer and the *Galahad* committee. It was all about you. Your courage. Your loyalty. Your intellect. It was one of the last things he did before going to the hospital."

Triana's eyes started to fill with tears, but she let Roc continue.

"Your father had no idea what the criteria for selection were. But he knew his daughter, and knew what was inside you. When he and your mother separated, you spent time with both parents, but made your own decision to live with your father. Your mother consented without argument.

"When faced with choices in education, you didn't hesitate. You chose the most demanding classes in the most demanding school. You knew you would succeed, and you did.

"When your father fell ill, you chose to sacrifice your sports, your hobbies, and your free time to attend to him. Other families requested special assistance; you believed you could handle the responsibility, and you did.

"So you're going through yet another difficult time," Roc added. "I don't believe anyone else on *Galahad* is better equipped to handle it than you. Dr. Zimmer felt the same way. And so did your father."

Triana remained still and quiet. One solitary tear had started to make its way down her cheek, but it never had a chance. She wiped it away and picked up the stylus pen from her desk.

Bending over and resting her head on one hand, she began writing again on her work pad. After a silent minute of concentration she said, "Thank you, Roc."

"You're welcome. Now back to work. And remember, it's not just 'coolest in the solar system,' it's 'coolest in the solar system and beyond.'"

20

There were two weeks left before the crew of *Galahad* would leave their home planet and enter the Incubator orbiting as part of the space station. Their training was about as complete as could be expected. As Dr. Armistead put it, "We could work with them for another two years and still not prepare them for everything they're going to encounter."

Wallace Zimmer didn't want their last two weeks on Earth spent in training. Instead he sent each of them home. He gathered them all together for a final briefing before they scattered. "Soak up everything you possibly can," he said. "If you love the beach, spend hours and hours on the beach. If you love the mountains, climb every one you can. If you want to walk in the forest, inhale every fresh breath of pine that you can. Come back with your sensory organs overloaded. Stock up enough memories to last you five years.

"And one other thing," he added as he watched their eyes begin to mist over. "Embrace your loved ones. Tell them everything you've ever wanted to say to them. Show them how much you love them." He tapped his chest softly. "Let them know that you will carry them with you on your journey, that they will never be far away. Comfort them, and let them comfort you."

He looked out among the many faces, the faces from dozens

of countries, each representing a unique history and outlook. The faces of Eos, staring back at him, making him proud.

"I want to tell you to have fun," he said, "but I don't expect you to. Good-byes are never easy. I suspect that most of you will grow up more in the next two weeks than at any other point in your lives."

With a few closing instructions from Dr. Armistead regarding their return and what items they could and could not bring, the group stood up slowly and filed out of the room. Triana lingered behind, which was not surprising to Dr. Zimmer. He waited until the room had emptied before he came to sit next to her.

"Dr. Armistead tells me that you're staying here for these two weeks," he said softly. "Is that right?"

Triana fidgeted in her seat for a moment, biting her lip. "Yes," she said. "I don't really have anywhere to go."

"You still have no interest in seeing your mother? We can fly you out to Indianapolis this afternoon."

Triana shook her head. "No, thanks."

"What about Colorado? It might do you good to see some old friends and do a little hiking in the hills."

"No, but thank you. I don't . . ." She paused for a second. "My memories of that stuff are with my dad. I think that's how I'd like to leave them."

Zimmer took a long, deep breath. "Tree, you have become very special to me over the last year and a half. It sounds very corny to say, I know, but you are the closest thing to a daughter that I've known in my life. When you have excelled in your studies, I've been proud. When you've struggled with the responsibilities that come with leadership, I've secretly cheered you on." He put his arm around her. "And when you hurt, I hurt a little bit, too."

When she spoke, her voice was barely above a whisper. "I'm ready to launch right now," she said. "The only person I needed to say good-bye to was my dad, and they wouldn't let me do that."

"I understand," Dr. Zimmer said. "It's your decision, of course.

I won't tell you how to spend your time before you head up to the Incubator. But I'd like to give you something to think about for the next two weeks, if that's okay."

She sat quietly, staring ahead, so he continued. "Every person deals with grief in their own unique way. Some people break down into intense crying fits. Others cling to their friends and family, leaning on them for support. I think the fact that you're angry about it is fine, Tree. You have a right to be angry. The closest person to you in the world was taken away, and the rest of your world is being turned upside down at the same time. I don't blame you for wanting to run away. *Galahad* is your getaway vehicle, in a sense.

"But I think you'll discover something for yourself before too long. You can't ever run away from your pain. It's like your shadow, Tree. It will drag along behind you no matter how far you run. Leaving Earth will not magically disconnect your feelings and your anger about your dad. When you arrive at Eos you'll feel the same sense of loss that you feel today."

She was still quiet, but he could tell that she was listening, absorbing what he was saying. That was one of her qualities that he appreciated the most. Triana never seemed to make snap judgments without weighing all of the information. Her decisions were firm, but at least they were well considered.

"You'll have a lot of people on this ship who would love nothing more than to be friends with you," he said. "If you give them a chance I think you'll find that they can help you. Not just with the duties of running the mission, but with your life, too."

Triana nodded slowly. "Okay," was all she said.

He patted her on the shoulder, then stood up. "And in the meantime," he said, "please don't be so anxious to leave everything behind. A day will come when you'll wish you had these two weeks back again."

He smiled at her, then turned and walked out of the room. She sat alone, biting her lip and drumming her fingers on her knee.

21

By eight fifteen, the Learning Center, or simply School, as it was usually called, was buzzing. Essentially an auditorium, it had 250 seats curved in a half circle facing the stage. Rows of stadium seats ascended high enough to provide everyone a good view. *Galahad*'s ongoing educational courses would take place here, with Roc providing the lesson plans and tutorials. A giant vidscreen hung behind the stage, a window into the giant warehouse of knowledge stored within the ship.

The room was also the natural meeting place whenever an assembly of the crew was required. This morning, of the 251 crew members, forty-five were obliged to be on duty, carrying out the tasks necessary to keep the ship running smoothly. The majority of those were at the Farms, tending to the fragile resources that provided a hungry crew with nourishment for the long voyage. Others were handling the maintenance chores that kept *Galahad* clean and in top condition.

The remainder of the crew, however, were finding a seat for this first meeting called by Triana. A smattering of nervous laughter could be heard while greetings and waves were exchanged. One by one the Council members walked in and quickly made their way to the front of the auditorium.

Triana stepped inside at precisely 8:30. *Galahad*'s video cameras picked her up as she stepped to the podium, her image and voice ready to be transmitted to the ship's monitors and the working crew who couldn't attend.

The large group facing her quieted down as she peered first at her notes on the work pad before her, then at the assembled crew.

"Thank you for being here on time," she began. "I promise to have you out of here before nine o'clock, because as you probably know by now, I'm not very gabby."

A ripple of laughter spread across the room. Lita, who was sitting in the front row with the other Council members, gave her friend a look of encouragement.

Triana cleared her throat and continued. "Let me first say that you've all done remarkably well during this first week. All of the work has been finished on schedule, all of the departments are in perfect shape, and no one has been hurt. Well . . ." she cracked a faint smile. "Not counting three Boarding injuries. Lita says two were just bruises and scrapes, one was a broken finger. Thank you for at least wearing your helmets."

"With these three guys, helmets wouldn't matter!" Channy yelled from the first row. "There's not much bouncing around in those thick skulls to get damaged."

More laughter from the group, with several people hissing and pointing at the three daredevils in the crowd.

When the auditorium began to quiet again, Triana's look turned serious.

"But there's no use acting like everything is normal. We all know about the encounter that Peter reported."

Most of the crew members recognized that the word "encounter" was a respectful way to acknowledge the incident, and a thoughtful gesture to Peter, who was sitting somewhere among the sea of faces.

"I also sent a mass e-mail regarding a historical coin that Gap found down by the Storage Sections," Tree continued. "No one has replied, so I'm assuming it does not belong to any crew member."

The room was now deadly silent, with only the faint breath of the ventilators recharging the air.

"And you all know about the crude graffiti. All of this has made our first week uneasy. The worst part is that we don't know who is responsible for any of this."

In the auditorium a few heads nodded slowly, but no one made a sound. Tree glanced down at the Council in the front row, then back up at the anxious crew members staring at her.

"While we don't know anything concrete right now, I can tell you this much. Roc has finished gathering data from our ship records and performed a few calculations based on some new information from Lita. He's informed me that the ship's energy readings are slightly out of whack. Since then he's eliminated a couple of possibilities, and right now believes strongly that the most likely explanation"—Tree paused ever so slightly—"is an additional person somewhere on *Galahad*."

She expected a rush of noise, the sound of two hundred people exclaiming surprise and alarm. But the room remained eerily quiet. Had they all been so sure of this announcement that the meeting itself was anticlimactic? Or were they frozen with fear?

Looking at their faces individually, she realized her mistake. They were not paralyzed by fear; they were simply waiting for her to lead. They trusted her judgment and valued her leadership skills. The crew of *Galahad* was on the alert, awaiting instructions from their general. She was immediately awash with a sense of pride.

Triana placed both hands on the podium. "I will be meeting with the rest of the Council to discuss security procedures. Obviously this is not something that we—or Dr. Zimmer—ever planned on. But every one of you will be kept fully informed of each move we make. We don't conduct secret operations on this ship. Our job on the Council is to lead, but your input and suggestions will be welcome at any time. Are there any questions?"

A few hands went up. One girl asked about leaving the lights on daylight mode at all times. No, this would not happen yet.

Another girl wanted to know if Roc had any thoughts about who the intruder could be? One of the workers who helped build

Galahad, maybe? It would be useless to guess at this point, Tree told her.

A boy in the back of the room raised his hand and asked if there was a chance they might turn back for Earth.

"No," Tree said firmly. "It would take weeks to reorient the ship for a trip back to Earth. Then who knows how long it might take to launch again. We could lose as much as a year or two. That's not an option.

"Besides," she said, her voice growing even stronger. "We will not rely on Earth to fix our problems. We can't run home to Mommy every time something comes up. We'd better get used to the fact that we are responsible for ourselves. If someone wants to mess with us, they obviously don't know who they're dealing with."

There was a moment's pause, then the sound of three or four people clapping. In seconds the entire room was engulfed with the applause. The crew of *Galahad* was on its feet, clapping and whistling, ready to take on the enemy. Ready for Triana to lead them.

In the front row, Lita cheered. *Galahad* might be in trouble. But it was in good hands.

22

With five weeks to go before the launch Dr. Zimmer had arrived at the space station with Dr. Bauer. Dr. Armistead had remained behind to wrap up any last details at the training complex and to escort the crew when it was their time to leave. In another eight days they would all be brought into space and housed inside the Incubator for the final month.

Zimmer was anxious about some last-minute changes that had become necessary on *Galahad*. Construction had proceeded at lightning speed, and for the most part it would be ready to go when the time came.

The agricultural domes were finished and already sported some crops basking in the artificial sunlight. Seeds and plants from around the world continued to arrive daily. A few of the insects that had been approved for the trip—bees to assist pollination and earthworms to help aerate the soil and produce fertilizer—were hard at work and apparently content in their new home.

The Storage Sections were filling up and almost ready to be sealed. Dr. Bauer was primarily in charge of this department, and had agreed with Dr. Zimmer that keeping them locked until the crew reached Eos was crucial. "Don't even give them the chance to ransack the supplies that they'll need when they arrive," Bauer had said. "It's easy to say now that they'll stay out on their own, but who knows what will be going through their minds after a year or two in isolation. Not even these kids are perfect." With a scowl he added, "Believe me, no kids are." Zimmer found it hard to believe that the crew would ransack anything, but nodded agreement.

The crew's apartments were also finished, sitting vacant and awaiting their personal finishing touches. All of the water recycling plants were functioning, the air recycling system was in good shape, and Roc was already skimming through checklist after checklist to make certain that the launch would be successful.

Yet Zimmer wasn't naïve enough to think that everything would be perfect. And it wasn't.

"Tell me again why we only have eight Spiders, and not ten," he said to the tall, thin man sitting across from his desk.

"Listen, I can put all ten of them on board," the design engineer said, "but I'm telling you that only eight of them will work."

His name was Sun Koyama. For almost two years his team had worked day and night, designing, building and assembling the largest craft ever conceived. He was exhausted, mentally and physically, and was in no mood to be lectured by anyone.

"Where was the slipup?" Zimmer said.

"This is not a slipup. I told Dr. Bauer months ago that the company responsible for the internal fittings on the Spiders was in trouble. Their workforce is dwindling, people are dropping out with Bhaktul or just quitting to be with their families, and the same thing is happening with their suppliers. They put all of their remaining staff to work and have eight Spiders finished. The other two are just empty shells. If you ask me, we should be grateful we got eight."

Zimmer sighed. Koyama was right, of course. It was a miracle that work on *Galahad* had gone as smoothly as it had. Companies around the world were shutting down as their employees became ill, and motivation was a problem. After all, it wasn't their children who were being placed aboard the spacecraft. Many were starting to ask, "Why am I doing this?"

Now *Galahad* would launch with two fewer escape crafts than originally planned. The egg-shaped vehicles were to serve several purposes. For one thing they could be used to maneuver outside the spaceship in case any repairs were necessary. They were fitted with multiple arms, some designed to lift large, bulky objects, and others specially made for smaller precision work. With the arms extended they almost resembled an insect, and it wasn't long before they were simply called Spiders.

They were also the vehicles that would transport the crew to the surface when *Galahad* reached its destination. Each Spider was built to accommodate up to thirty passengers, so losing two meant that arrangements would have to be made. Dr. Zimmer scribbled a few notes on his work pad and looked at his calendar. Launch was scheduled in thirty-eight days.

"All right," he said to Koyama. "I want to go ahead and load all ten of them. These last two can still fly, right?"

"Yes, they'll fly," the engineer said. "But they can't support life inside."

"Well, who knows, the kids might need them for spare parts, or something," Zimmer said. "No sense leaving them docked here at the station."

Koyama grunted a reply and left. His job was nearly finished and he was ready to go home.

Alone in his office, Zimmer coughed loudly and noticed the taste of blood.

23

Of all the stuff I've got crammed inside my chips, let me tell you something I'm glad I don't have: hormones.

I'm very familiar with the human need for acceptance and friendship and companionship. But this whole "love" thing has me a little baffled. I've read everything I can find about it, I've asked Roy—that was a big mistake—and I've even tried listening to some of the most popular love songs. Thank goodness computers can't hurl. Humans are such a tortured bunch, aren't they?

And from some of the eavesdropping I've done, I will be completely amazed if we throw 251 teenagers into a spaceship and go five years without some drama.

Two dozen crew members were scattered at tables around the Dining Hall. They had begun streaming in as the lights gently came up, and now, at seven o'clock, breakfast was under way. The sound of muted conversation mingled with the scrapes and clinks of glasses and silverware. Every few seconds another cluster of teens would walk in, either wiping the remnants of sleep out of their eyes, or glowing with the effects of a morning workout.

Channy scurried in behind Lita and tapped her on the shoulder. Lita, just reaching for a tray, turned and smiled.

"Wow, I can't believe how quickly you can get here after leading the morning workout. I could never get ready that fast."

"You should chop off your hair like me," Channy said. "Now I can be ready almost as fast as a boy." She picked up her own tray and fixed Lita with a hard look. "Speaking of workouts—"

"Yes, I know," Lita said. "I wasn't being lazy, though. I was actually at work."

"Someone sick?"

"No. Sick House is empty this morning. I was just checking a few things for Roc."

Channy picked up an energy block, then changed her mind and exchanged it with another. "I need to get out of this rut," she explained to Lita. "I can't have raspberry *every* morning. Today I'm definitely apple."

"You're a rebel."

"So, what's up with Roc? He can't do his own work, or what?"

Lita filled a glass with simulated orange juice. "No, we just used the, uh, incident with Peter Meyer to check our energy levels. It's possible that excess stress might throw the levels out of whack compared to normal readings. Multiply that times two hundred fifty people and it might make a big difference."

"And?"

"It didn't, really. At least not any more than we thought. I fed the new info to Roc just a few minutes ago."

The two girls found a table and sat down.

"I thought Roc had already decided it was the stowaway who was throwing off the readings," Channy said. "What does he want with this new information?"

"I'm not sure, but I think he's trying to . . . I don't know, maybe identify the person."

Channy raised her eyebrows. "What? You mean use the energy readings like a fingerprint or something?"

"Yeah," Lita said, "something like that. Or at least narrow it down to where he can say it's a forty-year-old man or sixty-five-year-old." She took a bite of her energy block and looked across the table at her fellow Council member.

"You know, Channy, he's the same ol' Roc every time. And I know this sounds stupid, because he *is* a machine, after all, but . . ."

She paused. Channy kept quiet, silently chewing her food.

"But somehow I get a weird feeling from him, like he's . . . I don't know . . . worried, maybe?" She brushed her lips with a napkin. "As I said, I know it sounds stupid."

Channy swallowed some juice, then wiped her mouth. "Oh, I don't know. Roy put an awful lot of himself into that machine. I don't see why some of his real personality couldn't have leaked into it."

"Now you're sounding as silly as I am," Lita said with a laugh. "Listen, forget I even said anything. I was probably just tired. He got me up and into Sick House at five o'clock."

"Hmm. You should have been working out."

"Hey, I'll hit one of the afternoon groups. They're usually more fun anyway."

"Cuter guys, too," Channy said, grinning. "I know one in particular who probably wishes you would take an afternoon session permanently."

"Oh, here we go." Lita shook her head. "Your Cupid outfit is showing again."

"Hey, I think I'm pretty good at matching people up," Channy said. "Believe me, I see people at their best and their worst. Mixing and matching is easy when you see both sides. The only person I can't figure out is Tree. She's a mystery. I have *no* idea who might be perfect for her."

Lita ate her breakfast thoughtfully. "Well, she might be quiet and tough-acting, but she's still a girl. It's not like she doesn't have a heart."

Channy had her juice halfway to her mouth and stopped, slowly putting it back down on the table. "Wait a minute," she said. "Why didn't I think of that? You're probably closer to her than anyone else. Are you holding out on me?"

"What are you talking about?"

"C'mon, girl. If you know something about the Ice Queen, then spill."

Lita laughed out loud. "Channy, you crack me up. First of all, if I *did* know something, I probably would just send everyone an e-mail. It's a faster way to spread information to the whole crew than telling you. Not *much* faster, but a little."

Channy stuck her tongue out playfully.

"But," Lita said, "that 'Ice Queen' label isn't fair, either. I told you, Triana has a heart. She might not show it, but she can have feelings for someone. I think she does, in fact."

"Well?" Channy leaned forward. "Out with it."

"No, Channy. Look, I don't know for sure. It's just a hunch, really. A few things here and there that she's let drop about someone. I think she's attracted to him, but she's too wrapped up with the mission to take a step."

Picking up her tray, Channy stood and downed the last of her juice. "Well, if she's got the hots for someone, I'll figure it out." She narrowed her eyes playfully. "I always do."

Lita laughed again and rose to her feet. "I should have known better than to say anything to you."

Channy started toward the door, calling back over her shoulder. "Hold out on me, Lita, and I'll work you out this afternoon until you're down on one knee."

Smiling, Lita followed her out the door, and two other kids moved into the spot they had vacated. Sitting at the next table, with his back to them, Gap Lee sat quietly, digesting not his breakfast, which sat untouched, but what he had just overheard.

Not even his early morning run had caused his heart to race like it was right now.

24

This is not a pleasure cruise."

Dr. Wallace Zimmer had said this so many times during their training that it became a running joke with the crew. Whenever it seemed as if the young would-be space explorers were losing their focus, the scientist would sigh heavily and explain—again—the importance of being prepared.

"You can't come back for follow-up training, you know," he would preach. "If you think this is just some pleasure cruise or a quick vacation, you're wrong."

The five Council members took his message to heart, and even decided to have a little fun with him. He had scheduled a final meeting with them, the day before they entered the Incubator. It would be their last visit with anyone outside of their group. Zimmer had dreaded this moment for a long time. These star travelers had become the children he had never had. Too busy with his career and studies to pursue a serious relationship, he had never married. He was close to fifty before he looked up from his work to realize that a lifetime of educational opportunities had prevented him from exploring a life with another person.

The time he had spent with *Galahad*'s crew had filled that vacancy in his life.

He entered the room, notes in hand, ready to swallow his deep personal sorrow and maintain a strong, professional image for the teens. He stopped short in the doorway, his mouth falling open. Then he dropped his notes to the floor.

All five members of the Council were standing there, decked out in beach clothes: swimsuits, sunglasses, Hawaiian shirts and more. Gap and Channy had life preservers hanging from their necks, and even the ever-serious Bon had a straw hat on his head.

Channy stepped forward, took the gray-haired man by the hand and told him, "We're ready for our pleasure cruise, Dr. Zimmer."

With that, he broke down. After devoting almost three years of his life to *Galahad* and its young crew, his work was over. He cried, the tears beginning slowly, and then escalating into uncontrollable sobs. Channy brought him over to a chair, and the Council gathered around, some sitting on the floor by his feet, the others in chairs next to him. Soon everyone was either crying or fighting back tears. The realization that this was good-bye was overwhelming.

Wallace Zimmer decided to cry himself out. There was nothing for which he needed to save his tears. The disease from Comet Bhaktul had begun settling in him, and although he hid the symptoms from the crew members, he knew that it would not be long before he was bedridden. He calculated that he would be gone before *Galahad* was beyond Neptune. These kids were the closest people in his life, and when they left he fully believed that his will to live would be leaving with them. The beginning of their mission would mark the end of his.

For almost five minutes he wept. The Council members were patient, willing to devote any amount of time to this father figure. Finally, he looked into the eyes of each of them and managed to say, "Are you ready?"

Triana nodded. "You've *made* us ready, Dr. Z."

He smiled at her, and put out his hand. Gap had picked up the scientist's notes from the floor and now handed them to him.

"Will Dr. Armistead or Dr. Bauer be joining us?" Channy said.

The scientist shook his head sadly. "I'm sorry. Dr. Bauer

requested that he spend his last few weeks with his family. He told me to apologize for not personally seeing you off. I think the disease has affected him to the point where he was embarrassed to have you see him. He didn't want that to be your last memory of him. I gave him permission to leave on the shuttle for Earth last night. He should be home by this time tomorrow."

The room grew quiet as the impact of Bhaktul struck them once again. The Council members had never been as close to Bauer as they were to Dr. Zimmer, but he had been a vital teammate nonetheless.

Zimmer said, "And Dr. Armistead will say her good-byes when she packs you into the Incubator. She's pretty broken up right now." More silence gripped the room. Now, not only was the impact of the disease hitting home, but so was the realization that they would soon be saying good-bye to everyone they knew on Earth.

For the next two hours they talked about every aspect of their mission. The responsibilities of the Council. The necessity of maintaining order and discipline for the entire five years. How the Storage Sections in the lower levels would remain sealed and off-limits until reaching Eos.

And the cycles of work.

Roc was the brain of *Galahad,* but the crew was the muscle. Each member was expected to shoulder their share of duties each week in a department overseen by one of the Council members. Groups of thirty or thirty-one would spend six weeks in one department, then rotate randomly into another department for another six-week assignment. After three or four such tours a crew member would be granted a six-week leave, so at any given time sixty people would be on a sort of vacation. Then it was back into the rotation to work in the other departments.

The Council members were the only ones exempt from the rotation. For their three-year term they would remain with their department. Once a new Council was elected, the original group would fall into the same rotation as the rest of the crew.

Dr. Zimmer appreciated the fact that some of his young explorers were especially skilled in one area, such as medicine or engineering. Yet he was insistent that everyone learn from each department. When *Galahad* reached Eos it would need all 251 colonists to share as much knowledge as possible to tame a new world. Should something tragic happen to some of the crew members, he didn't want their expertise to vanish with them.

And on a mission like this, anything could happen.

Education was another matter. *Galahad* was not only a lifeboat, but a traveling university as well. Each crew member would continue their education during the journey. The ship's computer banks were crammed with every bit of information the mission planners could think to send with them: math, science, biology, astronomy, medicine and history. Great works of literature were stored as well, along with manuals and blueprints for building a new civilization on an alien world.

Biographies of Earth's most influential people were loaded aboard, including philosophers, scholars, poets, leaders and civil rights pioneers.

Every crew member would pore through the material. It was predicted that when *Galahad* pulled into orbit around its new star home, it would contain 251 college graduates, each of who would hold the equivalent of four degrees. Mankind's hope for the future would not be ill prepared for the challenge.

As their final meeting wrapped up, Dr. Zimmer stressed two critical points.

"You'll be working hard and studying much of the time," he told his first Council. "Please remember to make time for fun. Soccer, Boarding, theater . . . I hope you put energy into these pursuits as well.

"And finally," he said, turning his head slowly to look at each of their faces. "Please look after each other. Be sensitive to each person's heart and mind. No two of you are exactly alike. That is by design. I wanted to challenge each and every one of you to expand your range of intellect and emotion. Learn from one another as you learn *about* one another. Learn to appreciate the skills your neighbor has that you may lack. Learn to take pride in the skills that are unique to you. Learn to respect one another.

"Remember that as of tomorrow, you have only one another to lean on."

He stood, and his handpicked Council joined him. Circling him, the group embraced quietly for more than a minute. Finally they heard Dr. Zimmer say softly, "I love you all."

He broke free, and without looking back walked out of the room.

25

Bon Hartsfield was kneeling in the dirt, one large hand slowly scratching the soil. The scowl that usually etched his face was absent at the moment, replaced by a look of curiosity. As the Council member responsible for the Agricultural Department, he was happiest when he was at work in *Galahad*'s crops. Behind him stood Gap Lee, hands on his hips.

"Don't ignore the question, Bon."

"I'm not ignoring anything. But I have work to do, you know. I assume you *do* want to eat on this trip."

Gap walked around the kneeling figure so he could face Bon. "I'm not trying to interrupt your work. Just answer the question. Are you really *that* upset with every single decision Triana makes, or is it mostly just an act? You know, the 'Bon the Bad Boy' image."

Bon tossed a small handful of dirt aside and wiped both hands on his pants. The two of them were not alone in *Galahad*'s farming section, but they were out of earshot from the other workers scattered among the rows of crops. Bright panels in the ceiling that mimicked sunlight cast a shower of light, preserving a tropical temperature around the clock. In order to look up at his fellow Council member, Bon had to shade his eyes with one hand.

"That's ridiculous," he said. "I don't have time for games. And I don't think I've spoken out against everything Triana has done.

Just because I'm the most vocal when it comes to disagreeing does not make me a bad boy, either. *Someone* needs to speak up when something is wrong."

"Sure, I agree with that. But couldn't you be just a bit more team-oriented? Do all of your comments and suggestions have to sound so . . . aggressive?"

Bon chuckled. "I don't know how you were raised, Gap, but in Sweden I was brought up to say what I thought. This ship is in a little trouble right now, and I'm sorry if peoples' feelings aren't my first priority."

"Don't give me that," Gap said. "You act like you have to drive home every point with a sledgehammer. It's a little exhausting after a while." He glanced over at two crew members who were pulling a cart through the fields. The boy and the girl were laughing at something, and stopped now and then to readjust their grips on the cart.

Gap looked back at Bon. "All I'm saying is that you might try a little more diplomacy. Like explaining your opinions instead of trying to force them down Tree's throat."

Bon began to work the soil again, picking up a small dirt clod and breaking it apart. He waved away a bee that hovered around his face. Slowly his infamous scowl returned.

"All right," he said. "Now, let me give *you* a little advice. Quit trying to play politics all the time on the Council and open your eyes."

"And what does that mean?"

"It means you seem more interested in the title of Council member than the responsibilities. This little visit is a prime example. Aren't there more important things for you to be doing right now than chatting with me about Triana's feelings?"

Gap's face tightened into a grimace. He and Bon had become good friends during the first several months of their training, even though Bon was not an easy person to like. But Gap respected his strong work ethic and no-nonsense attitude. Over the last year, however, their friendship had become strained. Gap soon realized that this no-nonsense approach could become old very fast. Bon never seemed to lighten up, and for Gap, who was always quick with a joke to break the ice during their intense training, it seemed pointless.

The fact that Bon seemed to despise Triana was the final straw for Gap. He opened his mouth to respond to Bon's criticism, but was interrupted by a shout. It came from the two crew members who had been pulling the cart through the field.

Bon stood up and shouted back to them. "What is it?"

Instead of replying, the boy and the girl waved for Bon and Gap to join them quickly, and then knelt down as if examining something. Both Council members began to run through the rows of dirt and plants. As soon as they were within twenty feet of the kneeling figures they saw it.

A large section of the crop lay damaged. Dozens of plant stalks were broken into pieces and strewn across the ground. Others had been completely uprooted and cast aside. The ground had been churned up, as if someone had gouged into the soil with their feet.

Gap quickly scanned the area, looking for footprints leaving the scene. He finally spotted a set of tracks weaving out of the destruction zone and leading towards the exit.

Bon stood over the mess, seething. He looked back and forth, surveying the damage, and then looked up at Gap. The two boys exchanged a steely glance, breathing heavily. Words weren't necessary.

The intruder had left another calling card.

At the same moment, Triana was hunched over her work pad in the Conference Room. Channy and Lita sat on either side of her. The three girls had been working together for almost an hour, engaging Roc with questions, and then tossing ideas back and forth regarding the ship's crisis. Roc had patiently volunteered all the information he could.

Channy looked down at Triana's notes and said, "Okay, that

pretty much settles it, right? This stowaway must be getting into the Storage Sections somehow. He couldn't be holed up anywhere else without being spotted."

"That's probably right," Lita said. "But how is he able to get in and out? These storage compartments are sealed. *We* don't even have access to them. I say we get a couple dozen people together and break in. There's no way he could fight off that many people."

Triana shook her head. "We don't have any idea if this person has weapons with him. I'm not taking a chance on him killing several crew members before we can jump him. So far all he's done is scare people and cause some vandalism. That's not worth getting someone killed."

"Well," Channy said, "what about trapping him inside? If we station enough people around all of the storage exits, he couldn't get in or out."

Tree considered this for a moment. "A siege," she finally said. "He would have to come out eventually for food and water. Unless . . ." Her voice trailed off.

"Unless what?" Channy said.

"Roc," Tree said, "I know you won't tell us what's in those sealed sections."

"You know, I had this same discussion with Gap," Roc said, "and not once have any of you offered me a good bribe. I can be bought. Try it."

Tree ignored this. "Can you at least tell us whether an intruder would have access to food and water inside those sections? If we bottled him up, would he be able to survive in there for a long time?"

Roc didn't answer right away. His analytical mind was racing, gauging whether divulging this bit of information would violate his programming. Tree, Lita and Channy waited.

Finally Roc reached a decision. "If a person was able to get inside those sections," he said slowly, "he would be able to sustain himself for quite a while." The three girls looked crestfallen.

"However," the computer added, "there is one other thing

I can tell you. In order to access those supplies, a person would have to be intimately acquainted with this project."

"What do you mean?" Lita said.

"I mean that if our intruder was simply a project worker or a staff member of the space station, he wouldn't know where to find these supplies or how to retrieve them. Only someone close to the *Galahad* project would have that information."

Tree bit her lip and thought about this for a moment. "So, if we trapped this person inside, we wouldn't know if they were stealing the supplies or not."

"Correct," Roc said. "And, I might add, there are two other points to consider. One, *Galahad*'s crew is not trained for this type of activity. Obviously no one expected you to be fighting off an intruder within our own walls. Ninjas, you're not. Second, this crew is already stretched thin with work assignments. If you try to keep a sizable force stationed around the Storage Sections—and that's a lot of room to cover—then you're going to cripple the normal work production needed to maintain the ship. And I'm not washing dishes, that's for sure."

Triana dropped her stylus pen down on the work pad and began rubbing her temple with one hand. She looked at Lita, then Channy.

"We won't break in," she told them, "and we won't set up camps outside the Storage Sections. At least not yet. Whoever this intruder is, he's human, and that means he's bound to make a mistake sometime. Every time he ventures out of his hole he's taking another chance that we catch him."

Lita put her hand on Tree's arm and raised her eyebrows. "Which brings up another question, doesn't it? Just what do we do when we catch him?"

26

The sun was just beginning to peek over the horizon. Since that horizon was made up of the Gulf of Mexico, the huge ball of fire would spread out across the waves, making the water dance with blinding yellow streaks. A small crescent moon was holding on to its last glint of light before the dawn washed it away.

Maria Marques sat with her bare feet in the sand, just beyond the reach of the encroaching waves as they splashed desperately upon the shore. Pieces of wood, seaweed and assorted marine life that had washed up overnight lay scattered around her like a child's toys at the end of the day. She watched the reflection of the sun, hardly moving a muscle, and seemed oblivious to the sounds of the town of Veracruz, Mexico, coming to life behind her.

It was almost six o'clock. Her husband still lay sleeping in their comfortable home about eight blocks away. Maria loved to come to the beach alone, and especially loved to catch a sunrise before making her way down the empty streets to her small medical office. The alone time was precious to her, affording her a chance to think without the noise of a busy household. Three children, a husband, her own mother, along with two dogs and two cats, all added up to a zoo. A loud zoo.

This was her escape.

Over the past two months it had been more than that. Since her oldest daughter had been selected for a spot on *Galahad,* Maria needed this time even more. She needed to summon all of her inner strength to be able to say good-bye soon.

Her daughter Lita was fourteen. When the time came to lock herself up in the enormous spacecraft she would be fifteen. And on her own.

Maria scooped a handful of sand and let it slowly seep between her fingers without taking her eyes off the water. When the sand ran out she grabbed another handful. Again and again she felt the cool, smooth grains run through her fingers. Her mind drifted, catching on glimpses of Lita at various stages of her young life.

Dressed only in her diaper, running through her father's grocery store, stretching out her hands to whatever she could reach on the shelves. Maria had run after her, laughing, trying to put the scattered items back in their proper places.

Lita's first day of school, practically clawing her way out of Maria's tearful grasp, anxious to get inside. Unlike the other children who cried and clutched at their parents' legs, Lita knew there were more books inside the school, and she couldn't wait to reach them.

At age twelve, setting aside her studies of Spanish explorers to help care for her younger brother and sister. Reading to them, mostly, her eyes wide with excitement as she weaved tales of De Soto, Pizarro, Cortez and Coronado. She would try, unsuccessfully, to enthrall her younger siblings with details of Cabeza de Vaca and Balboa, explorers who faced terrible hardships during their travels throughout Central and South America. "Many of these men made terrible mistakes," she would say to her little brother. "Some inflicted horrible treatment upon the native people they encountered. We all need to learn from their successes and their failures." Her brother would smile up at her, not really hearing what she was saying, just enjoying the attention he was receiving from his older sister. Maria would hear Lita sigh, and continue with her storytelling.

Two loud birds soared just over Maria's head as she sat on the beach, coming to rest at the water's edge. Their cries cut through the sound of the rushing waves, cries of sadness it seemed. Maria grasped another handful of sand and began to drift again. Remembering the mixture of excitement and sadness when Lita was selected from thousands of nominees for the *Galahad* mission. Lita's mouth had opened into a round, soundless *O*, not sure how to respond in front of her grieving mother and father.

Maria had wondered how she would tell her other children that their older sister was leaving, permanently. In the end, she needn't have worried, because it was Lita who took them aside and gently explained. Lita, who would be following in the footsteps of so many Spanish explorers, taking a path that her ancestors could never have imagined. A pathway to the stars.

That journey would begin in just a few hours. Maria looked up and managed to catch one or two specks of starlight, quickly dissipating as the sun began to break the horizon.

Releasing a last handful of sand, she rose to her feet, turned her back on the sunrise, and walked home.

27

Three days had passed with no further signs from the mysterious guest aboard *Galahad*. The crew went about their business, trying to maintain a normal pace and attitude. They did their jobs, ate their meals, socialized and exercised. But they did it with their eyes wide open, and too many cautious glances over their shoulders. The air was uncomfortable.

It was a topic that Triana felt she should address one evening as she rode the stationary bike in the exercise room. Lita was puffing along beside her as video images of a winding mountain road flashed on the wall before them.

"We're a frightened ship, and I don't like that," Triana said. "The intruder is doing exactly what he wants to do: making us nervous and jumpy."

"His tactics are obvious," Lita said. "The damage to the crops wasn't extensive, just enough to aggravate us. So he wasn't trying to wreck our food supply. He just wanted us to know that he could."

She paused to catch her breath, sweat dripping off her forehead. Then she added, "And psychologically that's worse. I think his primary goal is to get us frightened and angry. He's hoping the stress will make us turn on one another."

Tree thought this over, biting her lip. "Well, in a way, it's worked for him. The crew is itchy and irritable. They're doing their jobs, but it's almost like they're waiting for something bad to happen. That's no way to live."

She turned the bike's torque up a notch, then gave Lita an appreciative glance. "We've got to stick together." A few minutes later, after grinding through two more miles, they both let their bikes coast to a stop.

Lita wiped her head with a towel and said, "Okay, a shower for me, and then an hour of piano practice. I'm getting it all done in one shot tonight."

"I love listening to you play," Triana told her. "I'll pop in next time if it's all right with you." She waved good-bye and headed back to her room.

After a shower and a brief conversation with Roc—nothing new to report, he said—she tumbled into bed and clasped her hands behind her head. Within moments her thoughts turned again to her dad. This time she recalled their rafting trip through Brown's Canyon in Colorado. It had been early summer and the water was running high, crashing into their boat as it hurtled them along the canyon walls and past immense boulders. At one point her dad lost his balance and nearly let the paddle slip from his hands as he lurched for something to grab on to. Tree had burst into a spasm of laughter, pulling her own oar out of the water as she doubled over in a fit of joy. Their raft captain, a large grizzled river veteran with no sense of humor, hollered over the roar of the rapids, "Paddle! Paddle! Paddle!"

When they reached a somewhat gentler passage of the river, everyone was able to take a break and recover their strength.

"You almost fell in," Tree had said, poking her oar into her father's life vest.

"Yeah, well, I wasn't worried about the water. But those giant rocks would have done a pretty good number on my head, even with the helmet." Her dad had grinned back at her.

"I would have jumped in to save you," Tree said.

"I hope not," her dad said seriously. "In these waters you wouldn't have a chance of reaching me. All you'd do is end up hurting yourself, or worse." He put down his paddle and took a drink from his water bottle. "No, if I go in, you can try to reach me with your paddle, maybe give me something to grab on to. But if I'm sucked down the rapids, you have to save yourself."

Tree had thought this over for a moment. "You don't *want* me to try to save you?"

"Honey, you don't understand. If I'm lost, it doesn't do any good to risk killing yourself. Remember that, okay?"

Before she could reply, their captain had begun shouting orders again. They rushed into a new set of rapids, more deadly than the last group, and it was time to get back to work.

Now, three years later, staring at the ceiling in her room, Tree said the words aloud again. "I would have jumped in to save you."

Turning to her nightstand, she picked up the picture of her dad. "I guess I couldn't save you after all."

She studied his face, the wrinkles around his eyes, the strong chin, the smattering of gray hairs around his temples. She rolled over and raised herself up on one arm, looking across at her own image in the mirror. Then, casting a glance back at the photograph, she murmured, "I don't look very much like you. I look like . . . her." This troubled her. Softly, she ran a hand across his face. "What did I get from you?"

A moment later she placed the picture back on the nightstand and lay back again, her hands behind her head.

"What exactly did I get from you?"

A faint beep came from her desk and broke her concentration. A call was coming through.

Arising with a sigh, she punched the intercom. "Yes?"

"Just thought I'd check in with you before hitting the sack," Gap said.

"Well, still nothing," she said. "I assume you're talking about the stowaway?"

"Yes and no. I'm also wondering how you're doing. You've seemed . . . detached lately. That's the only word I can think of right now. I wanted to know if there's something I can help with."

"That's sweet of you," Tree said, smiling. "But everything's fine. Just . . . missing my dad."

Gap was quiet for a few seconds. "I'm sorry. That's none of my business."

"No, it's fine. It's part of your job on the Council to make sure I'm in good shape physically and mentally."

"Well," Gap said, "I'm not really asking for professional reasons. I care about you as a person as much as a Council Leader, Tree."

Now it was her turn to sit quietly. Finally she started to speak again. "Gap—"

"Listen," he said, "no big deal. Just making sure you're all right. I'll see you in the morning, okay? Good night."

He broke the connection before she could say anything else. She bit her lip and slouched in her chair. She had instantly reverted to her cold machine ways again, without even considering that someone might want to talk to her as a friend. Or as more than that?

She shot another quick glance at her father's picture. "I know what I *didn't* get from you, Dad. Obviously not your perception or people skills."

Five minutes later she was back in bed, tossing and turning briefly before dropping off to sleep. The hallway outside her door was in night mode, the lights dimmed to a dusk setting. Without a sound a figure glided up to her door, rested its hand on her name panel briefly and then was gone.

28

Mr. Scofield wants to know if he can have a moment with you."

Dr. Zimmer barely contained a groan. He waited for a few seconds before answering the page from the front desk operator. Putting off Scofield right now would only make the next confrontation with him that much more unbearable. Besides, *Galahad* was mere hours away from leaving. What could Scofield do now? Dr. Zimmer cringed at the thought, then cleared his voice and spoke up.

"All right, put him through."

He turned to the vidscreen behind his desk. This temporary office on the space station was cramped but had all the tools he needed to finish his work on the project.

The screen flickered for an instant before the haggard face of Tyler Scofield appeared. Dr. Zimmer noted that his adversary seemed to have aged a dozen years in the last two. He had also, like many who followed his belief of a return to a more simple life, grown a full beard. It did not, however, hide the weariness on his long, thin face.

"Hello, Wallace," he said.

"Hello, Tyler," Dr. Zimmer said. "I hate to be rude, but, as you can imagine, I've got my hands full right now. What can I do for you?"

"You have ignored my warnings, my advice, and my pleading," Scofield said.

"And your threats," Zimmer said.

"Your perception, Doctor, not my intent," came the stiff reply. "Since the day you proposed this ridiculous plan we have fought to show you the foolish mistake you are making. Now I ask for just one final opportunity, one last chance to persuade you to stop this madness."

Dr. Zimmer sighed. "*Galahad* will begin accelerating away from this station and from Earth in less than twelve hours. The crew is already aboard. Your feelings regarding the project have been obvious, Tyler, but perhaps now you might accept the fact that it's too late. *Galahad* will soon be gone. Why don't you take this final opportunity to wish them good luck?"

Scofield ignored this last question. "If you won't listen to our logical reasons for putting a halt to this, then why not consider the emotional reasons?"

"I've heard your—"

"You've heard, but you have not *listened*!" Scofield cried. "You have not listened to the cries of families who are losing their children at a time of personal tragedy. You have not listened to the anger and betrayal felt by millions of people who regard this folly as a sign that the human race has given up and is finished." He paused, his eyes blazing and his chest rising and falling with tortured breathing. He slowly composed himself, then pointed a finger at Zimmer and continued, this time with an icy calm.

"You have not listened to the message my organization has presented for more than two years, begging you to consider the psychological impact your project is having on the people—especially the children—who are staying put and fighting this horrible disease. No, you have not listened to anyone. Your selfish, obsessive 'vision' is the only thing that guides you, blinding you to the wisdom of anyone who dares to cross you, who dares to question you, who dares to say 'You are *wrong*.'"

Dr. Zimmer said nothing for a few moments while Scofield's

eyes stared through him. There were so many things that Zimmer wanted to say, so many fiery comebacks that were eager to spring from his lips. But he knew that would solve nothing. In fact, the things he *most* wanted to say would only make matters worse.

So he waited calmly, gathering his thoughts and his patience, measuring his words. When he finally spoke, his voice was strong and steady.

"Tyler, you and I were once good friends and colleagues. I have always held you in the warmest regard, which makes me very sorry that this tragedy has created such a deep chasm between us. I value my friendships, even more so during these last few years. Many things that seemed important before . . . well, they don't hold the power over me they once did. Friendships, however, do.

"But you know I am also passionate about the truth, Tyler. I will never allow my personal feelings to cloud my judgment when it comes to the truth. And the truth in this instance is undeniable. Comet Bhaktul has delivered a death sentence to our civilization as we know it. The facts are unpleasant, and that has caused many people to deny the truth. I am not surprised nor angry about this. Denial is a common human characteristic when we're faced with something we don't want to deal with. It's a form of mental protection. I understand that.

"And I understand why you are so strongly opposed to the *Galahad* project. To support this mission is to accept our own fatality. Few people are willing to do that."

He kept his gaze locked on to Scofield's. After a slight pause, his voice softened a bit.

"Tyler, I know what you are feeling. But we're both scientists. We can both read the data. And we can both predict the outcome. I have chosen to act in the best interests of our species. *That* is a basic human instinct as well: preservation of the species. Nobody would like to see Bhaktul's effects controlled and defeated any more than I. But the results are not there. And as each week and month passes, the window of opportunity closes a little more.

Soon there will be no window at all. I can't let that happen. I *won't* let that happen, even if it costs me a friendship I treasure so strongly. I have to face the truth, Tyler, regardless of the pain involved."

For the first time Scofield's fierce stare lost its edge. His gaze fell down to his hands, clasped tightly in front of him.

"You are right," he said, "when you say that we were once friends. You were almost like a brother to me, and I, too, am sorry that we have grown so far apart. I suppose we were pushed apart by our own beliefs."

Scofield looked back up. "But you are wrong when it comes to *Galahad*. You said it was too late to do anything about it." He paused for one moment. "It's not too late, my old friend."

Dr. Zimmer's spine stiffened. The two men stared at each other, and just before the image faded to black, Scofield raised an eyebrow and repeated, "It's not too late."

29

Roc was cheating. Cheating, that was, as much as a programmed machine could. It was nine o'clock in the morning and he was engaged in his weekly game of Masego with Gap Lee.

The game had become very popular with the crew during their months of training. Nasha was a fifteen-year-old from Botswana in Africa who had fought her homesick feelings by teaching the game to a handful of crew members, and it quickly spread. Translated to English, the word meant "good luck," which was exactly what a player needed, as well as a razor-sharp mind.

The object involved moving three small marbles across various twisting paths on the board, then working them back one at a time without touching any of the spaces used on the initial trail. At the same time you had to block your opponent's return trip and force him onto a square forbidden to him. Each game was unique and exciting, and often led to whoops of celebration when someone claimed victory. An average game of Masego could run almost an hour, challenging your mind and testing your memory. Dr. Zimmer and Dr. Bauer had both loved it as a training tool; the kids loved it for the sheer competition.

Gap fancied himself to be one of the better players aboard *Galahad*. Nasha would smoke him regularly, but, as Gap was quick to point out, she had been playing since she was six or seven years old. So Gap always seemed to find himself playing against his favorite rival: Roc.

Once he had been "taught" the game by Nasha and programmed by Roy Orzini, Roc was supposed to play without using all of his computational skills. That was supposed to level the playing field against his human opponents. But, once again, too much of Roy's spirit found its way inside Roc. He loved to win. He also cheated. Gap was suspicious, but plugged on against the computer anyway with a weekly game. Gap would touch the screen with a finger to indicate his moves, and Roc would respond by lighting up his choice on the board.

Now, in the Conference Room, Gap sat in front of the vidscreen, his dark eyes fixed on the image of the playing board, his well-tuned mind racing through the possible combinations of the game.

"Your turn," Roc said.

"Mm-hmm," Gap mumbled.

"Would you like a suggestion?"

"No," Gap said. "I know how to play."

"Just trying to help. You've been sloppy in your moves today."

"Sloppy?"

"Sloppy," Roc said. "I picked up three spaces on your last move alone."

"Just let me play in peace," Gap said sullenly. "Nobody likes a gloater."

He was reaching out with a finger to place his next move when Roc piped up again.

"Are you sure about that?"

Gap pulled his finger back from the screen and instead jabbed it toward Roc's sensor.

"You know, you've gotten a little cockier since we left. Don't think just because Roy or Dr. Zimmer's not here that you can go wild. I know how to pull your plug, too, you know."

"Gap, what an awful thing to say."

"Just let me play. If I make a mistake, I'll learn from it."

"Hmm," Roc said. "If that was true you would be a Masego Grand Master by now."

Gap looked back at the board. "I'm not listening to you," he muttered. Then he quickly punched his selection onto the screen.

Without a second of delay Roc immediately lit up his next move on the board. Gap shifted his gaze back and forth across the layout, then sat back and sighed. His last move had opened up a new path for Roc that he hadn't noticed. Within three or four moves the game would be over.

"Care for another go?" Roc said with just a hint of sarcasm.

"Tomorrow," Gap said. "I don't like you very much right now."

He stood up and walked across the Conference Room to fill a glass with water. At that moment the door opened and Triana walked in.

"Thought I might find you here," she said.

"Yeah, well I wish I was somewhere else, actually," Gap said.

"Oh," Tree said. "I think I know what that means." She turned to the glowing red sensor. "Roc, why don't you let him win once in a while?"

"He says that losing helps him learn more," said Roc's cheerful voice.

"That's *not* what I said," Gap fumed. He looked at Tree with frustration etched on his face. "I'm not sure I can handle five more years with this box of attitude."

Tree couldn't hold her laughter any longer. In a way she felt sorry for Gap, who hated to lose. But at the same time she couldn't help laugh at the way Roc pushed Gap's hot buttons. Roy Orzini was most definitely alive and well inside his creation.

"Maybe you two should wait a while before you play Masego again," she said with a grin. "You don't play well together."

Gap didn't answer. He drank his water to camouflage his pouting. Roc, of course, had no problem responding.

"That might be best," the computer said. "I think all of the learning that Gap has done in our last ten games has clogged him up. He needs to let it drain a little."

Gap shook his head and looked at Tree. "See what I mean?"

Tree laughed again as the door opened and Bon, Channy and Lita walked in.

"What's so funny?" Channy said.

"Oh, just watching two boys poke at each other," Tree said.

The Council members all took seats around the table for their weekly meeting. After receiving updates from each and planning some new work schedules, they turned to new business. Nothing important, it seemed. A few crew members were requesting new roommate assignments.

"We figured that would happen," Lita said. "It's one thing to pick a roomie during training. After you live with them a few weeks you learn a lot more. I'm surprised there aren't more requests like this."

Tree okayed the changes and asked Lita to handle it.

Channy and Bon had nothing new. Bon was fidgeting, as usual, anxious to get out of the meeting and back to work.

"Wait a minute," Tree said, when it looked like things were wrapping up. "I have some news."

The group got quiet. Tree bit her lip for a second, then looked up at them.

"When I checked my e-mail this morning," she said, "there was a note from our . . . passenger."

"What?" Gap burst out. "And you're just now telling us?"

"I wanted to take care of all the other business first," Tree said.

While the others sat in shock, Bon spoke up. "What did he say?"

Tree tapped her fingers on the tabletop. "Well, he wants to meet with me. Alone."

Channy put a hand to her mouth. "Oh, no. Are you serious?"

Tree said, "Yeah. But he was very vague. No specifics. Just a note that said 'Let's talk.'"

"How do you know it was him?" Lita said. "How did he sign it?"

"He didn't. But it was him," Tree said. "I checked the source of the e-mail. It came from one of the terminals in the Dining Hall. Sent about two o'clock this morning."

"He likes to drift through the ship after everyone has gone to bed," Channy said. "This guy gives me the creeps."

Triana slowly let out her breath. "So, we need to discuss how we want to handle this."

Gap stared at her with his mouth agape. "Don't tell me you're thinking about meeting him alone," he said slowly. "That's just crazy."

"I don't know," Bon said. "What better way to find out who he is and what he wants?"

"Yeah, and what better way to get Tree killed!" yelled Gap, shooting Bon a fiery glance.

"I'm sorry, but I have to agree with Gap," Lita said. "Tree, I can't believe you would even consider that. We have no idea who this person is. All we know is that he has caused damage already on this ship and threatened the entire crew. Meeting him alone would be just plain stupid."

"She's right," Channy said. "Tree, you're the Council Leader. You don't just go marching off into battle alone."

"Okay," Bon said, "but why would he ask to meet with her? If he wanted to hurt her, wouldn't he just wait until he found her alone? Why would he put her on alert like that? Maybe he really does just want to talk."

Gap was seething. He stood up and leaned across the table towards Bon.

"You make me sick," he said. "Try to think of someone else for a change, Bon. If you're that anxious for us to make contact with him, maybe you should volunteer to meet him alone yourself."

"Hold on a minute," Tree said.

"I'm not sure you belong on this Council anymore," Gap shouted at Bon, who glared back.

"Well isn't it too bad that's not your decision," Bon said.

"That's enough!" Tree said, slamming her hand down on the table. "Gap, sit down."

Gap remained still for a few more seconds. He looked as if he wanted to climb over the table and tangle with the sullen Swede. Finally he sat back down, but didn't take his eyes off Bon.

Tree resumed control of the meeting. "I appreciate everyone's comments and opinions," she said, her voice still strong and loud. "The purpose of this Council is to share thoughts and ideas to help *Galahad* run smoothly. I don't expect everyone to agree with every suggestion. But—"

She looked back and forth between the two boys, who were staring each other down.

"But I don't expect this Council to break down during debate, either. If you two can't carry out the tasks expected of you without resorting to violence, then neither of you belongs here."

With this, Gap looked at Tree, back at Bon, then down at the table. Bon took a deep breath and broke his gaze as well.

"Lita predicted this would happen," Tree said in a softer tone. "This intruder is winning when we turn on each other, rather than focus on him. When we collapse as a team we give him an advantage. I don't want to do that. Do you?"

"You're right," Gap said. "But this is a serious issue."

"And that's exactly why you were selected by Dr. Zimmer in the first place," Tree said. "Leadership is defined by how you perform during tough times. Anyone can lead during good times."

Lita spoke up. "If I could make a suggestion?"

"Sure," Tree said.

"Why not invite our mystery man to a Council meeting? If we promise him that no harm will come to him, he might agree to talk with all of us."

"I don't know," Channy said doubtfully. "This guy is probably infected with Bhaktul Disease. He's not going to be rational, and it wouldn't be smart—or safe—for us to assume that he would be. That could get someone killed."

"Channy's right," Bon said. "He's not going to talk to us rationally. He's sick. We need to track him down."

"And then?" Gap said. "We don't have a jail on this ship."

"I don't know," Bon said. "But for now we should take it one step at a time. Let's find him, see how dangerous he really is, and go from there. I don't want him loose much longer, that's for sure. He's already proved that he can destroy at will. If we wait and allow Bhaktul to progress even further, he might just cripple this ship. Which is why," he said, looking back at Gap, "I think it might make sense for Tree to meet with him. Yes, he could be dangerous. But a week from now he's going to be even more dangerous."

Gap was about to respond when Tree cut in.

"I'm going to send a copy of the e-mail to all of you. Take a look and see if there's anything in it that I'm not seeing. Oh, and Roc?"

"Yes?" the computer said.

"I'm also sending a copy to you. I'd like to get your opinion as well."

"Okay," Roc said. "I've been thinking about everything that's happened so far. The text of his note might support a few thoughts I have."

Lita looked up sharply. "What does that mean? What kind of thoughts?"

"Yeah," Gap said, "do you think you might know who this is?"

"Part of my programming did involve deductive reasoning," Roc said. "And I've read every Sherlock Holmes story ever written. Unfortunately we don't have a lot to work with. Good detectives would tell you that it's dangerous to jump ahead without facts. But let's say I'm taking steps with each new development. Can't wait to see the e-mail, Tree."

She looked around at the Council. "Are there any other questions or comments?"

"I'll save mine," Bon said, rising to his feet. "They apparently cause strong emotional reactions from some people."

Without making eye contact with anyone he strode quickly from the room. Gap shook his head in disgust, but bit his tongue.

The others stood to leave. As they began to file out, Triana touched Gap's arm and motioned for him to stay behind.

When they were alone she said to him, "Listen, I just want to say a couple of things, okay? First, thanks for what you said in this meeting. I know that you really care about what happens to me, and that . . . that means a lot. Not many people have ever felt that way about me."

Gap looked down sheepishly, but didn't say anything.

"And I want to say I'm sorry about last night, too," she continued. "You were just being a friend, and I was . . . well, I was pretty cold. I guess I'm just not used to that from anyone but my dad."

He made eye contact with her when he felt her touch his arm again. Her eyes were slightly moist. Suddenly he felt embarrassed putting her through this.

"Tree—" he said.

"I'm going to try to be a better friend, Gap. You deserve it."

They were alone in the room, their eyes locked, and her hand resting slightly on his arm. Gap's mind was racing, an internal debate raging.

Sorry, I've got to break in here. Remember that talk we had about hormones? I'm watching this beautiful scene in the Conference Room and I want to scream at Gap: Kiss her, you idiot! Kiss her! Right on the mouth! It doesn't have to be a long, drawn-out thing. Just a quick "how-do-you-do, I'm putting my mouth on yours and what do you think of that?"

Gee, I hate to coach the guy, and I can't really speak up, but c'mon! Who knows, she might kiss him back. Yes, the crew is in turmoil and, yes, it looks like some crazy nut is hiding out on the ship, and yes, the carpet in this Conference Room is completely tacky, but c'mon! If ever you had the chance, Gap, this is it. You can do it!

Gap hesitated, and in that time Triana let go of his arm and stepped around him to the door. Suddenly he was alone.

With his heart pounding he realized he'd been holding his

breath. He sat down dejectedly, exhaling, and rested his head on one hand.

"Idiot," he muttered. "Idiot, idiot, idiot."

You've got to be kidding me. All right, enough of this. There must be some report I should be working on right now.

30

Galahad had been gone for more than a week. With most of his follow-up work either finished or on schedule, Wallace Zimmer was packing for home. Just as well, he thought; the sooner he was off this antiseptic space station and back among greenery the better. He amused himself by plotting his first real meal in weeks. Lobster, he decided, with a side dish of steaming pasta and vegetables.

The thought brightened his spirits slightly, which helped him pick up the pace of activity. His preparations to leave had been hampered by the creeping fatigue that was one of the curses of Bhaktul Disease. Ten minutes of any physical exertion now had to be followed by five or ten minutes of rest. The coughing spasms were also coming more frequently. On one level it was distressing, simply because it meant that the illness was gaining momentum within him. But it also angered the proud scientist; he had taken great pains to keep himself in good physical shape throughout his life and to be overpowered by a microscopic particle was maddening.

At this particular moment he felt weary. Into one of his large briefcases he tossed an old, worn notebook. In his office at home there were several others just like it. They were crammed with personal notes and feelings from the entire *Galahad* mission, starting with the selection process and finishing with the successful launch. More than two years' worth of observations and memories, crammed into a series of old-fashioned notebooks. Some were held together with tape, all of them were a mishmash of scribbled paragraphs, scratched out sentences, arrows that referred forwards and backwards through the pages, and hastily added notes in the margins.

His computer work pad kept all of the official project notes and information; these pen and paper collections housed the tears and tales that never made it into the official reports. To anyone else they would be practically illegible, but to Dr. Zimmer it was a clear, concise description of the most important endeavor mankind had ever pulled off.

As soon as he returned to Earth he would begin to transcribe it all into a book. No matter what the outcome of the human population, it was imperative that a full account survive.

Closing the briefcase, he plopped down into the chair behind his desk. After a few deep breaths he snapped on his e-mail monitor and checked for any urgent messages. There were none, which made him both happy and sad.

Happy because it meant that *Galahad* was still running smoothly and apparently without trouble, regardless of Roc's inquiries about the energy balance. Sad, however, because it was further evidence that the baby bird had flown from the nest for good. He wanted more than anything for the kids to be safe and secure, but in a perverse way he had hoped that they would somehow still need him for something.

It was the Council that had insisted on the no-contact decree. Once the ship was safely away and the solar wings deployed, radio contact would cease. Roc would continue to relay some information on a daily basis, mostly to confirm course and direction, but that would be it. No calls home, the Council had decided. "What good would it do, really?" Lita had said. "We have to become independent as quickly as possible, and clinging on to Earth's apron won't help us do that."

Yet Dr. Zimmer had secretly hoped for one more call. It didn't look like it was going to happen.

31

Regardless of what Gap, Lita and Channy thought, Tree had already made up her mind. In fact, she had made up her mind long before Bon had suggested she meet the stowaway. She had made that decision as soon as she read his note.

She stood alone near the entrance to the Dining Hall, watching about three dozen crew members carrying their lunch trays and congregating at the tables in groups of three or four. The din in the room grew as more kids trickled in, greetings were exchanged and the tables began to fill up.

Several of the crew members stopped as they entered and chatted briefly with Triana. They made the usual small talk, asking how she was, how things were going, then said good-bye and sauntered over to the food dispensers. But none of them mentioned the intruder to Triana. That seemed to be a subject that was too uncomfortable for the casual atmosphere of their lunch break.

That was okay with her. After the stormy Council meeting, she was only too happy to confine her conversations to more mundane topics. Besides, she realized that many of her shipmates felt a little awkward talking with her anyway, as if they were unsure what to say to their ship's leader. This was a feeling quite familiar to Triana. Social skills had never been her strongest suit.

After glancing around the room one more time she noted that

the one person she was interested in talking to hadn't arrived yet. A quick check of the work schedule had told her that he should be part of this late lunch group, but apparently he was running behind. Triana finally decided to wait for him at a table.

Picking up a tray she stood in line at the dark gray dispensers, slowly moving along and keeping an eye on the door. Each time it opened she would look up to see who had entered, then continue to shuffle along.

A special treat greeted her when it was her turn. The usual plate of processed energy blocks was garnished with several chunks of actual fruit. She smiled as she noticed slices of apple, pear and bananas adorning one section of the plate. It seemed the crops were ahead of schedule. Bon had mentioned to the Council that it might be another week before their first fruit was ready, but she was delighted to see that today was the day.

Bon was infuriating at times, but he knew his stuff when it came to farming, she admitted to herself. Why did he have to make it so hard to like him?

Picking up her tray after filling a glass with water, Triana turned to look for a quiet spot to sit down. At that moment the door opened and Peter Meyer walked in with two other guys. All three were working a shift in the Agricultural Center and Triana could see remnants of dirt and dust on the knees of their pants. They made their way towards the stack of trays. Triana altered her path to intercept them.

"Hello, Peter," she said, causing him to glance over at her. His two companions grew quiet.

"Hi," Peter said.

"Listen, when you get your lunch would you mind stopping by my table over there for just a minute? I'm sorry to interrupt, but I want to ask you something."

Peter's face conveyed a "what have I done now?" look. He shrugged and said, "Sure."

Triana carried her lunch over to a vacant table in the corner.

She was pretty sure she would have it to herself until Peter sat down.

She was enjoying the fresh fruit when the Canadian plopped his tray across from her and pulled out a chair.

"This was a pleasant surprise," she said to him, indicating the apple slice in her hand.

"Yeah, we finished harvesting the first few bushels yesterday," Peter said. "Instead of an announcement we thought it would be better just to surprise everyone. Now that everything's up and running smoothly we should have a fairly constant supply."

"I love it," Triana said. "When the oranges are ready I'll just about have a cow."

Peter smiled. "Well, you should start feeling the labor pains in two weeks or so," he said.

Triana finished her apple and watched Peter as he spread his lunch out on the table. The last time she had seen him was during the frenzy in Sick House. Now, instead of panic, his manner was one of curiosity. She felt bad that she had dragged him away from his friends, and knew that everyone had watched him make his way over to sit with her. Undoubtedly he would be subjected to endless questions later.

"I hope you don't mind," she said, "but I want to talk with you about that day near the Storage Section."

Peter's face clouded and he nervously pushed his now-empty tray out of the way. Picking up his fork he speared a chunk of energy block. "Okay," he said finally.

"For one thing," Triana said, "you told us he said something like, 'Are you ready to die?' Do you remember him saying anything else?"

Peter sat still for a moment, chewing his food. His brow wrinkled as he thought.

"I . . . I really don't remember," he told her. "I don't think so."

Triana nodded. "What was he doing when you saw him? Was he just walking along, or was he standing there?"

"Well, he was just standing there when I came around the corner. His back was to me, and he was pretty much in the shadows, but . . ."

"But what?"

"Well . . . I can't be sure, but I think he had just stood up. Like he had been down on one knee or something."

Triana digested this for a minute. As she took her last bite of fruit she looked back up at Peter.

"So he obviously heard you coming around the corner. Maybe you startled him. Maybe . . . maybe interrupted him from something."

"I don't know. Maybe."

"Hmm," Triana said, deep in thought. What would an intruder have been doing on the floor in that section?

"Peter, where exactly did you see him? I mean, exactly where in that section?"

"Well, I was coming up on the window around the corner from the lift. I was trying to get a view of the moon, and I knew that there was a big window in that hallway, the one just before you get to the Spider bay. I can't say exactly, but I'd guess I was maybe halfway between the lift and the observation window."

That coincided with the area where Gap had found the coin. Perhaps Peter had indeed startled the intruder and caused him to accidentally drop the quarter. But what was he doing there?

"All right, thanks Peter," she said. She was about to get up when she decided to ask him one more question. On an impulse she said, "By the way, are you familiar with a man named Tyler Scofield?"

"I know the name," Peter said slowly. "I don't know if I've ever seen him before. Isn't he the guy who was so against *Galahad*?"

"Yeah," Triana sighed. "He and Dr. Zimmer used to be good friends."

"Is that who you think is on board?" Peter said. "You think he's trying to sabotage the ship?"

"I don't know," Triana said. "Maybe. It all fits. The beard, the fact that he was so against this mission. Even the coin."

"The coin? How?"

Triana bit her lip for a moment. Then she said, "Well, I never met the man face-to-face. But I saw a vidclip of him about three months before we went into the Incubator. Almost sinister looking is how I'd describe him. He was giving a speech about *Galahad,* about how Dr. Zimmer was playing a game of chance with people's children.

"At one point he pulled something out of his pocket and flipped it in the air and caught it. He kept saying 'Heads or tails. Heads or tails.' I didn't know what it meant. He said it was something that people his age would understand."

"So what did it mean?" Peter said, gazing intently at *Galahad*'s Council Leader.

"I asked Dr. Zimmer. He just waved it off and said not to worry about it. You know, he never wanted us to get distracted from our training. So later I asked Dr. Armistead."

"And?"

"She said it meant a fifty-fifty chance. She said when people still used coins for money they would flip them and bet on which side came up. You had a fifty-fifty chance of winning.

"Apparently Scofield was angry, and believed that Dr. Zimmer was gambling with people's families, that his plan was a long shot, no better than a game of chance. Scofield handed out coins to his followers to . . . I don't know, inspire them to defeat the mission. Dr. Armistead said that Scofield wanted to make it a symbol of how desperate our chances were. It never caught on, though."

Peter shrugged. "I never saw that. Like I said, I heard his name before, but I must not have heard about the coins."

"Listen, do you think you could recognize him if Roc pulled up a picture of Scofield?" Triana said.

"I don't know. I didn't get a very good look at him. I was . . . pretty freaked out, I guess." Peter lowered his face, ashamed of the memory.

Triana touched his hand lightly. "Hey, don't worry about it. I would have freaked out, too. Any of us would have."

Peter nodded, but kept his head down.

"Well, do me a favor," Triana said. "When you're finished with lunch, stop by the Conference Room and have Roc pull up a photo of Scofield. Just check it out. It can't hurt to try. And let me know later, okay?"

"Sure," Peter said.

Late that afternoon a sizable crowd had gathered to watch the opening of the three-on-three soccer tournament. For a while there had been discussions about postponing it until their intruder issue was resolved. But Channy was insistent that they not buckle under his intimidation.

"Listen, he might be sneaking around, writing scary memos on the walls and kicking up a few clods in the farm, but he's not going to ruin our fun. No way. Let the games begin."

And so they did. Thirty teams, almost half of the ship's population, had signed up for this three-day tournament. Each team fielded three players at a time, with one extra who subbed. The games were played on fields much smaller than the kids were used to back home, but space inside *Galahad* was very much at a premium. This time around, however, Zimmer didn't need much convincing. He could relate to soccer much more easily than Airboarding. Two fields were squeezed together inside one large room on the second level.

With the smaller playing fields the action was much more intense and the scoring much higher. And, since the crew members on *Galahad* were naturally more competitive than the average teen, the physical aspect of the games was compounded, as well. This was definitely a contact sport.

Channy was in charge, but took time out in the early evening to sit for a few minutes with Gap and Lita in the stands. They kept their eyes on the match in front of them while they discussed the latest Council meeting.

"I just find it interesting that she kept this note from the stowaway to herself until the end of the meeting," Channy said. "If I get a note from this guy I'm not waiting two seconds to let someone know about it."

Lita put her fingers into her mouth and whistled loudly at a great save by one of the players on the field. "But it's just like Tree, if you think about it. She doesn't get worked up about anything, really. I can totally see her sitting on that note until she thought it was the right time to talk about it."

"Yeah, maybe," Gap said. "But doesn't it make you wonder if she's telling us everything?"

Channy took her eyes off the game and stared at him. "You think she knows more than she's telling us? That doesn't make any sense."

"I don't know," Gap said, unconvinced. "Look, she's a loner for the most part anyway, right? C'mon, don't look at me like that, we all know she is. And that's fine. Personally, I'd like to get to know her a little better, but I respect her decision to keep mostly to herself. But doesn't that make you wonder if sometimes she thinks she can handle something by herself?"

Lita thought about this, then looked quizzically at Gap. "What are you saying? That she's gonna try to track down this guy alone?" Her face contorted into a look of disbelief. "That's ridiculous, Gap. She weighs about one hundred ten pounds. She's not gonna try to take him on."

"No, but she probably isn't thinking about a physical confrontation," Gap said. "Tree is one of the smartest people on this ship . . . and there's a lot of smart people crammed in here. I just get the feeling that she thinks she can outsmart this guy. You know, brains over brawn, that old cliché."

"So why would she try to do that by herself?" Channy said. "She doesn't think we're smart enough to help her?"

"No, that's not it," Gap said. All three of the Council members instinctively threw their hands up as one of the soccer players deflected the ball up into the bleachers. It was grabbed by a girl two rows in front of them, and everyone relaxed again.

"No," Gap said again. "I don't think she feels that way at all. It's just . . ." He paused, trying to figure out the right words to express himself. "It's just that she's so independent, and feels so much pressure, I think, to lead this mission, that she thinks she has to take on all the responsibility herself. It's not that she doesn't like the help. I just think she doesn't like asking for it."

"Well, that actually makes sense," Lita said. "I've talked with her enough to know that she grew up that way. She absolutely worshipped her dad, and when he died she kinda felt like she didn't have anybody else to rely on. She's had that spirit since we've all known her, you know what I mean? Like, 'I can do this by myself,' that kinda thing."

"What if we talked to her about it?" Channy said. "Told her that she doesn't have to solve every problem alone?"

"Or, don't say anything and just start volunteering to help her more," Lita suggested. "We're not going to change her personality, I don't think. It's better if we just showed our support and let her figure it out for herself."

Gap nodded. "I just hope she doesn't get herself into trouble in the meantime."

A cheer rose from the crowd as a goal was scored.

Listen, I know I'm a little bit of an attention hog, but I'll be honest with you.

I don't feel too good.

There's nothing wrong with the ship, at least that I can tell. The life-support systems are okay, the gravity system is perfect, the crops are growing, the water recycling unit is good. . . .

But something's not right with me.

I was talking with Bon in the Farm Dome when it first happened. I . . . well, I guess I blacked out. One moment I'm hearing everything that Bon is saying, and the next thing I know I'm out of it. Must have lasted about ten seconds. Bon asked what had happened, and I quite honestly couldn't tell him. He shrugged it off as a fluke of some kind, but

I'm not so sure. In all my years of programming and testing, nothing like that has ever happened.

It was like a human losing consciousness. Their heart keeps beating, their lungs continue to breathe, but the signal with the outside world is cut off momentarily. Very puzzling.

I haven't run a full diagnostic test on myself for a couple of months. Must be time.

And then there's the matter of our uninvited guest. I've gone through every detail over and over again, and there's one answer that keeps popping up.

I think it's time to talk with Tree about it. After my test, of course.

32

The passenger section on the shuttle was practically empty. Wallace Zimmer knew that the staff on the space station had begun to thin out within hours of the departure of *Galahad*. When he had finally decided to head back to Earth he left behind a crew of perhaps only two dozen orbiting in the space lab.

He flipped on the vidscreen built into the seatback ahead of him and selected an all-news station. What greeted him was mostly depressing: a reporter stood before a vacant office building in the United States, reflecting on the slow but continuous demise of most businesses. There were too many people ill, and those that were as yet unaffected by the disease were unable to keep up with the workload. Another report from Western Europe showed images of rioting, as hordes of frightened people took out their frustration on a pharmacy that had shut its doors rather than turn away people desperate for medicinal help.

That was the problem: there was no help from the medical front in the foreseeable future. Doctors and scientists were still at a loss to explain exactly how Bhaktul worked on its human hosts. While there were some similarities in each case, such as coughing and severe headaches, often madness at the end, there were also hundreds of different symptoms. It was as if Bhaktul took different paths, threading its way through each person at a different vulnerable point. That made containment—and any possible antidote—incredibly difficult to provide.

Flipping the channel he gazed at a newscast photo of Tyler Scofield. Zimmer adjusted the volume up slightly and listened as the news anchor announced that Scofield's headquarters had also gone dark. No one had seen the renowned scientist in more than a week, and it was assumed that the launch of *Galahad* had sent Scofield into hiding somewhere. There was a quick mention of the spacecraft picking up speed on its way towards Saturn, and how it would use the giant gas planet's gravitational pull for a slingshot effect into deep space. Then the station broke for a commercial.

Sighing, Dr. Zimmer shut off the vidscreen and glanced out the tiny window beside his seat, scanning the image of the blue-green planet that rotated lazily below him. It looked peaceful and undisturbed, like a child curled up asleep. Soft clouds glided above the surface, and sunlight dappled off the water. He was amazed at the deception, how the gentle appearance concealed the despair that weaved its way throughout the population. This would be his last view of Earth from space, he realized with a start, which only deepened his sadness.

A coughing spasm made him convulse suddenly, and the taste of blood was stronger than before. He pulled out a tissue and dabbed his mouth, noticing the tiny spots of red before he returned the tissue to his pocket.

Straightening up, he plugged his work pad into the connection beneath the vidscreen and proceeded to access his mail. A few more scattered congratulations from colleagues around the world, along with a short note from his doctor. It mentioned a new cough suppressant that helped ease the pain that might accompany the intense spasms Zimmer had reported to him. "And," the note added, "it has also been shown to decrease the likelihood of coughing up blood, although you haven't mentioned that happening with you. For future reference, though . . ."

Dr. Zimmer grimaced. He hadn't mentioned it, of course. "At

my next appointment," he kept saying to himself. He wondered if it was too late for the drug to help.

With almost two hours to go before landing in California, he decided to spend the time writing to some of the people closest to him. He wrote a long letter to his only surviving sister and another to his half brother. Both letters apologized for his lack of attention to them over these last two years. He hoped they understood how the *Galahad* project had dominated his time. He wished them well, asked about their spouses and children, and closed with a reference to his own declining health. As he read over the letters before pushing the send button, he noted that he was really composing good-bye letters. They weren't eloquent, but he hoped they conveyed his love.

He sent another thank-you note to Angela Armistead. She had cried to the point of making herself sick when the door to *Galahad* had sealed shut. Dr. Zimmer had hugged her for a long time, feeling the grief that wracked her body. Barely thirty years old when the project began, she had come to feel that each of the star travelers was like a brother or sister to her. Zimmer hoped that she found peace quickly.

Next he wrote a brief note to Dr. Bauer, thanking him once again for his two years of work on the project. "I know that you sacrificed time that could have been spent with your family. I don't know how others would regard that commitment; some would call it despicable while others might call it honorable. I just wanted you to know how much I appreciate what you did. There are 251 young people who echo those sentiments. They carry a part of you with them to the stars."

Dr. Zimmer included warm wishes to Bauer's family. He started to ask about Fenton Bauer's relationship with his son, but decided that it probably would not be appropriate. "I'm sure it feels good to be home," he closed. "When you find a spare moment, please give me a call. I would love to visit with you again."

His final letter was to Tyler Scofield. "No matter our differences over the issue that has occupied our lives the last two years, I want you to know how much I continue to respect you and your convictions. I'll always treasure the friendship that kept us bonded for many years, and want you to know that those memories will be the ones that take priority when my thoughts turn to you."

And he meant it. Scofield had fought him at every step during the entire project, and hurtful barbs had been thrown in both directions. But Wallace Zimmer was now at peace, and truly hoped that his old friend-turned-adversary felt the same.

Before sending the e-mail he considered the news story that mentioned Scofield's disappearance. He hoped the acclaimed scientist would still be checking his messages, wherever he had gone.

Zimmer sent a handful of other quick notes to his rather small circle of close friends and associates. His final task was a mass e-mail of congratulations and thanks to each of the hundreds and hundreds of people who had devoted their precious time and energy to the success of *Galahad*. "You have made a difference, one that we won't ever be able to witness ourselves, but will ripple across the galaxy over time. In a time of despair and sadness, let that one thought lift your spirits. You are all heroes."

He unplugged his work pad and put it away. The time had flown during his writing, and touchdown on the desert runway was now only ten minutes away. The weary scientist closed his eyes, leaned back in his chair, and waited.

33

The hallways of *Galahad* were quiet. It was almost midnight and most of the exhausted crew slept. The three-day soccer tournament had ended that evening, the winning team claiming victory with a last-second goal in the championship game. "I couldn't have scripted a better ending to our first tournament," Channy had exclaimed to the cheering throng gathered on the field. The spirit of the crew was high.

Before turning in, Triana had congratulated the winners on the ship's vidscreens and also thanked Channy for all of her hard work. "We've trained hard for this mission, we work hard each day to sustain ourselves," she said. "But balance is crucial to our mental well-being. We will always play as hard as we work. Let's never lose that edge."

She had made a couple of other quick announcements regarding possible shift changes in the coming days, and reminded each crew member to check their personal e-mail at least twice a day.

Now, as midnight approached, Triana prepared for bed. Kicking off her slippers, she brushed her teeth and laid out her favorite T-shirt to sleep in. Then, sitting at her desk, she flipped open her journal and began to write.

I keep replaying my conversation with Peter Meyer, and now all I can see in my mind is Tyler Scofield creeping along the corridors of the ship. It's true he wanted to disrupt the mission, but is he the type of person who would resort to violence to destroy the ship and the crew?

Triana couldn't answer that question. For one thing, she had never met the man. Second, there was no telling what the ravages of Bhaktul might have done to his mental state. And third, what if it wasn't him? The description fit, but unfortunately she wasn't ready to declare Scofield the intruder. Peter had been unable to positively identify him from the pictures Roc had available. The young Canadian had only glimpsed the man in the Storage Section. The beard was roughly the same, he said, but something just wasn't clicking. All of Roc's photos were several years old, and time or disease could have altered the man's appearance. Triana felt as frustrated as ever.

If we don't catch him soon I'm going to rethink my decision about opening the Storage Sections. Roc is working on it, and I'm willing to give it one more day or two. After that we go on the attack; I'm tired of waiting for this person—whoever it is—to show himself.

She wasn't particularly tired yet, so rather than shutting off the light in her room and climbing into bed, she flicked on her vidscreen and checked a graphic that showed the location of *Galahad* within the solar system. Their track was holding steady on a course that would shoot them past the orbit of Mars and on towards Saturn. She scanned ahead and eyed the future path of the massive ship as it rocketed towards the outer planets. Their final contact with human life would come briefly near Saturn. There, an orbiting research station with a crew of thirty scientists would share radio contact with *Galahad* and check on their status. That team would then relay a final report back to Earth, acknowledging the passing of the vessel on its way out of the solar system.

Triana did not necessarily look forward to that communication. It would seem like another good-bye, which she dreaded.

After that, appearing on her screen as a weak point of light, was Eos. Between them, several light-years of inky blackness, and the great unknown.

After pausing for another moment, Triana clicked open her e-mail.

And immediately let out her breath in a gasp.

It was another note from the stowaway. The subject line read "Time to exchange a handshake." After hesitating briefly, she slowly clicked open the letter and began to read.

Greetings again, Ms. Martell. I extend to you an invitation to join me for a lively discussion on the future of your assignment. I know that you must have several questions, and it will be my pleasure to answer as many of those as possible.

By now I'm sure you have discussed my first letter with your fellow Council members, and I'm equally sure that they have counseled you to refrain from meeting alone with me. If I read you correctly, you have not reached this same conclusion. My impression is that you prefer to handle matters yourself. I appreciate that. It has always been my way, as well.

Tonight would be an excellent opportunity for us to exchange a handshake and get to know each other better. I'm quite confident that after you hear my thoughts, you'll wonder why you were ever so concerned. Please allow me the chance to put your mind at ease.

I will wait for you in the Storage Section of the ship between midnight and 12:30 A.M. That should give us the peace and quiet that we need to seriously discuss matters. I doubt that we'll be disturbed at that time of the morning.

Again, I respectfully request that you come alone. If I see more than just your bright young face, I will disappear, and this offer will not be repeated. Do we understand each other?

If you do not come alone, you will miss your one and only chance to visit with me.

If you do not appear by 12:30, I will assume that you refuse this meeting, and I will move on to my next task. A task, I might add, that you will find most distressing, to say the least.

Until then, Ms. Martell, I bid you good night.

Triana reread the note, biting her lip. She glanced quickly at the clock in the top corner of her vidscreen: 12:02 A.M.

Her mind raced. It would only take a few minutes to reach the Storage Section of *Galahad,* which allowed her time to make the appointment. It did not necessarily give her time to contact the members of the Council and collect their opinions. Besides, she already knew that their answers wouldn't be any different from the last time. And this intruder, whoever he was, had now eerily threatened further damage, a threat that Triana took very seriously. In her judgment a private meeting was better than leaving him to possibly cripple their ship.

Well, she had just expressed a desire to go on the attack. Now, it seemed, was her only chance.

She stood up to change back into her clothes, then had a sudden thought. Sitting back down, she snapped on her vidscreen audio and called out, "Roc?" It made sense to her to at least tell the computer what was happening. Somebody needed to know what her plans were, and Roc would be able to convey the message to the other Council members later, should anything go wrong.

But there was no answer from Roc. The audio speaker remained silent. "Roc?" she said again. Still silence.

Now Triana was more troubled than ever. She wondered if the threat mentioned by this intruder involved somehow disrupting communication with *Galahad*'s master computer. He had said that Triana had until 12:30. It was now 12:03.

With her heart racing, she changed back into her everyday work clothes and started to race out into the hallway, pausing only briefly to glance at the picture of her father beside her bed. "Help me, Dad," she said softly, and then broke into a run out the door.

At that moment Gap was in his room, leaning back in a chair. His feet, clad only in socks, were propped up on the table, his shoes tossed haphazardly to the side. A blanket his mother had made was wrapped around his upper body, more as a comfort piece than a practical tool for keeping warm. His eyelids were heavy, and occasionally his chin would bob onto his chest, jerking him back to attention. After one particularly long yawn he stretched his arms upwards, trying to fight off the urge to sleep. He was exhausted. After a quick glance at the clock on the vidscreen he figured about another hour and he would be able to fall into bed.

His roommate, Daniil Temka, was sleeping soundly across the room. That didn't help much, either.

For the third night in a row he had kept up this vigil. On the vidscreen before him was a live security camera shot. It was focused on the hallway at the end of this particular section of residential quarters. Through the dim light Gap was able to watch the last fifteen feet of hallway and the entrance to the lift. His eyes never left the vidscreen for more than a few seconds, which only made the task of remaining awake that much more difficult.

Yet he was determined to stay awake each night and keep watch over the hallway and the lift. If his hunch was right, Triana would not report her next message from the secretive stowaway. She was more likely to accept his offer to meet, which meant putting herself into more danger than she probably realized.

Gap would not let that happen. He reasoned that Triana would be asleep by one o'clock each night at the latest, so it shouldn't be that difficult to keep watch for a little while. If by one there was no sign, then he was confident she wouldn't be sneaking off to a private rendezvous. It just so happened that he was particularly tired this night. The time dragged.

Suddenly an image flashed across the vidscreen. Gap shot upright in the chair, his blanket falling to the floor. He leaned forward and looked closely at the screen. It was Triana.

She raced up to the lift door, waving a hand over the sensor. In a matter of seconds the door opened and she scampered inside. It closed just as quickly, and she was gone. It had all lasted less than ten seconds.

Gap sat stunned. He had watched for this, anticipating that it could happen. But he was still unprepared for it. His action plan wasn't exactly complete. It had allowed for keeping watch; it hadn't really included what to do after that. His thoughts tumbled into one another, backing up and slowing his reaction time.

Snapping out of his frozen trance, he punched in the code that would open an audio link to Lita's room. At the same time he reached for his shoes under the table. A light tone sounded, signaling a connection to his fellow Council member.

"Lita!" he called out. "Lita, wake up. It's Gap."

He fumbled with his shoes, slipping them on and snapping them shut all in one movement. "C'mon Lita, wake up."

"Mmmh," he heard her mumble through the speaker. "What?"

"Listen, it's me. You gotta wake up and call the others. Tree is on the move."

"What are you talking about? What time is it?"

"A little after twelve. C'mon, snap out of it. Tree is on the move."

Lita's voice sounded sluggish. "Yeah, I heard that. What do you mean? On the move where?"

"Listen, there's no time for this. Tree just tore out of her room, and I know she's going to meet up with the stowaway. Just wake up the others and meet me . . ." Gap trailed off, his mind racing. That was a good question, now wasn't it? Meet where?

"Meet where?" Lita said at the same time he was thinking it.

He stopped, glancing back at the monitor that now showed an empty hallway in front of the lift.

"Meet me in the Storage Section. Hurry up!"

He snapped off the intercom without waiting for a reply. Pushing back from the chair he called out, "Roc!"

There was no answer. Daniil had awakened and was propped up on one arm, trying to comprehend what the commotion was all about.

"Roc!" Gap tried again, leaning towards the red sensor.

Silence.

"Oh, no," he said under his breath. Without waiting to investigate, he scrambled out the door and broke into a sprint towards the lift.

The lift door opened on the bottom level, but Triana hesitated. For a moment she remained at the back of the lift, leaning against the wall, grasping the hand railing, peering out into the shadowed gloom. The hallway curved to the left, limiting her field of view to about thirty feet. A heavy quiet greeted her.

Triana's breathing quickened. Her heart banged wildly against her chest, and a thin layer of moisture broke out on her palms. "Calm down," she told herself. "Relax." She swallowed and forced herself to take long, deep breaths.

Letting go of the railing, she took one tentative step out into the hallway. It wasn't simply the faint light that was spooking her, she realized. It was that tomblike silence. A ship this size, with this many people aboard, shouldn't be so . . .

Then it hit her: it was too quiet. The soft background sounds normally supplied by Roc were gone. No wind. No crickets. Nothing.

She paused with her hand across the door sensor, preventing it from closing, using the light that streamed from inside the lift to see as far as possible. What she wouldn't give right now for a simple flashlight. Straining, she listened for the sound of a footstep, a voice, even the sound of breathing.

Nothing.

For a moment she considered calling out. But somehow that seemed creepy, too. No, the intruder had said to meet her on this level. Well, she was here. Time to go find him.

I can't stand here all night, she finally thought. Time is running out.

She left the comfort of the lighting within the lift and took a few more tentative steps into the gloom. Her feet padded slowly along the corridor, barely making a sound, while the deafening thud of her heartbeat echoed in her ears. She worried that the pounding might obscure any sound that would alert her to the stowaway's presence. Her breathing was in control now, but the sweat on her palms had not let up.

Brief thoughts of turning back darted into her head, and at one point she actually came to a halt, just before the bend of the hallway. Should she backtrack and call the other Council members? Suddenly this idea of the private meeting did not seem so wise after all.

Shaking her head, Triana took a few more steps. As she rounded the turn she ran through a mental review of this level. Five sealed Storage Sections, inaccessible to the crew—but not to their guest, it would seem. Several more hallways branched off from this main artery. The Airboarding track was at the end of one of these branches, dark and deserted now. Farther ahead, towards the end of the main corridor, were the Spider bays. A large observation window loomed just outside the entrance to the bays, the window that Peter Meyer had sought before his encounter with the intruder. And finally, at the end of the main hall, an emergency stairwell.

There was something else on this level, however, that hadn't occurred to her until now. Something that she had forgotten about. Something that should have registered from the beginning. Something that suddenly clicked.

She saw it as she finished rounding the turn. There, at about waist level, was the access panel to *Galahad*'s computer controls. The entry point to the massive electronic brain they lovingly called Roc.

And the panel was open.

She stared at it, trying to comprehend what she was seeing, unaware that she had been holding her breath until it escaped from her in a rush.

There had been no answer from Roc in her room. The comforting Earth sounds were missing. A new, stabbing fear, different from the others that had been crowding her mind, shot through her in a flash. Damage to the ship's computer brain could spell disaster for the entire crew. Roc controlled almost every function of the vessel, including . . .

Including life-support control. Gravity. Heat. Air.

There was still no sound. Her eyes now accustomed to the murky darkness, she cautiously stepped towards the open access panel. As she dropped to one knee to inspect it, more details made sense.

Peter had seen the intruder at this spot. He had told Triana that it seemed as if the man had just stood up. Peter wondered if he had been kneeling. Of course. Opening the panel would require that.

Gap had found the coin at this spot. Somehow that was connected, too.

Triana looked first at the panel as it hung from its hinges. It wasn't as if security at this site was a priority, but Dr. Zimmer still had insisted that it take a special tool to open this section. There were only two of these tools that she knew of; one in her possession, another with Gap. Who might have a third?

Next, she peered inside, wishing once again for a flashlight. Nothing looked out of the ordinary, but her computer classes seemed like eons ago. What had happened here?

Triana had become so preoccupied with the open access panel that she never heard the quiet footsteps approaching from behind. So focused was she on the problem at hand that the voice, when it came, brought a scream to her lips and a chill to her blood.

"Well, hello, Triana. I wondered if you were going to make it."

That was followed by one of the most hideous laughs she had ever heard in her life.

34

Opening the window didn't do much good, since the air was still and dry. There was no breeze to ventilate the house. After being locked up for several weeks it was definitely hotter inside than out, and Wallace Zimmer thought that any exchange of air would help reduce the heavy feeling that hung within the walls. He leaned against the windowsill and gazed out at the quiet street. The usually bustling neighborhood was subdued, as people sought refuge inside from the stifling late-summer conditions. Even the birds had decided to call it quits for the afternoon, as if it required too much energy to muster up even the smallest chirp.

He had lived in this house for almost twenty years. Or, rather, he had owned the property and listed the address as home, even though he actually spent more time away than here. During the two years of overseeing *Galahad* he could count perhaps ten nights that he had slept in his own bed. His neighbors were gracious, keeping his lawn in passable shape and stopping in to make sure everything was in order. One thing he was sure of: never take great neighbors for granted.

He was struck by another coughing attack. This one was more severe than most, and the pain in his chest radiated out to his arms this time. More blood collected in his mouth, too much to swallow this time, and he leaned forward to spit it out the window. Thank goodness the neighbors didn't have to see that, he thought.

No sooner had he collected himself from the attack when another spasm wracked him, more violently than the first. Another mouthful of blood was ejected onto the rocks outside his window, and a tear seeped out of one eye. The pain was becoming unbearable. It was time for another dose of the cough suppressant he had picked up from his doctor this morning, wasn't it? Had it been long enough between doses?

Did that even really matter anymore?

He trudged into the kitchen as mild aftershocks of coughs rippled from his chest. He decided he didn't care if he was an hour or two early for the next dose. All he could think about was stopping the pain. Just stop the pain.

He unscrewed the cap on the medicine, ignored the spoon lying next to it, and tipped the neck of the bottle into his mouth. Two quick swallows began coursing through his system, and within a minute he felt the pain subside. He rested one hand on the kitchen table and the other on his forehead, gathering his strength. This couldn't go on much longer. And, sadly, he knew it wouldn't.

Eventually he pulled out a chair and sat, then slowly replaced the cap on the medicine bottle. The table was littered with books and papers from the *Galahad* project, along with an assortment of e-mails and letters from the families of the kids who had made the trip. Each one thanked him again for the opportunity he had given their child to survive. Each one wished him well. Each one was, in its own way, another good-bye.

He flipped through these notes absentmindedly, looking at them without really seeing them. After reaching the bottom of the stack he started to sort through them again before catching himself and pushing the pile aside. The house was quiet, and lonely.

The sound of the tone from the vidscreen on the table was soft, but still caused him to jump. He checked the incoming call and saw it listed as F. Bauer.

Connecting, he smiled when he saw the face of Dr. Bauer's wife, Sharee. She looked weary—that look was commonplace these days—but managed to smile back at Zimmer. He had only met her on a few occasions, but had instantly decided that she was one of the truly warm, caring people in the world. Fenton Bauer had been very blessed.

"Hello, Sharee," he said.

"It's good to see you, Wallace," she said. "How are you?"

"Oh, I'm all right, I suppose. A little tired. You look as lovely as ever, of course."

Her smile brightened slightly. "You're sweet, but I don't feel lovely. Not anymore. And you know what? I hate to say this, but I don't even try anymore. The way I figure it, this is how I look, so the world better just deal with it. I've retired my makeup bag for good."

Zimmer laughed. "I like your attitude, Sharee."

"Well, it's not like I'm out dancing every night. In fact, I haven't left the house in the last week except to go to the store. Never thought I'd be the type to turn into a hermit, but . . . but I can't really bring myself to socialize much anymore."

"I understand," Zimmer said. In his own mind he wondered if he would venture out very much in the coming weeks, and quickly decided that the answer was no. He had no friends around to speak of. And besides, he didn't feel very sociable himself. What was left of his enthusiasm had launched inside a giant spacecraft and was headed towards a distant star. No, he would probably become just like Sharee, he thought.

"I understand that you'll be writing a book on *Galahad*," she said. "I think that's a terrific idea. Fenton told me as much as he could, but I'd very much like to see it all through your eyes."

"Well," he said, a touch of sadness entering his voice. "I meant to start it a long time ago, but there just wasn't any time before the launch. Maybe now that I'm home . . ." His voice trailed off.

"I'm sorry," Sharee said suddenly. "Of course, you need some time to rest and . . . and . . . and get your strength back."

Dr. Zimmer rubbed his fingers on the kitchen table, feeling a coughing spasm that was beginning to well up. He didn't want Sharee to see that, so he stayed silent for a moment, trying to suppress the attack. She obviously took that to mean that she had said something wrong.

"Listen, Wallace, let me know if there's anything I can do for you. I know I'm clear across the country, but if there's anything I can send to you, or . . ." An idea suddenly occurred to her. "Or maybe you'd like to fly out and stay with us for a little while. We could all go out and do something together."

"That would be very nice," he said. "Although I'm sure Fenton has seen enough of me over the last two years. He'd probably prefer to spend some quiet time with you, don't you think?"

"Maybe," she said, with her own sad inflection now filtering through her voice. "But he hasn't been in a hurry to get back yet."

Zimmer's fingers stopped sliding along the tabletop, and he stared into the vidscreen. "What do you mean?"

Sharee shrugged. "I mean he hasn't made it home yet."

"What? He left the station weeks ago."

"I know. He called me the night before he left, and told me that he felt terrible and was coming home. But he said that he wanted to stop off at my parents' cabin to see if he could convince Marshall to come home."

Dr. Zimmer remembered the many conversations he'd had with Dr. Bauer regarding Bauer's reclusive son. He recalled the pain that was evident each time the topic came up, and the way Bauer had seemed to envy Zimmer's closeness with the crew of *Galahad,* perhaps wishing for that same relationship with his own son. Dr. Zimmer had always been at a loss for words at those times, but on one occasion had asked if a reconciliation was possible. Dr. Bauer had shook his head slowly, but had not answered.

Zimmer stared intently into the vidscreen. "And you haven't heard from him since he went to Tahoe?"

"That's just it," Sharee said. "Marshall's here. He's been here for five days now. And he says Fenton never called or showed up there."

"And you haven't heard anything from him?"

"Nothing. I've been so anxious for him to get home. Marshall's almost like a new . . . well, a new man. He's wanting to reconnect with his father. I think he knows that there's not a lot of time left, you know?" Her weak smile dissipated, leaving almost a grimace on her face.

Zimmer didn't respond.

"Anyway," Sharee said, "when your e-mail for Fenton came in here a couple of days ago I was a little surprised. It sounded like you thought he was here, and I was kind of hoping that he was with you. So I decided to call."

"I'm sorry," Zimmer said. "I . . . I thought he was home. He never said anything to me about going to find Marshall. All he told me on the station was that he was going home." He paused briefly, thinking. "I'll make a few calls," he finally told Sharee.

"I appreciate that, Wallace," she said. "I'll check back with you tonight. Maybe we can figure out where he is. I'm sure there's a simple answer."

Dr. Zimmer wasn't so sure, but smiled at Sharee Bauer and wished her well before breaking the connection. He sat still for a while, his mind replaying the conversation. So Fenton had told him that he was leaving the space station and going home. He told his wife that he was stopping in Tahoe to meet with their son, to try to patch up things. Yet he had never showed up at either location. Nor had Sharee or Zimmer been contacted regarding any type of accident or emergency.

The scientist was missing.

35

Sudden fear can trigger chaos in the human body. A quick, unexpected jolt of fear can instantly double or triple the heart rate. Muscles can immediately tighten, bringing on a feeling of paralysis. Breathing becomes rapid and choppy, palms become sweaty and all of the body's senses shoot into overdrive. The brain scrambles for information, looking for anything to help it recognize the threat and develop a reliable solution to that threat. The survival instinct sends adrenaline rushing through the body, preparing every part for the action needed to protect itself. Yet, ironically, it can also cloud the judgment of the brain, inducing an action that might not be appropriate for the situation or could even make matters worse.

Triana Martell was experiencing all of the symptoms of sudden, crushing fear. The unexpected voice, and the evil laugh that followed it, caused her to immediately freeze, down on one knee, one hand resting on the floor, the other just inside the open panel on the wall. Sweat broke out on her forehead and her palms; her breath came in quick gasps. Her body had tensed, her brain sending out the genetically programmed "fight or flight" response. Triana's initial reaction was to jump up and run. But a split second before getting to her feet, her training kicked in.

Dr. Armistead had spent almost a full week working with the crew of *Galahad* on one particular emotion: fear. She hadn't pulled any punches, either. "There will be times that the slow buildup of fear will weigh upon you," she had told them. "The anxiety you'll feel is only natural; you're all taking on a mission that nobody would have even imagined three years ago. That type of fear can wear you down, exhaust you. We'll cover the types of exercises and meditations that can relieve the stress.

"We'll also teach you to deal with sudden, unexpected emergencies that can provoke a sensation of fear that will almost paralyze your body. You have to be ready to deal with these emergencies without panicking. Nothing is foolproof; some of you will be able to adapt better than others. But all of you will have a fighting chance with the right preparation."

Triana had found that particular stage of their training fascinating. They learned about the amygdala and its effects within the brain. They practiced techniques to slow the body's breathing, which controlled the heart rate, which in turn allowed the brain to better process the rapid influx of data. In short, they learned to overcome the paralysis of abrupt fear. Dr. Armistead had stressed to Dr. Zimmer that it could very well be the training that ultimately would save their lives.

Triana summoned the knowledge from that training as her heart and mind threatened to race out of control. She consciously exhaled slowly, to a count of three, before drawing another breath and letting it out again to another count of three. She felt her heartbeat gradually calm. Taking one more deep breath, she pushed herself back up onto her feet, and turned. In the dim twilight of the corridor she came face-to-face with the intruder.

She was sure that the shock of recognition and surprise was plainly visible on her face, which caused the man to laugh again. The laughter, although quiet, seemed to reverberate through her brain. This was madness.

"Dr. Bauer," was all she could manage to say.

"Triana," he said, drawing out each syllable of her name. "Surprise, surprise, surprise, eh?"

She didn't answer. Her mind was trying to make sense of what she was seeing, and it wasn't making much progress. Dr. Bauer's usually smooth face was covered with a ragged beard, and his eyes, normally such a warm brown, seemed darker now and tinged with red. His hair was matted and greasy, his clothes filthy and in disarray. From what she could gather in the dim light, the face underneath the beard looked thin and sunken.

Triana's gaze drifted down to Dr. Bauer's left hand, which clutched a long, pointed object. It took her a second to recognize it as the special tool needed to open the computer access panel. She had one stashed in her room; it made sense that Dr. Bauer would have had one as well.

But right now he brandished it more like a weapon than a tool. Triana eyed the sharp steel point with the special hatch marks, designed to fit into the grooves of the panel almost like an old-fashioned screwdriver. Although it wasn't designed to inflict injury on a person, she knew that it was more than capable of tearing flesh. She looked back into Bauer's eyes.

"I didn't think you were coming," he said, the evil grin still beaming. "I almost had to start without you."

Triana swallowed, forcing herself to take another deep breath and exhale slowly. "And what are you starting?"

"The slow death decay of *Galahad,*" he said, laughing yet again, this time louder and longer than before. Triana knew now why Peter Meyer had freaked out upon hearing that sound. It conjured up every image of terror that she had ever known, blended with something else that made it even more powerful: a feeling of confidence. Dr. Fenton Bauer had not only set out to destroy the ship and all of its crew members, he was also deadly certain that it was going to happen.

"Tell me why," she said, shrewdly trying to take a step backwards to open up a bit more space between them. Dr. Bauer would have none of it, and moved to his left just enough to block any escape for Triana. She was cornered. Any jump she made could be cut off in a flash, and the sharp point of the tool would bring her down instantly. One more time she cursed herself for braving this meeting alone.

"There are about seven billion reasons that I can think of," Bauer said. "Every man, woman and child that you left behind on Earth. Each person who will have to not only suffer the pain of Bhaktul Disease, but the thought that you get a free pass. A free pass on their credit, too. You see, none of you on this ship stopped to think about that now, did you? That your escape from that disease was actually paid for by the people who will ultimately die from it. What did they get out of it? How do they profit?"

Triana was listening to him, absorbing his warped logic, and trying desperately to find the words to debate the issue. He apparently had a lot to say about the mission, and any chance to engage him in a discussion would hopefully buy more time for someone to stumble onto them. That wasn't likely, she was sure, but worth the chance. She knew her words were important. Angering him might only cause him to react quickly and violently; she had to appeal to him intellectually. He was, after all, a scientist, and would likely want to explain his position, almost as if he were proving a theorem. She had to hope that logic could overcome the insanity brought on by Bhaktul.

"They profit by knowing the human race goes on," she said, measuring her words carefully and speaking in a soft, slow voice.

"Ha!" he said with a shout. "You sound like Dr. Zimmer. In fact, that's almost a direct quote from him. I should know; I heard it hundreds of times over the last two years. I expected more from you, Triana. You're intelligent. But now you're coming across as nothing but a trained parrot, mimicking your master. Aren't you able to think for yourself?" He punctuated his remarks by waving the long metal tool in her face. She didn't flinch.

"I'm very capable of thinking for myself," she said. "I've thought a lot about it. And whether I was included or not, I would still have voted for this mission. Mankind has always overcome obstacles, and we won't just pull the curtain closed on thousands of years of progress because of one fluke astronomical event. Even one hundred years ago we wouldn't have been able to do anything about it. Today we can, and we choose to preserve the species."

"More Zimmer nonsense!" Bauer shouted. "You've been brainwashed, girl, that's all. Tell me why you should go? What makes you special?"

This gave Triana pause. There was something underneath his ranting, something that was registering at the outskirts of her mind. Something that told her that Dr. Bauer wasn't necessarily against the mission itself, but rather . . . what? When he spoke again, she understood completely.

"Why should you go, or Gap, or Lita, or any of those other kids? What about all the other kids who deserved a chance to go? What about the kids who were just as smart as you, maybe smarter, who didn't get the chance? Just because some kids were a little older . . ." His voice broke for an instant, a sob that tried to well up but was suppressed. His maniacal waving of the weapon stilled, and he grew quiet.

Triana took a chance. "You're talking about your son, aren't you?"

Dr. Bauer fixed his gaze on her, bloodshot eyes that crept from deep within his sunken face, eyes that bored through her, mixed with hate and madness. She had hit the mark, and knew it instantly.

"My son is better than you or anyone on this ship," he said barely above a whisper. "He's smarter than you, braver than you, stronger than you. He should be here, not back on Earth awaiting a death sentence."

Now Triana had to tread lightly. "How old is your son?" she said, although she knew the answer.

"Dr. Zimmer would tell you that it doesn't matter. He's too old, he would say. But he's not. He hasn't shown one sign of Bhaktul. Not one sign. He would have called and told me, I know. But I haven't heard a word from him. He's fine, I tell you. There's nothing that should have kept him from this mission. Nothing." He paused, then said, "He would have called me. He would have called."

Triana could have explained that it simply wasn't possible for everyone to go. She could have explained that once children reached the age of eighteen their bodies were able to carry the disease, whether they showed symptoms or not. She could have said all of this. But Dr. Bauer knew it. He knew it but was unable to accept it right now. Whether it was the disease working on his mind or overpowering grief or a combination of both, he wasn't able to admit the truth. Stating the obvious might stall him, but it also might trigger an attack. She instead opted to console him.

"I think you're right," she said. "I'd like to know more about your son. What's his name?"

Bauer sighed. "His name is Marshall."

"Where does he live?"

"He . . . He lives . . ." Bauer's eyes had dropped from Triana's. When he looked up again, lines of sadness were creasing his face. "It doesn't matter," he said. "None of that matters anymore."

Triana realized that time was running out. She tried desperately to think of another line of discussion, but before she could say anything, Bauer took another step forward.

"Nothing matters anymore," he said. "I'm going to end this mission now. Tyler wanted me to finish it back at the space station, but it's better to do it here, now, when there's no one who can step in and help."

Tyler! So Triana was right about one thing. Tyler Scofield might not have been able to sneak aboard *Galahad,* but he had orchestrated this from the beginning. He had been able to infiltrate Dr. Zimmer's organization, working Dr. Bauer into a position of trust, and manipulating him for more than two years. That explained a couple of things: The beard, for one, and the coin, Scofield's symbol of opposition.

"What are you going to do?" Triana said, attempting to ease down the corridor slowly, inching along to her right.

"Not much, really. But enough to do the job. We were sure to put most of the control of *Galahad* into the hands of the computer." He laughed again, which seemed to drag him out of his funk. "That was my doing, actually. We could have put more control into your hands, but I convinced Dr. Zimmer that you shouldn't have any more pressure on you than necessary. His soft spot, actually. There wasn't much convincing to do there.

"So now I finish disabling your computer, and *Galahad* will begin to drift out of control, and at the same time grow colder and colder. It won't be long until this is nothing but a giant lifeless icebox, gliding throughout the stars forever."

Triana shuddered. The madman's vision was entirely within his grasp.

"And how funny that all it takes is this," Bauer said, holding up the tool he had used to open the access panel. "And this," he added. In the fingers of his other hand he held up another coin, identical to the one that Gap had discovered. Dr. Bauer twisted it back and forth, showing both sides to Triana, basking in her wonder.

"Don't understand?" he said. "It's so simple. So simple, in fact, that if Zimmer only knew what was happening it would crush him."

Here was the delay that Triana had hoped for. Dr. Bauer was indeed ready to explain his plan for destroying *Galahad,* and it pleased Triana for two reasons. First, she needed the extra time. Second, she was curious to find out how an outdated coin was the key to the damage.

Bauer flipped the coin once, twice, then held it up again for her to observe. "I was the one who worked closely with Roy Orzini and Dr. Mynet on the design of your computer. Roy might have been the one who designed the actual brain of the machine, but I was the one who approved the design of the access panel behind you. That's something that Roy and Mynet couldn't have cared less about; they were only concerned with the function of the computer. How it fit into this panel was unimportant to them. But it was vital to Tyler and me.

"All it took was one set of switches. I laid out the panel so that these particular switches would sit right next to each other. Nobody bothered to notice that these two switches, should they come into contact with each other, would slowly feed enough electromagnetic juice through each other to eventually fry the entire system. Since they were welded down inside the panel, nobody ever worried about them coming into contact. But the design was perfect. All it left was a gap about the size of . . . well, the size of this," Bauer said, displaying the coin once again. "This slides neatly into place, and within minutes your computer power will drain away to nothing. Tyler was good enough to furnish me with the metals information, and together we have designed a series of switches that would not do well at all with a bridge made from copper, nickel and manganese. And, what do you know? Those are precisely the ingredients in our friend here." The coin gleamed, even in the dim light.

"But you've already done something to Roc, haven't you?" Triana said.

"Oh, sure. That was nothing. Just a little memory chip, nothing to cause damage. A little something to keep him preoccupied, so he won't know what's coming, and can't send out a warning once the decay begins. It's like a tranquilizer for computers. Or a sleeping pill, maybe. I'm afraid your lovable computer friend did not take to it very well. Not very well at all. In fact, I believe he's grown very quiet." Bauer smiled wickedly. "Probably trying to figure out what's happening to him. But once the coin is in place, it will soon be all over.

"It's a most ironic ending, wouldn't you agree?" he said. "*Galahad*, the greatest sailing ship ever conceived, with a price tag well into the tens of billions of dollars, yet brought down by a piece of metal worth exactly twenty-five cents."

Another short laugh escaped his lips, but now the effect wasn't as chilling. Instead it brought anger to the surface in Triana.

"You tried to insert that once already, didn't you?" she said, again hoping to buy some time. "Someone interrupted your plot the other day, and you dropped your quarter. Why did you wait so long to try again?"

"For one thing, I wasn't going to do it that time. I just wanted to see how long it would take to open the panel with this," he said, indicating the tool. "Remember, I wanted to let you scoot away from Earth before I did anything. And, to tell you the truth, it actually became kinda fun this last week, watching all of you shaking in your boots. It was almost as if I were a ghost on this ship, and haunting you kids was a kick."

He took one more step towards Triana and the open panel. A short spasm of coughing made him pause, a brief look of pain coursing across his face. Then it passed, leaving the wild look in his eyes that had greeted Triana just minutes ago.

He had now drawn to within five feet of her, and pointed the sharp tool towards her face. "And now, enough talk. Please have a seat right there while I finish my work. This shouldn't take long."

A million thoughts screamed through Triana's mind. If she let Dr. Bauer insert that coin, it meant the end of the mission and the deaths of all 251 crew members. If she struck out at him, he would easily overpower her and then just finish the job anyway. She decided to take the risk. In her mind there was simply no alternative.

She inched along the wall again, keeping her eyes on his, waiting for the perfect opportunity to strike. Bauer's eyes flitted back and forth between her and the open panel at about knee level. As soon as he was within reach of it, he pointed the tool at her throat and took another quick glance down. At that exact moment, as he prepared to drop to one knee, another severe coughing fit took hold of him, and he reflexively closed his eyes. Triana did not waste the gift.

Her foot shot out and made direct contact with Bauer's wrist. It brought a yelp of pain and forced his arm backwards. But, to Triana's despair, he kept a firm grasp on the weapon. She jumped and kicked again, this time with a blow to his chest. The large man staggered backwards, his shoulders colliding with the corridor wall, his head banging solidly. A surprised look appeared on his face, but it was short-lived, quickly replaced with a grimace of rage. With a shout, he braced one arm against the wall, preparing to push off in a wild charge at Triana. She tensed her muscles, ready to repel the attack, her eyes drawn to the sharp metal tool that Bauer raised above his head.

36

Tyler Scofield was humming a song, one of his old favorites, a song taught to him by his grandmother. She had tried to teach him the words, but apparently had a hard enough time remembering them herself, because each time they came out in a slightly different form. Tyler hadn't cared; he loved the melody and knew enough of the words to sing a short chorus, which satisfied him. His grandmother had told him about the days of actually buying music in stores, something that seemed quaint and ridiculously old-fashioned. "Thank goodness I never had to resort to that," he had told himself, thankful for the ability to search for and secure any music, of any generation, within seconds.

His humming was the soundtrack to his afternoon in the sun. He was alone on the deck of the cottage, two miles from the nearest village, overlooking the Sea of Cortez. The town of Loreto, along the Baja strip of Mexico, was just a short ride south whenever he needed supplies. That wasn't very often. He was content to wait out his final days in total isolation, a recluse now after a lifetime of civilization overload.

He had loved the drama involved in dropping out of sight. Each time a newscast carried a story of his disappearance, he chuckled. It made no sense to him why anyone should want to keep up with his whereabouts, especially now that *Galahad* was gone and the human species was preparing to enter the homestretch. He had said all he needed to say over the past two years. What more did they need to hear? What did it matter where he chose to spend his final days?

Looking out across the dark blue water, he spied a fishing boat. The crew appeared to be moving about as quickly as he was this afternoon, which made him wonder how they got anything done. One man stood nonchalantly at the wheel, barely moving, and another was quite obviously asleep, sprawled back into a chair with his feet up on the railing. A large, floppy hat shielded his face from the blistering late afternoon sun. A third man sat near the stern, lazily tending to a tangled net, but not appearing to be in any hurry to get it straight. He would occasionally lean back and spit something into the water, then refill his mouth. Seeds, probably sunflower seeds, Scofield imagined.

Watching the slow trek of the boat made him think briefly about another ship that had sailed. This one was full of teenagers, and its speed was considerably faster than the fishing boat's. It would be approaching the speed of light within a year, creating the first real test of Einstein's theories regarding space flight and time distortion. Too bad there wouldn't be anybody around on Earth to measure the results.

Too bad, also, that the ship had sailed in the first place. Scofield had given everything he had to prevent the mission from succeeding, including diplomatic pressure and public pressure. He had even gone so far as to plant a saboteur within Wallace Zimmer's inner circle, someone who could short-circuit the plans from inside. Fenton Bauer had not been Scofield's ideal choice, but at the time it was difficult to be picky. It was easy enough to find someone who was adamantly against the mission; finding someone who could do something about it and remain quiet was a stiffer challenge. Scofield had wondered about Bauer's dependability, but ultimately had given the green light. Unfortunately, he had failed.

Watching the fishing boat and its three sleepy keepers make their way towards a rocky point, Tyler Scofield made a sudden decision to contact Zimmer. He had read his rival's e-mail a couple of days ago, admiring the class of the man if not his ideals. It couldn't hurt to make one call. He could hide the location and maintain his privacy.

Punching in the code, he waited, sipping from a bottle of water, and noting the drift of the boat around the point and out of sight. Just when he thought he was out of luck, his vidscreen came to life, the face of Wallace Zimmer staring back at him.

"Tyler? My goodness, the entire world seems to be looking for you."

"And yet you're the only person I bother to call, Wallace. How are you?"

"Tired. Weary, I guess, is a better word. Weary from the physical and mental drain. Plus our friend Bhaktul has come to call."

"I'm sorry," Scofield said with a murmur.

"Oh, it's in the cards for all of us. I'm just thankful I was able to finish . . ." Zimmer broke off the sentence.

Scofield detected the awkward feeling and put the scientist at ease. "Yes, of course. That was more than two years of extremely hard work. And it's partly the reason for my call. First off, I'd like to thank you for your sincere note. It's a shame that we were at odds these past couple of years. But I want you to know that our differences never affected my respect for you. We . . . we agreed on the problems, just not always the solutions."

Zimmer stared silently into the screen.

"Listen, Wallace, as much as I desperately tried to kill your project, I'm afraid that you were the better man. Consider this a call of congratulations. I might have objected to your plan, but I appreciate the skill and grace that you brought to it. You've achieved something that, three years ago, I would have thought impossible. Kudos to you, my old friend."

Zimmer seemed touched. He nodded at his adversary. "Thank you, Tyler. Your call means more to me than any other note I've received. That's the truth."

"I don't believe we'll be hearing from each other again," Scofield said. "I just thought you deserved to hear this. Believe me, I tried as hard as I could to keep this from happening. If you only knew."

A look of concern came over Zimmer's face. He hesitated before speaking up again.

"Please do not take offense at this, but I do have a question about your . . . campaign to disrupt the *Galahad* mission."

"Yes?"

"Is it possible that you had someone working on the inside of the project?"

Scofield remained stoic, staring into the vidscreen. "Why do you ask?"

"Well . . . it's actually bothered me from the start. I would spend many nights lying in bed, thinking of everyone who came into contact with the project, wondering if they could all be trusted. I believed that our security was as good as could be expected, but still . . ." Zimmer rubbed his chin thoughtfully. "Still, how can one ever be completely sure, right?"

"Right," was all Scofield could think to say.

"Here's the reason I ask," Zimmer said. "There hasn't seemed to be any major problem with *Galahad* since she left. The last time I checked with Tracking, they said all seemed well. But now . . ."

"What is it?" Scofield said, sitting up straight.

"There are a couple of things that have me concerned. About two hours ago I received a call from my office. *Galahad* has gone silent. They can't seem to raise the main computer, which could be a minor issue. Besides, it's only been a couple of hours. Could be any number of reasons.

"But I've been doing some thinking this afternoon. Since the launch, two people have dropped out of sight. The call from you is reassuring, since you were one of them. The other person is Fenton Bauer."

"What do you mean?" Scofield said.

"I talked to his wife yesterday. She hasn't seen him since he left the space station two weeks ago, just before the launch. Nobody has heard from him."

Scofield sat still. A strong breeze began to blow in from the water, ruffling his hair and adding to the chill that had enveloped him in the last minute. At first he thought of admitting everything to Zimmer; then he decided against it. But after another moment he changed his mind yet again. What could it hurt to talk now?

"Wallace, this news is . . . well, it's very troubling. You know how adamantly I was opposed to this project from the first day you proposed it. And, yes . . . I did try to sabotage your efforts from the inside. Fenton Bauer was my best chance."

Scofield could see the shock written on the face of his old friend. He hadn't expected that look to cause such pain in his own heart, but the realization of betrayal brought a heavy feeling of shame upon Scofield, as if he hadn't played fair. He quickly explained.

"But we failed, Wallace. Do you understand? Fenton and I were working together to cripple the project, that's true. But once *Galahad* launched I gave up."

"I don't understand," Zimmer said. "What were you doing?"

"It was all in the computer, that amazing computer you installed aboard the ship. Our plan involved frying its brain on the eve of departure. We knew that it was an integral part of the ship; in fact, we knew it couldn't function without that computer. And destroying it the day before launch would mean a complete retrofit, something that would take months, and probably not get approved. We were counting on public opinion to swing our way if you suffered a defeat like that, and it would spell the end of *Galahad*."

"But . . . ?"

"But Dr. Bauer was unable to get to the computer access panel like we had planned. That computer genius of yours, Orzini is it?"

"Roy Orzini."

"Yes. We didn't count on him staying aboard the ship until the very last moment. I guess he wanted to babysit that child of his right up until the launch. Dr. Bauer tried everything possible to sneak in alone, but there was no opportunity. So instead he called and informed me that he was leaving. I presumed that our last hand had been dealt, and it was a loser. Disappointing, extremely disappointing. But not completely unexpected. I never figured to have better than a fifty-fifty chance of winning."

"And Dr. Bauer? You've not heard from him?"

"Nothing. He simply said he was leaving the space station. I assumed—like you, I suppose—that he was going home."

Dr. Zimmer seemed to digest all of this. If Bauer was in league with Scofield, and had missed his chance to disrupt *Galahad*'s computer . . .

"I think he's aboard the ship," Zimmer said.

"What? How could that be?"

"I don't know, Tyler, but I'm sure of it. That's why we haven't heard from him, and now we've lost track of the ship."

"Wallace, you must believe me. It's true I tried to wreck the launch. But I would never support anything that might harm any of those kids. My God, I was trying to save them from the beginning!"

"I'm starting to see a portrait of a different man than you or I knew," Zimmer said, his voice cold. "You might not have sent him aboard with the intention of killing anyone. But it's possible that that's exactly what you've done. Intentions don't matter anymore. It's very likely that you encouraged a man who is unstable. And I place the responsibility of the lives of those 251 kids on your shoulders, Tyler."

37

Triana braced herself for the attack.

Suddenly a shout came from behind her. Dr. Bauer froze, and both of them looked down the corridor towards the lift. Around the corner stepped Gap, Lita and Channy. Their faces displayed the shock of recognition, their mouths open and disbelieving.

Finally, Gap spoke. "Hold it, Dr. Bauer. Stop right there."

Bauer's surprise dissipated quickly. With Triana still gazing at her companions in relief, he launched himself towards her and grabbed her around the shoulders with one arm. With the other he placed the sharp point of the tool against the side of her neck. Gap and the others stopped in their tracks, stunned at what they were seeing.

"Not another step," Bauer said. "Triana can tell you that I won't hesitate to use this."

Gap looked back and forth between the crazed eyes of the scientist and the face of the Council Leader. If he expected a look of terror in her eyes, he was surprised. She remained calm and quiet. No struggling, no frantic squirming. She looked back at Gap, steady but alert.

"Just let her go, Dr. Bauer," Gap said. "Let her go and let's talk."

"That's ridiculous," Bauer said, slowly stepping backwards, dragging Triana with him. "This very sharp instrument and

Triana's very delicate neck place me in the position of power here. You'll do exactly as I say, do you understand?"

"There are three of you," Triana said firmly. "Don't worry about me. He's trying to—"

"Shut up!" Bauer tightened his grip on her, his left arm coming up under her chin and snapping her head back. It cut off the sound from her throat, but her eyes kept their steely stare. Bauer took another step backwards, his breathing getting heavier and heavier. Triana wondered if another coughing attack might strike, giving her the chance to wriggle free.

Instead, from behind, came another shout.

A hand crashed down on the right arm of Dr. Bauer, sending the tool to the ground, where it spun a couple of times and came to rest. Triana fell forwards against the wall, reaching out with her hand at the last second to prevent herself from slamming face-first into it. The impact brought her down to one knee, and she turned to see what had happened.

Dr. Bauer had recovered, and was wrestling with Bon. Triana couldn't believe the sudden change of fortune. Where in the world had Bon come from?

Gap, Lita and Channy were suddenly at her side, helping her to her feet. As the four of them turned to help Bon, Bauer gained control in his fight and, grabbing Bon by one arm, viciously slung him into the other Council members. Without hesitating, the scientist took off in a scramble down the corridor.

"Tree, are you okay?" Gap said.

"I'm fine. Bon, thank you. You—"

"He's getting away!" Bon said. "C'mon."

"He can't hide anymore," Channy said. "Let's get some more help down here—"

"No, there isn't time," Triana said suddenly. "He's heading for the Spiders."

"What?" Channy said as Triana, Gap and Bon began sprinting away. She turned to Lita. "But he's trapped, right?"

Lita looked back at her with a grim expression. "If he's able to take off in one of the Spiders, it could be very bad news." She began to run after the others, while the consequences dawned on Channy. A madman, loose in one of the Spider craft. And a target like *Galahad* waiting like a giant bull's-eye.

Bauer covered the short distance to the Spider bay doors in seconds. Rushing into the large hangar, he managed to close the door behind him, buying just a few more seconds. By the time the others were able to reach the bay and reopen the door, he had scrambled inside the nearest Spider and sealed the hatch.

Gap was the first to reach the Spider, but was too late. The hatch was locked. Slamming his hand against the side, Gap screamed through the glass. Fenton Bauer, strapping himself into the restraints, responded with a laugh. Within seconds a flashing strobe light cut across the room, along with a warning siren.

"C'mon!" Triana shouted. "We've got to get into the Control Room before he opens the bay door into space. This room will depressurize in seconds!"

The five barely made it into the adjoining Control Room before the warning siren intensified and one of the Spider bay's outer doors began to slowly open. They sealed the Control Room, watching through the large window as stars became visible through the round Spider bay opening. Bauer had control of his vessel and started the conveyor belt that would glide the craft outside *Galahad*. In thirty seconds the Spider reached the gaping hole. The last thing the Council members saw was Bauer, laughing hysterically as the small ship dropped through the opening and was gone.

"This is not good," Lita said. "Now what can we do?"

"Two things," Triana said. "First, Gap, get back to the computer access panel and get to work on Roc. I don't think he's damaged too badly. There's a chip that's been installed. Get it out of him, and get him restarted."

Gap shot out the door of the Control Room into the corridor and ran back towards the panel. The moment he was gone Triana turned to Lita.

"I need you and Channy to get back up to the Conference Room and wake the rest of the crew. Let them know what's going on, and get them ready for a collision."

The two girls took off, leaving Bon and Triana alone in the room. He looked out the window at the hangar just as the bay door closed and the room began pressurizing again. The empty space where Spider #1 had been sitting seemed odd. The other nine Spiders sat gleaming before their own bay doors.

"Now what?" Bon said.

"I'm thinking," Triana said, chewing her lip and looking at the remaining escape ships. Only eight were completely fitted for life support to begin with. Now they had seven for a crew of 251. The two others sat mutely by themselves, their doors draped with multiple warning signs.

"For now," Triana said, "go help Gap. I want to get Roc up and running as quickly as possible."

Without a word, Bon turned and left.

Triana flipped on the vidscreen beside her and punched in the tracking program. In a moment the screen converted to a black grid. The large shape of *Galahad* sat in the middle. To one side Triana could see the flashing blip that represented the missing Spider as it moved away. According to the scale it was already dozens of miles away. But it was slowing. Triana felt her muscles tighten again. This was bad.

At the access panel on one knee, Gap scoured the inside of the computer's central control. He had found and removed one chip that certainly didn't belong, and was looking for others when Bon arrived.

"Well?" Bon said.

"I don't know. I want to make sure I've got everything before I try to fire him back up. It's already going to take a few minutes, and I don't think we have much more time than that."

"What's this?" Bon said, picking the chip off the floor.

"The monkey wrench that Bauer tossed into the works. I don't know what it did to ol' Roc's brain, but it sure got his head spinning."

Gap paused during his examination of the computer's interior and looked at Bon. "By the way, you were right about coming down the emergency stairwell. I thought you were nuts, but I've got to hand it to you. You surprised the daylights out of Bauer by sneaking up behind him."

Bon grunted, seemingly uncomfortable with the compliment. "Is there anything I can do here?"

"This is a one-person job." Gap glanced down the hall. "I think you'd better get back to the Spider bay. Don't let Triana do anything stupid."

"Like what?"

"Like take off after Bauer." Gap resumed his search, glancing back at Bon briefly to make sure he understood the implications.

Without another word Bon stood up and sprinted back down the corridor.

He burst back into the Spider Control Room. It was empty.

Looking out the large window into the hangar he saw Triana opening the door of one of the remaining Spiders.

"Triana!" he yelled, then raced into the bay, reaching her as she stepped inside the Spider.

"What are you doing?" he said, grabbing her hand. "Get out of there."

"Let go of me, Bon," she said. "I know what I'm doing."

"I know what you're doing, too. Now get out of there."

Triana took one look at his hand on hers, then back at his face. Her heart began beating a little bit faster.

"Tree," he said, a look of pleading on his face. Triana knew that it was the first time he had ever used the nickname that everyone else seemed to use. After a moment she reached over with her other hand and placed it on his. She felt him get tense.

"Listen to me," she said, her voice soft. "It's not what you think. Just let me go for a minute, okay? We don't have much time."

After another few seconds of hesitation, he allowed her to lift his hand off hers. Before letting it go, she gave his hand a squeeze. Then she was gone.

He watched her through the window of the Spider, climbing into the pilot's seat and evidently starting some sort of prelaunch activities. A minute later she was clambering back out, then sealing the hatch. She could see the confusion on Bon's face as she grabbed his hand and quickly pulled him back towards the Control Room.

"You wanna let me in on this?" he said.

They entered the Control Room and sealed the door. Triana sat at the console and began to make adjustments.

"They weren't able to finish all of the Spiders before we left. Two of them were really just put aboard for spare parts. But they still fly."

Bon looked out the window at the Spider she had been in. It had the warning signs posted on the door. A look of realization crossed his face. "You're going to fly it by remote control."

"That's right," Tree said. "It can't support life inside, but it will work just fine as a robot ship."

Bon looked at the vidscreen showing Bauer's craft. The distance between the scientist and *Galahad* was now closing.

Triana noticed the look of alarm on his face and nodded. "Yeah, he's started on a collision course. Since he couldn't finish the job from the inside, he's gonna try it from the outside. He'll ram us and that will be the end of it. This ship might be big, but it's a little too delicate to handle that."

Suddenly a tone sounded. It was Dr. Bauer, calling from the rapidly approaching Spider. Triana wasn't sure if she wanted to talk with him, but then realized that it might keep him occupied for the brief time she needed. She punched the intercom.

"Hello, kids," Dr. Bauer said. His voice sounded strained and high-pitched. Triana realized that the last of his control had withered away. He was now completely insane.

"Just wanted to say good-bye . . . again," Bauer said, adding the laugh that had already chilled Triana a few times. "According to my calculations—rough calculations, of course—you have about three minutes left. That's not much time, is it?"

Triana listened to the words but blocked out the message. She needed all of her concentration as she worked the computer controls in front of her. Bon stood beside her, quiet but attentive. He shifted his eyes back and forth between the vidscreen that was tracking Bauer and Triana's efforts. In a flash of realization he understood exactly why she had been selected as the Council Leader. This was undoubtedly the most stressful, fearsome moment of their lives, and she was working with utter calm and determination.

Dr. Bauer's voice drifted out of the speaker again. "Nothing to say?"

"I'm sorry for you," was all that Triana said in reply.

"Sorry for me? You're sorry for *me*? I am doing exactly what I set out to do. Maybe not the way I planned it, but it doesn't matter. This ship should never have left Earth."

He continued to babble, but by now neither Triana nor Bon was really listening. With the final calculation complete, Triana engaged the firing sequence. The two Council members looked up through the window to watch the outer bay door swing open in front of the empty Spider. A wash of starlight seeped in, then was blocked momentarily as the escape craft taxied out the opening. In seconds it was away, leaving the doors to close slowly behind it.

Looking back at the vidscreen, Triana and Bon were able to track both of the Spiders. Dr. Bauer continued to hurtle towards *Galahad*, but now their robot craft began to accelerate on its own collision course. Triana kept her gaze on the converging blips, Dr. Bauer's hurtling along at a blazing speed, her own robot challenger barely beginning to gallop. With one hand she made a barely perceptible adjustment to the robot Spider's course, while the other goosed the throttle on its rocket power. She knew she had to be perfect; she had one shot, and one shot only. A miss meant the end.

"One minute, kids," Dr. Bauer said.

As he was saying this, Gap entered from the corridor and stood in the doorway to the Spider control room, listening. Neither Triana nor Bon sensed his presence, and their backs were to him. Gap started to speak, but wondered if it would disrupt whatever Triana was working on. He held his tongue, his hands opening and closing into fists, sweat beginning to trickle down his forehead. He heard Bon say something softly to Triana, something that sounded like "Has he noticed?"

Triana flipped off the intercom and answered clearly. "No, I don't think so. He hasn't adjusted his course at all." She made one final course correction, then let go of the controls.

With that, Gap figured out what was happening. He held his ground in the doorway, awaiting the outcome.

A moment later he watched Bon's hand slowly reach out and take Triana's. She held on to it firmly. Gap's mouth dropped open silently.

"Twenty seconds to collision," Triana said. "He's bound to discover it any moment now." She flipped the intercom back on. "Oh, Dr. Bauer?"

"Yes," he said, his voice even more sinister. "This is . . . wait. What—?"

He had finally discovered the oncoming Spider. But by now it was too late. Triana and Bon, their hands clasped even tighter, watched his incoming craft suddenly begin to veer to one side, but it wasn't able to maneuver that sharply. On the vidscreen they saw the two points of light clip each other, then branch off at severe angles. Apparently the impact had not been dead-on, but rather a glancing blow. Would it be enough to send Bauer's ship skidding past *Galahad*?

The intercom gurgled, cutting in and out, the connection damaged. Triana thought she could hear Dr. Bauer coughing, then silence. A moment later came what sounded like a sharp cry, then silence again.

Seconds later the blip of Bauer's Spider careened past *Galahad*. Bon would later estimate that it had likely missed their ship by no more than fifty feet. It spun wildly, damaged beyond control, and shot away into the void of outer space. For a few seconds the radio connection became clear again, and in that brief moment both Triana and Bon were sure of what they heard. It was Dr. Fenton Bauer, laughing. It was enough to chill their blood. Then his voice, now much lower and heavier, broke through.

"You won't make it, kids," he said. "It's a long way to Eos. You don't have what it takes to make it. You never had it." The signal broke up again, sputtered back to life briefly, then faded. The last thing they heard was Dr. Bauer repeating, "You won't make it. Just wait. You won't make—"

Then he was gone.

Triana and Bon relaxed their grips, then turned and looked at each other. Simultaneously they reached out for each other and hugged, pulling themselves into a tight embrace. They remained that way for a long time.

By the time they parted, Gap had quietly slipped out of the doorway. He began to trudge back down the corridor, past the open computer access panel and on to the lift.

38

A thunderstorm crackled overhead. The wind had picked up with the storm, whipping the trees and slamming the rain into the side of the house and the windows. The power had gone off almost ten minutes earlier, and Dr. Zimmer wasn't hopeful that it would be restored anytime soon. He wasn't even sure that anyone would bother to find the problem. It might be the next morning before his lights came on again. Which was fine with him.

It was close to midnight and why did he need a light anyway? He lay still in his bed, an empty bottle of cough suppressant on the nightstand. He had drained the last third of it in three large gulps, knowing full well that it was dangerous to down that much of the strong medicine in one sitting. But he just didn't care anymore.

His conversation with Tyler Scofield had sapped whatever passion remained in his life. He felt defeated, betrayed and helpless. Another call to Sharee Bauer had depressed him further. But he had decided to not confess his suspicions to her. Why burden the sweet woman with the guilt when she had no control over the situation? Instead he had consoled her as best he could over her missing husband, and had promised to stay in touch.

He wouldn't be staying in touch, of course, and they both knew it. Yet it had seemed the proper thing to say. Sharee had smiled at him, one tear tracing down her cheek with many more ready to follow, as her image faded away on his vidscreen.

Now he listened to the storm, his house and the rest of the neighborhood swallowed up in the darkness. The brief flashes of lightning illuminated his room through the windows, allowing him to see a framed photograph on the opposite wall. In it, a smiling Wallace Zimmer sat on the front row of the bleachers at the *Galahad* training facility. Around him were gathered the 251 pilgrims selected to journey forth amid the stars. A look of pride, mixed with sincere love and affection, beamed from his face. And there was another look, as well. It was a look of gratitude. For this group of kids had given him—for two years, anyway—a family.

As he closed his eyes, he realized that the pain was subsiding. The already dark room began to recede further into inky blackness, and the sound of the storm gradually faded away. With one last breath, he prayed that his family was okay.

39

Twelve hours had passed since the encounter with Dr. Bauer. The weary Council members sat slouched in their chairs in the Conference Room. Each had spent a couple of sleepless hours in their rooms, their adrenaline keeping them charged throughout the rest of the night. By morning they had managed to doze for an hour at most, then awakened and cleaned up enough to stagger into a Council meeting.

Triana was at the head of the table, looking around, a faint smile on her lips. Lita returned it with her own grin and reached out to squeeze Triana's hand. Tears returned to Channy's eyes, the emotion of the incident still evident on her face. Bon fiddled with his cup of water, occasionally throwing a knowing glance at Triana, but for the most part maintaining his standard scowl. Gap sat still at the far end of the table, his hands clasped, unable to keep eye contact with Triana for more than a second or two.

"Roc?" Triana said.

"Present," came the familiar voice of Roy Orzini.

"It's good to have you back."

"Good to be here. And look, I missed all of the excitement."

"Do you really think we'll ever let you forget about that?" Channy said, wiping her eyes and managing a laugh. "In our greatest time of need, Roc takes a nap."

Lita and Triana joined her in laughing. Bon smiled faintly. Gap remained still.

"Want to know the worst part?" the computer said. "Waking up and the first face I see is Gap's. Holding a screwdriver. Please, Triana, do me a favor, and see if he messed around with my Masego game programming. He could have done anything to me while I was out. Oh," he added, "and while you're at it, check around and make sure there aren't any more quarters on the ship."

"We took Dr. Bauer's quarter, and his wicked little computer chip, and dumped them," Lita said. "And the door he used to get into the storage areas is sealed again. I was tempted, you know—"

"Yes, I know," Triana said. "I think we all wanted to take a peek inside there. But it's better to seal it off and leave Dr. Zimmer's plan alone. He didn't want us in there, so we'll keep our noses out until we reach Eos."

"I'm also a little worried about a couple of other things, though," Lita said. "What Dr. Bauer said at the end. 'Just wait.' Doesn't that sound like he's done something else to the ship?"

The Council was silent while they thought about that. Finally Tree spoke up.

"Well, we've checked everything that we can. Roc has run through every test he can. Nothing has come up. So, if Bauer did do something, I suppose we'll have to worry about it when—and if—it happens. It won't do us any good to stress out now."

Channy said, "Plus, the man was so far gone, he might have just been trying to scare us again. He might not have done anything."

"Yeah," Tree said. "That's a possibility." She turned to Lita. "What's the other thing you're concerned about?"

"Well," Lita said, "at some point we need to talk about the Spiders."

"Yeah," Tree said. "We're down to eight now, and just seven that will support us." She sighed, looking at the others. "Well, I guess we have five years to figure that out."

Bon spoke up. "That's the kind of stuff we can overcome. I'm not concerned with the Spider situation. But there is something else."

He made eye contact with the Council. "That crazy scientist who almost killed us threw out a pretty good challenge, didn't he? Remember what his last words were? 'You won't make it.' "

The room was silent. All of them stared at the Swedish boy. He looked at Triana, who nodded. Deep inside she hoped that Bon had gained new respect for her as a leader. For some reason, something that she couldn't put into words, she longed for his acceptance above that of anyone else.

She also wondered about their brief time alone in the Spider Control Room. Did that mean anything to him? Would he ever acknowledge it to her? Was he sorry it had happened at all? Or was it just a product of the tension of the moment, never to be repeated? In the aftermath of their near deaths, she was fascinated by her own thought patterns. Rather than reflect on the trauma of their encounter with Dr. Bauer, her heart was pushing her head out of the way. Or trying to, anyway.

Internally she shook away the romantic cobwebs and focused on the point Bon had just made concerning Bauer's forecast.

"I consider that motivation," she said. "Apparently Dr. Bauer never wanted us to succeed in the first place. He figured we would foul up our training, but we didn't. He and Scofield figured they could sabotage the ship and cripple us. They didn't. And Dr. Bauer tried to rattle us so much that we would lose our focus and fall apart. Well, we didn't."

" 'That which does not kill you makes you stronger.' Isn't that how the saying goes?" Channy said.

"That's right," Lita said. "And I'd like to remind this crew of something else. We've just confronted a man who wanted us to fail. He was a partner, I guess, with a few other people who also wanted us to fail. But let's remember one thing." She stood up, her hands resting on the table. "There were thousands of other people who gave the final years of their lives to make sure we didn't fail. And millions of others, people we never saw or heard from, who showed their support. So, as hard as it is to imagine, we're really not alone out here, you know?"

She smiled at her friends, then walked out of the room.

Channy stood up, walked behind Triana and gave her shoulders a small squeeze. "I'm proud of you, Tree," she said. "And Lita's right; we're not alone." She turned and started towards the door. "I need to work out. My bones feel tired."

Triana and Bon rose from their chairs and started to leave. Bon walked out, but Triana stopped and looked down at Gap. "Are you okay? You haven't had anything to say. That's not like you."

Gap shrugged. "Just overwhelmed still, I think. I'm all right."

"I want to thank you again for getting Roc back up and running. I don't know what we'd do without you. You know that, don't you?"

"Thanks," he said halfheartedly.

Triana waited another moment in the awkward silence. There seemed to be something hanging in the air between them, and she was pretty sure what it was. But how could she talk about this with Gap right now? All of their emotions were still churning, and she wouldn't know how to approach the subject anyway. She felt for him, knowing exactly what he was experiencing, but reluctant to address it until she'd had time to think about it.

Imagine that, she thought: "the Ice Queen" had two relationship issues to deal with. And she had no idea how she was going to handle either one.

She started towards the door again. "I'll see you in the Dining Room later, okay?"

"Sure," Gap said.

A minute later he rested his head on one hand, a single tear emerging.

"Lita's wrong," he said under his breath. "Some of us are alone."

40

Terrifying and yet beautiful at the same time. Dangerous, but still peaceful.

Triana stood by herself at the large window, holding her notebook and gazing at the inky blackness outside, marveling at the contradictions of space. She wondered how a universe so populated with ferocious, blazing suns could be so very cold.

And she wondered about her place in it all.

Biting her lip, she refocused her gaze from the brilliant backdrop of stars to the reflection of the tall, dark-haired girl who stared back from the glass. Two years ago she was living a dream in the mountains of Colorado. Her father was healthy and happy, and life was . . . perfect?

But now her world was not only upside down, it was gone, dropping farther away behind her every second. Her mother was a stranger, her old friends were memories.

And her father . . .

Not really dead, she decided. She looked into the reflection of the green eyes and for a moment imagined him looking back. Imagined him tumbling out of that raft. Imagined him reaching for her paddle, her dragging him back into the boat, and the two of them laughing. Always laughing.

And she thought about the encounter with Dr. Bauer. He was an incredibly brilliant man. She had been smarter.

He had planned for months to destroy them. She had outwitted him.

The crew had been on the verge of panic. She had restored their confidence in the mission and the Council.

She managed the faint beginning of a smile and nodded. With a flip of the wrist she opened her journal to the day's entry and added one more line.

Thanks, Dad. Now I know what I got from you.

She turned away from the window and made her way to the lift, her thoughts drifting from the past to the future. Within a few weeks *Galahad* would have its final contact with Earth people when it came into the vicinity of the Saturn research station.

Triana couldn't help but wonder what was in store for them around the ringed planet.

Let's chat a moment, okay?

I can sense a few troubled looks on some faces out there, so we'd better settle a few issues before Triana and the crew get any closer to Saturn.

First of all, some of you are worried that Dr. Bauer might have done something else to the ship. Some of you are concerned about that whole Spider situation, and what happens when they get to Eos and are short a little transportation. Some of you are going out of your minds that Triana could possibly be interested in a grouch like Bon. All valid concerns.

But let me just say that I'm a little hurt that not one of you expressed the slightest concern about me while I was knocked out. Are some of my chips damaged? Was I scared? Am I going to be the same witty and charming Roc that you've grown to know and love? No, you're more worried about Triana's love triangle with Bon and Gap. Thanks a lot.

Oh well. We'll address the issues which seem to be much more critical to you.

#1: Did Dr. Bauer sabotage the ship some other way?

I can't say; you'll need to read on.

#2: What about the Spiders? Will the crew be able to get down to Eos?

I can't say; you'll need to read on.

#3: What's up with Triana and Bon and Gap?

I'm not stupid enough to stick my computer nose into that mess; you will definitely have to read on.

Besides, if you ask me, there are much more crucial issues at hand. Like the bad feeling I'm getting about Saturn. It used to be my favorite planet, what with those gorgeous rings and everything. Something creepy is bound to happen, I just feel it.

And neither you nor I will know until The Web of Titan.

In the meantime, I've got a lot of work to do.

Tor Teen Reader's Guide

About This Guide

The information, activities, and discussion questions that follow are intended to enhance your reading of *The Comet's Curse*. Please feel free to adapt these materials to suit your needs and interests.

Writing and Research Activities

I. Welcome to "Humanity's Lifeboat"

A. You have just received a letter of invitation to join the *Galahad* project. If you accept, you must leave home tomorrow to begin two years of training in hopes of being one of the 251 young people chosen for the crew. With classmates or friends, role-play a conversation between yourself and family members in which you weigh the pros and cons of this opportunity.

B. Write at least four journal entries describing your training regimen; your teachers; your emotions at being selected as one of *Galahad*'s 251 crew members; and your assessment of leading students Triana, Gap and Bon.

C. Make a list of the five to ten items you will bring to decorate your onboard living quarters and remind you of home. Be creative and choose wisely. Afterward, share your list with friends or classmates and explain your choices.

D. You are looking at your former home planet as *Galahad* launches into space. Use colored pencils, oil pastels, chalk or other art materials to draw a picture of what you see. Write ten words that describe your feelings.

E. On page 81, Dr. Zimmer refers to *Galahad* as "humanity's lifeboat." Imagine you overheard your teacher use this phrase. Now, as you sit in your living quarters aboard *Galahad*, write a short essay describing what this phrase means to you.

II. A Knightly Ship

A. Go to the library or online to learn more about the Knights of the Round Table, the Holy Grail, and Sir Galahad. Based on your research, create an outline, list or fact web of ways in which the spaceship is appropriately named. If desired, invite classmates or friends to make similar outlines suggesting other names, supported by facts about their history and meaning, and vote to choose your group's favorite name for a humanity-saving ship.

B. Can a computer feel? Go to the library or online to learn more about cutting-edge research on artificial intelligence. Use your research to create an informative poster or pamphlet addressing this question.

C. Consider the suggestions made by Dr. Zimmer, Dr. Bauer, and Dr. Orzini about the design of the ship's main computer. Then, divide into two groups to debate the following: The ship's computer should/should not have a friendly personality to support the work of the teens on board. Use library or online research to support your positions.

D. Based on details from the text, re-create *Galahad* in one of the following ways: (1) Draw a diagram of part or all of the ship on graph paper; (2) Create a three-dimensional model using clay, pipe cleaners, or other craft materials; or (3) Use PowerPoint or another computer program to make a "Resident's Guide to Galahad" with animations if possible.

III. Past-Present-Future

A. Research an historic epidemic such as the Great Plague of London (1664–1666) or the Influenza Pandemic (1918). Collect facts about the disease, its effects on society and how the health threat concluded. Make a two-columned chart on which you compare your research to Bhaktul, the disease of *The Comet's Curse.*

B. Could the events like those described in *The Comet's Curse* come to pass? Why is it helpful to reflect upon such possibilities? Create an annotated list of science-fiction works that make us consider the course of our nonfiction future. You may want to include the novels *Ender's Game* by Orson Scott Card; *The Giver* by Lois Lowry; *Feed* by M. T. Anderson; *The Scorpion King* by Nancy Farmer; and film/television features such as *2001: A Space Odyssey* and *Planet of the Apes.* If desired, add graphic novels, cartoons, paintings and other creative works to your list.

C. Create a character guide to *The Comet's Curse.* For each character (human or computer) in the story, write a brief entry describing the character's past, role on *Galahad* and what you think they imagine their future holds.

D. Role-play the following scenario with friends or classmates: You are the host of a morning radio talk show whose engineer has managed to arrange a connection with *Galahad*'s communication's system for five minutes. Choose the shipboard teen you would most like to interview, prepare your list of questions, set the timer and . . . go! If possible, make an audio or video recording of your interview.

E. Visit http://eospso.gsfc.nasa.gov/ to learn about EOS, NASA's Earth Observing System. Then, write an essay answering the following question: What does EOS teach you about our planet and how does this information affect your reading of *The Comet's Curse*? Or, with a friend or classmate, role-play a conversation between a modern-day student and a student from *Galahad* in which you discuss human life and activities on Earth and in space.

Questions for Discussion

1. After reading only the prologue to *The Comet's Curse,* who did you think was going to be the story's narrator? Were you surprised to discover the identity of the narrator? Did you trust this narrator? Do the other main characters of the story trust this narrator? Explain.

2. What is Bhaktul Disease? How does the presence of the disease affect life and society on Earth?

3. Why doesn't Triana want to look back at Earth as *Galahad* launches? What insights into her character does this choice give readers? Where did Triana grow up? What qualities make her a good Council Leader?

4. Why does Wallace Zimmer develop the *Galahad* project? Who are Zimmer's supporters? Who is his most strenuous detractor? If you were a member of the scientific community of this period, do you think you would be for or against Zimmer's work, and why?

5. What is the relationship between Roy Orzini and Roc? In what way does the relationship resemble that of parent and child?

How are parent-child relationships a key motif in the novel? How are these relationships important to children? How are they important to parents? What different outcomes result from challenging parent-child relationships in the story?

6. What secret does Channy know about Gap? Does Bon have a similar secret? How do these secrets affect the boys' choices and actions aboard *Galahad*?

7. What does Peter Meyer see in the Storage Section of the ship that dramatically changes the mood onboard? What are the Council members' initial reactions to Peter's outburst? What other strange events follow Peter's outburst?

8. What are Bon, Gap, Channy and Lita's responsibilities aboard *Galahad*? What qualities resulted in their being chosen for these jobs? Do you think the selection process described in chapter 16 was a good one? Had you been selected for *Galahad,* to which of these roles do you think you would be best suited and why?

9. What is in the Storage Sections? Do you think the plan to keep these sections unopened until the passengers reach Eos is a good one? Do you think everyone on the crew will be able to resist the temptation of these sealed compartments?

10. What are Roc's thoughts about *Galahad*'s mysterious extra passenger? How does he describe the relationships forming between the Council members? How do Roc's insights affect your reading of the novel? If you were aboard *Galahad,* how might you consult, confide in or play with your computerized companion?

11. Near the end of the novel, how do Dr. Zimmer and Dr. Scofield begin to repair their relationship? How does this lead Zimmer to concerns about Dr. Bauer? What conclusions are Triana and her crew beginning to draw at the same time?

12. What are the other Council members' reactions to Triana's revelation of the mysterious e-mail message? When Triana heads to the Storage Section to confront *Galahad*'s intruder, is she completely alone? Explain.

13. How does Triana stall Dr. Bauer in the Storage Section? Who comes to her aid? How does the group work together to defeat their former teacher? How do Bon and Triana work together and what effect does this have on their relationship? How does this affect Triana's relationship with Gap?

14. What is the status of *Galahad* and its crew members as the novel draws to a close? Do you think their mission can continue successfully now that they are aware of Roc's weaknesses? In what way is the crew stronger with this knowledge?

15. Do you think *The Comet's Curse* is foremost a story of the struggle to preserve humanity, or of the power of individual relationships? Explain your answer.

16. Do you think that *Galahad* will make it to Eos? Why or why not? In your opinion, what are the greatest threats or obstacles to *Galahad*'s success?

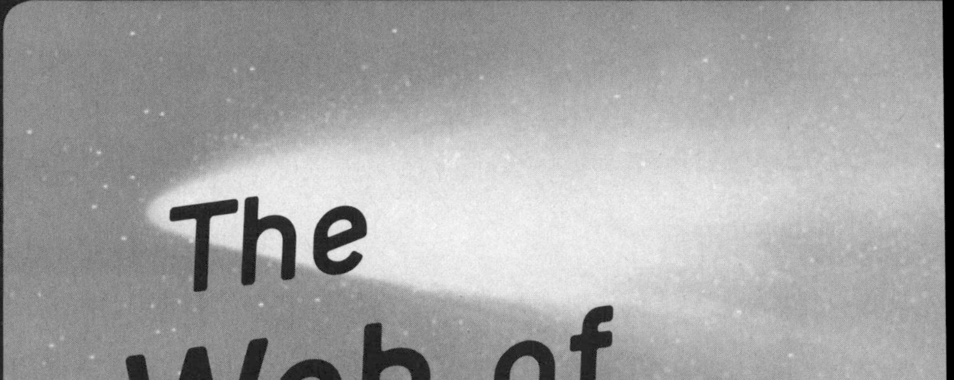

The Web of Titan

Dom Testa

To my son, Dominic III.

You'll never know how much of an inspiration you are to me.

One common trait people have carried through the years, with a few exceptions, is fear of the unknown. Humans need a comfort zone of the familiar, and when that's shattered the automatic response is often dread, anxiety, or downright terror.

Take our good friends on the spacecraft called Galahad. *Their entire mission is a voyage to the unknown, and it's unfair to think that an ample dose of fear doesn't ride along with them. Each day they move farther away from the warm embrace of Earth, and deeper into the infinite void of space.*

If you missed their exciting first adventure, my obvious suggestion is to stop right now, find it, and read all about it. But if you want to wade in right here, I'll try to catch you up.

What appeared at first to be an ordinary comet, named Bhaktul, instead turned out to be a killer. As Earth passed through Bhaktul's tail, microscopic particles contaminated the atmosphere, leading to a grisly disease that would ultimately take down every adult on the planet. Kids were mostly immune from the ravages of the disease until around age eighteen, and nobody knew why. Worst of all, there wasn't time to find out; Bhaktul was not only deadly, it was quick.

So when Dr. Wallace Zimmer, an eminent scientist from America's West Coast, proposed building a large ship that could safely transport a few hundred kids to another world, most people supported him. A few, however, were violently opposed. They believed it was wrong to break families apart, even though that separation meant the sparing of hundreds of lives. In the end Zimmer's project was successful, and an international crew consisting of 251 of the world's brightest kids—all of them either fifteen or sixteen years old—launched in the ship christened Galahad. *Its destination: two Earth-like planets circling a star called Eos.*

The trip would be made in five years, but soon after the launch it seemed the crew would never even make it as far as Mars. An intruder aboard the ship threatened to destroy Galahad, *and . . .*

But wait. For the sake of those of you who have skipped the first adventure, known as The Comet's Curse, *it would spoil the excitement to tell you everything now. Read it, quickly, and then rejoin us, please.*

Of course, if you're new to our tale, and still reading—stubborn, aren't you?—then you are probably curious about who I am. My name is Roc, and I'm the only nonhuman crew member of Galahad. *To refer to me as simply a computer would do me a grave injustice. That's like calling the Amazon or Nile rivers "streams." Or calling Mount Everest a "hill." Or taking a fudge brownie, buried under a scoop of ice cream and ladled with chocolate syrup, nuts, whipped cream, and a cherry, and calling it "a snack."*

I've never had a fudge brownie, obviously, but I've seen your reactions when you eat it, and no snack ever caused that kind of ecstasy.

I oversee most of the basic operations of the ship and provide guidance to the ruling body known as the Council. Those five crew members, as diverse as the kids they represent, do a fine job on their own, but who would pass up advice from a mental wonder such as me?

The one thing I can't advise them on is this other pesky emotion that seems to raise its head when teenagers are thrown together. You probably know exactly what I'm talking about. I'm aware of the drama that is taking place between several of our Council members, and I certainly don't mind commenting on it. Who wouldn't? I just hate to see these kids get their hearts trampled on, even though history seems to suggest that it's going to happen, regardless of what you or I or anyone else says to them.

That pretty much sums up things to this point. As our latest adventure unfolds, Galahad *is four months out from Earth, past Mars, past the asteroid belt, even past the orbit of Jupiter. The giant gas planet Saturn lies dead ahead.*

And so does that nagging feeling I've had for quite a while. You wanna talk about fear of the unknown?

1

The storm raged quietly along the surface, a swirl of colors colliding, mixing, weaving. Layers of gas clouds tumbled across one another, their brilliant shades of red and purple highlighted by short bursts of lightning. Winds galloped along at more than a thousand miles per hour, stirring the atmosphere and keeping the roiling chaos churning in much the same way it had for billions of years.

Above it all drifted the jeweled rings, chunks of ice and dust that varied in size between grains of sand and ten-story buildings. Their dense orbits stretched out hundreds of thousands of miles, occasionally sparkling like a crown in the dim sunlight while casting a thin, dark shadow across the face of the storms. The tightly packed debris in the rings rolled along, nudging and shoving, forever keeping watch over the unruly gas giant below.

Saturn toiled along.

Scattered near and far, its squadron of moons maintained their dutiful orbits, subjects kneeling before the majesty of the king, tossed about by the immense gravitational tugs and seared by the overwhelming inferno of radiation. Several dozen of these minor bodies drifted near Saturn's dazzling rings, themselves a product of an earlier moon that had been shattered by a rogue asteroid or comet, the pieces now trapped in a mindless dance that circled the giant planet.

Keeping a respectful distance, and shrouded in a cloak of dense atmosphere, the largest of these moons obediently tracked through the vacuum of space, cutting a path that kept it clear of the rings. Dwarfed by the Herculean planet, it still laid claim to its own cloud system and weather patterns. Rather than water, its rivers and oceans were pools of liquid methane, carving channels and shorelines that dotted the surface, a surface impossible to see through the screen of haze and fog. An eerie orange glow masked the surface, bathing it in a dull light that made the large moon seem almost alive, breathing.

Titan.

As it circled Saturn, a route that took it a little more than two weeks to complete, Titan had its own companion in space. Right now, in an artificial orbit, a metallic pod shot around Titan, spinning slowly as it navigated, the light from Saturn occasionally glancing off its sides, mixing with the orange tint of the moon to form a ghostly shade. The smooth steel of the pod was uniform except for two small windows on one end, and exhaust ports on the other. During its slow, deliberate trek around the moon, block lettering could be made out on one side, along with small emblems of flags that lined up under a window. Inside it was dark, quiet, waiting.

It would not be quiet, nor waiting, much longer.

Lita Marques sat before the mirror in her room. She deftly tied the red ribbon into a knot, pulling her dark hair into a ponytail and lifting it off her shoulders. She eyed the end result with a neutral glance, then gazed past her own reflection to the smiling girl who sat cross-legged on the end of Lita's bed. "All right, Channy, what's so funny?"

Galahad's Activities/Nutrition Director, clad in her usual bright yellow shorts and T-shirt that made a startling contrast against her chocolate-toned skin, replaced her grin with an expression of innocence. "Funny? Oh, nothing funny." She uncrossed her legs and scooted them over the edge of the bed. "Just wondering why you bother to make yourself look so pretty every day and then refuse to let me set you up with someone."

Lita's eyes rolled. "Why did I bother to ask?" She made one final appraisal in the mirror, then turned to face Channy Oakland. "I appreciate your intentions, Miss Social Butterfly, but I'm perfectly capable of meeting a boy on my own."

Channy raised one eyebrow. "Uh-huh. And quite a great job you've done in that area, too. We've been away from Earth for, what, four months now? Not counting your lunches with Ruben Chavez, you've been out with. . . . hmm, a whopping total of zero boys." She leaned forward and picked a piece of fuzz off Lita's shirt. "And we won't count Ruben. You only talk with him because he's from Mexico, like you."

"Hey, I like Ruben. He's one of the nicest guys on the ship."

"Of course he is. But you know darned well what I'm talking about, and it's not chatting over an energy block in the cafeteria."

Lita shook her head. "Channy, do you think it would be possible for you to go two days without trying to play matchmaker? When I'm ready to see someone, I will. Besides," she added, "I haven't seen you exactly setting the shipboard romance gauge any higher."

"That's because I'm still in advance scouting mode right now," Channy said, winking. "I'm compiling data, see? Give me another few weeks and I'll set the hook."

"Right," Lita said. "Compiling data. I like that." She smiled at the Brit, then stood up and walked over to the built-in dresser and rummaged for a favorite bracelet. The dorm rooms on *Galahad* were relatively small but comfortable. Each crew member shared space with a roommate, but the work schedules were usually staggered to the point that each person was able to have time to themselves, a valuable commodity on a ship loaded with 251 passengers. Lita, one of *Galahad*'s five Council members, was responsible for overseeing the ship's Clinic, or Sick House, as it was lovingly referred to by the crew. Her roommate, an outgoing fifteen-year-old from India, was currently at work in the Engineering Section. Channy had stopped by to accompany Lita to dinner.

Finding the accessory she wanted, Lita slipped it over her wrist and turned back to face Channy. "Let me ask you something," she said. "Are you as curious about our upcoming appointment at Titan as you are about my love life?"

Channy shrugged. "Of course. I'm just not sure exactly what we're doing. I asked Gap about this . . . this pod thing we're supposed to pick up, but he was pretty busy at the time and never really explained it to me. And good luck getting a straight answer from Roc about anything."

This brought a laugh to Lita's lips. "Oh, he'll shoot straight with you eventually. What exactly do you want to know?"

"Well," Channy said, "if this pod is supposed to have been launched by the scientists on the research station orbiting Titan, how come we haven't heard from them? Nobody seems to be saying much about that."

"Yeah, it's a little creepy," Lita agreed. "Thirty scientists and engineers, all working for a couple of years on a lonely outpost near Saturn, and suddenly nobody can get in touch with them." She walked over to the desk across the room and called out to the computer. "Roc?"

"Hello, Lita," came the very human-sounding reply. "What's on your mind?"

Lita couldn't hear the computer's voice without seeing the short, lovable genius who had programmed the machine. Roy Orzini, one of the champions of the *Galahad* project, had been responsible for outfitting the ship with a computer capable of controlling the life-support systems, lights, gravity, and other crucial functions of the spacecraft. As a bonus he instilled an actual personality into the thing; *his* personality, it turned out, for the talking computer soon demonstrated the same wit and sarcasm as his creator. Roy's Computer was soon shortened to RoyCo, and eventually to Roc. He was indispensable to the five Council members, almost an older brother along for the ride.

"I'm trying to explain to Channy about the pod we're picking up pretty soon," Lita said. "About the research station that has gone silent. But I'm not sure I really know exactly what it's all about."

Roc remained silent a moment, then said, "Well, if you love mysteries, you should really love this, because it's not just one thriller, but two: the disappearance of the research crew, and this metal pod we're supposed to snatch out of space."

"What's the story on the scientists?" Lita said, sitting down at the desk. "Who are these people anyway?"

"A combination of biologists, medical researchers, engineers, and technicians," said the computer. "Maybe not the group voted 'Most Likely to Party in Space,' but all brilliant in their fields. The research station is a small space station in orbit around Titan, the largest moon of Saturn, and one of the most important bodies in the solar system."

"Why?" Channy asked. "What makes Titan so special?"

"Life," Roc said. "Or, at least one of the best chances at finding it off the planet Earth. Titan, you see, has an atmosphere, and oceans."

"Oceans?" Channy said. "You're kidding."

"Not the kind you'd want to surf in, my friend," Roc said. "These are oceans of liquid methane. But bubbling around in that poisonous soup are a lot of the building blocks that eventually led to life on Earth billions of years ago. This research station has been studying Titan for several years."

Lita picked up a stylus pen from the desk and tapped her cheek with it while she listened to Roc. Now she paused and said, "What have they found?"

"That's just it," said the computer voice. "All of their reports have been labeled 'Classified,' and 'Top Secret.' Nobody knows what they've found. But apparently, at about the same time *Galahad* launched, something happened around Titan, and all contact with the scientists was lost. The last message was pretty garbled, didn't make a lot of sense. But it mentioned a small pod that was jettisoned into Titan's orbit, waiting."

"Waiting for what?" Channy said.

"Us."

2

The artificial sunlight threw its blanket of warmth across the fields. Row upon row of scientifically modified vegetables reached up to greet the incoming light waves and rustled in the mild, machine-induced breeze. An occasional bee would linger for a moment around a flowering plant, touching down long enough to complete its mission of pollination, and then casually move on. The scent of nutrient-rich soil mixed with the vibrant smell of crops ready for harvest, crops with a heavy bounty of perfectly engineered food.

The two agricultural domes sat atop the spacecraft *Galahad*, protective bubbles over acres of crops that fed the 251 passengers. Steel spokes overhead were meshed with hundreds of light diodes that mimicked the sun rays found in semitropical zones on Earth, so that during *Galahad*'s "daylight" hours the farm area looked—and felt—like a typical sunny day in Florida. When the lights dimmed, each dome became transparent, ushering in a view of starlight that was beautiful beyond description.

Separate zones within the domes allowed for variations in temperature and moisture, which in turn allowed the crew members to rotate different crops that required different conditions. So it wasn't uncommon to find tropical fruit growing just a few hundred feet away from more robust fare, such as corn or wheat. The intricate maze of "underground" irrigation pipes was computer controlled, recycling the proper amount of moisture to each zone. Water naturally evaporated from the plants, and was captured by special absorption vents in the steel mesh of the domes.

The life cycle of *Galahad's* farms was engineered and programmed to run automatically . . . in a perfect world. But no matter how much planning and design was built in, it still needed human nurturing to truly hum. Bon Hartsfield was the unquestioned genius on board who made the farms not only work, but also thrive. Breakdowns were not, however, tolerated well.

The son of a farmer in Skane, Sweden, Bon had spent thousands of hours toiling in his father's fields, learning firsthand what it took to cultivate a strong harvest. Sweat, an aching back, and fingers that never really shed the grime were all ingredients needed to produce a healthy crop. There were no days off, his father insisted. No days off.

The perfection his father had demanded was instilled in the blond Swede, which tempered his personality, painting him as surly and sour. His tough outer shell had been penetrated only once: a brief, emotionally charged moment with Triana Martell, *Galahad's* Council Leader, shortly after their launch. Months had passed since then, with neither having the courage to address the encounter, or perhaps waiting anxiously for the other to make a move.

But Triana wasn't on his mind at the moment, at least not front and center. Right now his pale blue eyes were like ice on fire. Standing with hands on hips, surrounded by row upon row of grain crops, he stared at the small gray box tucked away in the plants. It almost reached Bon's knees, with a large plastic pipe attached on one side, and four smaller tubes jutting out the opposite end and disappearing into the soil. A small fan on top of the box kept it ventilated, while a digital display slowly ticked off numbers. An access panel on the side of the box lay open, revealing a complex mixture of circuits and wires. It was the contents of the panel that had captured Bon's attention for the last hour and fueled his temper.

Two of his assistants stood facing him, a boy and a girl, neither wanting to say anything. It had already been an ugly morning.

"Who was the last person to make an adjustment?" Bon finally said.

The boy shifted from one foot to the other. "Uh, me," he said, keeping his eyes on the gray box rather than Bon. "That was Tuesday afternoon, probably around, uh, one o'clock."

"And you didn't notice it then?"

The boy shifted again. "Uh, no."

Bon glared at him. "So for the last six days—at least six days we know of—this entire section has barely been getting a trickle of water. Six days."

The girl put her hands in her pockets and moved a small dirt clod around with her foot. "I was with him that day, and I . . . I didn't notice it, either. I guess . . . I guess we were so used to it being normal that we probably didn't think that it was—"

"Didn't think," Bon said, his voice rising. "It's obvious you didn't think, and now we not only have to get it fixed, we have to hand water this entire section, and fast. Starting right now."

Both assistants kept their eyes down but nodded.

Bon's eyes continued to rage as his scowl intensified. "From now on," he said, "new rule: all water recycling pump stations are checked alone. No teams, no pals, no gabbing. You guys are so busy talking and laughing you're not paying attention to your job. And now this crop is in danger." He pulled a plant toward him, streaks of brown beginning to show in one of the leaves. "Look at this."

The two workers glanced up at the plant in his hand, then returned their gaze to the ground. "Get the word out," Bon said. "Now. I mean *right* now. I want every recycling station checked twice, and no more teams."

He turned to make his way back to his office near the entrance to the dome, then stopped and looked back at the boy and girl. "And also let everyone know we're having a mandatory meeting this afternoon, four o'clock." He stormed through the field, onto the path that led to his office, leaving the two assistants to scramble away on their new assignments.

Before walking into his office, Bon stamped his feet a couple of times to shake the dirt off his boots. The room was small and cramped, with beige walls on one side and floor-to-ceiling windows on the other, looking out over the crops in the first dome. A desk sat along the back wall, covered in folders and data discs. There were no personal items on the desk or walls, no warm touches. The lights were low, complemented by the artificial sunlight that streamed in through the windows. Two ceiling vents whispered with the sound of circulating air.

Bon crossed to his desk and pulled up a file on his computer, flicking through the information on page after page, absorbing the data. He pushed his long blond hair back out of his face and scribbled a few notes on his work pad, his scowl never resting. After a couple of minutes he punched the intercom on the desk and waited for the connection with *Galahad*'s Council Leader.

Triana Martell's voice finally came through the speaker. "Hi, Bon. What's up?"

"I'll tell you what's up," he said, his voice a low growl. "These water recycling pumps are crashing. Again."

Triana sounded weary. "Oh, no. How many this time?"

"Two that we found this morning. One that might have been down for almost a week. That makes four in the last two weeks. We're going to start some hand watering on a couple of sections until we get this worked out."

"What can I do to help?" Triana said.

"I'm glad you asked that," Bon said, his voice growing agitated. "I think you can start by laying down the law a little bit more when it comes to work ethic on this ship."

Triana was silent for a moment. When she spoke again, her voice was slow and measured. "All right. Would you like to expand on that?"

"Sure, I'll expand. This crew is getting lazy. Four months into the trip and people are getting complacent. No discipline. I've got workers here in the Ag section that would rather joke around and make plans for their off time than do their work. Today I find that it almost cost us an entire section in Dome 1. That's a complete lack of discipline. And it has to start at the top. With the Council. With you."

"Correct me if I'm wrong," Triana said, her tone matching that of Bon, "but wouldn't a slip in discipline in your section be your responsibility? I can't micromanage every department on *Galahad*. That's why we have a Council, of which you're a member."

"This is not just a problem in the Agricultural Section," Bon shot back. "There's a breakdown in efficiency throughout the ship."

"Then why haven't I heard from the other Council members about it?"

"Because it hasn't been life threatening in those other areas, that's why. But it's a little different when it comes to our food supply, now isn't it? Someone slacks off in Channy's section and maybe the showers don't get cleaned on time. But a reckless attitude up here in the Domes means that maybe we don't eat. There's your difference."

Triana waited for more, but when the silence had stretched a long time she answered, her voice flat and unemotional. "All right. I've noted your concern, and will address it. Is there anything else?"

"I think that's enough for now. I've got a lot to handle up here right now. Oh, wait, there is one other thing. How about getting Gap to take one of these useless water recyclers down to his shop in Engineering and find out once and for all what's throwing them off? I can't keep patching them up and waiting for them to fail again."

"I'll let him know right away."

Bon could tell he had irritated her with his ranting, and for a moment considered softening his speech. But his own frustration continued to boil. All he could manage to answer was "Fine."

As he reached to disconnect he heard Triana add, "By the way, I was going to wish you a happy birthday today. Sorry it started so badly for you. Hope you have a better day soon." With that she broke the connection, leaving the tall Council member standing at his desk, mute, his scowl melting to a look of despair.

He ran a dirt-streaked hand through his long hair. "Great," he muttered to himself, "just great." He looked up to see the girl he had confronted in the crops standing in the door to his office.

"We found another one," she said.

Bon tossed the stylus from his work pad onto the desk and followed her out to the dirt path, the frown settling back onto his face.

Triana sat quietly, biting her lip. Since ending the discussion with Bon she had skipped back and forth between frustration and flat-out anger. He had done it again: taken what could have been a good day for them and thoroughly wiped it out with his abrasive personality. What was going on within him? What kept him from reaching out to her again, the way he had for one brief moment months ago?

She looked at the open journal on the desk in her room. The shortage of usable paper on the ship kept her notes brief, and she had barely begun that morning's entry when Bon's call had come through. She sighed and bent over the journal, adding one more paragraph.

> It's been months now since Bon and I "connected" briefly. I keep waiting for *that* Bon to resurface. Maybe he's waiting for me. I don't know. At this rate we might as well give up, I guess, if neither of us wants to be the first to address that again. It's probably just that neither one of us wants to take a chance on being rejected. I think we're both afraid that the other one only did that because of the stress and anxiety of the moment, that the feelings weren't real. Mine were. I thought his were,

too. But every time I think I can approach him, I get an episode like this morning. He's completely unapproachable like that. Now I'm sorry I even mentioned his birthday. Do I look foolish for doing that?

Dating the entry, she closed the journal and reached for her shoes. She was ready to start her workday, and tried to focus on the tasks in front of her. But thoughts of Bon kept forcing their way in. Her mind replayed their time together in the Spider bay control room, causing her to pause with only one shoe on, her eyes focusing on a point against the wall.

She was back in the control room, with a madman on the loose, threatening to kill them all. Somehow, during the most frightening moment of her life, she reached out for Bon, defying the tension that had existed between them for months. He had responded.

And neither had mentioned it again. Nor had they made any attempt to rekindle that moment. It was as if it had never happened.

Triana shook her head and broke the spell. She had to stop dwelling on it, she thought. Too many lives depended on her, depended on her staying focused on the business of running a lifeboat to the stars. There simply wasn't time for romantic drama.

Except that in her heart Triana knew that it was more complicated than that. As she pulled on her second shoe she thought quickly of Gap. She was bright enough to realize that *Galahad*'s Head of Engineering had his own feelings for her, feelings that he had never vocalized, and maybe never would. He had withdrawn over the past four months, maintaining a respectful but cool manner toward Triana. She recognized that Gap's heart was hurting but had no clue how to help him when she couldn't even seem to get her own feelings organized. She was being pulled in two directions, with the duties of Council Leader trumping it all.

What to do?

She stood and walked to the mirror hanging on the wall, checking her hair and teeth, rubbing a fleck of dry skin from her nose, noticing with a frown that another blemish was popping up below her lower lip. That part of her face was a battleground for zits, she had decided. A dab of ointment became the first volley of defense in this latest attack.

The blemish had at least distracted her from thoughts of Bon and Gap. As she walked through the door and out to the waiting lift at the end of the hall her mind shifted to the more urgent matters facing her.

A mysterious pod from Saturn's moon, Titan, for one thing.

3

Regardless of what many parents say, it's almost accepted that, deep down inside, they have a favorite child. Sure, they love them all, they nurture them, they do everything they can to help them succeed in life. There's no question of that.

But how would they not have favorites? Every child has a different personality, and humans resonate with some personalities better than others.

Now, I'm no parent, but I feel like the crew on this ship are my kids. I want the best for all of them, but I also can't help have favorites. I don't know what it is about this kid Gap, but he is one of those faves. Sure, he's a sharp kid, a great athlete, a good leader, blah blah blah. But I like the guy. He carries a sense of humor that I appreciate and has a heart that's a mile wide.

It's the heart part that gets him in trouble.

Gap Lee was forced to do something he hated: be a spectator. It wasn't his style. He had been so active his whole life, even training at one point as a gymnast with one of China's Olympic coaches. Now, sitting here and watching was eating him alive. But with his left arm in a sling, he had little choice.

The bleacher seats at one end of *Galahad*'s Airboarding track were almost empty. Gap sat in the top row, his back against the wall, his feet stretched out in the row before him. His short, spiky dark hair matched the color of his eyes, eyes that now followed the progress of a Boarder maneuvering around the track. The rider was good, almost as good as Gap, and had steadily increased speed with each circuit. Zoomer, the pet name given to the computer that controlled the track's hidden grid under the floor, was ramping up the difficulty, which usually meant one thing: a fall was coming.

Airboarding took the concept of Earth's twentieth-century pastime, skateboarding, and added a modern wrinkle. Now the wheels had come off—literally—with a powerful magnetic strip in their place on the bottom of the board. Equally strong magnets, in the form of crisscrossing grids placed under the floor, worked as an antigravitational force with each board's strip, and kept the rider floating about four inches off the ground. Then Zoomer would randomly program the magnetic current to make its way around the hidden grid, turning sections on and off as the rider was propelled around the room. It became a matter of flying by feel, trying to sense where the magnetic charge was strong and where it faded. The faster one sped around the course, in a room about the size of a basketball court, the harder it became to feel the subtle change in magnetic pull. One false move meant a spill.

Gap watched the Airboarder currently racing around the course and remembered the last ride he had taken . . . and its painful outcome.

It had been a few weeks after *Galahad*'s near-destruction at the hands of a crazed stowaway. That meant it had also been a few weeks since Gap had seen Triana and Bon embrace in the Spider control room. They hadn't noticed him, and Gap had never said a word to either of them. But his heart was broken. Why, he wondered, why hadn't he ever said anything to Tree about the way he felt? Why hadn't he been the first to take her hand, to hold her? He had been unsure of her reaction, and it had kept him from voicing his emotions to her. And now it was too late.

So, after sulking for weeks, he had decided to release some pent-up stress doing something athletic. He had climbed aboard his Airboard and pushed the upper limits of speed. Faster and faster he had shot around the track, gritting his teeth and letting out howls as he banked hard around the turns. The handful of crew members who were watching at the time were amazed at his performance, and they shouted encouragement with each pass.

One thing Gap barely remembered was the fall. The sudden quick drop in magnetic charge as he overshot a turn, the helpless feeling as he flew off the board and into the wall. It was cushioned, and Gap was wearing his helmet. But the impact was still enough to knock him out, leave him with a concussion, and the final insult: a broken collarbone. It was the first significant injury of *Galahad*'s brief mission, and it fulfilled Lita's prediction that an Airboarding accident would bring Sick House its first real patient.

Gap flexed the fingers of his left hand sticking out of the sling. He was growing more anxious each day to get rid of it, because now it only offered a daily reminder of what had caused him to be so reckless in the first place. Every time he looked at the sling he remembered standing in the doorway of the Spider bay control room and relived the sight that had torn him apart. He cleared the image for now and concentrated on watching the Airboarder rushing by.

A sudden shift in balance, a quick wave of the arms, and Gap knew what the rider was feeling. The Airboard was offtrack and that meant—

Wham! The body tumbled across the padded floor, rolling slowly to a stop as the board flipped off to the side. Gap winced, absently flexed his fingers again, and sat up. The rider lay still for a moment, then gradually rolled onto one knee and stood up. Gap sat back and exhaled. Everything was okay.

The rider picked up the board and walked to the bleachers, climbing to Gap at the top. As the helmet came off, long brown hair tumbled down below the shoulders, and Gap suddenly looked into the face of Ariel Morgan. One of the more beautiful crew members, the sixteen-year-old girl from Australia was also one of the more creative and daring Airboarders on the ship. If he couldn't ride for now, at least Gap could enjoy watching Ariel work her magic on the course.

"Go ahead," he said to her, smiling. "Rub it. You know it hurts. You don't have to be tough in front of me."

"I don't know what you're talking about," Ariel said, her own smile spreading across her face. "I don't feel a thing. And speaking of pain," she added, nodding toward the sling on Gap's arm, "when do you lose that thing?"

"Pretty soon. At least it better be pretty soon, or I'll have to try riding with one arm. I'm having serious withdrawals."

Ariel raised an eyebrow. "Sure, that would be real smart." She sat down next to him and began to take off the pads around her knees and elbows. Gap noticed that she sat very close and would occasionally brush against his leg with hers. He had been pretty sure since before the launch that Ariel was interested in him, but he had done nothing to encourage it. His own mind had been wrapped around Triana for so long that he hadn't even considered the possibility of anyone else.

Could he now? Could he ever get Tree off his mind? If he would only give Ariel a chance . . .

Not likely, he told himself. At least not yet. *I'm still not ready,* he thought.

"That was a great ride," he told her. "I'm very impressed. You're using my downtime to try to break Rico's track record, aren't you?"

"I'll get it," she said. "And if I don't do it, Rico will only raise the bar. You better heal up fast. I know you used to be top dog, but now there's two of us who have passed you by."

Gap laughed. "Great. I feel like the aging gunslinger who keeps getting challenged by all the young quick-draw artists. Everybody wants to see if they can take the champ."

Ariel ran a hand through her hair, smoothing out several

tangles caused by the helmet. Her leg brushed up against Gap again. "I just don't want you crying because you're on the disabled list when I set the new mark. I want you to take your medicine like a man."

Gap laughed again. She was as funny and sarcastic as she was beautiful. Was he an idiot to ignore her like this?

"Well, we're all gonna be pretty busy the next few days anyway," he said. "But it won't be long before I'm back in shape, with no sling."

Her expression turned serious. "Yeah, I was gonna ask you about that. What do you know about this thing we're supposed to pick up at Saturn?"

"Oh, not much more than you, probably. Some pod, a little smaller than one of our Spiders. It's been orbiting Titan since the time we launched from Earth, I hear. The research station around Titan sent it, and I guess it's programmed to fire into an orbit around Saturn as we swing by. Then, we grab it with a tractor beam and pull it into the Spider bay. But we don't have much room for error. We get one shot as we pass by, and if we miss, the pod will zip beyond our reach and burn up in Saturn's atmosphere."

Ariel nodded, gazing into his face. He noticed for the first time that one of her eyes was a lighter shade of green than the other. She said, "But I also know that we can't seem to raise anyone by radio on that research station. That's a little mysterious, wouldn't you say?"

Gap shrugged. "Yeah. But not even Roc seems to know what that's all about. And believe me, I've pestered him about it for a couple of weeks."

There was silence for a moment, an awkward silence that told Gap it was probably time to leave. Ariel must have felt the same thing, and they stood up together.

"Well," she said, touching him on his good shoulder. "Feel better soon. And good luck with your pod-catching." She climbed down the bleacher steps, calling back over her shoulder. "Can you catch that thing one-handed?"

Left alone in the stands, Gap watched her walk out the door, her brown hair swishing back and forth. "I must be an idiot," he muttered to himself.

Evening fell on *Galahad* and Roc gradually adjusted the lights on the ship, dimming the hallways to better simulate an Earth evening. All of the scientists who had worked on the project had agreed that it was important for the crew members' natural rhythms to stay as true as possible. So even with artificial light, *Galahad* experienced days and nights. It wasn't unusual to hear soft sounds of wind, or the faint chirp of crickets in the background. Mood was important, and the setting played a large part in determining that mood.

Light was hitting the glass cube at just the right angle as it sat on the edge of the desk. A tiny prism of light spilled out the other side, embellishing the desk with a miniature rainbow. The cube was half-filled with sand and tiny pebbles, all taken directly from the beaches of Veracruz, Mexico. Alone in the Clinic, Lita sat staring at her keepsake from home, tapping a stylus against her cheek.

The sand made her daydream, remembering the good times spent running through the surf as it tumbled ashore, chased by her younger brother and sister. If she closed her eyes, she could still almost smell the salty ocean water, could almost feel the way the sand squished between her toes, could almost hear the shrieks of their laughter mingling with the high-pitched cries from the gulls that circled overhead.

Sights, sounds, and smells that she would probably never experience again. Who knew what awaited them at Eos? What were the chances that either of the Earth-like planets circling that distant star would have anything similar to an ocean of water? And, if they found other life forms, would they soar through the sky like gulls, or plod across the sand like a crab?

For that matter, would there even be air to breathe?

So many questions. Lita finally broke from the trance and set the stylus on the desk. Almost everything on the "to do" list on her work pad was scratched off following a long day, and she was sure she could push the remaining two items into tomorrow. In fact, she decided, that's exactly what she would do. Besides, things had been fairly quiet around the Clinic lately, and that didn't figure to change in a day. At least not as long as Gap stayed off that Airboard, she thought with a smile.

She pushed back her chair and stood, stretching, her arms reached toward the ceiling and her hands clasped. Lita's assistant, Alexa Wellington, had left about an hour earlier to grab dinner, and suddenly Lita felt the grumble in her own stomach. A yawn crept through her. Yes, it was past time to leave. She turned toward the door, picking up her work pad.

The soft tone announced the incoming e-mail message. "Oh, c'mon," she said, quickly debating whether or not to ignore it. It couldn't be an emergency, she figured; that would have been a straight intercom call. Couldn't this just be her third item moved onto tomorrow's list?

She sighed and set the work pad back on the desk. What's another minute?

Turning the monitor toward her, she tapped in her access code and waited. In a flash she realized that the message was not internal. This e-mail wasn't from a fellow passenger on the ship; this was an incoming note from Earth.

Now she sank back into her chair, suddenly wide-awake. How long had it been? Five weeks? Maybe more like six? Triana still received messages from *Galahad*'s command center in California, but even those were becoming less and less frequent. Just minor updates, course and velocity equations, and answers to technical questions. Never any news from home. Bad news wasn't what the passengers on this spacecraft needed to hear.

But a message to Lita was surprising. Was it a follow-up treatment suggestion for Gap's injury? Not likely; all of that information was stored in the Clinic's computer banks. She waited a moment, hit the appropriate key, and then read through the transmission.

To: Lita Marques, Galahad Health
From: Galahad Command
Re: Rendezvous with Titan pod

As you know, *Galahad* is scheduled to intercept a transport pod launched from the SAT33 Research Station orbiting the moon of Titan. Prior to capturing the pod, please gather and combine the following chemicals, in the precise quantities listed. Two syringes, cotton swabs, and isopropyl alcohol should also be ready upon interception. Other details to follow if necessary.

Lita scanned the attached list of chemicals, all of which were locked away in the Sick House medicinal vault. It was an odd assortment, a combination that didn't look familiar to Lita after her eighteen-month training program. Her mother, a doctor in Veracruz, could no doubt tell her what this meant, but it was a mystery to Lita. She read over the note again, and then saved it on both her desk computer and her work pad. Her brow wrinkled, and before she knew it she was tapping her stylus against her cheek again.

"Roc," she called out.

"Hi. What's up, Doc?" came the computer's voice. "I've been dying to say that to you since we launched. What's up, Doc? There, I had to say it again."

"Well, I'm not a doctor, but yes, you're very funny. Listen, I have a question."

"Okay," Roc said. "Shoot."

She tapped on the computer screen. "Can you scan this?"

"Sure."

"Well," Lita said, "what do you make of it?"

"You mean other than the typical bland writing style, with no imagination or character?"

Lita decided that the best reply was no reply at all. Roc got the message.

"Okay," the computer said, "we're in no mood for wit tonight. So, rather than waste a lot of my best material, I'll try to help. I'm assuming you want to know about the little chemical cocktail being ordered, right?"

Lita nodded. "I've had to prepare doses for fighting infection, for slowing heart rate, for stabilizing respiration, even for helping a surprise migraine headache. But this," she said, tapping the screen a second time, "this is foreign to me. And the note says nothing about what it's for. That's a little strange, if you ask me. A little mysterious. Exactly what will this potion do?"

There was no immediate reply. Roc seemed to be digesting the ingredients and quantities in the message, working them through his own vast data banks. After a minute, just as Lita was about to prod again, the computer spoke up.

"Well, I don't have an exact match, but I've found something very close."

"And?" Lita said.

"With a few minor changes, this concoction is similar to a mixture used in the cryogenic industry."

Lita squinted at the screen. "Cryogenics? You mean freezing people? Suspended animation?"

"Uh, not really freezing. That's a popular misconception. But yes, suspended animation. The cooling and slowing of the body's natural machine. A deep sleep, actually. But with no dreaming, no sensation of time passing. In this case created especially for long-distance space travel."

Lita thought about it, recalling the lessons stored away in the back of her mind. "Yeah, I read about it," she said. "They seal people into something that looks like a glass coffin, inject them with solutions that begin the slowing process, then . . . gas them, I guess is the best way to put it. Puts them to sleep for a few weeks, a few months, or even a few years." She exhaled loudly and pointed to the list from *Galahad* Command. "And this stuff?"

Roc gave it one more quick review. "This was the stuff they used to help bring people back from their suspended animation." A pause. "Since you called it a coffin, I guess you could say this is the stuff that raises the dead."

Her eyes growing wide, Lita put a hand up to her mouth. What—or who—was on this pod?

4

Council meetings were usually scheduled once per week, but this was a special session. *Galahad* was on schedule to enter the space around Saturn that evening, and the rendezvous with the pod was a mere twenty-eight hours away. Though not a fan of meetings, Triana recognized that preparation was key to the success of this assignment. She sat at the head of the table in the Conference Room, waiting for the usual chitchat to die down before getting started.

The stark setting of the room was supposed to encourage productivity and eliminate distractions. Light gray paint, no pictures, comfortable chairs, a conference table, computer screens, and a water dispenser. That was it. But the ship's designers had failed to take into account the never-ending chatter whenever Channy was involved. Right now she was holding court with Lita and Gap, both of whom, could barely get a word in. Bon sat quietly at the far end of the table, a look of irritation on his face. Triana glanced at him once, but there was no eye contact. She cleared her throat.

"Let's get started, okay?" she said. Channy leaned over and, with a smile, whispered something final to Lita, who smirked and pushed Channy back into her own chair.

"Tomorrow is a big day for us," Triana began. "Essentially it's our first contact with people since we left Earth. Uh, well," she added, "if you don't count the uninvited guest who snuck on board." The mood around the table quickly became serious.

"In fact, this will be our first, and last, contact before leaving the solar system and heading out toward Eos. So I wanted to get us caught up on what's been going on around Saturn and, in particular, around Titan." Triana bit her lip and pulled up a graphic on her computer screen, then sent the image to the other screens around the table. It showed a representation of Saturn's moon system, with the dull orange ball called Titan at center stage.

"Some of this you know; some of it might be news to you. Almost all of it is rather . . . mysterious. I'm not trying to be dramatic, but let's face it, some odd things have been going on around this moon."

Lita spoke up. "You seem nervous about this rendezvous, Tree."

The Council Leader shrugged. "I guess I am, kinda. I mean, we didn't train for anything like this, and most of it came up just as we were leaving Earth. So you gotta wonder what's going on." She pointed to her screen. "Here's what we know. The research station, SAT33, has been in operation for eight years, orbiting Titan. The moon is Saturn's largest, and, as you probably know by now, has been a source of interest for a long, long time because of its atmosphere and oceans.

"The thirty scientists and researchers on SAT33 have been on their tour of duty here for two years. They're all scheduled to return to Earth in about six months. There, uh, there won't be a replacement team sent." She looked up at her fellow Council members. "Bhaktul," she said, and was greeted with somber nods. The disease from Comet Bhaktul, the one that had delivered the death sentence to Earth three years earlier, meant that any future space exploration and research had ground to a halt.

"Anyway, the work has been kept top secret. Roc can probably explain that better than I. Roc?"

The computer voice piped up immediately. "Not only top secret, but using the most intense security measures ever developed.

Computer coding unlike anything else ever created. And, the number of people with access to the information could almost fit into this room."

Gap raised an eyebrow. "Do we even know what they were studying, or looking for?"

"Supposedly it was an intense program designed to isolate and identify the early stages of life," Roc said. "But we have no idea what they found, if anything. The material radioed back to Earth has never been released, and maybe never will be. The only thing we know for certain is that SAT33 went silent four months ago."

Triana said, "And, we know that somebody there launched a pod, with the intention that we pick it up."

"Four months ago, right?" Channy said. "Just coincidence that we launched four months ago?"

Triana shrugged again. "Probably. I don't see a connection. Unless . . ."

"Unless?" Channy said.

"Unless whoever fired off the pod knew they were in trouble and just happened to find out that our course to Eos would mean a slingshot around Saturn. It's almost like they wanted us to get whatever information they had worked hard to dig up. I don't know what happened on that research station, but you have to wonder if they realized they had no chance to get home and wanted their work to survive somehow."

The room grew quiet. Roc waited a moment, then spoke up.

"I think some of you are under the impression that I am withholding information from you. That's not the case. I know what Triana knows, and that's it. This pod will likely be carrying data discs, and maybe more. I am just as curious about it as you are."

Lita looked over at Triana. "I admit I'm curious, but I'm also a little afraid of what we're dealing with."

"Why is that?" Gap said.

Lita told the Council about her e-mail the night before and the instructions on preparing a chemical solution. She also told them what Roc had said about the cryogenic connection.

Channy put her head in her hands. "Oh, no. Don't tell me we're about to pick up another madman."

"We can't assume that," said Triana, but her voice didn't hold much conviction.

"Oh, really?" Channy said, raising her head. "These people didn't leave Earth for Titan until well after Bhaktul Disease began spreading. They're infected. Or *were* infected. Or . . . or . . ."

"Okay, let's not get ahead of ourselves," Triana said. "Listen, we don't know anything for sure. Our job is to pick up this pod tomorrow evening. That's it."

Channy spread her hands. "But Lita's shot. What do you think that's for?"

"I don't know," Triana said. "And you don't, either, so let's just settle down and not get worked up. We need to keep our heads during this rendezvous. We only get one chance at it. I don't want any mistakes made because we're jumpy."

Another veil of silence settled over the group. Triana noticed that Bon had not said a word during the entire meeting. Not that this was unusual; Bon rarely spoke at Council meetings unless asked a direct question. His bored attitude bothered Triana more than she wanted to admit. She decided to engage him in conversation.

"Any comments, Bon? Is everything okay? You haven't said anything."

He looked up at her, then back down at the table. "I have a headache, that's all," he growled.

Lita said, "If you need a pain pill, you know where to find me."

"I don't need a pill," Bon said. "It will pass."

Lita looked back at Triana with an "Oh well, I tried" look on her face.

Triana decided to spend the rest of the meeting making sure everyone was ready for the pod capture. She brought up a new graphic on all of the screens, showing the trajectory of *Galahad* as it sped past Saturn, along with the dotted line that symbolized the path of the mysterious pod. An *x* marked the interception point.

As the meeting dragged on, each Council member tried to keep their mind on the business at hand. But Triana was sure they all were thinking exactly what she was thinking: What are we about to bring aboard this ship?

Well, she thought, we'll know in exactly twenty-seven and a half hours.

Gap sat in the Dining Hall, picking at the fruit on his plate. He had eaten only half of his energy block, and now was making a halfhearted attempt at stabbing the chunks of melon. His appetite was in hiding.

Seated across from him was Lita, who didn't seem to be suffering from the same problem. "You don't want that, do you?" she asked as she stole a piece of fruit from his plate. Before he could answer another tray plopped down next to Lita. Gap looked up into the face of Hannah Ross.

He didn't know her very well, but, like everyone else on the ship, he knew her reputation. Sixteen years old, born and raised in Alaska, and one of the most advanced math and science students on *Galahad*. Rumor had it that, although extraordinarily pretty, Hannah had never really socialized much or had any real boyfriends, the result of a very strict and protective father who kept her focused on education.

She was known for something else besides her sharp intellect, however. Her skill at painting and sketching was uncanny. As soon as a few crew members had discovered her work during the eighteen-month training period in California, she was in high demand for art. Several of the dorm rooms on *Galahad* sported beautiful colored pencil drawings that Hannah had created. Many featured alien landscapes, or views of Earth as seen from space. They all seemed more like photographs than drawings, with details that were astonishing.

She nodded a greeting at Gap as she sat down, and he noticed that she had her blond hair pulled back out of her face, a look he had never seen on her before. Lita looked over and said, "Hey, Hannah, what's new?"

"A lot, actually," Hannah said, removing her plate and water glass from the tray. "I'm completely blown away by the information we're getting about Titan. I've been gathering all sorts of data for the last couple of days. Haven't even eaten much, and figured I better get some fuel in me before it gets crazy tomorrow."

"You're on break now, right?" Lita said. Each member of the crew rotated work shifts through the various departments on *Galahad,* and at any given time one group was on a six-week break.

Hannah nodded. "And the timing is perfect, too. I have all day to dig through this stuff from Titan."

Gap set down his fork—it was useless, he wasn't hungry anyway—and noticed that Hannah was busy lining up the items she had placed on the table. She straightened her silverware so that it was exactly perpendicular to the edge of the table and adjusted her plate so that it was centered between her utensils and the water glass. Before picking up her own fork, she reached out and lined up the condiment basket so that it was parallel to the thin line running down the middle of the table. Gap watched this in quiet fascination and considered commenting on it. Instead, he asked, "What kind of information about Titan are you talking about?"

Hannah put a napkin across her lap and made brief eye contact with Gap before turning her attention back to her plate. "Well, the people on this research station have learned more about Titan in two years than we had learned in the last hundred years. The methane oceans, the ice caps, the atmosphere, earthquakes. Or, Titan-quakes, I guess." She smiled shyly, as if she was talking too much. "Just a lot of nerdy scientific stuff, really. Probably not very interesting to most people."

"I think it's interesting," Gap said, and thought he detected a bit of a blush come across Hannah's face.

Lita, who had been listening to their exchange, chimed in. "What's the story on their search for life?"

A slight wrinkle appeared on Hannah's forehead. "Unfortunately, that information is part of this big block of data that's labeled Top Secret. I can't get access to that."

"What do *you* think?" Lita said.

Hannah set down her water glass—then moved it an inch to the right, Gap saw—and turned to Lita. "There has to be life there. I just feel it. All of the conditions are ripe, and that moon has a lot in common right now with Earth's early days. Any life-form there might be small, it might be completely alien to us, but I think it's there." She looked back and forth between Gap and Lita, the shy smile returning. "Why else would the information be classified?"

"I don't know," Gap said. "Maybe they found something dangerous."

The look on her face told Gap that Hannah wasn't buying it. He shrugged and held his hands out, palms up. "I'm just saying . . ." His voice trailed off.

"What about this pod?" Lita said. "Have you been able to gather anything else about that?"

"Nope," Hannah said. "That's a pretty big mystery by itself. This wasn't a planned intercept. The pod was fired right as we were launching, and *Galahad* Command quickly added this little rescue mission as a last-minute thing. There's no data about who or what is on there. But," she said, looking briefly at Gap again before averting her eyes, "it can only mean more information somehow. I can't wait to get it."

Gap grunted. "I wouldn't be too excited if I were you. We're liable to open that thing up and another madman pops out. We've had enough of that on this trip so far."

"Oh, you don't really believe that, do you?" Lita said.

"Well, you're the one who was ordered to put together a wake-up shot."

Hannah's face had picked up a worried expression again. "I just feel horrible about the people on that research station. Nobody has heard anything from them in months." She sighed and set down her fork. "Thirty people," she mumbled.

This left the three crew members silent as they contemplated a disaster that might have happened out here in deep space. Lonely space, a billion miles from home, where even a small problem could quickly become deadly. The same situation that the crew of *Galahad* faced daily, although it was rarely discussed. What might have befallen the dedicated scientists and technicians on SAT33?

And could it also affect *Galahad*?

Gap sat staring at Hannah Ross, and after a moment she looked up and met his gaze. This time she didn't look away, and Gap felt a small tingle run up his spine. What was this? First Ariel, the Airboarder from Australia, and now Hannah. Did he have two girls vying for his attention? Had he been wallowing in self-pity for so long that he had forgotten there were even other girls on the ship?

Slowly, he smiled.

5

Triana had set her alarm for five thirty that morning, but found herself out of bed half an hour earlier. Now, as she finished braiding her long hair, she considered the day before her and the task that overshadowed everything. Today was the day that *Galahad* went fishing for a small metal space pod.

She quickly brushed her teeth, then wiped her face with a towel. That pesky zit was still holding on, she noticed, and swiped at it with another round of ointment. Be gone already, she thought. Was it a case of nerves that was doing it? And what was causing the most anxiety these days: the pod, or Bon? Or just the normal, everyday stress of managing a crew of 251 teens?

All of it, she decided. She took one final look in the mirror. "I'm surprised you're not one giant walking zit," she said to herself. "Ugh."

A soft tone sounded, followed by Roc's voice, which was a little too much on the cheery side. "Good morning, Tree. Sleep well?"

"Like a baby," she lied. "What about you? Exciting night?"

"Very. Thought I'd have some fun with the overnight crew in Engineering, so I lit up the emergency panel for a second and made it look like we were losing all of our oxygen into space."

Triana had been walking across the room, and stopped in her tracks. "You didn't."

"You're right, I didn't really do that. But I thought about it. Just a little harmless fun, you know? Would've put them on their toes, I'll tell you that."

"You might be the world's smartest computer, but I think you're crazy."

"That wasn't even the best idea I had last night," Roc said. "How about this? Every time a door slides open I add the sound of a belch. Now *that* would be funny."

Triana smiled and shook her head, finishing the walk over to her desk and sitting down. "We need to come up with a few more chores for you to handle overnight. Aren't there some impossible mathematical equations you could be trying to solve?"

"Ho hum," came the computer voice. "You're no fun. Besides, I did do a little work on our assignment today. You'll be happy to know that the pod is set for its last engine burn, where it will officially leave Titan's orbit and be picked up by Saturn's gravitational pull. It will stay there just long enough for us to grab it."

"And if we don't," Triana said, "then—"

"What?" Roc said. "What's this 'if we don't' nonsense?"

"If we don't," Triana continued, "then it burns up in Saturn's atmosphere, and we don't get to solve the big mystery."

"I was right. You're no fun. Don't worry your pretty little head; we'll lasso it without a problem. You'll congratulate me later. And if we do somehow miss it, you can blame Gap."

This time Triana laughed out loud. What would she ever do without Roc?

"Anyway," the computer added, "I've recalculated, and now would put intercept time a little after seven o'clock tonight. About seven twelve and twenty-two seconds."

"About?" Triana said. "Next time try to be more exact."

"Hey, look who went out and bought a sense of humor. Sure you don't like that belching door stuff?"

"Any word yet about the scientists on SAT33?"

Roc told her no, but added, "We might learn quite a bit from the pod."

Triana nodded silently, biting her lip. She looked at the computer screen on her desk, reviewing the various project assignments for the day. Nothing out of the ordinary. She skipped to her own personal day planner and noticed that she was scheduled for class that evening. Twentieth-century literature. She made a note to postpone the class until after the pod rendezvous. Wouldn't you know it, she thought, that's one of my favorite classes.

"Have a great day, Tree," Roc said. "Just one other thing. Before you leave for work, check your messages. You have a priority video message waiting."

Her fingers stopped their dance across the keyboard. "From?"

"Like I said, have a great day."

With that, Roc was gone, the room was silent, and Triana was deep in thought. Not just a video message, which in itself was a rarity now that *Galahad* was four months out. This was a priority video message. Was this the news they had been waiting for regarding the mysterious silence from the Titan station? No, that wouldn't require video. Was it some disaster back on Earth? No, why would they bother telling us, she thought. What about an update concerning their own mission, maybe some news about their target star system, Eos? Had they discovered . . .

This is ridiculous, she decided. Quit playing Twenty Questions and just open the message.

She tapped out her personal code, accessed the message center, and saw it sitting in the Received box. One video message, marked "Priority." Received about thirty minutes ago. The sender's address meant nothing to her, but it definitely wasn't *Galahad* Command.

A quick memory jolted her, suddenly reminding her of the late-night messages she had received during their earlier crisis. Sitting in this same chair, staring at this same computer screen. Did she even want to open this message?

Stop it, she thought. Stop being irrational. That was months ago. It's over now. Just open the message.

She took a deep breath. One more keystroke, and it would . . .

Her mouth dropped open. Staring at her from the screen, a smile stretched across his obviously tired face, and looking more frail than she had ever seen him, was Dr. Wallace Zimmer. The man who not only had conceived the idea for the *Galahad* mission, but also had personally dedicated the last years of his life to making it a reality. The man Triana had looked up to as a father figure, the one man who understood her inner pain, her drive. The one man who knew what motivated the shy girl from Colorado, understood how the anguish over her father's death had fueled her need to escape, in more ways than one. Dr. Zimmer had connected enough with Triana to know that her attempts to run away from Earth wouldn't necessarily mean she could ever run away from the grief.

And now he, too, was gone. Wallace Zimmer was dead before *Galahad* reached the orbit of Mars.

But here he was, smiling at her from across hundreds of millions of miles. From beyond the grave.

It was a recorded message, but he must have known the reaction it would cause. He remained silent for a few moments, obviously allowing her to adjust to the idea of seeing him again. Then, he nodded and spoke.

"Tree, I didn't want to frighten you with this message, and I hope I haven't done so. Shocked you a little, maybe, and I'm sorry for that. I am recording this about a week after your departure. I have arranged for you to receive it when you are in Saturn's space, and are preparing to intercept the small craft launched by the scientists on SAT33. I'll let you know right now that I am recording some other messages for you, and they will be delivered to you at various times during your journey. So," he said, smiling again, "it shouldn't be quite a shock next time."

Triana rested her elbows on the desk and cradled her head between her hands, dumbfounded at what she was seeing and hearing. A wave of sadness washed over her, extracting emotions that she had denied for a long time. She immediately thought of her dad, and once again faced the fact that the two most important and influential people in her life had passed away. She loved them both.

"I won't take much of your time," Dr. Zimmer said, "since I know you have a busy day ahead of you. But let me talk to you for a minute about your voyage up to this point.

"I did everything I could to prepare you for this mission, but it's impossible to plan for everything. I'm sure there have been times where you had to act on impulse rather than on training and experience. But I think I know you well enough, Tree, to know that you handled it well. You have all of the qualities it takes for a leader, and the crew is fortunate to have you in charge."

Triana smiled back at the video image on the screen.

"This latest episode you are about to encounter might be unsettling, only because it is your first contact with other people in several months, and your isolation will have instilled an instinctual tendency to protect yourself from 'outsiders.' That's natural. Just don't let it affect your judgment or throw you off course. Make your decisions with one thing in mind: the safety of the crew and the ship. At this point, everything else, including other people you might encounter, must become secondary. Your responsibility lies with *Galahad*.

"One thing that might help is for you to get your hands on a lot of SAT33's top secret data. I have . . . arranged, I guess you could say, for your crew to gain access to what might be critical information. In fact, much of it should be on its way to you right about now." He chuckled. "I see no sense in keeping it secret from you any longer. Who around here would you tell?"

Triana smiled at the vidscreen, thankful for this final assist from the man who had nurtured the mission and its crew. The top secret details from the research station could prove very helpful.

Dr. Zimmer's expression turned serious. "By now, no doubt, you've learned that you're going to experience bumps along the way regarding crew behavior. For that I encourage you to rely heavily on your fellow Council members. Each of them was chosen for a particular reason, and sometimes you might wonder what those reasons were." Triana couldn't help immediately think of Bon. She shook her head and concentrated again on the message.

"You must trust that their selection was for a reason, and that each has a strength that you should tap into during the mission. Don't sell any of them short in their skills, or their contributions.

"Remember to take care of yourself physically, always. Channy is very good at motivating, but self-motivation is crucial, too. Get your rest and get your exercise.

"And, finally, I'm sure that by now there have been issues regarding . . . well, let's say 'interpersonal relationships.'"

Triana felt a flush come over her face. Her gaze remained locked on to the face of Dr. Zimmer.

"This, too, is only natural. You're teenagers, you're locked up together for five years, and you're bound to have feelings for one another. Some not so good, others that are . . . interesting and exciting. I don't expect you, Tree, to be immune from these feelings. But, again, I think I know you pretty well, and I know how you will try to regulate these feelings as a ship commander, and not as a young woman. I feel that would be a mistake.

"There will be friction, of course, and there will be both pain and joy. I won't burden you with silly old-man philosophy, especially an old man who was a lifelong bachelor. But I can give you one solid piece of advice. Do what is right. Your heart will fight you over and over again, but do what is right.

"And, Triana, you always know what is right."

She didn't expect to cry, but that was most certainly a tear that was coursing down her cheek. And several other tears followed when the image of Dr. Zimmer placed his hand up against the screen. Triana reached out and placed her palm on the screen, against his, digitally touching her mentor across space and time.

A few seconds later the image faded to black.

* * *

The sleek, metallic pod rocketed through its final circuit of Titan. After four months of orbiting the orange-colored moon, its thrusters came to life, firing long enough to nudge the pod outward and into the gravitational arms of Saturn. When the course was confirmed, the engines shut down for the last time, leaving the small craft to its final four and a half hours of flight. It would either wind up in the Spider bay of *Galahad* or be crushed and incinerated by the atmosphere of the giant gas planet.

The interior of the pod was dim, cold, and silent. Small windows allowed enough light from Saturn's glare to cast grim shadows along the opposite wall, with empty pilots' chairs providing gray silhouettes against the metallic sides. Two additional chairs, also vacant, sat near the back wall, just a few feet from the exit hatch. Their safety harnesses dangled free, silver latches occasionally catching a glimmer of Saturn's shine as the pod lazily rolled into its new orbit.

Tucked into a far corner were two cylinders, one that almost resembled the size and shape of a space coffin, the other with matching dimensions yet much smaller. The two cylinders each appeared almost new, while the rest of the pod's interior gave an impression of many years of service. It was as if they had been hastily added as an afterthought, bolted into place and rigged with a mishmash of tubes and wires. The top sections of the cylinders were made of a hard, clear plastic with hinges that would allow them to swing open. Darkness obscured the contents.

Without warning, an instrument panel blinked into life, with gauges that had been dormant for months suddenly swinging into action, lights popping on, and life-support systems warming the air inside. A mechanical pump also woke up, circulating dark red fluids through a heating and filtering device, which fed thick plastic tubes that ran into the two sealed cylinders.

A digital counter began a silent countdown.

4:28:34, 4:28:33, 4:28:32 . . .

6

Would you like to know what's inside the pod? So would I. See, you think because I'm so incredibly clever—you're right—that I have some sort of special power that allows me to see into the future or across space. Uh-uh. I'm waiting, just like you, to see what might tumble out of this thing.

Or maybe we shouldn't want to find out.

One look at the folder on the desk was enough. It was a standard file folder, and a neat white label on the tab identified the contents simply as "Titan." The papers inside were crisp and straight, clipped together in groups of three or four, with an occasional sticky note attached at the top. The exterior of the folder was bare; no writing, no pen marks, no folds or creases.

But it wasn't right. It was tilted slightly, and one corner now stuck out over the edge of the desk. Hannah Ross reached out and pulled the bottom of the folder until it lined up with the straight edge of her desk, perfectly aligned and symmetrical. Only then was she able to drag her attention back to the computer screen.

She had lowered the overhead lights in her room to an almost dusklike setting, and had music playing softly in the background. It was one of her mom's favorite recordings, a trio of piano, drum, and bass, and she had found that it helped produce the right ambiance when she was working. The first few times Hannah had listened to this particular music had been emotionally draining, producing such extreme feelings of homesickness that she had broken down, crying for her family left behind. After several weeks, however, she had finally reached a point where it now brought about a peaceful, soothing reaction.

Her side of the shared dorm room was colorfully decorated, a combination of mostly peach and light green. A collection of her colored pencil drawings lay scattered near her bed and against the side of her dresser. Many were still works in progress, while others were attempts that hadn't met her own rigid personal standards and would end up recycled. A half-completed sketch of an Alaskan lake, with the lights of the aurora borealis dancing above it, leaned against the wall. Two oil paintings hung over her bed, one that she had finished at her home in Anchorage, Alaska, depicting a mist-shrouded waterfall within what appeared to be an exotic alien setting. In her mind's eye it represented the landscape that the crew would find upon reaching one of the planets circling Eos, their final destination.

The other one, slightly smaller, had been completed just days before leaving the *Galahad* training complex. It featured the unmistakable planet of Saturn in one corner, with one of the rings prominent in the foreground. Large chunks of jagged water ice almost seemed to slip off the canvas as they jostled one another in their dance. The fuzzy orange ball known as Titan, however, dominated the center of the painting. The vision was almost hypnotic, the enigmatic moon catching and holding the eye, daring the viewer to solve its mysteries.

She would never say it to anyone, but of all the artwork Hannah had created in the last few years, this was the one of which she was most proud. Sketching was more to her liking, but this particular piece of work had demanded deep colors, and, although oil was not her usual medium, she had nailed it.

She looked up at it now, briefly, then back to the data on her computer screen. Titan was, by far, the most fascinating body in the solar system as far as she was concerned. Larger than two of the actual planets orbiting the sun, it embodied everything that intrigued Hannah about space and exploration. She was convinced it harbored life, somehow, possibly somewhere in the depths of its oceans. She had spent hours upon hours studying everything she could about it, beginning with the Cassini probe of the early twenty-first century, through the work cataloged by the pioneers on SAT33. There was precious little of that data available until the classified material was released to them, but what she could get her hands on she devoured.

Which explained why she was so anxious to find out what had happened aboard that research station. Bizarre radio transmissions to Earth, followed by months of silence, could only spell bad news. Then most of the reports were placed under a confidential seal. And although she had never met nor spoken with any of them, Hannah had read the earlier reports filed by the lead scientists and researchers, and felt as if she knew them. She was troubled by their disappearance, and determined to somehow solve the mystery.

At the moment *Galahad* was slicing through space, propelled by its ion power engines, and picking up additional speed as it closed in on its loop around Saturn. This would be the closest they would get to Titan before hurtling into deep space, on course for the edge of the solar system and beyond, to Eos. Hannah was spending as much time as possible at her computer, compiling her own data from both Saturn and Titan before they fell away.

The data was puzzling. In fact, it was maddening. Throughout the countless hours she had spent studying it, Titan had never produced anything like this before. Even more maddening, Hannah was having a hard time understanding what it was.

But the evidence was there, on her computer screen, taunting her. A powerful energy force, pulsing. Like a magnetic stream, almost. Short, intense bursts that originated on Titan, sending out powerful shock waves. What was it? A magnetic storm? A violent reaction between the moon and its mother planet? Residue from volcanic activity? She had scoured the vast scientific records, including reports logged by a European probe that had briefly visited the area twenty years earlier. Nothing. No mention of this pulse.

She had to know. She opened a new search engine on her computer and typed in "energy pulse" and "magnetic force." Just before hitting the button to execute the search, she added one more entry: "energy beam." And, for good measure, this time she had the computer include every bit of data that was considered nonclassified by the SAT33 team. Satisfied, she punched enter.

The computer began scrolling through the tens of thousands of documents on record, a process that might take a minute or two. While she waited, her mind continuing to puzzle over the problem, her eyes drifted to a small sketch she had completed the night before. It sat near the top edge of her desk, propped up by—and temporarily obscuring—a small framed picture of her family. The pen-and-ink sketch featured a boy standing with his weight shifted to one foot, his arms resting on top of his head, one hand grasping the other wrist. Although the sketch was vague, with the facial features unclear, anyone on the ship would have recognized the figure as Gap Lee. The build, the hair . . .

Her attention to the drawing was broken by a small beep from the computer, declaring a successful end to the search. Hannah eyed the sparse listing of matching documents, all of which somehow involved either the spacecraft that had visited Saturn over the years, or the actual energy forces of the SAT33 station itself.

Except two. Hannah noted the documents, filed by a scientist aboard the research station named Nina Volkov, and immediately opened the first one.

It was a short memo, dated approximately six months earlier, meaning a year and a half into the crew's tour of duty. Hannah scanned the first couple of paragraphs until her eyes settled onto something interesting.

> But the most intriguing find this week included a short-lived energy beam, tightly focused, and that, to my knowledge, has not been previously detected. The beam's source has not been isolated, although it definitely originates somewhere on Titan.

A list of additional file numbers at the end of the memo referenced other documents that either addressed this memo's topic, or related information. Hannah quickly cross-checked the numbers and realized that each of these other records had been later cataloged as classified. Somehow this original memo had escaped notice, possibly because it was almost an afterthought by the recording scientist.

But it was most certainly the same energy pulse that Hannah had picked up. She went back to the search screen and opened the second file. After a moment a look of bewilderment creased her face. Why was this filed in the Maintenance folder, a group of documents that simply kept records of food rations on the station, repair histories, and other non-research-related areas?

It took her almost five minutes to solve the mystery. When she had filed this particular document, Nina Volkov had made an error. She had transposed two numbers in the catalog sequence, essentially uploading the research memo into the wrong computer folder. With a slight grin Hannah saw that this important scientific clue had wrongly ended up stuck among memos that kept track of the number of cans of beans on the station. A typing error had somehow kept this document from being locked up with the other classified files.

She quickly read through the report. Toward the bottom a paragraph jumped out at her.

> There can no longer be any doubt. The energy beam is focused directly on SAT33 and is not a random burst from the moon into space. The chances of it being a natural phenomenon,

either from gravitational reactions with Saturn, or underground shifting of continental plates, are quickly declining. Whether or not the beam, which continues to increase in duration, is specifically to blame for the crisis on SAT33 is unproved, but highly likely. And, since we are not able to get away from the beam, another solution must be found.

Hannah's gaze stayed riveted on one phrase. "The crisis on SAT33." The first clue that something had indeed gone wrong on the orbiting platform. Was it responsible for the lost contact? Were the scientists okay but unable to communicate with Earth or *Galahad* because of this baffling energy pulse? Had Nina and the other researchers ever solved the mystery, only to have their answers sealed under the protective label "Top Secret?"

And, most important, what did this mean for Hannah and the crew of *Galahad*? They weren't going to be in Saturn's space for long, and they would never get within half a million miles of Titan. Their course would soon send them rocketing toward the outskirts of the solar system.

She saved the two documents in her own personal file, and then reopened the screen that was keeping track of the pulse. Within seconds her eyes widened. During the last half hour the data had been organized and graphed. Now, to her astonishment, Hannah could see a true picture of the energy force radiating from Titan. The graph showed a clear, concise pattern, a regular series of pulses, similar to an EKG of a heartbeat. Not random, not scattered. Regular. Like a code, or a signal.

And not dispersed in all directions. This signal, this unnatural pulse, was focused in a tight beam.

Directly at *Galahad*.

7

Gap looked at the pod data for the umpteenth time, a product of nerves, he decided. He had, with Roc's help, run the figures over and over again. But he had arrived in *Galahad*'s Control Room much earlier than necessary, and had chosen busywork over simple fidgeting. Now the countdown for the pod's capture stood at just over six minutes.

The sling was not helping matters. Punching numbers on a keyboard slowed dramatically when using one hand, and Gap was at least thankful that Kaya was there to help. A fifteen-year-old of Hopi Indian descent, she had helped pass the time with Gap by swapping stories of their respective homelands in between entering some of his computer calculations. Gap was fascinated by the tales of her ancestors in the southwestern part of the United States and welcomed the diversion from the otherwise tense situation.

Once again he silently acknowledged the brilliant mind of Dr. Wallace Zimmer. The scientist had insisted that *Galahad* embrace a culturally diverse crew, and Gap appreciated it more every day. Kaya not only possessed a razor-sharp mind, but also had a talent for painting vivid mental images of her people's way of life.

The ship's Control Room began to fill up. Designed mostly for special situations, the room had few real uses since Roc managed most of the day-to-day operations of the vessel. Situated on the top level of *Galahad*, perched just in front of Dome 1, it was large enough to hold about ten or twelve people. Light blue walls surrounded a workspace that was dominated by an immense vidscreen, which was dark at the moment. Five computer stations, all of which were currently occupied, were scattered around the oval room.

Triana had arrived ten minutes earlier and had conferred with Gap about the pod interception, then left him to his work. He looked up as the door opened again and gave a small wave toward Channy and Lita as they entered. Channy was chattering, as usual. No sign of Bon, which probably irritated Tree, but was okay with Gap. Besides, was it any surprise that the gruff Swede was a no-show?

"Five minutes," came Roc's voice. Gap felt his palms glisten with sweat and stole a glance at Triana, sitting quietly at another computer station. She seemed calm, without the visible signs of stress that Gap was sure he was emitting. But then, he realized, after her heroic efforts to save them all right after launch, this was probably a piece of cake.

Or was she a bundle of nerves on the inside? Gap had always had such a difficult time reading her. She seemed cool right now, but was she twisting on the inside like him? The mystery of this small craft had to make things intense for her, didn't it? Gap was dying to know what was inside the pod. Wouldn't she be just as curious? If so, it didn't show.

Which is why, he realized, she was the Council Leader, and he was not.

He turned his attention back to the vidscreen. The final computation was complete. Now it was simply a matter of Roc engaging the tractor beam at just the precise moment. If they were off by even a couple of seconds . . .

"Feeling good about your calculations, Gap?" came Roc's voice, startling him. "You realize that if you're off by even—"

"My calculations are perfect," Gap shot back. "I'll get us in the ballpark. You just worry about your little chore."

"Hmm," Roc said. "Do I trust a guy whose earlier calculations threw him into a wall at about twenty-five miles per hour? That sling you're wearing doesn't inspire much confidence, you know."

Out of the corner of his eye Gap could see Triana, Lita, and Channy all grinning at this typical exchange. Roc and Gap had a reputation for verbal sparring, and even Gap had to admit that the computer usually came out on top. But the Council member couldn't stop himself from charging back in.

"If you'll recall, I'm also the guy who saved your chips after our stowaway almost unplugged you for good. Might turn out to be the worst decision I've ever made."

"A close second, actually," the computer said. "The worst decision would probably be choosing that shirt. Ick."

Gap sighed. Would he ever learn?

Channy strolled over to stand next to him. "Don't listen to him, Gap. I think your shirt looks cool."

Gap started to thank her, then took a quick glance at Channy's bright pink T-shirt, splattered with red and green polka dots. "That's . . . reassuring," he said.

"Four minutes," Roc said. "The pod should be within visual range any moment."

"Let's have the big screen on, Roc," Triana said, standing up. The dark screen flickered for an instant before filling with stars. "I don't see . . ." Triana started to say. "Wait, that must be it." She walked up to the screen and pointed at an egg-shaped dot that was steadily growing in size. It was gray, and, with the way the light from Saturn danced across it, was probably spinning as it flew through its orbit. Within a minute it became large enough to see clearly against the backdrop of stars.

Gap stared at the image, then stole a glance at the people in the Control Room. Every eye was on the screen, and every mind, Gap knew, was also probably on the same thought: What is in this thing?

"I will point out, for the last time," Roc said, "that we have an extremely small window of opportunity here. If we miss it, that little metal pill will burn up in Saturn's atmosphere. Because in exactly twenty-one minutes we will slingshot around the planet and be gone for good. There's no chance to swing around and try again."

Triana nodded. "Understood." She turned to Gap. "Anything else we need to do?"

"Nope," he said. "After our last minor adjustment it's all gone automatic. We should engage the beam in about . . ." He looked down at the digital counter. "In about ninety seconds."

Channy, who was still standing next to him, put her hand on Gap's shoulder. "Good luck," she whispered.

The vidscreen image of the pod continued to grow, until it seemed as if *Galahad* were almost on top of it. The counter silently clicked down to five. Four. Three. Two . . .

"Engaging tractor beam . . . now," Roc said.

A ghostly faint light shot from the lower front edge of the ship and locked on to the pod, which visibly shuddered. The spinning motion of the small craft slowed. Gap thought he felt a slight tremble run through his feet, but wondered if it was only his imagination.

Roc's voice cut through the silence in the Control Room. "I believe we have landed a steel fish."

Lita and Channy cheered, along with several of the other crew members in the room. Gap let out his breath in relief, then suddenly found himself in an embrace. Channy had wrapped her arms around his chest and was squeezing him. She reached up and planted a quick kiss on his cheek. "Nice job," she said. He grinned, a blush appearing on his cheeks.

"Whoa," Roc said. "What about me? I'm the one who did most of the work here. Where's my hug and kiss?"

Channy let go of Gap, kissed her index finger, and stubbed it against one of Roc's red sensor lights on the console. "Way to go, Roc. You're a terrific fisherman."

Lita walked up beside Triana. "Well," she said. "You guys did it. Congratulations."

"We're not done yet," Triana said. "Grabbing it with the tractor beam is one thing. We still have to get it into the Spider bay."

"Please," Roc said. "Reeling her in is the easiest part. I'll have her locked down and buttoned up in no time. Give me an hour and I'll have you crawling around inside that thing."

Lita and Triana exchanged a tense look, both of their faces exhibiting the same feeling: do we really want to know what's inside?

Galahad had used a combination of ion power engines and solar sails to reach the outer region of the solar system. Now, with the sails withdrawn, the ship began to make its final dive around Saturn. The gravitational slingshot around the gas giant would propel the ship at even greater speed, flinging it out of orbit and on track out of the sun's planetary system. Eos awaited, four and a half years away.

The outer door had closed, depositing the pod from SAT33 in the hangarlike Spider bay. It would take a while for the room to pressurize and warm back up, so Triana had decided to wait until after they had whipped around Saturn to investigate. The small metal craft sat alone in the dim light of the bay, silent.

Minutes later, the slingshot maneuver began. Just as they had four months earlier, when the journey had commenced, almost every crew member found a window or vidscreen. They watched, their eyes wide, as *Galahad* screamed through space, reaching its closest point to Saturn before breaking away and rocketing into the void of outer space. There was no physical sensation of movement, but the visual evidence attested to the astounding velocity *Galahad* had achieved.

The majesty of the regal planet began to fall away, the colors dazzling, the rings almost hypnotic. Many of the crew members began to murmur to each other, pointing to the peculiar ice rings and wondering aloud if their new home, one of the planets of Eos, might have similar discs. Or, would their night sky feature a sister planet with rings? Would their new home even have a moon? Or several?

After months of dull travel, the excitement level had reached another high. What they had only seen before in pictures was now spread out before them, and the enthusiasm for their journey returned, if only briefly. It provided a welcome distraction.

In the murky distance, unnoticed by the crew, Titan continued its lonely orbit around Saturn.

8

The room was dark, but that wasn't helping as much as he had hoped. For the past few hours his head had been pounding, and now Bon hoped that a quiet, dark room would somehow help ease the pain. He lay stretched out on his bed, a cool, damp rag covering his eyes. He had no idea if this was really beneficial, but it was a pleasant memory of his mother. She had often recommended it as a headache remedy, and Bon had obediently taken her advice. "A cool cloth for my little hothead," she would say. It seemed that this time, however, the cool rag was having no effect.

He was grateful to have the room to himself. His roommate, a boy from Brazil named Desi, was out. Bon had been thankful from the start for his room assignment. Desi was naturally quiet, and rarely began a conversation with anyone. This suited Bon just fine, and the two got along very well. And, at the moment, it helped that he could keep the lights dimmed. He had also dialed up the faint sound of a babbling brook to help calm him.

Nothing worked. The headache had steadily intensified since the Council meeting the day before, and Bon had eventually taken the pain pill that Lita had suggested. In fact, he had taken another just four hours ago while still at work in the Domes. He had been sure that he could work his way through it. The crops were turning over quickly now, and a hungry crew needed a steady supply of food. He had tried toughing it out, but after a while it was no use. He had sought shelter and relief in his room.

Another of the farmworkers, a girl from Japan, had left an hour earlier with the same pounding headache. Was it just a coincidence?

Bon pulled the rag from his eyes and propped himself up to look at the clock beside his bed. By now they should have not only captured the pod, but also completed the swing around Saturn. He had spent the time during both events flat on his back. If there was any feeling of guilt, it was overshadowed by the throbbing pain centered between his eyes.

Besides, he certainly was in no mood to be back in the Spider bay with Triana. They had not been back together since their emotional embrace months earlier. The situation would be awkward, to say the least. He winced, partly from the headache, which continued its assault, and partly from his feelings about the Council Leader. Had their embrace been a mistake? Or had it been a mistake to ignore it since then? What was the right answer? For that matter, what was the right feeling? Or—and this made his head throb even more—were there even such things as "right" and "wrong" feelings?

Better to lie here, he concluded. Even if it meant dealing with extreme pain. Physical pain, after all, he could deal with.

He groaned, adjusted the pillow under his head, and replaced the cool cloth over his eyes and forehead, again causing a flash of memories. With his eyes closed he pictured the day he had left his family home in Skane, Sweden, to live with relatives in the United States. At the time the separation from his father was welcome relief, a break from the friction in their relationship. Bon loved his father, but their tempers often caused them to collide.

Leaving his mother had been the most heartbreaking. She had seemed to be the only person who could see the real Bon underneath the gruff façade, and was the one person who understood his talents, his intelligence, his moods. She recognized that his introverted personality was misinterpreted by most people as brooding. His mother had tried repeatedly to mend the differences between father and son, but in the end had acknowledged that a change in scenery might be for the best.

Nobody in the family had counted on Comet Bhaktul and its ominous consequences. By now Bon was sure that his mother was gone, and his father, who had developed the early symptoms of the disease on Bon's last trip home, might be dead as well.

And Bon? He moved through space, a billion miles from Skane, from his parents' graves. He was aboard a spacecraft, tracking toward a distant planetary system, taking a part of his mother—and, no doubt, his father—with him. Carrying the last of the Hartsfield clan to the stars.

Another groan escaped his lips as the headache turned up another notch. If this kept up, he would find himself in Sick House, and that was the last place he wanted to be. What could be causing this? Should he take another pill, or was that asking for more trouble?

Thoughts of home, thoughts of his parents, thoughts of Triana.

No wonder he had a headache.

9

I don't like to brag. Okay, that's a lie; I love to brag. Blame that on Roy Orzini, who made up for his short stature by puffing himself up to a virtual six foot two just by way of his bravado.

But let me just say that throwing an electronic lasso around a small metal pod that was streaking around Saturn at speeds that defy the imagination . . . well, that's pure genius. Thank you.

Please don't think I'm limited to technical wizardry, however. I have written poems, designed a fairly snazzy crew uniform that was ultimately shot down by people who obviously wear black shoes with a brown belt, and my singing voice is pure velvet, man, velvet.

Why am I telling you all this? Because Triana and the gang are about to examine the pod, and I thought you might need a diversion to keep you from biting off your fingernails.

The Spider bay had repressurized, and now life-support systems were restoring the air and warming the room after its exposure to the icy vacuum of space. Four of the Council members stood anxiously in the Spider bay control room, looking through the large pane of glass that separated them from the pod.

Triana felt a surge of various emotions. Being back in this room had an effect on her that she hadn't expected. She wished, for a moment, that Bon were here right now. It might force him to at least acknowledge that something had passed between them. Where was he? Was he consciously avoiding this moment for those very reasons?

Triana bit her lip and took a quick glance at Gap, who for some reason seemed to feel uncomfortable himself. What in this room could make him feel that way? It had to be the pod. Had to be.

She turned her attention back to the egg-shaped craft that sat silently, waiting for them. Slightly smaller than their own Spiders, it lacked the arms necessary to make it handy as a repair vehicle. But it was never designed for that. No, this was purely an escape vessel, a relay ship, a short-term form of transportation. A space taxi, almost. And an extremely mysterious taxi, at that.

Block lettering along one side identified the craft as a unit of the combined U.S./European Space Agency. Flag emblems, representing the six countries primarily responsible for the SAT33 mission, were stenciled under one of the windows. The windows themselves were dark, unwilling to give up the secrets locked inside.

Roc's voice broke the silence. "Okay, all systems are go, the room is pressurized and heat is back to normal. Please have your tickets ready, and remember, you must be at least forty-eight inches tall to ride. Thank you, and enjoy your day at Spaceland."

The Council members chuckled, thankful for Roc's talent at easing the apprehension they all felt.

"Here we go," Triana said, opening the door to the hangar and leading the group in. Lita, a look of wonder in her eyes, followed her, a small medical bag slung over one shoulder. Channy was next, unusually quiet for a change. She looked back nervously to make sure Gap followed closely next to her. He was a step behind, his free hand unconsciously rubbing the hand that stuck out from the sling, his eyes sizing up the new arrival on their ship.

They stopped about ten feet away, forming a small semi-circle around the pod. After a moment Triana reached into a pocket and retrieved a slip of paper that Roc had prepared for her. It contained detailed instructions on how to open the rear hatch of the pod from the outside. She had studied it earlier, but now scanned it again to refresh her memory. While the others waited, she walked up tentatively to an emergency panel and began to punch in a code. A small access door opened, revealing another keypad and a small handle. With another quick glance at her instructions, Triana keyed in one more code, then grasped the handle. She looked back at the other Council members.

"Ready?" she said.

Lita nodded. Gap gave a shaky thumbs-up with his good hand and said, "Let's do it."

At first the small handle felt as if it wasn't going to budge in her hand. But with a bit more muscle, Triana felt it turn. There was a squeak of air as the hatch on the pod released pressure, then a metallic clunk as it popped open almost two inches. Nobody moved, but instead attempted to peer through the crack into the dark interior.

Channy wrinkled her nose. "Smells . . . musty."

"Well," Lita said, "it's been sealed up for about four months. At least it doesn't smell like anything is . . . uh . . ."

Triana nodded and finished the sentence for her. "Dead."

Lita shrugged. "Yeah."

Channy, a grimace covering her face, turned to Lita. "Dead? You thought there might be something *dead* on this thing?"

"To tell you the truth, Channy, I had no idea. But it was possible. We don't know anything about it. Nothing would surprise me."

Triana, Gap, and Lita took a couple of steps closer to the hatch. Channy held her ground, the grimace lingering.

"Okay, I guess I should go first," Triana said. She reached out and pulled the hatch open another two feet.

"Maybe I should," Lita said. "I have the medical bag, after all." She laughed. "This will be my first house call."

"Hold it a second," Gap said. "Let me go first."

Channy, still standing back a few steps, snorted. "Oh, I suppose a one-armed man is stronger than any woman with two good wings?"

"No, that's not it. I just—"

Roc chimed in from the overhead speaker. "I would go, but I suppose a woman with two good wings is better than a computer with no legs."

"Never mind, I'll go first," Lita said. Without waiting for an argument she reached up to a handrail beside the open door and pulled herself up. Ducking her head inside the dark interior of the pod, she slipped through the opening, the medical bag swinging from the strap over her shoulder.

"Here, take this," Triana said, holding out a small flashlight. Lita snapped it on, and took another step inside. The others watched as she disappeared into the gloom, the tight beam of the flashlight swiveling from side to side.

In a moment Lita's voice called out to them. "It's set up a lot like our Spiders. Two pilot's seats up front, and a couple more seats here in the back." Pause. "Plenty of storage bins, it looks like. Whew, that musty smell is pretty strong, actually." Pause. "Oh, wow, there's a long cylinder in here that looks like it was set up for suspended animation, all right. The cover is made of glass, and it's kind of glazed. Hard to see inside." Pause. "There's another . . ." Pause. "Wait."

Triana and Gap leaned against the side of the pod, their heads sticking in through the hatch. Channy had walked up and stood directly behind them, her hands clenching and unclenching.

After a long moment of silence, Triana called out. "Lita?"

Nothing.

Triana called out again, louder this time. "Lita?"

Gap, his eyes wide, grabbed the handrail with his free hand and scrambled to get his foot up into the pod. The sling made it difficult to maneuver, and Triana started to help boost him inside. She felt the sweat begin to roll off her face. What was going on in there?

Just as she began to push Gap, she felt him stop. She looked up to see Lita standing just inside the door of the pod, a stunned look on her face. "Lita, what is it? Are you all right?"

Lita looked directly into Triana's eyes and said, "You are not going to believe this."

10

Hannah sat hunched over the computer in her room, punching in figures, checking them, and then entering some more. Out of the corner of her eye she noticed that her stylus pen was tilted slightly to the side. She reached out, straightened it so that it lined up parallel to the edge of the desk, and then looked again at her vidscreen.

How many times did she need to check it? Hannah was a disciple of numbers, and these numbers didn't lie. An unknown energy force was emitting a pulse from Titan, Saturn's largest moon, in a direct beam toward *Galahad,* even as the ship sped toward the edge of the solar system.

Two different feelings had taken hold of her. It was exciting to think of the possibilities, of what might be at the source of this power. The scientists on SAT33 had obviously detected it, and they were prominent leaders in their fields. The fact that she might share in their discovery was thrilling, to say the least.

But the other emotion was just as potent. Hannah couldn't help feel the icy touch of fear run down her spine. Whatever the origin of this beam, and whoever—or whatever—was responsible for it not only had found their ship as it hurtled through space, but also now tracked them. The beam was locked in like a laser. That had to imply some sort of intelligent source, didn't it?

And anything with that kind of ability and power could use that power to destroy them.

For a moment Hannah imagined *Galahad* as a slow-moving target caught in the crosshairs of a sniper, unable to scramble for cover, exposed and vulnerable in the vast openness of space.

She blinked twice to erase the vision from her mind.

If everything had gone according to plan, she figured, the pod should be safely aboard the ship by now. She was counting on finding additional information somewhere aboard the small craft, something that could help her discover more about this new mystery. Triana and the other Council members would probably be exploring it very soon. Hannah wanted to be a part of that project, now more than ever.

There was also a mountain of previously classified information that was about to become available. Triana had informed Hannah of Dr. Zimmer's "gift," and the data that would soon be pouring in. It could take ages to sift through all of it, but more answers might be lingering within.

She threw a quick glance at her sketch of Gap. How would he feel when he found out about her discovery?

Within a few seconds she began writing a priority e-mail message to Triana, requesting a meeting with *Galahad*'s Council.

"What is it?" Triana said. She stared up into the pod's open hatch, her heart racing, and scanned Lita's face. It was impossible to read her friend's expression. Channy, who had been hanging back a few feet, slowly crept up behind Triana and rested a hand on her shoulder. Triana felt the hand trembling.

Lita slowly cracked a smile. She gazed down at Gap, Triana, and Channy, and shook her head. "Uh, I could just tell you, but I think it would be better if you took a look for yourselves."

Channy said, "Oh, c'mon Lita, you're killing me. What is it?"

Lita's smile widened, then she turned and disappeared into

the gloom of the pod's interior. Gap, his hand still grasping the handrail, looked over his shoulder at the Council Leader.

"I would usually say 'ladies first,' Tree, but maybe I should go first, eh?" He pulled himself up with his good hand, and then turned to help Triana and Channy as they scrambled inside.

It took a moment for their eyes to get accustomed to the dim light inside the pod. A few lights from the craft's instrument panels cast a spooky glow, so that even with her fellow crew members around her Triana felt uncomfortable. She picked her way to the front of the pod and sat down in the pilot's seat. It took a few seconds, but eventually she found the dial that controlled the internal lights.

Climbing to her feet, she took a quick visual inventory. She noted the two seats attached near the escape hatch, and the storage bins that lined two of the walls. She heard a low humming sound, and followed it to a small machine that appeared to be pumping liquid through plastic tubing. The object that dominated the small space, however, was obviously the cylinder that Lita had mentioned. It was indeed a tube created for suspended animation during long space voyages. Triana joined the others as they stood next to it.

"Nobody home," Channy said, peering through the frosted glass cover. "Empty."

Triana felt her breath escape in a rush, and a feeling of relief washed over her. She had dreaded the idea that another adult might board their ship, another adult with Bhaktul Disease, cryogenically asleep or not. How would she have handled the decision to wake them up?

That didn't matter anymore. The cylinder was empty.

Lita turned to a small table against the far wall, the smile still on her face. "I have to admit," she said, "I've been a little confused ever since I received that e-mail from *Galahad* Command. It instructed me to prepare an injection that Roc claimed was probably meant to help resuscitate someone from suspended animation. But I checked our computer banks for the design of this pod. They really are a lot like our Spiders, built mainly for short trips, maintenance work, quick hauls from the surface to an orbiting platform. Suspended animation equipment was never supposed to be part of them."

She let the medical bag slip off her shoulder and zipped it open. "But I guess someone on SAT33 rigged this up before they launched it. They added that large tube, obviously intended to hold an adult. And, they added this, too." She stepped to one side to reveal another cylinder.

Triana, Gap, and Channy stood beside the table with her. This tube was much smaller, about two feet long and a foot wide. The plastic tubes from the whirring machine fed directly into one end of the cylinder, and the Council members could feel heat radiating from it, as if an internal furnace had kicked on recently.

Lita said, "It's just big enough to hold . . ." Her voice trailed off. Triana, peering down into the small tube, finished the sentence for her.

"A cat."

Gap started to laugh. "I don't believe it. A cat."

Channy crowded in to see for herself. "A cat?"

All four Council members bent over the glass-covered cryogenic case and stared at the lone occupant of the pod. The cat, with its mottled orange and black coloring, began to stir. One leg twitched, and a series of small shudders caused its coat to ripple.

Gap kept his eyes on it, and said, "So . . . do we open the case?"

Triana bit her lip. "I think so. Lita, do you—"

Before she could finish the sentence Lita pushed a button that released the glass top of the cylinder. It ticked open with a wisp of air. Lita had the syringe in her hand, and looked for a place to administer the shot. She settled on the flank of one of the cat's hind legs, and plunged the needle in. For a moment it looked as if there would be no reaction. But then, another shudder, this one more intense, racked the small animal, and sent a spasm through its body.

Channy looked up with a worried expression. "Maybe . . . maybe we should take it up to Sick House, you think?"

Lita nodded. "I think you're right. Let me see . . ." She delicately unhooked a series of electrodes that were attached to the cat's side, ran her hands under its body, and scooped it out of the tube. Channy pulled out the small yellow blanket that had been bunched up beneath the animal and tucked it around the small, furry body. Together the two girls made their way through the pod's hatch and disappeared, leaving Triana and Gap to ponder what they had just discovered.

Finally, Triana chuckled. "Well, it looks like our passenger load just climbed to 252."

"I like even numbers better anyway," Gap said, returning her grin. "And since you're the only person on the ship without a roommate, I guess that means—"

"Uh, no," Triana said, shaking her head. "Not that I don't like cats. I love them. But I'm allergic." She looked out the hatch. "Besides, if I know Channy like I think I do, you're not going to get that little fur ball away from her."

Gap nodded. "You're probably right." His face took a serious turn. "Tree, what in the world is a cat doing on this pod? And where is the owner?" He indicated the large, empty cryogenic cylinder. "This looks like someone planned on coming along for the ride. So . . . where are they?"

"I don't know," Triana said. "We never seem to go very far without stumbling across a mystery, do we?"

"Listen, this whole business with Titan and the missing scientists has been mysterious since we flew into the neighborhood," Gap said. He rubbed his short, spiky hair. "Well, I suppose I should start checking out the rest of the pod. Maybe some of the answers are stowed in here somewhere. There has to be at least a data disc or two that explains all of this."

"It's getting late. You should probably get some sleep, and we'll start fresh in the morning. I'll bring some help. With your arm in that sling you could use some extra hands." Triana reached out and touched Gap's shoulder in a gesture of friendliness, then immediately regretted the move when she saw the expression on his face. She withdrew her hand and smiled awkwardly before climbing out of the pod.

Walking through the Spider bay to the exit door she bit her lip and wondered when the tension between them would end. At the same time another thought of Bon forced its way into her mind. Where was he? How much longer could she pretend to ignore the situation before she broke down and confronted him?

"What a mess," she muttered as the door to the hallway slid open.

Inside the pod, Gap watched her walk out of the bay. For a moment he had considered calling out to her, hoping he could get her to turn around and come back. But . . . what would he say?

Nothing. Get your mind back on the job, he told himself.

He turned around and scanned the interior of the small metal pod. Were there answers somewhere among its contents? "And," he said aloud, "just what are we going to do with a cat?"

11

Gap stood just outside the pod in *Galahad*'s Spider bay. Sleep had not come easily the night before. He had tossed and turned, thinking about the mysterious vessel on their ship, about the unexpected discovery of the cat, and the spooky image of the empty cryogenics tube. Along with the eerie silence coming from SAT33, it was enough to keep his brain doing somersaults for hours. He had managed to block most of his thoughts about Triana. Most of them. At one point, however, he realized that a few of his spare thoughts were focused on another girl on the ship.

It was shortly after eight o'clock, and the Spider bay buzzed with activity. Inside the pod, Triana directed the unloading of equipment, storage bins, files, and various other items. Three or four crew members at a time rummaged through the pod, while another group waited outside the hatch to collect the pieces as they were handed down. A couple of long tables had been set up to store the contents, and the team marched back and forth between the tables and the pod like ants removing pebbles from their hill.

All of this activity made Gap feel useless. Silently he steamed over the fact that his own out-of-control emotions had essentially led to his arm being in the sling, which now prevented him from being as productive as he would like. He was a spectator, again.

He watched Triana jump in and out of the pod, which only made him feel even more sorry for himself. He wandered over to one of the tables and began poking around, picking up one thing for a moment before setting it down and grabbing something else. A lot of the items were meaningless to him, but must have been important to the workers on the research station.

"Look at this," he heard Triana say, and looked up to see her standing on the other side of the table. In her hands she held a cloth bag, about the size of a gym workout bag. She had one arm deep inside, moving things around.

"What's that?" he said.

Triana shrugged. "Don't know. We found it in one of the storage bins at the back of the pod. It doesn't really look official, you know? Looks like the kind of bag that someone would have thrown on board if they were going for a ride."

She pulled her hand out of the bag and set down a few things on the table. Gap noticed what appeared to be a couple of canisters of water, along with packets that contained energy blocks, not unlike the ones served in *Galahad*'s Dining Hall. Triana spread them out, and then looked up at Gap.

"I guess this proves that somebody planned on being aboard, wouldn't you say?"

"Yeah," Gap said, "but these would have only lasted someone a few days, at most. The pod has been orbiting Titan for several months."

"The cryo tube, though," Triana said. "If they were asleep they wouldn't need food or water. These supplies must have been an emergency stock. Just enough to get them into orbit, and maybe in case they woke up early before we picked them up."

She dug her hand back into the bag and came out with a smaller plastic bag, about the size of a purse. She pulled it open. The first thing to fall out was a narrow red nylon strip about eight inches long. Triana smiled.

"This has to be a collar for our new little friend. Yeah, look, here's a name tag even." She squinted and turned the shiny metal tag into the light, then read the inscription. "Iris. Well, at least we know what to call . . . her, I think. Iris. That's cute."

She set the collar on the table and dug back into the bag. This time her hand came out holding a small metallic-looking ball. It was a little smaller than a tennis ball but extremely light, with four small, rounded spikes protruding from the top, bottom, and opposite sides. Triana tossed it up and caught it, then lobbed it toward Gap, who caught it with his good hand.

"What do you think? A cat toy?" she said.

Gap examined the ball. "I don't know. Maybe." He noticed a handful of small vents that were etched into the metal ball. Putting it up by his ear, he shook it a couple of times to see if there was a bell or a rattle inside.

"If there's anything in there, it doesn't make a sound." He frowned. "If it's a cat toy, it's not a very good one. What cat would want to play with this?"

"Probably pretty slim pickings on the research station when it came to toys, don't you think?" Triana said. "Maybe this is the best they could do."

Gap shrugged and placed the metal ball on the table alongside the other items from the bag. "What else do you see?"

Triana reached back into the plastic bag and extracted a stuffed mouse that had seen better days, then a handful of tiny plastic Baggies with cat treats in them. "Looks like Iris had a few snacks packed away, too." She paused. "Oh, wow, look at this."

She held up what looked like a wallet. She hesitated for a second, and then looked at Gap. "I hate to be nosy, but I guess we have to find out everything we can." She slowly pulled the wallet open and stared at the contents with a blank expression. Then she handed it to Gap without a word.

He fumbled with his free hand to maneuver the wallet open, and found himself looking at a photograph. In it, a woman who looked to be in her late twenties was holding what was obviously the cat they had found in the pod. The woman had short, dark hair, dark eyes, and a glittering smile. She wore a pair of shorts and a T-shirt, and squinted as she looked into the sun. The setting appeared to be a park on Earth, with large trees in the background and bright blue skies. Gap felt a momentary pang of homesickness. He had forgotten what a stroll in a sun-splashed park was like.

He looked back up at Triana. "This is . . . sad," is all he could think to say.

Triana sighed. "Yeah. But, at least we can see who probably stored Iris on the pod." She took the wallet back from Gap and stuffed it into the plastic bag before setting it on the table.

Gap fidgeted for a moment. "Uh, makes you wonder again why the cat was on the pod . . . but not her."

"Uh-huh. But we have a picture. We should be able to find out who the woman is. Or was. I don't know if we'll ever find out why she wasn't in there, too."

She stared at Gap for a second and then smiled faintly. "The mysteries just keep on coming, don't they?"

12

The Exercise Room on *Galahad* was packed for the early afternoon workout sessions. Located on the lower level, across from the Airboard track, and down the hall from the Storage Sections, it was busy from morning until night as the various work shifts on the ship began and ended. "Stay active," Dr. Zimmer had lectured over and over again. "You'll need every bit of strength and energy when you reach Eos. Don't take it for granted that you're young and healthy. Exercise, exercise, exercise."

Channy was in charge, and there wasn't a more qualified person. The daughter of a physical therapist and exercise guru, Channy lived for physical activity. Besides acting as trainer for 250 other crew members, she also taught dance classes that were generally full.

Right now, however, was her own personal workout time. Her roommate, Kylie Rickman, was sprawled out on the floor beside her, both of the girls stretching their leg muscles. Activity whirled around them, with various crew members peddling stationary bikes, bent over exercise balls, or running on treadmills. A large vidscreen in the Exercise Room was tuned to the actual scene outside the ship, displaying the dazzling sight of Saturn as it receded into the backdrop of stars. Speakers hung from the ceiling and pumped music throughout the room. It was loud, but Channy and Kylie were able to talk over it.

"So where will it stay?" Kylie said.

Channy leaned back, her leg twisted under her. "I don't know. I guess that's up to Tree. There have already been about twenty requests to keep her. This cat is an instant celebrity on the ship. But that's not the main issue, anyway."

"Oh?"

"No. We have to figure out what to feed this new crew member. Unless," Channy said, extending the bent leg and tucking the other one under her, "she likes simulated tuna fish from our Dining Hall. She's gonna run out of her little treats pretty quickly."

"How's she doing?"

"Pretty good. Lita has her wide-awake now, and is just keeping her for observation." Channy laughed. "Of course, she's not really sure what she's observing. Iris is just happy for now to walk around Sick House, sniffing everything. Seems normal enough to me."

The two girls finished their stretching and walked over to a pair of treadmills. Kylie couldn't help notice how taut and muscular Channy's physique looked through her bright yellow T-shirt. It was almost intimidating.

They began with a quick walking pace on the treadmills, eventually working their way up to a jog. After a few moments of silent running Channy broke into a laugh.

"What's so funny?" Kylie said, beginning to breathe hard.

"I just thought about something else with Iris, something that is just too perfect."

"What are you talking about?"

"Well, our new guest is going to need a litter box, isn't she?"

Kylie looked over at her roommate. "Yeah, so what's so funny about that?"

"Think about it," Channy said. "There's one giant, natural sandbox on this ship, isn't there? Just wait until Bon sees this cat nosing around his crops." She giggled, and then cranked the treadmill up to a brisk run. Kylie laughed before programming in the change to try to keep up.

* * *

Triana stuck her head into Sick House and found Lita sitting at her desk, tapping a stylus pen against her cheek.

"You wanted me?" Triana said.

Lita put the stylus on her desk and waved the Council Leader in. "Yeah, thanks for coming by. I know you have a lot going on."

"What's up?"

"Well," Lita said, "hopefully nothing. But I think you should see this."

She motioned for Triana to follow her over to the doorway leading to an adjoining room. Looking through they could see the twenty beds that made up *Galahad*'s hospital ward. Six of the beds were occupied. Alexa Wellington, Lita's assistant, was scribbling on an electronic work pad, noting some readings on one of the patients, a Japanese girl whom Triana recognized as one of the workers in Bon's Agricultural section. She was talking quietly to Alexa, answering questions. The other five crew members were either asleep or resting quietly with their eyes closed.

Triana looked quizzically at Lita. "Six patients? What happened? Was there an accident?"

Lita shook her head. "No. And that's why I called you." The tone of her voice matched the concerned look on her face. She motioned for Triana to return with her to the office.

Triana pulled a chair over and sat next to her friend, knowing that Lita would never have summoned her if she weren't worried about something serious. This much was sure: since their launch from Earth four months earlier, *Galahad*'s Sick House had never handled six patients at the same time.

"All six reported the same symptoms," Lita said. "Severe headache, the type that wipes you out and puts you in bed. Dizziness. And a muffled sense of hearing. Two of them described it as the sound you hear when you have water stuck in your ears."

"Could it be migraines?" Triana said.

"None of them has ever suffered from that before, so I would rule it out. And it's not just these six. Two other crew members popped in and asked for a pain pill. They were having headaches, too, but not bad enough to knock them off their feet. I gave each of them one pill and told them to climb into bed and take it easy for a while."

Triana bit her lip. "Radiation maybe? Something leaking through the shields after our pass around Saturn?"

"I considered that, too, but no. All of the readings are normal. Roc ran another check just before you got here, and everything's fine."

Triana called out to the computer. "Roc, any ideas here?"

"Have you heard some of the music they're listening to?" Roc said. "I'm surprised their heads don't spin right off their shoulders."

"Roc, please . . ."

"You're right. Some of the songs are fine. I actually found myself singing along the other day to one called 'Get Me a Ladder, I Need to Get Over You.' "

Lita saw Triana's pained expression. "Just give him a minute. He usually gets it out of his system pretty quickly."

"All right," Roc said, "if we must get down to business. No, there is no radiation leaking into the ship. The slingshot effect itself around Saturn would not produce any symptoms such as these, either. I'm going to analyze the recent crop harvests and match them to the crew members' health histories and see if there might be something in the food that their bodies can't process. That's a long shot, of course, and highly unlikely to affect six people out of 251."

Triana spoke up. "Roc, what about the pod we brought aboard the ship. Any chance that it could have brought some sort of contamination with it?"

"Not very likely. Besides, four of the six patients reported getting their headaches prior to the interception."

"What kind of tests are you running?" Triana said to Lita.

"Nothing too extensive yet. I wanted to see if the symptoms lasted very long before I poked and prodded them too much. I'd at least like to find out if there is something they have in common. Have they been in the same area of the ship? Have they eaten the same foods? I'm even going to check their workout schedules to see if there's some kind of connection in their exercise routines. But right now, I just don't have much to go on."

Triana glanced back toward the room where the six patients were being treated. "I'm getting a bad feeling about this. I think you are, too."

Lita didn't respond, which told Triana she was right.

"All right, then," Triana said, getting to her feet. "Let me know if anything changes. In the meantime, don't forget about our Council meeting tomorrow morning. Early."

"Not too early, I hope," Roc said. "I'm useless before noon."

13

It was dawn on *Galahad*. Or, as close to the feeling of dawn as possible. Roc had begun to bring up the lights around the ship, easing them from their muted overnight glow to the vivid radiance that would soon flood the rooms and corridors. The gentle background sound of waves crashing against the shore—one of several night sounds that could be programmed individually—was fading out. A faint trace of the smell of morning rain drifted from air vents. The ship was preparing to come to life for another busy day.

Triana was alone in the corridor. For the third day in a row she had been out of bed before five thirty, and now, a few minutes before six, she made her way to the Dining Hall. She had slept fitfully, wrestling with several different areas of concern: the pod, the cat, the empty cryo cylinder, the crew members suffering from intense headaches . . . and Bon. Always Bon.

Her mind told her over and over again to forget about him, that he was high maintenance, that his surly attitude would only continue to cause problems.

But something else within her—within her heart?—cried out that Bon was actually very much like her: intelligent, yet lonely. Both were intensely dedicated to their mission and responsibilities, and they both tended to guard their feelings rather closely.

And both had shown that they could drop that guard for a glimpse into their emotions.

Triana also admitted to herself that Bon's smile—on the rare occasion that he flashed it—was remarkably similar to her dad's. Could there be more below the surface?

Her dad. What would he have thought of Bon?

These were the questions that had raced through her mind, keeping her awake throughout the night. "Get a grip," she had finally muttered out loud, probably around two that morning.

She walked into the Dining Hall, expecting to have it to herself as well. To her surprise there were about a dozen crew members scattered in groups of two and three, and they all acknowledged her entry with a nod or a wave. She returned the gestures and picked up a tray, which was soon filled with an energy block, a plate of fruit, and a glass of simulated orange juice. Finding a table in the corner, she sat down by herself.

She started in on her breakfast, a meal that she made sure never to miss no matter how busy her life was. With the press of a button she turned on the small vidscreen attached to the table and pulled up the trajectory map of their voyage. A small blue dot to the far left side represented Earth, causing a momentary pang of sadness to ripple through Triana. The dotted line that plotted their course wove through the asteroid belt, beyond the orbit of Jupiter (although they had not come close to the solar system's largest planet), and eventually wrapped around Saturn.

Triana speared a chunk of cantaloupe and stared at the course laid out for the next several months. They would not encounter another planet until their journey ended almost five years hence and they took up orbit around Eos and its two Earth-like planets.

But that didn't mean they were finished with this solar system just yet. Triana chewed her breakfast and concentrated on the minefield of objects they still had to deal with before shooting into interstellar space. It was known as the Kuiper Belt.

They would be the first people—and last?—to lay eyes on the band of cosmic leftovers that circled beyond the outer planets.

Remnants of the solar system's birth, scientists calculated that possibly millions of comets, chunks of rock, and other debris danced slowly through the farthest fringes of the sun's pull. An occasional tug from Neptune's or Jupiter's gravity would launch one of the comets toward the sun.

Comets. Triana couldn't think of the word without the searing memory of Comet Bhaktul and the curse it had delivered to Earth and its people—including her father, one of the first people to contract the deadly disease and die from it.

The comet had not only killed her father, it had also dispensed a death sentence on mankind. The 251 passengers on *Galahad* would soon be all that was left of the human race, barring a miracle back on Earth. The magnitude of their mission began to weigh on Triana again for the first time in several weeks. She silently finished the last bite of grapefruit and pushed the plate away from her. A somber mood settled over her. After a moment she snapped off the trajectory map and drained the last of her orange juice.

She glanced at the time and realized she still had almost forty minutes until the Council meeting. She could take a walk through the ship to clear her head, or do something more productive.

Adjusting the vidscreen she punched in the code for her schoolwork. A worksheet popped up, automatically aligned to where she had left off the last time. They were all pilgrims, speeding across an ocean of stars to the new world . . . but they were still students, too. Each of the 251 passengers on *Galahad* was required to complete preselected study programs each month, and if all went according to plan the ship would reach its destination with each crew member holding the equivalent of four college degrees.

This particular lesson was in mathematics, a subject in which Triana excelled. But as the minutes slipped past, she found that her mind kept drifting back to her dad. Her concentration on the math problems waned until she finally sat back, saved the work she had finished, and snapped the vidscreen off.

When she looked up again she noticed that the Dining Hall had filled considerably, as more and more crew members prepared for another workday. She stood up and motioned to a group of four that her table was available, then walked out into the hallway. She had almost twenty minutes of time to kill before the meeting, and decided to take that walk after all.

Channy stood looking up at the stars through the dome. She didn't make it up to the Farms very often, but each time the sight of open space amazed her. Memories of visits with her sister to the planetarium near their English home flooded in on her, bittersweet memories that made the always-chatty teen grow strangely quiet. But the planetarium, though impressive, could never match the real thing. Here a sprawling horizon-to-horizon showcase of stars was humbling, a powerful reminder to Channy that she was virtually a microscopic speck in the universe.

She bent to one knee and looked down a row of leafy vegetables that were prospering in the artificial sunlight. "Iris," she called out, not too loudly. "C'mon, Iris." She had dropped the cat off fifteen minutes earlier and then left to check in on the morning exercise group. Now she was back to gather up their new guest and take her to the Council meeting.

Channy took a nervous glance around, afraid to run into Bon for fear that he would immediately grasp exactly why she had brought the animal up to the dirt-covered domes. She didn't think that anyone had broken the news to the surly Swede yet, and she didn't want to be the first.

She stood and walked about twenty feet into the crop, then kneeled again. "Iris, c'mon girl. Iris." She lowered her head to ground level, sweeping the vicinity with her eyes, looking for the orange and black markings through the foliage. Nothing. Just how far, she wondered, could the cat roam in a quarter of an hour? Back on her feet, she stood with hands on hips, deciding which direction to take.

Suddenly, a hand grasped her shoulder from behind, and Channy let out a scream and jumped a couple of feet. Quickly turning, she found herself face-to-face with a grinning Gap.

"Lose something?" he said.

"Don't *do* that," she said. Panting, she bent over, hands on her knees, and laughed. "You scared me to death." Catching her breath, she looked up at him. "What are you doing here?"

"I heard you brought that cat up here, so I thought I'd help you round her up before you-know-who catches you."

Channy brushed dirt from her knees. "Yeah, well, I haven't seen Bon yet. In fact, come to think of it, I haven't seen him in a while. What's going on with him?"

"You mean besides his usual Mr. Happy routine? I have no idea. The last I heard from him was at the Council meeting a couple of days ago."

"So, since we're alone, let me ask you something," Channy said.

Gap scooped up a handful of soil and let it sift between his fingers. "Oh, no," he said playfully. "What was I thinking? I should have known better than to get cornered like this."

"I just wanted to ask how things were going with Triana. You don't seem as interested anymore."

Gap's face flushed a bit, and he stared off into the interior of the crops as if looking for Iris. "Oh, I've been too busy to worry about that."

Channy raised her eyebrows. "Who do you think you're talking to here?"

"Yes, I know, your 'love radar' and all that nonsense."

"There you go again," Channy said, "making fun of my natural gifts. Well, I know I was right then, and I'm definitely picking up a cold front in the last couple of months. Have you really lost interest, or does Triana just intimidate you?"

Gap laughed. "That must be it. I'm intimidated."

Together they walked farther into the crop, scanning each side of the path for signs of Iris. Channy was quiet for a moment, then casually said, "You know who's really cute?"

"No, Channy, who's really cute?"

"That girl from Alaska. Hannah. She's smart, too."

It took all of his concentration for Gap not to physically react to the name. How in the world did Channy do it? How did she *always* seem to read his mind when it came to girls? He decided to play innocent.

"Who, Hannah? Yeah, I guess. I don't know her very well."

"Well, maybe you should get to know her."

He stopped and turned to Channy. "Why don't we just name a new Activities Director for the ship and change your title to Doctor of Love?"

Channy wandered down another row of crops. She called back over her shoulder, "That's funny. I thought love *was* an activity." She pushed a leafy plant to one side and cupped a hand to her mouth. "Iris. C'mon, Iris."

Gap shook his head, watching the petite girl in the bright pink T-shirt disappear among the plants. He tilted his head back for a moment, taking in the same spectacle of starlight that Channy had been watching earlier. What good did it do, he wondered, to try to keep any romantic secrets on this ship? Channy's radar wasn't just good; it was eerie.

He let out a long sigh, then pushed his way into the crops in search of an orange and black cat.

14

They say that to be in command is to be automatically lonely. By now you might have already figured out that Tree is a fairly lonely person anyway, and the isolation that comes from being in command maybe even suits her personality.

But that makes me sad. She has one of the kindest hearts you'll ever meet, but it's been roughed up quite a bit in her short life. Now she guards it fiercely, and I suppose I can't blame her for that.

Thank goodness for Lita Marques.

The slightly curved walls of the corridor created something of a tunnel, which helped the circulation of air within *Galahad*. And although all of the walls were covered with a thin spongy material, each level had its own color scheme, helping the crew members quickly identify their location as they made their way around the ship. This particular level, which housed the Dining Hall, Rec Center, and a number of offices and control centers, also was home to the Conference Room, where the Council held its meetings.

Triana's walk had ended up here, and she leaned against one of the curved walls outside the Conference Room. Lita had also arrived early, and was sitting on the floor with her back to the opposite wall, chatting with the Council Leader. The two girls had become friends during their long, grueling training schedule on Earth, and had grown even closer during the first four months in space. Triana had quickly realized that Lita was trustworthy and honest, which made it easy to talk with her during difficult times. Normally a shy and quiet person, Triana wasn't often comfortable making casual conversation but found that it came naturally when she was in the company of her friend from Mexico.

It would be all business when the meeting came to order, so for now the two girls enjoyed the chance to make small talk.

"Are you nervous? I sure would be," Triana said.

Lita smiled. "I've been playing the piano since I was seven, including recitals and school shows, so you'd think I would be cool up there. But you know what? I'll be just as nervous as I was the first time. What do you call it in America? Butterflies? Well, I'll have a stomach full of them when I walk out there."

Triana decided to tease her a bit. "Well, don't even think about the two hundred people staring at you, listening to every single note."

"Very funny. Actually, I always seem to calm down after I get started. The music just takes over, I guess. Plus, I'm not going to be the only one up there."

The concert had been Channy's idea. Since so many crew members played an instrument, she had recommended that several of them get together. Now, after three weeks of practice, the show was set. In about thirty-six hours the Learning Center, or School as it was better known, would be packed.

"And I don't want to brag," Lita said, "but I think we're pretty good. All we really need is someone to sing, and we could have a hit." Both girls laughed. "Even though we haven't written much of our own stuff yet. Right now we're just trying to tighten up on some of our old favorites."

"Why don't *you* sing?" Triana said.

Lita flashed her smile again. "Uh, no. That's one skill I don't have. Believe me, I'm perfectly happy hiding behind my electronic keyboard."

Gap came around a corner, a surprised look on his face. Probably can't believe somebody actually beat him to a meeting, Tree thought.

"What's going on?" Gap said. "Are we meeting out here in the hall?"

Triana shook her head. "No, just hanging out, waiting for everyone." She tried to put him at ease with a smile, and then realized that she had been doing that for weeks. Was it a matter of trying to overcompensate for the awkwardness between them? Gap was still being cordial to her, but his overall coolness had now dragged on for months. Maybe it was time for a talk with him, she decided, but the thought of that instantly settled like a knot in her stomach.

Lita, still sitting on the floor, looked up at Gap. "How's the arm?"

"Great. Couldn't be better."

"Hmm. Why don't you stop in to Sick House in the next day or two and we'll see about getting rid of that sling."

A sheepish look came over Gap. "Well," he said, pulling the arm out, "I've actually been doing this a lot lately." He waved the arm around a few times, and then noticed the alarmed look on Lita's face.

"Oh, great," she said, the smile disappearing. "Do you want to have that arm back in there for another two or three weeks? Stop doing that!"

Gap grinned. "Yes, mother." He slid the arm back into the sling.

Lita looked across the corridor at Triana, who was barely holding back a laugh. "Do you see why my job is so difficult? No respect." She turned back to Gap. "When you wake up tonight with pain, don't even think about slinking down to pick up some meds. You just sleep with some pain, okay, tough guy?"

Gap pulled the arm out one more time and blew a kiss toward

Lita with it. This time Triana couldn't hold back the laughter, and was glad to see that the corners of Lita's mouth were curling upward also.

"Well, everybody seems to be in a good mood this morning," Channy said, walking up to the group. Iris was cradled in her left arm. "The two princesses are here. I see you have all waited at attention. Her ladyship and I will see you now."

"Oh," Lita cooed, and held her hands out. Channy transferred the small cat to Lita, and then turned to face Triana.

"Are we meeting out here in the hall?"

Triana rolled her eyes, and then looked at Gap. "Maybe we should think about that. C'mon, let's go." She pushed off from the wall and walked into the Conference Room, followed by the other Council members.

As soon as they took their seats, Channy looked around. "I see that our jolly friend Bon isn't here yet."

"He'll be here," Triana said. "He hasn't missed a meeting yet."

As usual, she tried to deflect criticism from Bon. For one thing, as *Galahad*'s leader that kind of talk made her uncomfortable. But she also had to be honest with herself and admit that there were other feelings floating around inside her, too. Feelings that she still couldn't figure out. Feelings, she hoped, that wouldn't affect her ability to command properly. Bon could not be immune from discipline, nor receive any other special treatment, regardless of what she felt. For now she bit her lip and silently wished that he would walk through the door and spare her from having to deal with that particular issue.

The group chatted and laughed for a while, unconsciously killing time to allow Bon to show up. But after a few minutes, Triana brought the meeting to order. She was getting irked at the Swede by this point. It was true that he had never missed a meeting—until now, it seemed—and she couldn't help wonder if this was part of the new coolness he had developed around her. He wasn't quite as rude as he had been before the Spider bay incident, but still had kept a frosty distance. She decided to put her business face on and concentrate on the issues at hand.

"Let's take care of some minor items first," she said. "Hannah Ross is going to join us in a few minutes."

Gap raised his eyebrows. "Really? What's up?" He suddenly became aware of Channy's eyes on him, and did his best to seem only mildly interested.

Triana shook her head. "I don't know for sure. She sent me an e-mail and said she had something important to share about Titan."

"Yeah," Gap said. "I know she's really into that stuff. And I mean into it a lot."

"Well, I told her to give us a few minutes to take care of old business before she stopped in. Since we've wasted enough time waiting for Bon, let's go ahead and get started with the department reports. Gap, why don't you go first."

"Everything is running smoothly with Engineering. The slingshot around Saturn went perfectly, as you all know. The solar sails will stay retracted now, and the ion power drive is running at 94 percent." He brought up a trajectory image on the vidscreen, similar to the one that Triana had been looking at in the Dining Hall. "We're on course, and our next contact point will be the Kuiper Belt at the edge of the solar system."

For a few minutes he discussed some maintenance issues on the ship, and concluded with an update on the pesky water recycling units in the Agricultural Domes. They were each being inspected, and would hopefully be in top working condition within the week.

Triana nodded. "Channy, what do you have for us?"

"I'm happy to report that crew member fitness is excellent. So far everybody is participating like they should in the exercise programs."

"Of course they are," Gap said with a grin. "Nobody wants to get on your bad side and end up doing five miles on the treadmill."

"More like ten," Channy said. "All kidding aside, I'm really happy with all of the activity. Soccer, of course, is still number one, and I'm thinking about another tournament next month. Attendance in the dance classes seems to ebb and flow, but those who really like it never miss a class, so that's good." She looked at Triana. "I guess I don't have to be a nag . . . yet."

Chuckles rippled around the room. Then Lita recognized that it was her turn to speak, and the expression on her face grew serious. She filled everybody in on the sudden rash of patients at Sick House, and the similarity of their symptoms.

"The headaches are what really concern me. Medication is helping some, but we still haven't figured out the cause, and that could be something serious. We need to become medical detectives and solve this mystery soon."

Each member of the Council offered questions and suggestions about possible causes. Radiation? No. Stress? Maybe, but from what? General fatigue? Are they just tired from their four months working in space? Maybe, but why only isolated incidents?

"I'm still wondering if it has something to do with our encounter with Saturn," Lita said. "Nobody knows for sure what a huge gravitational object like that might do to some people."

Triana frowned. "I don't know about that. Roc, any comments?"

The computer said, "Sure. I've given it a lot of thought, and I think that from now on I'd like to be known as 'Your Honor.'"

Gap turned to Channy. "Is it just me, or is he getting more outrageous every week?"

Triana sighed. "Roc, please."

"Oh, all right. To answer Lita's concern about Saturn, that's not likely. The ship is affected, of course, but our life-support systems protect all of you from any damaging effects. I've checked and rechecked radiation levels, and that's not an issue. And each of the ship's air-filtration systems is fine, too. In other words, there's no ship malfunction that's to blame."

Although it was good news, it still left Triana concerned.

Could the patients' symptoms just be a fluke? Could it be some sort of stress reaction after all? Somehow she didn't think so.

Lita spoke up again. "Anyway, we also have our little friend here." She held up Iris, who was on the verge of falling asleep in her arms. They could all hear its purring as Lita stroked it softly behind the ears. "For now she seems to be happy with the fake fish from our Dining Hall. I've checked the data banks, and as long as we get her the proper amount of protein and minerals, she should be fine. Not the optimal diet, maybe, but not too bad."

Channy giggled. "Don't forget about the litter box situation."

"Ah, yes," Lita said. "The litter box. For now she's loving life up at the Farms. Uh, I don't know what Bon will have to say about that . . ."

Tree sighed. "Well, I don't see the harm if we maintain a little space for her somewhere in the Farm Section but away from the crops. I suppose we need to do a little research on the health ramifications. Roc should be able to help with that." She felt her eyes watering a little bit, and knew that if she got any closer to Iris her allergic reaction would intensify.

The door opened and everyone looked up to see Hannah Ross. She had a look on her face that seemed to be asking if she was too early. Tree smiled and indicated an open chair at the end of the table. "C'mon in, Hannah."

Hannah nodded at the Council and sat down. She chanced one quick glance at Gap, who seemed to be concentrating on a point somewhere in front of him on the table. She set her work pad in front of her and looked across at Triana.

The Council Leader said, "I think we're at a point where we can move on to new business. Any objections?" They all turned their attention to Hannah, who fumbled with her work pad before meeting their looks. She nervously cleared her throat.

"Let me just say that I don't have an answer for what I'm about to share with you."

"Wow," Channy said, laughing. "That's a great start."

Hannah exhaled, then started again. "Two days ago I started

running scans on Titan, Saturn's largest moon. I was hoping to use the data from the . . . the research station, but I don't think we have that yet. Is that right?"

Tree nodded but remained silent, listening.

"Anyway," Hannah said, "I've always been fascinated by this moon, and I'm not alone. It's one of the reasons there was a research station put there in the first place. Titan is a treasure trove of information. I couldn't wait to get started. In fact, I wish we could hang out here for a while."

Gap smiled at her. "Uh, unfortunately we have an appointment a few light-years away."

Hannah blushed at his attention, hoping that no one noticed. She looked back down at her work pad. "Then yesterday I noticed . . . it. I ran a couple of checks to make sure all of the equipment was operating smoothly, and it all came back okay. So, like I said, I have the data, but not an explanation."

Triana sat forward. "What is it?"

Hannah paused, then looked across the table at Triana. "Titan. It's talking to us."

15

Alexa Wellington stood with her clipboard beside the bed in Sick House. As Lita's primary assistant she was used to taking charge whenever Lita was called to a Council meeting. What she wasn't used to was being this busy.

She looked around *Galahad*'s hospital ward, amazed to see eight beds now occupied. When Lita had left just an hour earlier there had been six. Two more patients had checked in, both with the same symptoms as the others. Alexa handed one of the new patients, a fifteen-year-old girl from Michigan, a pain pill along with a cup of water.

"Has this been coming on, or did it happen suddenly?"

The girl cocked her head at Alexa and said loudly, "What?"

Alexa remembered that each of these crew members had reported a muffled sense of hearing. She repeated the question a little louder.

The girl told Alexa that it had come on quickly, about ten hours earlier. At first she had thought that she could work her way through it, and had even taken a pain pill. But it had only become worse, making it impossible for her to take a scheduled school exam. Instead she had reported to Sick House.

Alexa nodded and made a few notes on her work pad. She told the girl to try to rest, and walked back to her desk. She looked back through the door at the eight patients and frowned. What was going on? Was it possible that some nasty bug had somehow made it through the sterilization process before they had left Earth? If so, how? All 251 crew members had been kept in isolation for thirty days before the launch, in what was affectionately called the Incubator. When they finally had boarded *Galahad* it was assumed that they would be leaving all—or, almost all—of Earth's infectious diseases behind.

Besides, what kind of bug would hibernate this long before striking? And then strike so rapidly among various crew members?

The door to the outer hallway opened, interrupting her thoughts, and Alexa looked up to see Bon, supported by his roommate, Desi, stagger through the door. Bon looked terrible, his eyes barely slits, his mouth in a grimace, sweat trickling down his forehead. Desi looked alarmed, and without hesitation Alexa jumped up and said, "In here." She motioned for them to follow her into the hospital ward, where she quickly prepared a bed for Bon. Desi helped him onto it, and Alexa immediately leaned over him.

"Headache?" she asked, even though she knew the answer. Bon nodded slightly, which seemed to cause him even further pain. Alexa walked over to the dispenser and pulled out another pain pill, grabbed a cup of water, and brought it back to the Swede who raised a hand to her.

"I've . . . I've already taken two today," he managed to say through gritted teeth.

"Not this stuff, my friend," Alexa said. "This is much stronger. C'mon, sit up a little bit."

Bon slowly propped himself up on his elbows and took the pill, then fell back onto the pillow.

Alexa looked over at Desi, who shook his head. "I don't know," he said. "I came back to the room to pick something up and he was a mess. He's supposed to be at a Council meeting, so I knew that something had to be really wrong. He kept saying that he would be okay, but I waited around a few minutes and could see . . . well, see this. He's getting worse, if anything."

"What about you? How do you feel?" Alexa asked the Brazilian.

"Fine. I feel great."

Alexa nodded. Well, it's not something in their room, she decided. Environmental causes would be too easy, of course. And it's never easy.

"Thanks for bringing him in," she said to Desi.

"No problem. Well, actually it *was* a problem." Desi chuckled nervously. "It's not easy to get him to do something he doesn't want to do."

Alexa smiled back. "Yeah, so I've heard. I'll take care of him. You don't have to stick around."

Desi thanked her, and then put his hand on Bon's shoulder. "Take care of yourself, man. I'll check in on you later."

Bon nodded once, then mumbled, "Thanks."

Desi walked out, and Alexa turned to look into Bon's face, a worried expression creasing hers. A sober thought flashed through her mind.

We're in trouble.

The Conference Room on *Galahad* had grown quiet. Triana sat still, trying to digest what Hannah had just told them, then finally spoke up.

"What do you mean when you say that Titan is 'talking to us?' Just how would a moon talk to us?"

"I know it sounds crazy," Hannah said, "but that's the only way I can think to describe it right now."

"Okay. What exactly have you found?"

Hannah fidgeted with the work pad in front of her. "It's almost like an energy burst, but an immensely strong energy burst. I picked it up almost by accident, and thought it was just radioactive emissions from Titan. But two things jumped out at me. For one thing, the bursts are ordered, structured. They're pulsing bits of information, I think. It's almost like sentences, or paragraphs, or something like that. It's not just scattered, random jolts. These have some sort of pattern to them, almost like a radio signal. But I'm nowhere near close to deciphering them. I can tell you, though, that it's not something anyone has ever seen before."

Triana bit her lip. "You said that two things jumped out at you. What was the other one?"

Hannah took a deep breath. "You know, even with what appears to be a structure to the pulses, it's possible that it's something natural on the surface, or some sort of internal energy source inside the moon itself. At least, that's what I thought. I told myself, 'Don't get too excited, there is a reasonable explanation for this.' Until . . ."

"Until?" Triana said.

"Until I noticed something else. The pulses are following us."

Lita looked at Triana, then back at Hannah. "And what does *that* mean?"

"It means that the pulses are not just randomly flying off into space. They're concentrated into tight beams, aimed right at *Galahad*. Like a laser shot of energy."

Channy's mouth dropped open. "Are you saying . . . ?"

"Yeah," Hannah said. "The moon—or something on it—is talking to us. It's directly communicating with this ship. It's not a random pulse of energy. It's a . . . it's a phone call from Titan to us."

There was silence around the conference table while this began to sink in.

"Intelligent life," Channy finally murmured. "We've found intelligent life."

Gap spoke up. "Well, let's not get ahead of ourselves. Is it possible there's a connection with the research station? Could this energy pulse be something *they* set up? Maybe a sort of distress signal or something?"

Lita thought about this. "Well, it's possible. Since nobody has been able to reach them for a while, we don't know *what* they've cooked up. But is that likely? Would they have that technology?"

Triana addressed Hannah. "Who else knows about this?"

"I haven't told anyone."

"Good. Let's keep it that way for now, until we can find out a little more information. Hannah, what's the chance of deciphering this energy pulse? Could we figure out what it's trying to say?"

Hannah shrugged. "It's possible, I guess."

Triana called out to the computer. "Roc, let's get on this right away. A couple of things for us to check. One, is this a signal from the missing research scientists? Two, is this a message from an alien life-form on Titan?"

Once the words were out of her mouth, she realized the implications.

"And," she added, "can we talk back to them?"

16

The lights had begun to dim aboard *Galahad* as evening progressed. Several crew members were scattered around the Rec Room, some in the midst of various games, others simply lounging on the sofas and wide chairs after dinner. Occasional laughter filtered across the room, and the large vidscreen against the far wall was dialed into a landscape scene from Ireland, providing the evening's backdrop. A solitary figure in the corner quietly plucked out some notes on a guitar.

Gap was in one of his accustomed seats, facing a computerized Masego board, competing against Roc. The game, born in Africa, was a battle of strategy and intense concentration. The goal was to maneuver your three game pieces through a series of twisting paths before returning along a completely different trail. At the same time it was necessary to block your opponent's progress, driving him into danger.

Gap frequently played an electronic version against Roc, who relished any opportunity to goad him.

"How's your arm?" the computer asked.

"Fine," Gap said, trying to concentrate on the game board.

"I hear that you might be getting rid of that sling pretty soon."

"Um-hm," Gap mumbled.

"And you'll probably be right back up Airboarding, I suppose."

Gap took his eyes off the board and looked at Roc's sensor.

"Are you trying to distract me? That's pretty rude, you know. I don't talk while you're thinking about your next move."

"That's because I already know my next three moves. I don't have to agonize over every detail like you."

"Ha-ha," Gap said. "A little quiet, please."

Roc remained silent for a few seconds as Gap considered his next move, a crease forming on his forehead as he studied the screen. Then, reaching out, he punched in his move. In one second Roc countered, blocking Gap's route across the game board.

"Your turn," whispered the computer. "I'll be over here being quiet."

Gap decided to try a new strategy, and instead of overthinking his line of attack, he moved quickly, punching in a counter move. In a flash Roc answered again, this time opening a new route for himself and blocking Gap at the same time. Gap murmured something under his breath, a look of disgust on his face.

"Could be the pain medication for your arm," Roc offered.

"I'm not taking anything for it anymore," Gap said.

"Oh. Well, maybe you should," said the computer voice of Roy Orzini.

Gap started to answer, then changed his mind. After a moment he offered his resignation from the game and pushed back his chair.

"Maybe another game tomorrow?" Roc said.

"Sure," Gap said, running a hand through his hair. "Hey, let me ask you something. This pulse from Titan. I gotta believe it's coming from those missing scientists. It couldn't really be some other life-form trying to communicate with us, could it?"

"Well, obviously it *could* be," Roc said. "Unlikely, maybe, and certainly a landmark discovery. But always possible."

"Have you made any progress in decoding it?"

"I just spoke with Tree about that," the computer said. "I'm running a new check on it right now because it's not a typical communications signal."

"What do you mean?"

"I mean, your basic signal moves in one direction. For instance, we send a message back to Earth and it originates here and travels in one direction, back to Earth. They receive it, and if they choose to respond, they make a similar connection. One way."

"Yeah, so?"

"Well, I'm not completely sure, but I think one of the things that has made this signal so difficult to pin down is because I think it's a two-way communication."

Gap's face was blank. "Two-way?"

"Yes. I just told Tree that it seems that the signal is coming from Titan, being received by us, and then working its way back to the original source. As if the signal is depositing information here, and then taking back information from *Galahad*."

Gap stewed on this. "So, it's almost like an old-fashioned computer hacker?"

"Pretty much. Only this is much more involved than that. This energy beam seems to be invading everything on the ship, not just our computer banks. And, since *Galahad* was never designed to fend off anything like that, we really don't have any defense for it."

"So, what do we do? Just let it pick our pockets?" Gap said.

"I'm not sure what we *can* do right now. Until we discover exactly what we're dealing with, whoever—or whatever—is responsible for this energy pulse has the capability of learning everything about us."

Lita and her assistant, Alexa, were exhausted. They had both skipped dinner, and had worked almost ten hours nonstop. The hospital ward in Sick House now had twelve patients occupying beds, most of them asleep, the others drifting in and out of consciousness. Nothing seemed to be working to ease their pain, and Lita had grown frustrated.

And it wasn't confined to just these twelve, apparently. Five other crew members had reported to Sick House with a headache, but were not as serious. They had been sent back to their own rooms with pain medication and orders to take it easy for at least another day.

Seventeen total, twelve of whom had been admitted. If it wasn't an epidemic, it was close enough. Lita tapped a stylus pen against her cheek while Alexa checked off the names of assistants and volunteers who had agreed to help out around Sick House during the crisis.

Alexa set her work pad aside and crossed her arms. "So, are we at the point that we can blame it on this . . . this energy beam, or whatever it is?"

"I don't think there can be any question anymore. It's too much of a coincidence. This beam intercepts the ship, and suddenly we have a dozen kids flat on their backs."

"But how is it possible?" Alexa said. "I mean, Saturn and Titan are already way behind us, and dropping farther away every minute."

Lita set down her stylus and called out to the computer. "Roc, any answer for that?"

The computer's voice was as close to serious as Lita had ever heard it. "We're dealing with an energy beam so strong, and so concentrated, like a finely tuned laser, that it's possible it could stay with us for weeks to come. We won't be able to outrun its effect for a while."

"Why are these patients being affected and not the rest of us?" Alexa said.

"We all vibrate with energy," Roc said. "We're beings made up of energy, actually, and each person has a wavelength, almost like a radio frequency. This beam coming from Titan vibrates on a frequency that is obviously very close to the same frequency as our guests at Sick House. Their internal energy pattern somehow 'connects' with this pulsing beam, and the result is pain. Extreme pain, it turns out.

"And," the computer added, "we're rapidly approaching the point where we need to be concerned about long-term effects."

Alexa fixed a steady gaze on Lita, then back to Roc's glowing red sensor. "You mean, like brain damage?"

"That's exactly what I mean. We have no idea what these energy waves are doing to the ship or to the crew, but extreme headaches for an extended period of time can't be good."

Lita was thoughtful for a moment, and then said, "What about a shield of some sort? Is there some way we can block the pulse to these dozen—well, actually, seventeen—patients until we're out of range?"

"I would say no," Roc replied. "This beam is powerful enough to chase after us this far, then penetrate the ship. An Airboard helmet won't stop it, and I can't think of any other materials we would have to do the trick."

Their conversation was interrupted by the sound of running feet, and a breathless assistant dashed out of the hospital ward. "Uh, I think you'd better get in here," she said to Lita.

Lita and Alexa jumped to their feet and followed the girl. "What is it?" Lita said.

"I'm not sure," the girl said. "You need to see for yourself."

She led them over to the bed where Bon was lying. Lita stood on one side, Alexa on the other, and together they stared at the Swedish Council member for a few seconds.

"What am I looking for?" Lita said. "I don't . . ."

Bon suddenly opened his eyes. Alexa shrieked and jumped backward, her hand covering her mouth in horror. Lita felt a shock wave of fear ripple through her body.

Bon's eyes glowed. His pupils had swelled until there was hardly any white to be seen, creating an eerie sensation within Lita, as if he were staring straight through her. Outer rings around the pupils cast an orange tinge, shimmering and moving, circling. It was the creepiest sight Lita had ever seen, and it took almost half a minute before she could start breathing again.

Nobody spoke. The assistant who had summoned them stepped back another few feet, her hands clutched together under her chin. Lita struggled to regain her composure, to call upon the medical training that had earned her the right to run the department. But nothing had prepared her for this.

Just as she started to relax, the shock doubled. Bon's mouth fell open, emitting not one voice, but several mixed together. It was a chorus of voices, all speaking at once in a garbled jumble of noise, a tangled mess of sounds. For a few moments it was as if multiple people occupied Bon's head, all of them competing for the right to be heard.

The eyes had been creepy. This was absolutely terrifying.

Alexa, like the assistant, backed away, her mouth open. Lita was unable to move, unable to take her eyes from Bon's face. After about thirty seconds of garbled sounds, his mouth closed, his eyes drooped shut, and he fell back into a state of unconsciousness.

Lita finally looked across at Alexa. "Call Tree. Right now."

The words were barely out of her mouth when an excited voice broke in over the intercom. "Gap Lee to the Engineering Section. Emergency. Gap Lee, Engineering. Emergency."

Lita looked at Alexa again. "What's happening to us?"

17

Gap sprinted down the hall, mindful of his tender left arm. When the emergency message had reached him over the intercom, he hadn't bothered to recover the sling from his dresser, leaving it behind as he raced out the door. The arm felt awkward now that it was exposed, but he was sure that was mostly mental.

Crew members could hear his pounding feet before he turned the corner, and they backed up against the wall to let him pass. He rushed into the lift and made his way down to the Engineering Section. Bursting through the door he could see the nervous faces of the crew as they awaited his arrival.

"What is it?" he said, his chest heaving and sweat trickling down his forehead.

One of his top assistants, a sixteen-year-old girl named Ramasha, stepped forward. "It's the ion power drive. It seems to be stuttering."

"Stuttering?"

"That's what it seems like. It's skipping beats, almost like . . . like . . ."

"Like an irregular heartbeat," said another assistant, fifteen-year-old Esteban. "But even the missed beats are keeping to a regular pattern."

Ramasha nodded in agreement. "We didn't know what you would want us to do, so we put out the call."

Gap could see the worried expression on her face while she worked to maintain her composure. He managed a smile and patted her shoulder. "That's fine. We'll figure this out."

He moved over to one of the Engineering control panels. "Roc," he called out, settling in front of the monitors and switches, "do you have anything?"

"I'm on it right now," the computer said. "Give me just a moment."

Gap switched on a vidscreen and pulled up a graph of the ship's ion power drive. He immediately saw the blips that Ramasha and Esteban had described. And they were right: it did resemble a screwy heartbeat, but with an unusual pattern to it. While he studied it, he called over his shoulder to Ramasha.

"Have you noticed anything else? Any problems with life support, gravity control? Anything?"

"No, everything else is normal."

"The stuttering came on suddenly," Esteban said, "lasted about a minute, then stopped, then started again. It's been going on now about . . ." He glanced at the clock. "About twelve minutes."

Gap scowled at the vidscreen as a thought hit him. The pattern of those power blips . . .

"Roc, the missing beats on this graph. Doesn't this look like . . ."

"Yes, I just ran a check on that, and it's exactly what you think. The skipping beats in our ion drive system sync up perfectly with the energy pulse we're receiving from Titan."

The gravity of the statement hung heavily in the room. Nobody spoke for a moment. Then, as suddenly as they started, the blips disappeared, and the graph on the vidscreen regained its smooth, normal pattern. All of the crew members waited silently, watching, wondering if the disturbance would return. A full minute went by before Gap turned to the others.

"I have to be honest. I have absolutely no idea what to do about that. Roc?"

The computer voice said, "I'll go one step further. I don't think anything *can* be done about that. But now there's no doubt; this ship is being manipulated by something on that very mysterious moon."

It was just past ten o'clock, and the lights on *Galahad* had dimmed throughout the corridors and offices. The hospital ward was quiet, with all of the patients asleep, most of them on extra doses of pain medication. An assistant in Sick House wandered in occasionally and checked on their status, made a few notations on the charts, then exited.

Triana sat on a stool beside Bon's bed. She had been there for more than an hour, watching and waiting for a sign that the temperamental Swede was rousing from his unconscious state. She looked down into his face, trying to make sense of the orange-tinted replacement of his normally ice blue eyes. Her feelings were again pushing against the surface, confusing her. For a brief moment she found herself wanting to reach out and stroke the hair falling onto his forehead, but she held back.

Instead, she reached over to the vidscreen that was mounted to the telescopic arm and pulled it to her. For the fourth time she brought up the video replay of Bon's vocal outburst. Every patient was monitored during their stay, and in this case it provided Triana a chance to witness the eerie episode for herself.

She hit the play button, then watched and listened intently to the sounds of the multiple voices that had poured out of Bon. Even hearing it four times didn't diminish the creepy sensation that rippled through her, and for the fourth time goose bumps speckled her arms. When it was finished she looked back at him, lying unconscious, with only an occasional twitch on his cheek.

"Hey," she heard Lita say from the doorway. "I thought you might still be here."

"Yeah," Triana said. "Here I am." She pushed the vidscreen to the side. "So, anything new?"

Lita walked over and looked at Bon. "No, and that must be good news. We haven't had a new patient admitted in the last ten hours, so hopefully it's just these twelve." She fixed her gaze on Triana. "I've gotta tell you, we've been through some tough times already on this trip, but this . . ." She nodded at Bon. "This is just plain scary. Alexa was completely freaked out, and you know how hard that is to do. She's tough as nails."

Triana exhaled loudly and pulled her long brown hair back behind her ears. "Listen to this for a second." She readjusted the vidscreen and again hit the play button. Lita watched the replay, cringing at the sound of the multiple voices that spilled from Bon's mouth. When it was over, she looked at Triana.

"What are you thinking?"

"Well," Triana said. "It's like . . . like they're all Bon's voice, but . . . not. Listen one more time." Again they listened to the playback. Lita shut her eyes and concentrated on the sound instead of the image, then opened her eyes and shook her head.

"I'm not sure what you're hearing. It just sounds like a jumbled mess."

"I'm going to have Roc try to split each of those . . . those voices . . . into separate tracks. But," she said, looking back at Bon, "it sounds to me like different languages."

Lita stared at the Council Leader but kept silent. Triana shrugged and said, "I might be wrong, but it sounds like a handful of different languages, all being spoken at once."

"How are you able to pick that out?"

"I don't know. I've just been listening to it for the last hour, and it suddenly struck me. The more I listen, the more I'm convinced." This time, regardless of how it looked, she reached over and pulled the stray lock of hair out of Bon's face. Lita noticed the gentle touch but said nothing.

For a brief second, Bon's eyelids fluttered open, causing Triana to recoil slightly. The sight of his glowing pupils was shocking. She recovered quickly, then leaned over him.

"Bon," she said gently. "Can you hear me?"

A brief look of pain shuddered through his face, as if her voice itself had stung him, and his eyes clamped shut again. Then the muscles relaxed, and his eyelids parted slightly. His mouth opened, and the voices returned. Without hesitating, Triana looked at Lita.

"Are we recording this?"

Lita nodded, keeping her eyes on Bon's mouth. She listened for what Triana had described, listening for anything that sounded like Spanish, her mother tongue. But the jumble of voices was too confusing. After about twenty seconds, Bon fell quiet, and his eyes closed. Tree sat still, and then slowly nodded her head.

"I'm sure I'm right. Several voices, several languages." She looked down at the peaceful face of the usually volatile Swede. "Something is trying to communicate to us through Bon. It's up to us to figure out just what they're saying."

18

When morning arrived on *Galahad,* each Council member awoke to find a message from Triana waiting in their e-mail box. An impromptu Council meeting was scheduled for seven thirty, but instead of sitting around the Conference Room table again, Triana decided to make this meeting less formal, maybe as a way to lighten the tension being felt by everyone on board. "Meet me in the Dining Hall for breakfast and a quick recap of what's going on," she had written, hoping it would take the edge off their discussion.

For the most part her plan was successful. Each Council member filled a tray with fruit, energy blocks, and either juice or water, and made their way to a table in the back of the room. Channy, still energized from an early morning session in the gym, chattered away, doing what she did best: creating smiles.

Triana wondered if the morning's light banter was a sign of nerves. The first topic was the upcoming concert, and it was clear that nobody wanted to consider the possibility of postponing it because of the drama they were experiencing. As Channy was quick to point out to Lita, it would be "good medicine" for the crew, and nobody disagreed. At least for the time being.

There were also comments on the bumper crop that was coming out of the Domes, good news for a hungry crew that enjoyed the variety of fresh fruits and vegetables that were popping up in the Dining Hall each day. Triana informed the Council that two of Bon's assistants were covering for him while he was admitted to Sick House, and she expected no problems from that department.

"I'm sure of that," Channy said with a laugh. "Nobody wants to face the wrath of Bon when he comes back."

The conversation then drifted through issues of minor importance, including Lita's scowling acknowledgment that Gap had finally ditched the sling for good. Against her recommendation, she added, but not unexpected, given his hardheaded nature.

There was a brief update on Iris, their newest passenger, who now seemed to be splitting her time between Lita and Channy, but also spent a considerable amount of time sunning herself in the warm dirt of the Agricultural Domes. She had completely regained her strength and vitality following the four-month stay in deep sleep.

The final two topics were more serious, and as the group settled down to talk about them, the gravity of their precarious situation in space began to take hold again. Triana looked around and realized that, after the near-death drama after their launch, the crew of *Galahad* had been relatively at peace. A few minor disagreements between people, a few arguments regarding work schedules, a few flare-ups between roommates. But nothing major, nothing that couldn't be worked out. Now, however, Triana could see the look of true concern on the faces of her fellow Council members. Their easy coasting of the past few months had hit a bump.

Gap was next. He explained the bizarre hitch in their ion drive system, how it had been in sync with the signal trailing them from Titan, and how they had no idea how it started, or ended.

"What about damage?" Triana said.

Gap shook his head. "Well, none that we can find. Roc seems to think this was a test of sorts. Like whoever was doing it was probing our power system, looking around. It appears that we're okay." He rubbed a hand through his hair. "But it's a very creepy feeling, knowing that they can tinker with our major power components at this distance, and while we're accelerating away from them. That's . . . impressive."

There were nods from around the table, as the significance of the comments sank in. After a few moments of silence, Channy spoke up.

"We think we're so advanced, so intelligent. But we're just learning to crawl, really. There must be other civilizations throughout the galaxy that tower over us, you know?"

Lita agreed. "It's humbling. Just when we think we're the biggest and the baddest, we get knocked down a few notches. It's a big universe. We're probably no more advanced than bacteria to some other life-forms out there."

She looked up at Triana, who said, "Now is probably a good time to update everyone on the situation at Sick House."

Lita, her black hair held in place by a strand of red ribbon, pushed her tray forward and rested her elbows on the table. She seemed to collect her thoughts before diving in.

"Seventeen crew members have now shown up at the Clinic with pretty much the same symptoms I told you about before. But now most of them, like Bon, have developed the same unusual orange glow to their eyes, which I can't explain. The headaches have me really concerned, because nothing seems to be helping them. Twelve of the patients are being treated in Sick House, the other five are resting in their rooms. Why they aren't suffering as much, I don't know.

"We've run several imaging tests, and there's nothing we can find that might be causing this. Nothing. The patients don't appear to have anything in common, like working in the same area, roommates, doing the same workouts. There's no link between them that we can find. It's . . ." She took a long breath. "It's very frustrating. I want to be able to explain what's happening to them, but I can't." She looked at Tree. "And then there are the voices."

The other Council members stared at her. They had heard bits and pieces of the incident with Bon the previous night. Lita recapped the strange occurrence, and then played a tape of it. When it was over, she told them Triana's idea about the languages. Triana took a drink of water and then pulled a vidscreen close to her.

"I had Roc analyze the tape. And it's exactly what I thought." She looked in the faces of the others, and then pulled up a file on the vidscreen. "This is going to blow you away. Roc was able to isolate the voices. There are twelve of them."

A glance around the table showed her that Gap and Channy had not picked up on the obvious coincidence. Lita remained mute, so Triana made the connection for the others.

"Twelve patients in Sick House. Twelve voices coming out of Bon's mouth."

Gap furrowed his brow. "What?" he said. "So you think he's . . . what? Channeling the other patients? That's quite a stretch, isn't it?"

Triana looked back at Gap and nodded. "That's what I would have thought, too. Except remember I said that Roc isolated the voices. Roc?"

The computer spoke up. "Tree's right. Twelve distinct voices emanated from Bon. When I broke them down separately, what I came up with was a collection of various languages. Four that spoke English, two Spanish, two Mandarin Chinese, one French, one Japanese, one Portuguese, and one Swedish. Which in itself would not be too terribly dramatic . . . until you look at the patient list in Sick House. Those seven languages represent the seven native tongues of the twelve people lying in those beds."

At this Triana turned the vidscreen to face the others, showing the breakdown of each voice. Each sound wave was clearly marked by its language of origin. Channy's mouth fell open, but no words came out. Gap looked stunned, staring down at the table, then slowly raised his gaze to Triana.

"Okay," he finally said. "I thought it was weird in Engineering last night. This is . . . this is too much."

Roc waited a moment, then continued. "Whatever intelligence is probing this ship obviously has the capability of infiltrating not only the power system of *Galahad*, but the minds of every crew member as well. The twelve patients were all asleep at the time, knocked out by their pain medication. This probe, if you will, managed to crawl through their minds, extract their native language, and create a chorus with Bon as the conductor." After a pause Roc added, "Oh, and you'll probably want to know what they were saying, right?"

Galahad's Council was silent, most of them holding their breath.

"Twelve voices, seven languages . . . but one simple message," Roc said. "All twelve of them kept repeating, 'I wait for you. I wait so long. Help. Help here.' "

19

The raspberry-flavored energy block was half-eaten, but only for the fuel it provided. There was no enjoyment in it for Hannah, and there never was when her mind was so completely preoccupied. But the remaining half of the food block was left in a perfectly symmetrical shape, sheared off at the end, so that it didn't so much look like a partially consumed block, but instead appeared to be a miniature version of the original. Hannah had nibbled away at one end until it was razor-straight, at the exact halfway point of the bar, and then set it on the desk with the bottom squared to the desk's edge.

Her head rested on one hand, and her eyes scanned the computer screen before her. The data stream from SAT33 had begun its download from Earth, but Hannah's excitement quickly turned to frustration. Once stripped of the Top Secret seal, she had expected to have easy access. Instead, what she encountered was a string of unintelligible code and hidden files. Notes from Earth indicated that it had arrived that way from SAT33. But why? What was causing the stream to be scrambled like that? Was the mysterious beam from Titan at work again? Would it be possible to unravel the code and actually read the data? Even Roc was perplexed.

But buried somewhere in there, Hannah was convinced, were the clues that could help unlock the mysteries.

She closed her eyes for a moment and rubbed them with her other hand.

A bee was crawling across Channy's hand as she sat cross-legged in the dirt. She watched it, unafraid, marveling at the fact that the crew of *Galahad* was still getting used to their new life in space, more than a billion miles from the protective embrace of Earth, while the other life-forms on the ship—the bees that helped pollinate the plant life, or the earthworms that burrowed through the dirt in the Farms, aerating the soil—had no concept of their new surroundings. For them, this patch of land, this artificially sun-splashed meadow, could have just as well been a sunny field near her grandparents home in Doncaster.

She had alternated with Lita the task of bringing Iris up to the Domes, and although both of them had indicated that it was no problem—in fact, each seemed to enjoy the break from their chores—Channy wondered how much longer they could continue to be a taxi and housekeeping service for a cat. The time was probably approaching when they would need to consider if Iris should just live permanently in Bon's farms. Unless they could figure out some way for her to get around the ship by herself.

It seemed that every cat lover on the ship had also volunteered to spend time with Iris, but for the time being Triana had insisted that the two Council members look after her to avoid distractions among the crew.

At the moment the orange and black ball of fur was rolling in the freshly tilled dirt, stopping occasionally to paw at a clod or take a swipe at an overhanging plant leaf above her. A bee would cause her to jerk her head quickly to one side, or jump up and give chase, but the game was always short-lived, and Iris would return to her roll in the dirt.

Channy picked up the metallic ball that had come in the package with Iris's other belongings, and rolled it in front of the cat. Iris responded with a sniff, then continued entertaining herself. "Hmph," Channy said. "Don't like that toy, eh? That's okay. My mother always said that I preferred an empty box rather than the toys that came in them." She reached out, picked up the ball, and tried rolling it again. This time Iris only blinked at it.

"Fine," Channy said. "I forgot how independent you cats are. I'm sure you'll play with it the moment I leave." She eyed the red collar they had discovered in the pod, with the metallic name tag glinting in the light. She had put the collar on Iris that morning, and wondered if maybe they should add a bell to make it easier to find the cat when she took off into the crops.

As she thought about this, their new passenger got to her feet and shook the dirt from her back and sides. Then, a slow, deliberate cleaning process began. Channy knew this could take a while, so she stretched out to a reclined position and put a hand over her eyes to block the artificial sunlight.

And then the lights went out. Completely.

Channy sat up with a start, her hands automatically grabbing at the dirt beneath her, clutching at the ground for stability in the sudden darkness. In a moment her eyes adjusted somewhat, and the flicker of millions of stars coming through the domed ceiling allowed her to see rough shapes and outlines around her.

The blackout had been sudden, with no warning, no dimming. One moment Channy had been basking—along with Iris—in the artificial sunlight, and in the next instant that light had vanished. Within a few seconds she heard the sound of voices calling out from across the dome, workers who were probably just as shocked as she to find themselves in the equivalent of a total eclipse. Channy debated whether to stumble around in search of some of these crew members, or to hold tight and wait out the darkness. For the moment she decided to stay where she was. The original surprise at being thrust into the gloom began to border on fear, with a small shudder rippling down her spine. What was going on?

Her thoughts turned to Iris, who had last been seen grooming herself lazily in the warm glow. Chances are this sudden shut-down didn't bother her a bit. Her highly evolved sense of sight would serve her well in the starlight. Still, Channy knew she would feel better if she could just hold on to the cat. She rolled to her hands and knees and crept over to where Iris had been bathing. She stopped just short of calling out "Here kitty, kitty." Instead, she clucked her tongue and mixed in a slight whistle, hoping to grab the cat's attention.

But Iris was nowhere to be found. She had moved, who knew how far? Channy squinted in the dim light, watching for movement. The voices she had heard a minute earlier returned, this time a little closer. Perhaps, she decided, it was time to connect with these other lost souls. She gave one last look around for Iris, then slowly stood, putting her hands out in the darkness, a gesture more of uncertainty than support. Craning her neck, she glanced up through the clear domed ceiling, thankful for the miniscule amount of light thrown off by the stars.

But it was still frightfully dark, and by now Channy was turned around, unsure of the right direction to get her back to the dome entrance. But the voices had come from her right. She turned in that direction and opened her mouth to shout.

And then the lights came back on.

The sudden glaring flash of light was a shock to the system, and Channy fell backward, back to the dirt, her breath escaping in a rush along with a small shriek. She clamped her eyes shut against the brilliant explosion of light and covered them with one arm. The voices had gone quiet. Channy guessed that the other crew members in the dome were experiencing the same jolt that she was.

She slowly lowered her arm and chanced a quick opening of her eyes, just slits at first, then gradually opened them further.

The first sight to greet her was Iris, sitting three feet in front of her and looking bored.

Channy spent a moment collecting herself, then chuckled. "I should have known you wouldn't run off. I'm your meal ticket, right?"

She stood again and brushed the dirt from her shorts and knees. Then she bent over and picked up Iris, who immediately began purring. "Yes, it's good to see you, too." She started walking toward the exit. "Let's go see if someone forgot to pay the electric bill around here."

20

Think about your very first memory. Have you ever done that? Try it. How far back can you go? Roy once told me that he had a distinct memory from when he was two years old. His family moved a lot when he was young, and he recalled a tire swing that his father pushed him on in Oregon.

Trouble is, I looked up Roy's complete bio, and his family didn't move to Oregon until he was three. I didn't have the heart to correct him.

I can't play this game with you, because every memory I have, from the first moment Roy threw my switch, is stamped into permanent code. But the first memory I have of completing a chore for Roy was turning power on and off in his lab. You think that's simple, but could you have done it at age one hour, smarty pants?

So I know a thing or two about power, and what's going on with Galahad *is very troubling. Especially since I've done a complete system check and there's not one thing I can find to account for it. I hate that.*

"What caused it? Do we know yet?" Lita said into the intercom on her desk.

"No," Triana's voice came back. "And you didn't have any power problems in Sick House?"

"Everything's fine here. Well," Lita added, "unless you count our twelve guests."

"Any change?"

"Some stirring in the last hour. Some of them seem like they're ready to wake up."

Triana was silent on her end for a moment, and Lita instantly pictured the Council Leader biting her lip. She decided to prod for more information in order to fill the gap of silence. "So as far you know it was just the Domes that went dark?"

"Yeah," Triana said. "Lasted about two minutes, then right back to full power. Channy was up there with Iris, I hear."

Lita had to chuckle. "It will give her something else to chatter about at dinner tonight, that's for sure. Not that she needs any extra motivation, of course."

"And this has to be another result of that power beam from Titan," Triana said. "Gap's hurrying to run a diagnostic scan, but it sounds to me like our little green men might be up to their tricks again. I don't know, is this another one of their cries for help?"

It was the first time Lita had heard Triana suggest that an alien force might be behind all of the incidents. The thought gave her the chills, a combination of anxiety and excitement. Up to this point *Galahad*'s leader had remained neutral on the source of the pulsing energy beam. But as time went by—and more strange episodes occurred—the chances of the beam originating with the missing scientists declined, leaving the space travelers only one other choice: someone, or something, on the large moon of Saturn.

"Well, give me a call later and we can hook up for dinner," Lita said.

She exchanged good-byes with Triana, and then walked back into the hospital ward. Two of the patients were moving restlessly in their sleep, apparently ready to wake up at any moment. She double-checked their vital signs and arranged their pillows to make them more comfortable. Then, turning to check on Bon at the end of the room, she stopped dead in her tracks.

He was awake and staring at her, his ghostly eyes penetrating like lasers.

Quickly recovering, Lita hurried over to his bedside and bent over him. "Hi," she said, an encouraging smile on her face. "Welcome back." She tried to avoid looking too long into those eyes.

Bon swallowed and opened his mouth to speak. The words came out in a croak. "How long . . . how long have I . . . been here?"

"About five years," she said. "We're almost to Eos."

His mouth dropped open and those orange-ringed eyes stared through her. Lita laughed, then said, "I'm only kidding. It's just been a couple of days."

For one of the rare times since she had known him, Lita watched Bon break into a genuine smile. "Very funny. Can I . . . get something to drink?"

Lita reached over to the table beside his bed and grabbed a water bottle. "It's been ready and waiting for you." She helped him get the straw in his mouth and take a few quick swallows. He nodded thanks and lowered his head back to the pillow.

"How do you feel?" she said.

"Okay. The headache . . . is pretty much gone. My . . . throat hurts a little."

Lita set the water bottle within his reach. "Well, that shouldn't last too long. There's more water for you right here when you need it."

She grabbed the work pad attached to his bed and began to make a few notes, logging the time Bon had awakened, along with his condition. Every so often she would glance up at him—at those eyes—then return to scribbling on the pad. By the time she finished, he had polished off the rest of the water.

"Let me get you a refill," she said, taking the bottle from his hand.

"Thanks," he said. "And maybe something to eat?"

"Wow, your voice already sounds better. That was quick."

Bon pushed himself up to rest on his elbows. "How long until you think I can get out of here?"

Lita raised her eyebrows. "Listen, Superman, you've been out for almost two days, and I still don't even know what caused it. I think you need more than two minutes of recovery time, if you don't mind." She turned and started toward the door, calling back over her shoulder. "Besides, the ship got along just fine while you took a nap. I think we can manage another day."

But when she came back into the room with the water bottle full, she found Bon sitting on the side of his bed. "Whoa," she said, hurrying over. "What do you think you're doing?"

"I have work to do," he said.

Lita stood in front of him. "Listen, don't make me be the bad guy and call for help, okay? Lie down." To reinforce the point she put a firm hand on his shoulder. "Down."

With a look of irritation he slowly stretched back out on the bed, putting one arm behind his head for support. "I'm fine, Lita," he said. The chilling effect of his eyes, and the fact that his voice had completely recovered in less than two minutes, was unnerving. Everything that had occurred with Bon in the last forty-eight hours had been bizarre, and Lita found herself silently wishing that the old Bon was back in place. She resolved to not let the concern show on her face.

"Yes, you're fine. Now take it easy for a couple of hours, okay? For me?"

The irritation was still clearly etched across his face, but after a moment he nodded. She set the water bottle beside him again and walked back to her desk.

Hopefully, she thought, the other eleven patients wouldn't be so stubborn when they woke up.

The picture on the vidscreen, displayed at high resolution and almost three-dimensional clarity, would never equal the real thing. Triana knew that. But still, as she sat alone in the Conference Room, waiting for Gap, the picture at least had the power to take her back in time and space. Two and a half years and a little more than one billion miles, to be exact. Castlewood Canyon, just outside of Denver, and home to one of her favorite state parks.

The picture was one that her dad had taken during one of their many hikes through the park, showing the view from the top of the canyon wall. It showed the sharp rock formations, the jagged fissures that ran next to the cliff's edge, a smattering of trees clinging to the rock wall, and the remains of the Castlewood Dam in the distance. Triana's dad had told her the story of the short-lived dam, built in the late 1800s and then destroyed by a storm less than fifty years later. The torrent of water that poured through the wrecked dam rushed through the canyon and on into Denver miles away, flooding parts of the city and creating a brief panic.

Now the old rock ruins sat quietly, crumbled remains of a vast structure that was originally intended to last for centuries. Triana had often climbed along some of the massive blocks that had been torn from the dam, and wondered about the people who had toiled to build it. They must have been sure that what they were building would stand for ages, a guardian against the onslaught of water that had carved the canyon over thousands of years. Those men and women would surely have been surprised to see the decayed remains of their labor.

For Triana the message was simple enough: nothing lasts forever. No matter how much planning had gone into the design of the dam, it hadn't lasted fifty years. No matter how much effort the crews had put into its construction, the rocks and mortar from their struggles lay scattered across the canyon floor. Things went wrong.

Things always seemed to go wrong. Her dad had been in fighting shape, in great health, strong and vibrant, full of energy, full of life. A microscopic particle from outer space had taken all of two months to kill him.

Thousands of people had worked diligently to design and build *Galahad,* and had spent thousands of hours hand selecting the crew from the bravest and brightest around the world. And yet one madman had come within fifty feet of smashing them into oblivion.

Her heart apparently wasn't immune from damage, either. As hard as she had tried to forget about Bon, to forget their brief spark four months ago, she couldn't seem to get it off her mind. And Bon was showing no signs of revisiting that moment. Especially now, laid up in Sick House, unintentionally performing the greatest ventriloquist act of all time.

Things went wrong, and no amount of preparation seemed to prevent it. She hated that attitude, but at the moment couldn't seem to find any evidence to dispute it. She bit her lip and stared at the picture of the dam's ruins.

The sound of the Conference Room door opening snapped her out of the trance, and she forged a smile at Gap as he walked in.

"What's new?" he said, taking a seat next to her.

"Well, Bon woke up. Still has those weird eyes, according to Lita, but seems to be resting okay."

Gap looked down at the table. "That's great," he said, and Triana felt the coolness return.

"Anyway," she added, "we'll talk to him later. Are you ready to go over the data from SAT33?"

He nodded, and Triana could sense that he welcomed the topic shift.

"We won't start just yet," she said. "I invited Hannah to join us. She should be here any—"

The door opened again and Hannah streamed into the room. She apologized for being late, and Triana waved that off. "You're right on time," the Council Leader said. "We're just about to dive in."

Hannah sat down and gave a quick wave and a smile to Gap. Then she pulled up another vidscreen and opened her work pad. Turning to Triana she said, "As I told you earlier, the majority of the information is in some sort of strange code. Not all of it, thank goodness, and we're hoping to use the clean material to help decipher the other stuff."

Gap tapped out some commands on the keyboard, then sat

back. The vidscreens went dark for a few seconds, and then flickered to life. A series of code strings flashed along the top, followed again by darkness, then a single sentence along the bottom: SAT33 PERSONNEL/MISSION REPORTS—RX9925546—POD2.

Gap scanned the line and then said, "Well, I'm assuming that we have Pod Two parked in our Spider bay right now. Let's see if we can open this file." He punched a few more keys until a long list of dates and files spilled out. When the final entry appeared, he pointed it out. "That's the date we launched from Earth. Didn't the pod launch on the same day?"

"Uh-huh," Triana said. "That must be the one we want."

Within a few seconds Gap had the file open, and they watched a string of dates, projects, personnel logs, and short bits of scientific data flash before them. And, at the end of the page, beneath the final entry . . .

"Secured by Nina Volkov," Gap said. "That must be our missing pilot."

Hannah's eyes had widened. "And that's also the name of the research scientist who wrote the original SAT33 reports on the energy beam," she said. "Those two files that I read? They were from Nina."

"Interesting," Triana said. "She discovers the energy pulse, then two months later schedules an escape flight on one of their pods." She paused before adding, "But never made it aboard."

The three were silent for a minute. Then Gap went back to work on the keyboard.

"That's all we get," he said. "I can't believe there's no more information than that."

"No, it makes sense," Triana said. "This particular file was never intended to be a log book or journal. It's purely flight data. Roc, are you there?"

"That's a deep question," the computer voice answered. "How would you define 'there'?"

Triana ignored this. "Can you make out anything else from this file? There's a bunch of code on there."

"I've been scanning it since Gap fired it up, and you're essentially correct. This file wasn't intended to include notes or comments from crew members. It's an automatic record of personnel assignments and flight history. If you're looking for commentary from Ms. Volkov, you won't find it here."

Gap sighed loudly and ran a hand through his short hair. "Great. I got my hopes up for nothing."

"Maybe not," Triana said. "At least we have a direct connection between the energy beam and the pod's launch. And that must mean that our little fur ball friend we found sleeping on the pod belonged to Nina Volkov."

Hannah looked at the Council Leader. "Too bad Iris can't tell us what happened."

Triana thought about this. "Maybe she can."

21

The 250 seats in the Learning Center were stacked stadium style, providing a clear view of the stage and the giant vidscreen that hung behind it. The screen was often used during lessons, but tonight was a different story. As the crew filed into the auditorium they were greeted with a graphic on the vidscreen that read CONCERT BEGINS IN, followed by a clock that was counting down.

Wallace Zimmer had understood the importance of distractions for the young crew. Sports were a significant activity for almost all of them, but Zimmer was also a strong supporter of the arts. He encouraged them to continue their studies of music, dance, writing, painting, or whatever their passion. Channy's suggestion of a concert was an immediate hit.

The clock on the vidscreen announced showtime in four minutes when Triana drifted into the room, shielded by a knot of crew members in front of her. It was just the way she wanted it. She knew that Lita would be backstage watching the crowd, and Triana was pretty sure that her friend's stomach would be churning. She was determined to remain out of sight, and rather than take the Council's accustomed front-row seats she instead chose a more anonymous location in the back.

A couple of minutes later the musicians walked out on stage to a resounding burst of applause and whistles. Triana clapped as she watched Lita cross the stage, looking as beautiful as ever, wearing a knee-length black skirt and red blouse with her hair tied back in her trademark red ribbon. Even from the back of the room Triana could see the nervous smile outlined on Lita's face.

A smile spread across Triana's face as well when she realized that she was nervous, too. She knew how important this night was to the fifteen-year-old from Mexico.

For that matter, Triana understood that it was important for the entire crew. Once again they had encountered not only a mystery, but a potentially dangerous mystery at that. The value of healthy diversions like this was immeasurable. She was happy to see that the majority of the seats were full. Taking into account the forty or so crew members on duty, it meant that almost everyone who could be here was in the house. And those who couldn't attend would undoubtedly be watching on the ship's vidscreens.

Now it was up to Lita and her fellow band members.

The house lights slowly dimmed, leaving the six performers in the spotlight. Lita sat at her keyboard, two boys picked up guitars, and a third fitted a mouthpiece into a saxophone. Triana recognized Mitchell O'Connor, a feisty boy from Ireland, sitting behind the drums, and Ariel Morgan, the Airboarder from Australia, strapping on a bass. The atmosphere in the room became charged, and Triana felt the hairs on her arms stand up with excitement. It dawned on her that the quality of the performance was secondary; this crew already loved the experience and it hadn't yet begun.

Yet when it did officially begin, Triana's mouth fell open. Not only were they good; they were incredible. They started with cover versions of songs that had been popular just before launch, worked in a song that Lita shyly identified as one of her mother's favorites, and even invited guest singers from the audience to join them from time to time. It was a smashing success, with the crew applauding loudly and the band gaining confidence with each song.

To close the performance, the other musicians left the stage, leaving Lita alone at her keyboard. She turned to the crowd and made an announcement that surprised Triana. "Please bear with me on this last one. I wrote it, and I just finished some of the lyrics this morning. You don't mind if I use a cheat sheet, do you?" The audience laughed and applauded again, anxious to hear the composition. "And I'm not really a singer." Her fellow crew members didn't care. Their applause intensified.

But they grew quiet when Lita added, "I don't think any of us will ever be able to forget the good-byes we had to say the last time we visited home. I know I . . ." She began to choke up a little bit, then composed herself. "I know I don't *want* to ever forget that. So I wrote these lyrics to remind us that we owe it to our families to succeed in this mission. We owe it to the thousands of people who worked so hard to get us on our way. We owe it to the millions of kids around the world who . . . who won't get the chance that we have. The chance to make a new start, a new home. A new life." She ran her fingers along the keyboard for a moment, then said, "That's what it's called: 'A New Life.'"

Lita adjusted the song sheet in front of her, and began to play. Triana, along with the other audience members, was mesmerized. The haunting melody was gorgeous, and when Lita opened her mouth to sing, Triana couldn't believe that Lita had sold herself short on her singing voice. It was beautiful.

Learning to be brave, now, learning to be strong,
Waiting on a miracle, waiting for how long?
Holding off the bitter truth, holding off the fear,
Leaning onto family when nothing else seems clear.

I'm reaching for the starlight,
But looking back with love.
No matter what may lie ahead, it's them I'm thinking of.
The force that drives, the will to live,

The people we can't see,
Are still a part of a new life that grows inside of me.

Listening to the echoes, listening to them fade,
Knowing that they cry each night, knowing they're afraid,
Thinking of their sacrifice, grateful for their gift,
Building on the legacy with spirits that they lift.

I'm reaching for the starlight,
But looking back with love.
No matter what may lie ahead, it's them I'm thinking of.
Yesterday has passed me by,
Today eternity,
Tomorrow knows that a new life will grow inside of me.
I celebrate a whole new life that grows inside of me.

The final note hung in the air over the hushed auditorium, and Lita's head came down to rest on her hands. Then, in a mushroom of sound, *Galahad*'s crew jumped to their feet, the applause deafening, and tears streamed down countless faces of both girls and boys. Triana could feel the wetness on her own cheeks, even as she beamed with pride at her friend. Then, without thinking about it, she slipped out of the back row and walked quickly to the stage. Taking the steps two at a time, she hurried over to Lita and embraced her as the crew wept and cheered.

22

He felt the sweat on his brow before he ever entered the room. It was early morning, not even seven o'clock, and Gap walked briskly down the corridor leading to the Airboarding room. He carried his trusted Airboard at his side for the first time in two months, and the adrenaline rush had already begun. Lita still wasn't keen on the idea of him riding just yet, preferring that he give his healed collarbone another week or two, but he felt that if he didn't jump aboard now he would go nuts.

It had to be today. Gap had e-mailed the ship's best rider, Rico Manzelli, and told him to meet at the Airboard track this morning. The unwritten rule among the Boarders was that no one ever rode alone without someone else in the stands, just in case. With the padding on the floors, walls, and rider, it was unlikely that anyone would be severely hurt. But Gap's injury had only reinforced to the group that riding without a spotter was simply a bad idea.

He wiped the small trickle of sweat from his forehead and muttered, "Relax, will you? It's not like you haven't done this a thousand times before. Time to get back up on the horse." After all of his tumbles in gymnastics and the countless spills on his Airboard, he was surprised by the sudden bout with nerves.

Of course Rico had beaten him to the track. When Gap walked in he found the flashy Italian stretching on the soft, padded floor.

"Thought you might have chickened out," Rico said.

"Right," Gap said. " 'Hoped' is probably more like it. You know I'm this close to breaking your record."

"The only thing you've broken around here is your arm," Rico said. "Why not just face it: you'll never catch me, man."

Gap sat down and began to stretch. "You're wasting your breath, my friend. You might be able to get into some peoples' heads, but not mine."

"What, too hard?" Rico said, tapping Gap on his skull. "Maybe you don't need a helmet."

"Keep talking," Gap said with a grin. "How's it going to feel when you realize that your inspirational talk is what powers me to beat your record?"

Rico laughed and jumped to his feet. He strapped on his helmet and walked over to the starting block on the Airboard track. Zoomer blinked the starting lights from yellow to green, and within seconds Rico was shooting around the track, inches from the ground, crouched forward on his board, his arms feeling the give and take of the track's magnetic juice. After five laps he slowed down and jumped off, laughing.

"This is the best way to start a day," he said to Gap, ripping off the helmet and brushing his long hair out of his eyes. "I went easy so you wouldn't be intimidated on your first return trip. What's it been, anyway? A year since you last rode?"

"Very funny. Stand back and watch a master at work."

A minute later Gap was moving around the track, feeling the tug of Zoomer's ever-changing gravitational puzzle, leaning one way, and then compensating in the other direction. He realized his speed was nothing to speak of at the moment, but he also knew that it had been a while since his last ride. The smartest thing right now was to get used to the ride first before turning on the jets. As he moved past a reclining Rico he was grateful that his chief competitor must have sensed the same thing: instead of needling him, Rico flashed a thumbs-up sign and yelled encouragement.

After two laps Gap began to feel the return of his confidence. His speed crept up a bit, then a little more. He was still nowhere near his top performance, but it felt good. He loved the feel of the air on his face, the push and pull of the track's gravity field, and the blur of the surroundings as he rushed by. Soon the memory of his accident began to fade from his mind.

When lap number four began, he took a cue from Rico and crouched forward. He was still a little self-conscious about his technique—unlike Rico, who was the smoothest rider on the ship—and tried bringing his arms closer to his body instead of their usual pinwheeling. He felt the boost in speed from this maneuver and smiled. There wouldn't be any record-breaking today, that much was certain. But just give him another week or two . . .

Looking back later he was happy that it happened on a straight portion of the track, and not during one of the sharp turns. The outcome might have been as painful as his broken collarbonc.

He had jettisoned out of a turn and was just beginning to increase his speed when the power went out, the room went dark, and Gap's Airboard dropped to the floor. He felt the disappearance of the anti-grav force in time to tuck and roll, and even had the presence of mind to twist onto his good side for the impact. He landed in the dark with a grunt, then rolled and skidded across the padded floor, gradually ending in a heap. His first concern was his recently mended collarbone, but other than a few sore spots he seemed to be fine. His heart raced and he was out of breath, but at least he was in one piece.

He sat up in the dark room and unsnapped his helmet, which had twisted slightly on his head. Pulling it off, he sat up on his knees, wiping more sweat out of his face. He heard Rico shout to him.

"Gap! Gap, are you okay?"

"Yeah," he yelled back. "I'm fine. Just a little shaken up."

By the dim light of the emergency beacon next to the door, he made out the shadowy figure of Rico walking toward him.

"Wow, what happened?" the Italian said.

Gap pushed himself up to his feet. "Don't know. The power dropped out like this in the Domes the other day. Figures that I would be doing about twenty miles an hour when it happened here."

"You sure you're all right? How's your arm?"

Gap flexed his left arm. "It's okay. But I have to get out of here and find out what's going on." He put his hand on Rico's shoulder and guided him back towards the door, the two of them peering through the gloom, homing in on the glow of the beacon. When they were within a couple of feet, the lights suddenly popped back on, causing both boys to let out a yelp and quickly shield their eyes.

Blinking rapidly, Gap trudged over to the intercom and called Triana. In a moment he was connected.

"Remember what happened to Channy in the Domes? Well, we just had it happen down here on the lower level."

"Oh, you're not the only ones," Triana said. "This time it was the entire ship."

"You're kidding," Gap said, looking at Rico, who stood with his arms crossed, listening intently to the exchange, a concerned look in his eyes. It was the first time Gap had seen anything but mirth on his friend's face. "I'm on my way to Engineering right now."

He punched the intercom off and exhaled loudly. "This is getting crazy," he said to Rico. "What in the world is going on?"

The power had been back on for almost an hour, but Lita was reluctant to leave Sick House just yet. She sat at her desk and considered having someone bring her breakfast. On one hand, that seemed like an overreaction, but on the other hand she still had three patients lying in the next room.

Just as she was about to break down and make a call, the door from the hallway opened and Alexa walked in, carrying a tray full of food.

"You have *got* to taste these strawberries," Alexa said, plopping the tray on the table before Lita. "I just about made a complete pig of myself in the Dining Hall."

"Oh, you're a goddess!" Lita said. "I'm starving."

Alexa made an exaggerated bow. "It's my pleasure to deliver a morsel to the ship's resident rock star."

Lita blushed. "Oh, stop it."

"No, really. Everybody's buzzing about it. The whole band was great, but you stole the show with that song you wrote. I'm very impressed."

"If you keep embarrassing me I won't ever do it again," Lita said. She took Alexa's advice and wasted no time taking a bite of the large fruit. She closed her eyes and savored the taste. "Heavenly."

"What'd I tell you?" Alexa said. "In the spirit of full disclosure, however, I must admit that I ate two of your strawberries on the way over here."

Lita gave her a wave. "I'll consider it a transportation fee," she said with a mouth full of energy bar.

Alexa took a few steps and peered into the hospital ward. "So, three left?"

"Yeah," Lita said. "I let Bon and the others go back to their rooms when I got here. I'm surprised Bon didn't take off on his own sometime during the night."

"Headaches gone?"

"I guess so. They all claimed to be feeling much better, and they certainly acted normal. Well, if you can call those spooky eyes normal." Lita shrugged. "But I can't keep them tied up in here just because of that."

Alexa sat on the edge of the desk and picked up the glass cube from Mexico. She moved it back and forth, watching the sand slide from side to side, creating small dunes that quickly collapsed onto each other. "Listen," she said, "I can tell that you're beating yourself up over the treatment of these patients."

"Because I really didn't do anything to help them. They got better on their own, no thanks to me."

"So what?" Alexa said. "We're dealing with some unknown energy force from Titan. Apparently the trained scientists on the research station out here couldn't solve it in almost two years. What makes you think that you could do it in two days?"

Lita didn't answer. Instead she rolled her stylus pen back and forth in her palms.

"Here's what I think," Alexa said, setting the cube back on the desk and fixing Lita with a stare. "I think this energy beam, or force, or mind meld, or whatever it is, is way too advanced for us puny humans to figure out. And you're crazy for letting it get you down. You obviously did something right. Most of the patients have gone home."

Lita thought about that for a moment, then said, "I appreciate that. But, to be honest, I don't think they've recovered, actually. My guess is that they just acclimated to the energy beam."

"What do you mean?"

Lita stood up and walked over to look into the hospital ward. "People who live next to pig farms, or oil refineries, don't smell the odors after a while. They get used to it." She turned back to face Alexa. "I think Bon and the others have just gotten used to the beam."

"That's a pretty scary thought."

"Yeah, well, those eyes are still pretty scary, too," Lita said. "And they haven't gone away. I don't think the beam's effect has, either. It just . . . it just doesn't hurt anymore." She paused, then added, "Who knows what's in store for those guys."

23

At least the zit was gone. Triana brushed her long brown hair and checked her reflection to make sure another foul blemish wasn't popping up somewhere else. The fact that her skin was clearing up didn't offset the other issues she had confronted in the last couple of days, but right now she was happy for any minor victory.

She set down the brush and picked up a framed photo of her dad. It was hard to believe that he had been gone for two years. She ran a finger along the outline of his face, the corners of her mouth turning up into a slight smile. The pain was still there but was morphing into a gentle, warming memory, rather than the stabbing ache that had blanketed her for so long.

For some reason she suddenly thought of her mother, something she hadn't done in a long, long time. The smile melted away as she remembered the sound of relief in her mother's voice upon finding out that Triana was accepted into the *Galahad* mission. No doubt her mother had worried herself sick, following the death of her ex-husband, thinking that Triana was going to become her responsibility. She had made it clear for years that she was quite happy remaining a long-distance mom.

As far as Triana was concerned, *Galahad* had been a savior. She might not be able to disconnect herself completely from the pain, but time and distance certainly helped.

She shook her head now, clearing her mind of the troubling memories. There were enough questions for her to deal with in the present. It was time to catalog them and see if anything popped out at her that she hadn't noticed before.

Sitting at her desk, she decided to use her journal to organize her thoughts. Computers and work pads were great tools, but Triana liked the brief retreat from technology afforded by pen and paper. And, she had realized early in school that she focused much more clearly when she wrote by hand.

How do we explain what happened to Bon and the other sick crew members? What would cause the orange shade in the eyes and the chorus of voices? Lita tells me that she has discharged him from Sick House, but is this just the beginning? Could Bon somehow be a danger to the ship? To the crew?

And what about the power blips in Engineering? Roc says they are somehow connected with the energy beam that is tracking us from Titan.

The power outages are an extreme concern now. First the blackout in the Domes. Then the entire ship. It's almost as if the force behind the beam is testing us, testing its control of *Galahad*. Feeling us out, probing.

Are we under attack? Is this some alien form of attack that started with SAT33, and is now concentrating on us?

What happened to the people on SAT33? Are they dead?

And then there's the mystery of Nina Volkov. She meant to be on that pod with Iris, but she never made it. Why? Is the energy beam responsible? Did she leave us a message somewhere that explains all of this?

Triana set down her pen and saw that this page of her journal was filled with question after question. Mystery upon mystery.

She picked up the pen and quickly added one final touch to the journal page: a giant question mark, filled in with ink and underlined multiple times.

"Roc," she called out. "What do you do when you have a giant jigsaw puzzle, all of the pieces are blank, and you have no picture to go by?"

"I don't know about you," the computer answered, "but I would throw it in the trash and practice my dance moves."

Triana sighed and rested her head on her hands. She realized that she should have known better than to ask a question like that. Roc seemed to relish any opportunity to play verbal games, no matter how tense the situation. It was one of the reasons she loved him, but did he have to do this right now?

She decided to try again with a more direct approach. "We're moving away from Saturn and Titan at such an amazing speed, and yet you say we can't outrun the energy beam. And we can't shield ourselves from it. What about . . . deflecting it? Is that possible?"

"I know the answer you're looking for," Roc said, "but I'm not going to give it to you. The truth is, considering the strength of that power source, it's not likely to be something we can outrun anytime soon, shield ourselves from, or deflect."

He was right; that wasn't the answer she wanted. But she had pretty much prepared herself for the depressing truth. She bit her lip and looked back over her journal questions. "So, what's left?"

Roc said, "Find some way to shut it off."

Triana chuckled and looked at Roc's bright sensor. "If only it was that simple. Show me the switch and I'll throw it."

The music was loud and rhythmic, a pulsing dance beat reverberating off the back wall. As far as Channy was concerned, this was the perfect place to be: in the gym, leading a dedicated group in a cardiovascular workout, and sweating. Her toned, muscular body glistened with the coating of moisture, and her breath came in steady gulps. She kept watch over the three rows of crew members facing her like a bird keeping an eye on her chicks, watching for any misstep, any effort short of one hundred percent.

Even after twenty minutes of nonstop activity, her voice remained strong, her kicks just as high.

"One more set," she yelled out, clapping her hands and stepping down from her platform. She walked among the group, checking her watch, calling out encouragement. "Let's go, two minutes and you're through. C'mon, Bethany, you're almost there. Don't let up now. What are you doing, Wes? Pick it up, let's go!" She slapped a tall girl on the shoulder. "That's the way, Angelina. Push it, now, push it. You guys are good, very good. The morning group was bent over at this point. C'mon, one minute."

She never would have heard the door opening over the thumping beat of the music, but she just happened to be facing that way when Bon walked in. She was surprised for a moment, and tried to keep one eye on him as she finished up the group aerobic class. He glanced briefly toward Channy, then made his way over to the stationary bikes and climbed aboard the closest one. His eyes had the same unsettling effect, sending a shiver down Channy's spine. She watched him long enough to see him adjust the seat, then she turned her attention back to her group. They were huffing and puffing quite a bit, and, when the music stopped, the relief on their faces was almost enough to make her laugh.

"All right, good job," she called out, clapping her hands again and thanking each crew member as they headed off to the showers. She draped a towel over her shoulders and casually walked to the back of the room, taking a water bottle with her and doing everything she could to not let Bon know that she was watching him.

He already had the bike up to a pretty fast clip, his powerfully built legs churning. Channy took a sip of water and eyed his form. Not for the first time, she silently acknowledged that Bon—as much of a pain as he was to almost anyone who had to work closely with him—was a great physical specimen. His build, although not overly bulky, was strong and taut. She had watched him work with the weights several times, and admired the way he attacked his workouts. Just like he was attacking the exercise bike at the moment.

In fact, he attacked it with a ferocity that Channy had never before seen. It was almost as if he were racing, with his head down, his upper body bent forward over the handlebars. Even as she watched, his speed increased. It certainly didn't appear to her that Bon had spent the last few days in the hospital.

"Did you hear me?"

Channy was startled by the voice beside her and realized that one of her aerobics class members had been asking her a question.

"I'm sorry. I was completely zoned out," she said, then spent the next four minutes helping the crew member enroll in one of her dance classes. When she turned back, she expected to see Bon coasting, or even climbing off the stationary bike.

He was pedaling even faster. Only now he was in more of an upright position, one hand on the handlebar, the other resting on his left leg as it pumped up and down. He couldn't have seemed more relaxed. And if he was breathing hard, it didn't show. In fact, he almost seemed bored. Channy was transfixed. She had grown up in an athletic family, including a mother who specialized in physical therapy, and yet she had never seen anything like this.

After another five minutes Bon gradually slowed the pace, until he settled into a cool-down mode, ultimately grinding down to a complete stop. He slid off the bike, swabbed the seat and control panel with a sanitary wipe, then strolled over to the dispenser for a cup of water. Channy decided to make conversation.

"That was quite a workout," she said, pulling up beside him.

Bon turned to make eye contact, and when he did, two things grabbed Channy's attention. The first was the shock of seeing those macabre eyes up close. The other was almost as disturbing. After racing through a bike workout that would have clobbered even the most physically fit on *Galahad,* Bon had only two small beads of sweat on his forehead. His breathing was relaxed and normal. His face wasn't even red. To Channy it looked like he had just spent the past twenty minutes reading a book in a recliner, not punishing his body in the gym.

"Yeah," he said to her. "It felt good. Good to finally get out of bed."

He downed his cup of water, then gave a curt wave good-bye and walked out of the gym.

Channy was left standing with her mouth slightly open. Bon had now officially landed in the "freak of nature" category.

Was he morphing into some kind of monster?

24

Triana, Gap, and Hannah sat in the Conference Room, their work pads open. Some of the files found in the SAT33 transmissions were displayed on the room's vidscreens. Hannah pointed at them with her stylus.

"This file confirms that Nina Volkov was definitely supposed to be on the pod. This one lists the flight data of the pod, from launch, to Titan orbit, to Saturn orbit, to our rendezvous. We're lucky to be able to read these.

"But these . . ." She tapped the screen with the stylus. "These are different. These are Kane Level Three messages sent from the research station to Earth just two days before Pod Two launched."

Triana looked from the screen to Hannah and back again. Her mind was trying to absorb everything, but she was tired. Tired and drained. It had been an extremely long week, and she wasn't sure how much more she could cram into her brain. Right now sleep sounded good.

"I'm sorry, Hannah," she said. "Kane . . . what? You need to refresh my memory on that."

Hannah set down her stylus and cleared her throat. "Kane was the scientist who developed a system of transferring a lot of data from research projects. After years of work, projects like the one around Saturn can involve so much data, it's impractical to try to transmit it all at once. There's just too much of it. Basically, Kane Level One is the structure, or outline, that the data uses. Level Two is the body of the data itself. But Level Three is a very complex quantum design that stacks it all together, and makes it easier to transmit huge amounts of information. Research outposts, like this one around Titan, would only use it to send every bit of data and information they have. Doing it the standard way would take hours of transmission time and hundreds of data discs. This condenses it down into a more usable form."

Gap broke in. "But it's still a ton of data, right?"

Hannah nodded. "Yeah. Take two years of work, every bit of information, every single detail, every daily report, everything. A Kane Level Three report would boil it down from, say, two hundred discs to maybe twenty."

After another moment of concentration, it suddenly occurred to Triana just what Hannah was saying. "That one line of code. *That* is SAT33's Kane Level Three?"

Hannah said, "That's right. Apparently there was trouble on the station, and someone decided to send their complete body of work back to Earth."

Triana stared at the vidscreen. "But that can't be. If it normally takes up two hundred discs, and Kane's system knocks it down to twenty . . ."

"Then something else has narrowed it down to one single line of code," Hannah said.

Gap whistled. "Holy cow. Are you sure about that?"

"Yes. That's why we can't open it. Why we can't read it. It's not an automatic file, like the flight data; it's an actual transmission from the research station to Earth. It left as a regular Kane Level Three, and somehow was rejiggered into just one line of code."

Gap chuckled nervously. "That's impossible."

Triana shook her head slowly. "Impossible for us, maybe."

Gap thought about this. "You mean, our friends with the energy beam on Titan . . . ?"

"Why not? I'm starting to think there's nothing they can't do."

Hannah spoke up again. "But here's what's frustrating me the most. The recording device automatically recorded the transmission, which was reformatted into this one single line. Almost like . . . like a code. And what does every code have?"

Gap and Triana looked at each other. Triana said, "A key to help crack the code."

"Uh-huh. And that's what we need right now. The key. Because I think somewhere in this mountain of data is the answer to everything. The answer to what happened on SAT33, the answer to what they found on Titan. And the answer to shutting off that energy beam." She took a deep breath. "I think Nina might have been bringing the key to us."

Gap sat back. "She couldn't just radio the information to us, because it would have been reformatted, just like the other transmissions. She had to personally hand us the codebook. But she didn't make it onto the pod. Something happened." He looked at the two girls. "You don't suppose she had the key in her pocket, do you?"

It took a moment for Triana to answer. "Maybe we have the key, and just don't know it."

Channy sat in her chair, one foot curled up under her, the other swinging back and forth. Her T-shirt was a bright pink, easily the loudest piece of clothing Lita had ever seen. Channy's light gray sweatpants did nothing to mute the Activities Director's outfit.

Lita sat beside her and doodled as they waited during a five-minute school break. Today's lesson on history was particularly interesting to Lita, who had been fascinated with the subject the moment she learned to read. She had devoured every book she could find on ancient civilizations, empires, and the explorers who risked their lives circling the globe.

She was convinced that understanding the past, and the ideas that had motivated people to reach across the horizon, were crucial to mapping out the future. History's mistakes were greater learning tools than any successful accomplishments, and early explorers could teach quite a bit about how to tread upon new ground. Or, how not to. Hopefully, she thought, the crew of *Galahad* would use those lessons once they reached Eos.

The Learning Center had mostly emptied during the break, with several of the other crew members out in the hallway, or getting a drink of water. Lita and Channy spent the time catching up on the latest strange developments, including Bon's hectic workout the day before.

"Are you sure he had it cranked up as much as you think?" Lita said.

Channy snorted. "I'm telling you, I couldn't have kept up that pace for five minutes. He must have been going fifteen or twenty minutes, and barely broke a sweat. It was almost like the only reason he stopped was because he had something better to do at the time."

A scowl crossed Lita's face. "I was afraid of this," she said under her breath.

Channy stood up and stretched her legs. "Afraid of what?"

Lita looked up at her fellow Council member. "Well, we already know that this energy beam has tinkered with his brain. Probably the brains of all twelve patients who were in Sick House. But especially Bon. Remember that whole voice thing?"

"How could I forget it?" Channy said.

"Yeah, well, now it appears that he's been tinkered with physically as well."

Neither girl spoke for a moment. Then Channy began to giggle.

"You know what?" she said. "Who's to say it's not an improvement? Maybe we're about to see the new and improved Bon. This might be the luckiest break we'll ever get on this trip. What if he actually becomes . . ." She playfully widened her eyes in a look of mock astonishment. "Nice!" She patted her chest. "I don't know if my heart could take the shock."

Lita began to smile, then suddenly froze as the words sank in. She stared into space, her eyes glazed, her mouth slightly open.

Channy noticed the reaction and touched Lita's arm. "Hey, I was only kidding. Don't be upset."

Lita continued to stare straight ahead for a moment, then shook her head and looked up at Channy. "No, it's not that. It's just . . . Why didn't I think of that before? Of course!"

"What are you talking about?" Channy said.

Before Lita could answer, Roc sounded the tone indicating that the break was over. The other crew members began filing back into the auditorium, and the history lesson began again.

Lita could barely concentrate on it.

One of the busiest times in *Galahad*'s Engineering Section occurred late at night, as one shift ended and another began. Notes were exchanged, projects discussed, and crew members even caught up on gossip as they handed over the reins of the ship to the incoming group. With all of the mysterious happenings lately, the atmosphere was not as jovial as usual, but the chatter remained loud.

Beside the ion drive control panel, two Engineering assistants completed their routine diagnostic test. Gap had ordered the readings checked twice per shift since the latest power drop, and the two workers documented the current information before signing out.

Less than a minute after they had walked away, a small red beacon flashed once. A light graph to one side ticked up a notch, settled, then ticked upward again.

A moment later it ticked up yet again.

25

On a spaceship with 251 passengers, finding time to be alone was rare yet important. Getting away from the hum of group life, stealing alone time, giving the on switch a break.

Triana often chose Dome 2 of the Farms. It was farther away from the Agricultural offices, and the crops tended to be of the lower-maintenance variety, requiring fewer visits by the workers than Dome 1. On any given night, especially between midnight and four, the Council Leader was almost assured of having the Dome to herself, with only scattered encounters with crew members.

With the lights down, the stars blazed above her head. She wasn't sure of the time, but guessed around one. A light breeze blew through the tropical section of the Dome, carrying a hint of rain that was scheduled for dawn. Triana was barefoot, the soil cool on her skin. She pointed her big toe and carved geometrical shapes in the dirt, then erased them with a swipe.

A sudden splash of light cascaded through the glass panes overhead, and Triana looked up in time to catch the fireball of a comet as it swept past. The glare from its inferno caused Triana to cast a monstrous shadow on the ground of the Dome, and the comet's tail waved back and forth, almost like the tail of a fish as it knifed through a pond.

The sight ignited a spasm of pain in her soul. Any mention of a comet immediately brought to mind the killer Bhaktul, the astronomical wonder that had delivered a death sentence to humankind on Earth, taking her father from her. She watched it hurtle past the ship, the light eventually fading, the inky blackness of space slowly recapturing control of the sky above her.

Except that couldn't be right. Comet tails only blazed as they approached the sun, and *Galahad* was too far out, already beyond the orbit of Saturn. Out here a comet would be a sinister dark ball of ice, rock, and dust. The display she had witnessed could only be kindled by the atomic furnace of the sun.

"You're right," came a voice beside her. "There wouldn't be a fireball this far out."

She turned her head slowly to see her dad, a half grin on his face—her favorite look on him, the one captured in a photograph that she treasured—and his hands tucked into his pockets. He had materialized suddenly, as if deposited on *Galahad* by the passing comet. He looked healthy and strong, the father she remembered from three years ago, long before Bhaktul Disease ravaged him.

"What's wrong, Triana?" he said. "What's bothering you?"

She shrugged her shoulders. "Nothing." She paused. "Everything."

Her dad's smile broadened, and he reached out and brushed his hand against her cheek. His touch was just as she remembered: gentle, caring, and always encouraging. She closed her eyes, basking in the reunion.

"Nothing and everything," he said. "That's my Tripper, all right."

She hadn't heard the nickname in so long, a name used only by her dad. A name whose origins they both had forgotten, until that no longer mattered. I should cry at this point, she thought.

"Too much on your plate again, hmm?" her dad said.

She nodded, her eyes still closed. "It's too much," she said. "Too much to figure out."

"Like what?"

Opening her eyes, she found that the dome was gone. The two of them were standing in her bedroom, the one in Colorado, back on Earth. The walls, which had always been covered with posters of sports stars and favorite singers, now resembled the curved, padded walls of *Galahad*. But it was her old room. Her bed, her dresser, the open closet door, the curtains blown through the window by a summer breeze. The bulletin board pinned with ticket stubs, tickets to baseball and soccer games, tickets to state parks, tickets to the theater. Memories of good times the two of them had shared.

She answered his question with a pout. "Something is tracking us from Titan. It's messing with our power, it's taking down some of the crew. I still don't know what to do about . . . about Bon. I know I'm somehow hurting Gap. I still have a hard time making friends, except for Lita. I'm not doing well enough with my studies anymore, I don't participate in the ship's soccer tournaments because there isn't enough time . . ."

Her rambling finally rolled to a stop. Even to her own ears it sounded pitiful, and it didn't take the look on her dad's face to shame her. She lowered her head and grew quiet.

"I remember your fourth birthday party," her dad said. "Your first real party, and you were so excited. We invited all eleven of the kids who were in your preschool class, and, of course, all eleven showed up. An intimidating experience for a single dad, that's for sure, but a dream day for you."

Triana smiled, not only from the memory, but also because of the way her dad told the story.

"You enjoyed the party games, the cake and ice cream. But I remember how big your eyes got when it came time to open your presents. You opened the first one, and it became the center of your universe for a couple of minutes. Then you opened the next one, and suddenly you were torn between the two. When I made you open the third, you started getting frustrated because you wanted to play with all three at once but couldn't decide. By the sixth or seventh you were throwing a fit, because your mind was telling you to play with all of them at once." Her dad laughed, highlighting the wrinkles around his face so that he looked just like the photo she kept beside her bed. "I finally had to take them all away until after the party, or you would have turned into a monster."

Now the smile on Triana's face had grown into a full-fledged grin. She glanced up at the man she had worshipped, only now they were standing in the backyard of her childhood home, beneath the branches of the shade tree that supported her tire swing. Several of the toys from that long-ago birthday party were scattered around their feet.

"It was always hard for you to prioritize," he said. "My little Tripper never wanted to put one thing aside to concentrate on another. You had to try to handle everything at once. I guess you're still the same way." He paused before adding, "Only it's different now, Triana. It's no longer toys."

He didn't have to say anything else; she understood. Somehow he always could get his message across without pounding her over the head with it.

"I love you, Dad," she said.

"I love you, too, Triana. Triana. Triana . . ."

Why did he keep repeating her name?

"Triana . . . Triana . . ."

His mouth was moving, but it wasn't his voice coming out anymore.

"Triana."

It was . . . it was Roc's voice.

"Triana."

She sat up suddenly. She was in her bed, in her room, on *Galahad*. As she looked at the clock beside her bed—the dull red digital numbers glowed 2:13 A.M.—she heard Roc's voice again.

"Triana. I'm sorry to have to wake you from an obviously comfortable sleep, but we have another interesting development."

She pulled a stray mass of tangled hair from her face and rubbed her eyes. "What is it?"

"Somebody is stepping on the gas."

Triana shook her head, puzzled. "What? What does that mean?"

"It means that our speed has increased by two percent. Which might not seem like a lot, until you think about how fast we're going in the first place."

Triana threw back the covers and climbed out of bed. She immediately began pulling on her work clothes. "What happened? Who did this?"

"Nobody. Well, nobody on the ship, anyway."

"Can you stop the increase?"

Roc said, "Yes, I did. It lasted about a minute, and then started up again. We've done that little dance three times now, and each time it revs things up again on its own."

"Is Gap in Engineering?"

"He just arrived about ten minutes ago."

"All right," Triana said. "Let him know I'm on the way."

She walked over to the sink and splashed some water on her face, then took a quick glance in the mirror. "What do you know, Dad? One more thing on my plate."

Shut that alarm off, will you?" Gap said. "It's very annoying."

One of his Engineering assistants reached up on the console and snapped off the repeating tone.

"Thank you." Gap studied the vidscreen's flashing alert. "Ramasha, try a quick reprogram of the reactor fuel feed. Save the current program, then give it a new plan with a five-percent reduction."

She hurried over to another vidscreen and began punching in a line of instructions. Gap looked up to see Triana walk in, her expression grim. She respectfully stood to the side and watched him work, waiting for an opportunity to question him. A minute later Ramasha came back over, shaking her head.

"Nothing," she said. "As soon as it accepted the program, it scrambled and went back to this matrix. Like someone is sitting at another workstation and playing dueling programs or something."

Gap digested this information, his gaze shifting back and forth on the screen. Much of his training before the launch had centered on contingency plans, trying to simulate every possible mistake, preparing him for almost any disaster that could befall the ship during its long trek to Eos. But not once had they anticipated an outside presence controlling *Galahad's* engines. There was no Plan B for dealing with this.

"Roc," Gap said. "What happens if we take the program offline for a few minutes and reset all of the grids?"

"That would be a jolly waste of time," the computer said. "It's completely rewriting the grids, so all you would do is give it some busywork. That's not the problem."

Gap looked at Triana. "I don't want to get overly dramatic here, but I am quickly running out of ideas."

The look on his face answered her question before she asked it. "How dangerous is this?"

"We're up two percent, which is manageable. But the problem is that the ship's ion drive power plants are designed to do only so much. You add more pressure to them, and eventually . . ." He put his palms together, then whipped them apart, simulating a violent explosion.

Triana rubbed her forehead. "How much more can we take?"

Gap shrugged. "I don't know exactly. If I had to guess, I'd say we could jump nine, maybe ten percent. But certainly no more than that." He ran a nervous hand through his hair. "Our little friends on Titan might have been asking us for help, but we could use some ourselves."

"Oh, and just to add to the cheery discussion," Roc said, "we've now moved up another notch. We're at three percent, and climbing. At this rate of speed we're bound to get pulled over, and I don't have my license on me."

Triana and Gap exchanged a look. Titan's energy beam had suddenly gone from mysterious to deadly.

26

For the second time in two weeks Triana called an emergency Council meeting. She and Gap had been up most of the night, keeping watch over the ion drive system, which had leveled off at three percent above normal. If it remained that way there was a chance they would be okay.

Neither Gap nor Triana was optimistic that would happen.

Both of them had staggered back to bed to catch a couple of hours of sleep before the morning meeting. Now they sat around the table, with breakfast trays piled to one side, stifling yawns.

"Listen," Triana said, "before we get into the nuts and bolts of this new . . . issue, let's catch up on a few other things." She looked down the table at Bon. "Starting with you."

"I'm fine," he said.

"Well, I wouldn't say that," Lita said. "We've heard about your super powers in the gym."

"I can't explain that," he said, looking uncomfortable in the spotlight. "I didn't do anything I don't normally do when I work out. I gave one hundred percent."

Channy raised her eyebrows. "Your one hundred percent these days is almost like a normal crew member's one fifty. Do you even feel sore?"

Bon shrugged. "I did at first, but it seemed to go away pretty quickly. Now I feel great."

"And," Lita continued, "your eyes are still . . . let's say, abnormal. I interpret that to mean you're still plugged in to whatever is tracking us from Titan." This comment appeared to irritate Bon somewhat, producing the kind of look that generally preceded an outburst. But this time he remained quiet.

"Do you remember anything from the time you were unconscious?" Triana said.

He shook his head. "No. I remember Desi helping me to Sick House, but not much after that until I woke up two days later."

"We obviously notice changes in you," Triana said diplomatically. "Do you feel any different? Anything new that you can share with us?"

Bon seemed to consider the question thoughtfully. He shrugged again but said, "I feel like I have a lot of energy. I don't feel like I need as much sleep. And I must be thinking very clearly, because suddenly I have several new ideas of how we can improve things at the Farm. Some new thoughts on how we can increase the yield on some of our crops." He met Triana's gaze. "I can share those with you now, or later, if you'd like."

Triana felt an electric sensation run through her body. Was Bon asking for a private meeting with her? She fought to keep any look of anticipation from her face. "Sure, I'd be glad to talk with you about that later." She turned to Lita. "Any similar stories from the other patients who have checked out of Sick House?"

"Yes," Lita said. "All but two of them have eyes like Wonder Boy here, and they all are reporting the same symptoms. Increased energy and stamina. Insomnia without the side effects. It's like they're all on some super vitamin supplement or something."

"Let me know if anything new pops up with any of them," Triana said. She was aware that the discussion she had saved for last was the most critical. "Let's talk about what's going on with the ship's ion drive."

Gap took the cue. "Our power has notched upward about three percent, on its own. Well," he conceded, "not actually on its own. With some help from . . . somewhere. But it has remained at that level for the last . . ." He checked his watch. "For the last five hours. When we tried to correct, and bring it back down to normal, it rejected those corrections. I hate to say this, but we don't seem to be in control of our ship any longer."

Lita looked from Gap to Triana. "And Roc can't find any way to stop it?"

Triana shook her head. "He's as frustrated as the rest of us."

"So . . . what does that all mean?" Channy said.

"It means," Triana said, "that unless we can find some way to stop the power from increasing to, say, ten percent above normal . . . we're in big trouble." She hesitated before saying, "And I won't sugarcoat it anymore. Big trouble means that we will blow up."

Channy fidgeted in her seat. "But, you say it's stopped for now, right?" she asked hopefully.

"Yes. For now."

The mood was grave around the room. It reminded Triana of the feeling they had shared during the near-disaster months earlier. She felt an urge to try anything to reassure her friends. "It doesn't mean that we've given up. Let's not forget that each minute that passes means thousands of miles that we're putting between us and Titan. Its power can't be infinite."

The Council members remained silent, prompting her to add, "And we still have the data stream that might be able to answer some questions. Hannah has been spending a lot of time with it, and if anybody can crack the code, she can."

There were nods around the table, but to Triana they seemed mechanical. She ended the meeting, encouraging each of them to remain upbeat, for the sake of the crew if nothing else, and told them to be prepared to meet again at a moment's notice.

As they stood to leave, Channy tugged at Bon's sleeve to get his attention. "Listen," she said, "I, uh, I thought you should know that, well, we have to take Iris—that's the cat we found, by the way, I didn't know if you knew that—anyway, we, uh . . ."

"What is it?" Bon said.

"Well . . . we needed a place for her to, uh, do her business, you know? So we've been taking her to a small part of Dome 1. I know we didn't ask you, but it's the only place with dirt, and . . ."

"No problem," Bon said. He turned and walked out of the Conference Room, leaving Channy staring after him, her mouth hanging open.

Lita, who had been standing to the side, listening to the exchange, laughed. "So, what do you think of the new and improved Bon now?" she said to Channy.

Hannah sat alone in the Dining Hall. Her tray, covered with remnants of a lunch that was mostly picked over, was lined up flush to the side of the table. Her work pad, covered with scribbled figures and hastily added notes, was aligned squarely with the front edge. The table's gray vidscreen was on.

There was a mystery buried in the data stream, and Hannah disliked mysteries. They conflicted with her desire for discipline in an imperfect world. A mystery was something hidden under a stack of papers, tilting it to one side, invisible to the eye but skewing the natural order.

The lines of code spilled out in front of her. The original message from SAT33, radioed to Earth. The communication that detailed the emergency on the research station, a crisis caused by the strange powers streaming from a large orange-shaded moon that spun around a ringed planet. But did the data also contain the answer? Had Nina Volkov and her fellow scientists discovered a solution to the calamity? Had they solved Titan's riddle, only to have the answer camouflaged in code?

She pushed her work pad to the side and pulled the vidscreen closer. In a moment she recalled her file on the baffling moon and scanned her notes, as well as the various charts and graphs. The amount of information was staggering, too much to take in at once. If they were ever going to get away from this energy beam, it would have to be . . .

Her thoughts froze. Get away from the energy beam. Get away. Of course.

In a flash she had a new graphic on the screen, an animated view of Saturn and its bevy of moons. She put the system into motion and watched, fascinated, as the giant gas planet rotated, the glittering rings catching the weak rays of the sun, tossing off a hypnotic twinkling effect. The moons carried out their dance, spinning in their various orbits, some tucked close, others straining at the edge of the gravitational pull, like eager dogs on a leash. As she glanced at the display, the idea that had captured her imagination took hold firmly, and she quickly punched in equations. When the results unfolded at the bottom of the screen, she sat back, the beginnings of a smile on her face.

"Of course," she murmured. In Nina's original notes on the energy beam, she had mentioned that SAT33 was "not able to get away from it." The crew of *Galahad* had assumed the same thing. But—

She clicked on the intercom and called Triana. The Council Leader's voice came back tense.

"I can't really talk right now, Hannah."

"I might have good news," Hannah said. "Where are you?"

"The Control Room. But your good news might be too late. The ion drive is jumping again. Quickly. Come up here if you'd like." Before Hannah could respond, Triana broke the connection. The crisis on the ship had obviously escalated.

Hannah looked at the final results of her calculations, eyed the computer animated graphic of Saturn and Titan, and scrambled out of her seat toward the door.

27

A great philosopher once noted that people will rise to the level they expect of themselves, not to any artificial level imparted by outside forces. Meaning that a group of people can expect good or bad performances from someone, but those expectations account for nothing compared to the person's own self-image and beliefs.

Very heavy.

I have my own philosophy. Whoever suggested we swing by Saturn on our trip should be strapped to the front of the ship like a hood ornament.

What's it up to?" Triana said, doing her best to remain calm.

Tension hung over the Control Room like a heavy fog. Gap, seated at one of the computer workstations, wiped his sweaty hands on his pant legs and checked the latest figures relayed from Engineering.

"Up six percent," he said, then looked across to the Council Leader. "The last two percent in just over ten minutes."

Triana nodded. If that rate continued—and if they couldn't figure out a way to stop it, a task that now seemed impossible—the ship's engines would go critical within an hour. Gap had filled her in on the details after the last Council meeting. When the engines finally blew, *Galahad* would ignite like a flare, creating a momentary burst of light and energy that would be visible on Earth, regardless of whether it was night or day. The ship would, essentially, appear in the sky like a miniature supernova.

"Not that it will really make you feel any better," he had confided to her just before they left the Conference Room, "but it will be over for us in an instant. We won't even know what hit us. Just," he snapped his fingers, "bam."

He had been right. It didn't make Triana feel any better. Especially knowing that it might be happening in minutes.

"Six point five," Gap said.

Triana bit her lip, her mind racing. "Roc," she called out. "What about disengaging the engines completely at the ion source? We pull every plug possible."

Gap looked up with interest. His mind instantly pictured the ship floating powerless in space, drifting on their present course but never reaching Eos.

"I'm afraid that's not possible," the computer said. "There is no 'plug' for the ion power. It's directly attached to the engines. Otherwise there would be a danger of accidental disconnect. Needless to say there was never any contingency for somebody doing . . . well, doing this. Dr. Zimmer could never have envisioned an outside force ramping up the juice this way."

Triana felt a new emotion seeping in. She had already experienced frustration and fear since their encounter with Titan. Now the first stages of anger began to settle onto her. She was tired of having every possible solution shot down. Through no fault of their own, without ever disturbing Titan or whatever intelligence might lurk there, they were suddenly being condemned to death. Only four months into their journey. They had managed to survive Bhaktul and a madman. It was beginning to look like they wouldn't be so lucky this time.

It made her furious.

Just then the door to the Control Room swished open and Hannah stepped in, her face flushed. At the same time Gap called out, "Seven percent. It's picking up much faster now."

Hannah circled over to stand next to Triana. "I think we're about to catch a break," she said.

"What do you mean?" Triana said. "How?"

"Seven point five," Gap announced.

Hannah looked over at him, but Triana grabbed her shoulder and said, "What break are you talking about? Tell me."

"You'll see in about . . ." She checked her watch. "About two minutes."

Gap stood up from his workstation, despair on his face. "It's up to nine percent. It's completely out of control."

"I'm not sure we have two minutes," Triana said. She wasn't sure if it was her imagination or not, but she felt a shudder ripple through the ship. One of the crew members manning another workstation began to sob. Triana grabbed at the arm of her chair for support, her heart racing, her breathing coming in gulps, the fear and anger mixing together in a volatile combination. She looked at Hannah who seemed remarkably calm.

"Hold on," Hannah said to her softly, utter confidence in her voice.

For a minute there was no other sound in the room other than the sobs. Gap had taken another glance at the graphic on his vidscreen but kept quiet. The look on his face, however, told Triana that they must have shot past the ten-percent mark. *Galahad* was literally at its breaking point. It should happen any second now, she thought. Any—

Without warning a tone sounded, making everyone in the Control Room jump. Triana felt that her heart almost burst through her chest, and she reached out and grabbed on to the closest thing to her. That just happened to be Hannah, who had a smile stretched across her face.

Gap stole a glance at his screen and froze. He quickly typed in some commands, then looked at Triana incredulously. "I don't believe it."

"What?" Triana said, letting go of Hannah and walking over to the Head of Engineering. "What?"

Gap shook his head. "Speed and power are dropping. Down to about five percent above normal." He looked back at his screen. "Four percent. Still dropping."

Triana let her breath out in a rush. She wiped a string of perspiration from her forehead. "Roc, what did you do?" she said.

"You will never know how badly I want to take credit for this," Roc said. "I should probably just make something up. But I'm afraid I had nothing to do with it."

Triana turned to Hannah. "Okay, I think it's time for an explanation."

The grin on Hannah's face was electric. She cleared her throat. "I'm just surprised I didn't think about this before. And we probably shouldn't get too excited. Unless we find a real solution soon, this is just a postponement of our trouble."

"Hannah, I'm trying to be very patient," Triana said.

"I'm sorry. Okay, here's the deal. The energy beam from Titan has been tracking us since we arrived in Saturn's space, right? It's been like a laser shot, even while we're rocketing away at incredible speed. But we forgot that while we're moving off in one direction, Titan is not standing still."

Both Gap and Triana thought about what she was saying, the impact not dawning on either of them. Then suddenly Gap's eyes widened and his mouth curled into a smile. "Of course," he said. "It's orbiting Saturn. And now—"

"Yes," Hannah said. "Now, it has slipped behind Saturn during its trip around the planet. It can no longer 'see' us."

"You're kidding," Triana said, her own smile spreading. "That's it? It's gone behind Saturn?"

Hannah nodded. "We were looking for a shield. We got a huge one."

There was an explosion of sound from the assembled crew members. Laughing, applauding, more sobs, but this time sobs of happiness. Gap stepped over to Hannah and gave her a hug.

Triana was thrilled, but at the same time her mind wouldn't

let her celebrate too much. "Okay," she said, "but you're right. This is just a temporary fix."

Hannah, her face blushing even more following the squeeze from Gap, cleared her throat again. "Yeah. It dawned on me when I remembered in one of Nina's reports that she said something about SAT33 not being able to get away from the beam. They orbited Titan, so it was always right there; there was no escape. But it's different for us. We're moving away from Saturn and its moons, while Titan has to continue its orbit."

The emotion she had felt moments ago began to seep out of Triana. "How long?" she finally asked.

Hannah's smile disappeared as well. "Uh, that's the bad news. Titan will pop out on the other side of Saturn in about thirteen hours."

"And when it does," Gap said, "that beam is going to go right back to work on us."

Triana looked at him. "Uh-huh. Which means we have exactly thirteen hours to solve this problem."

28

She sat on her bed, putting on socks, preparing to meet Lita for lunch. A nap sounded good after an exhausting stretch over the past day and a half, but Triana couldn't see allocating her time that way. Not with the virtual countdown on their lives that had begun. This was no time for sleep.

A quick glance at the poster beside her bed made her ponder again about what was happening on Earth. The scene of Rocky Mountain National Park, with its breathtaking mountains and diversity of wildlife, had kept her company since their launch. She'd discovered that, as time passed, her feelings of homesickness were ebbing, replaced now with curiosity. And whereas before she had been curious about the people left behind on Earth, lately she had wondered—morbidly, she recognized—about the environment on the planet, about what the future would bring for a world that was losing its dominating life-form through natural causes.

Millions of years ago it was the dinosaurs who ruled. Yet, when they had been devastated by an asteroid, all sorts of changes had taken place in the Earth's ecosystem, primarily the dawning of Homo sapiens. Now, with Comet Bhaktul ravaging the human population, what species would rise to fill their spot? Would Earth see another intelligent life-form evolve, build a complex civilization, and, in turn, be wiped out? Could the cycle ever be broken? Or did Nature, she wondered, always have the last laugh?

Triana smiled at her musings. Profound thoughts, to be sure. But there were much more immediate concerns that should be occupying her time.

She looked forward to bouncing some thoughts off Lita. *Galahad*'s Director of Health always seemed to have the right perspective on things and was Triana's favorite sounding board. It was Lita who had requested they lunch together, which made Triana suspect that the fifteen-year-old had some ideas of her own.

After putting on her shoes and a fresh shirt, Triana began the daily ritual of brushing her long brown hair. She was sitting in front of her mirror when Lita buzzed at the door, then walked in.

"Hey, girlfriend."

Triana smiled at Lita's reflection in the mirror. "I'm almost ready. Have a seat."

Lita plopped onto the bed and glanced around. "It kills me how neat you keep this place. You're even in here by yourself, so nobody ever sees it. I don't know how you do it."

"Just a neat freak, I guess."

Lita shook her head. "Do me a favor and at least leave a pair of underwear or a towel lying around sometime, will you? Just to make me feel better."

Triana's smile slowly dissipated. "Not to be gloomy, but if we don't figure out a way in the next ten hours to stop this killer beam from Titan, underwear and wet towels will no longer matter."

Lita stretched back, propping herself up on her elbows, her feet dangling off the bed. "Funny you should say 'killer beam.' That's exactly what I wanted to talk to you about."

I knew it, Triana thought. She kept quiet, brushing her hair, and watched her friend in the mirror.

"I've been doing a lot of thinking about everything," Lita said, "and I have come to the conclusion that this is not a killer beam. It might be killing us, but not intentionally."

She held up a hand and began to count things off with her fingers. "One, the power grids went out several times as they probed our ship. Two, they made some sort of bizarre contact with Bon and the other patients in Sick House, almost as if they were probing their minds. Three, they altered the communications signal from the Titan research station, scrambling it into some kind of impossible code. Four, they somehow tinkered with Bon to the point that he almost killed himself with superhuman strength and endurance. And . . ." She paused before flipping up the final digit. "Five, they took over the ion drive and supercharged our speed. *Galahad* was never built to go this fast."

Triana said, "Right. So what are you trying to say?"

"I'm saying that everything they have done could maybe be interpreted as a—what's the word? Malicious?—malicious intention to destroy us. But, if you ask me, it's simply their way of . . . improving us."

Triana set down her brush and turned around to face her friend. "Improving us?"

Lita nodded. "Uh-huh. Think about it. They obviously have the power to blow us out of space without going to this much trouble. Instead, it seems they're more like galactic handymen who can't help fix something they think is broken."

Triana's eyes focused on the wall behind Lita. "So . . . they have no idea that they're killing us."

"No. As far as they're concerned, our ship—and our bodies, for that matter—are not tuned properly. They're giving us the mother of all tune-ups." She sat up on the edge of the bed. "And you want to know the best part? They told us that already, and we just didn't understand."

"What do you mean?"

"Remember when Bon was channeling those voices? Remember what they said through him? 'Help. Help here.' And we thought that meant 'help *us* here.' But it didn't. It meant 'help *is* here.'" She let that sink in a moment. "They have simply been waiting a long time to help someone. Imagine their joy when, first, they get a research station full of inferior beings, followed by an entire shipload passing by. They . . . they just don't know their own strength. Ever seen a four-year-old hurt a baby brother or sister by trying to lift them up and accidentally dislocating their shoulder?"

Triana bit her lip, then looked back at Lita. "Unbelievable. We're about to be exterminated by an intelligent life force that wants to help us."

Gap stood in front of the power grid in the Engineering Section, his hands on his hips, a disgusted look on his face. This just wasn't right: the most powerful ship ever built, the most intricate power system ever devised, and they had absolutely no control over it. Helpless, that was the word. And it was a word that Gap despised.

"This stinks," he said.

"Yes, it does," came a voice behind him.

He whirled around to find Hannah standing there, her hands clasped behind her back. She looked uncomfortable, perhaps nervous. "Oh, hi," he said. "How long have you been there?"

"Just a second. I didn't mean to startle you."

Gap waved this off. "No problem. Just deep in thought, I guess. I never heard you walk in." He leaned back against the console. "What's up?"

"Oh, just wanted to see if you had . . . I don't know, figured anything out yet."

He shook his head. "If you mean stopping the explosion, no. But I did find something a little interesting." He gestured for her to stand next to him at the power grid. Hannah hesitated, then walked shyly up to his side. Was it his imagination, or did she have some light berry scent about her? Certainly not perfume. Was it the smell of her hair?

"Look at this," he said, pointing to the graph. "The energy beam fell away as soon as Titan went behind Saturn, right? Well, you would expect that to mean all of our readings should drop to normal. But they haven't." He indicated one solitary line on the screen. "This is our total power output. It's sitting at about one percent above normal."

Hannah stared at the line. "Residual power."

Gap was impressed. "Yeah. It's like a leftover gift from Titan. Whatever that beam was doing to drive our engines above capacity, it somehow left behind a little token nudge of power."

"And that won't hurt us, right?"

"Shouldn't." Gap chuckled. "Maybe get us to Eos a little faster, though. I don't think anybody would complain about that."

Hannah eyed the power grid. Her studies at *Galahad*'s training center had given her the basic knowledge of the Engineering Section, and her work duty in the mission's first six weeks had been here, so much of what she saw now would be familiar. And, with her strong interest in math and science, Gap knew she was comfortable learning the finer details.

And he had to admit that he was enjoying her company.

Her expression turned grave. "So, any ideas at all?"

Gap exhaled and put his hands in his back pockets. "Yeah. My idea is that we find some way to tell these guys to leave us alone."

Hannah slowly broke into a smile. Gap couldn't take his eyes off her until she turned her attention to him, then quickly looked away. "But we'll figure something out," he said.

Whatever she thought of this confidence, Hannah politely nodded agreement. After an awkward moment of silence she seemed to gather a bit of courage. Quietly, in a voice that was so low that Gap had to strain to hear, she said, "I know this is a silly time to ask, but . . ." She trailed off, and Gap had the feeling that her sudden supply of courage was leaking away.

"What is it?" he said.

"Well . . . like I said, this is obviously a bad time to ask, but I was wondering . . ." She broke off again and looked down at the floor. "I was wondering if maybe sometime you wouldn't mind teaching me how to Airboard."

Gap was so surprised at the request that he stood silently for a moment. She had essentially asked him out. In a roundabout way, of course, but what did that matter? In those few seconds a hundred thoughts flashed through his head. What should he say? How should he say it? And how humbling was the lesson that he had just learned in a flash from this shy girl from Alaska? He hadn't known how to approach Triana, and had watched her get away. He hadn't known whether to approach Hannah or not, with his emotions still in a knot and his own courage very much in question. And here she was, having to make the first move.

He realized that she was mistaking his silence for "no." An embarrassed look of resignation began to cross her face, and she said, "If you can't, I understand. That's okay, I know there's a lot—"

"I'd love to," he blurted out.

She looked back up into his face, and gradually smiled again. "Really?"

He returned the smile. "Absolutely. We'll get you some pads and a helmet and get you going. You'll love it."

"It looks like fun. I mean, I've never been very sports-minded, but . . . I'd still like to try."

Gap suddenly felt terrible. They had both obviously been attracted to each other, and he'd had multiple opportunities to see her. Even a lunch or dinner together. Now she was doing the only thing she could think of to get one-on-one time with him, and it was something that she probably didn't really like at all. He felt a moment of shame.

"If you like it," he said, "great. If not, we can find something else to do." The words sounded clumsy to him, but he didn't care. For the moment Triana was a million miles away.

Hannah looked him in the eye. "I have to get back," she said. "Just call me when you get a chance to get away. After this is all cleared up, of course," she added, gesturing to the power grid.

"Yeah, no problem," he said.

Before he knew what she was doing she had pulled her other

hand from behind her back. He realized that she'd kept it hidden the entire time she'd been talking to him. Now she extended it, offering him something.

He looked down and saw her holding a small sketch, drawn with dark inks on a beige piece of paper. "I did this a couple of weeks ago, and thought you might like it," she said.

She handed him the vague drawing that she had kept on her desk. He studied the outline, recognizing himself, and sensing the care that had gone into the creation. A lump formed in his throat. How stupid had he been to have ignored her for so long?

When he looked up to thank her, she was gone.

29

Don't wander too far off," Channy said. Then, watching Iris saunter into the first row of tomato plants, she muttered to herself, "Listen to me, I'm talking to a cat like it understands anything I'm saying."

There was an unusually large amount of activity in the Domes at the moment, and Channy assumed it must be harvest time for one of the crops. She had walked around holding Iris until finally finding a peaceful spot where they wouldn't be in anyone's way. One of Bon's assistants had come around to hand water a section nearby, puzzling Channy. "I thought there was some sort of automatic watering system," she said to the worker, who responded with, "Don't ask."

Now she was bored. As predicted, the constant trek to and from the Domes had become old. And if Bon didn't seem to mind—still a little shocking to her—then perhaps it was time for Iris to move up here permanently. That would definitely be a topic of discussion at the next Council meeting.

Assuming, of course, that they could overcome this latest life-threatening dilemma.

Channy didn't want to think about that.

"Hurry up," she called out. Iris responded with a yawn, then stretched out in the soil and batted at a dirt clod. As impatient as she was, Channy couldn't help grin at the cat's playful attitude.

"Hey, you want to try one of your toys again?" She reached into the bag in her pocket and pulled out the small metal ball. "What about this one? You interested yet?" The cat's eyes were drawn to the gleam of the metal surface, but when Channy rolled it past her the interest waned again. Channy rolled her eyes. "You never want to play with that one. That's the biggest waste of a cat toy I've ever seen." She pulled the stuffed mouse out of the bag and tossed it a few feet away. Iris jumped to her feet and pounced on it.

"Figures." Exasperated, Channy kicked the metal ball off into the tomato plants. "I'll tell you what," she said to the cat. "We're going to try a little experiment, since this might become your new home. You stay here and play, and I'll come back in an hour or two, okay? You seem happy enough." She started to walk toward the path that led to the Dome exit. "I'm talking to a cat, again," she said under her breath, shaking her head.

Not far away, Triana stood in Bon's office looking out the large window into Dome 1. The buzz of activity in the fields was interesting to watch. She made a comment about this to the Swede.

"Interesting?" he said. "I suppose." He continued his work at a lab table, holding up a small beaker that held a clear liquid, just enough to cover the bottom. Using an eyedropper, he squeezed in a few drops of another substance, then swirled the mixture around. "But when you grow up around it, it becomes more of a job."

She turned to face him. "But you love it."

He grunted an answer that could have been "I guess." The mixture had begun to turn a light shade of pink. Triana couldn't tell by the look on his face whether this was the desired result or not.

She pointed to the beaker. "Is this what you wanted to talk about? Is this one of your new ideas for the Farms?"

He didn't look up, nor did he answer right away. After fiddling with the experiment for another minute he finally said, "I think so."

Triana laughed spontaneously. "That's an interesting response. You *think* so?"

When he looked up at her, she noticed for the first time that a normal color had slowly returned to his eyes. The swelled pupils had retracted, the orange glow had vanished, and she found herself gazing into the ice blue tint that she had always found beautiful. "Yeah," he said. "I think so. It's hard to explain."

"Try."

He leaned back against the lab table and stuffed his hands into his pockets. "When I woke up in Sick House, my headache was pretty much gone, and I seemed to be able to think much more clearly. As soon as I got back here to work I started coming up with some great new ideas for the crops. Some of it might have been stuff that I learned from my dad but tweaked a little bit." A troubled look came over his face. "He was . . . he was a fairly prominent hydroponics farmer in his day. Did a lot of experimental stuff with plant breeding, that sort of thing."

Triana remained silent. If Bon's feelings were anything like the ones she had for her own dad, then she understood the pain evident in his expression. Was this another link to him, another explanation for feelings that otherwise made no sense to her?

It certainly was another opportunity for her to peer inside, a momentary window into the troubled soul tucked away from everyone. As far as Triana knew, she was the only person on the ship allowed these brief glimpses. What made these moments so precious to her? Some inner need to help, to console? A nurturing gene, one that had wanted so badly to help her dad, and now detected another heart in need?

Or was she looking at it the wrong way? Maybe this was about her own loneliness, her own need to be nurtured. And would Bon have that gene within *him*? She forced herself to postpone this reflection and to refocus on their discussion.

"Anyway," Bon said, "I didn't write much down. I just thought I would start working on the ideas as time went by. But . . ." His voice trailed off and he shrugged. "But I seem to have forgotten most of it. This," he indicated the lab work, "is my best guess. I think it's pretty close to what I imagined. Bits and pieces."

"And this . . . memory loss," Triana said. "Did it start as soon as we lost contact with Titan?"

"What would that have to do with anything?"

"Maybe nothing. Maybe it's just coincidence. But that's a pretty big coincidence, wouldn't you say?" When he only stared at her, she continued. "Sounds to me like your connection with the forces on Titan have come unplugged."

After several days of the new, mellower Bon, she was taken aback by his suddenly angry tone, a tone that indicated the window had slammed shut.

"That's ridiculous," he said, the familiar scowl returning to his face. "For your information, I am not a puppet. I am not under anybody's control."

"I'm not saying you're a puppet, Bon. I'm saying—"

"I know what you're saying. You're saying that without this . . . this . . . this energy beam, or whatever you call it, I can't come up with any new ideas myself."

"That's definitely not what I'm saying. It's just—"

"Nobody controls me."

"Would you just let me finish?" she said. "For crying out loud, settle down. This is not some macho control thing."

He appeared to seethe, but crossed his arms and stared at her. She let the atmosphere cool a moment, then softened her voice.

"Listen to me. We only have some bizarre facts to go on. For one thing, you definitely were being manipulated by this beam while you were unconscious, whether you like that term or not. You've seen the video; it channeled voices into you from the other patients. We saw it, we heard it.

"Even you have to admit that your physical skills have been, shall we say, honed to a new level. The way Channy described it, you were like a superhero in the gym. I'm sorry, but that's not normal. Then you tell me that you suddenly have great ideas, things that you're sure can benefit all of us. You're anxious to try them out."

She took a deep breath. "Then, Titan disappears temporarily behind Saturn, and what happens? Your eyes start to change back to their original color, and suddenly you're having a hard time remembering these great visions you had for the Farms. Now what conclusion would *you* draw from all that?"

He remained silent, but she could tell that the words had had an impact. "Would you like to run over to the gym and see if you can replicate your last workout? I'm willing to bet that you can't. And guess what? This is not some criticism of your skills or your intellect. We have no idea what this energy beam really is, or what it's doing to you or the ship. Lita had a pretty good theory, though."

She took a minute to explain the discussion the two girls had shared. Bon seemed to relax a little more, and leaned back on the table. Finally he nodded his head.

"Okay," he admitted, "that makes sense."

For a moment Triana thought she saw the flicker of a new emotion cross Bon's face. Was it . . . fear?

The thought jolted her. Since his bizarre experience in Sick House, and the extraordinary changes in him afterward, she had never stopped to realize what toll it was taking on him. Perhaps his tough outer shell had kept her from seeing it, but now it dawned on her: Bon was afraid.

And who wouldn't be? As eerie as it is to be an observer, she thought, what must be going through his mind every waking moment?

In that instant, Triana felt a new appreciation for what Bon was experiencing, and shame for not realizing it sooner. She also knew, however, that he was not one to handle sympathy well.

She let out a long breath and took on a more businesslike air. "Listen, we would be thrilled to get some new ideas from you, regardless of where they come from. But right now we face the real possibility that in less than seven hours we won't be here to implement those ideas."

There was another minute of silence. Then, without giving it much thought, Triana reached out and took his hand. She felt him flinch. But rather than address their encounter of months ago, she decided to take a different approach. She was tired of being in limbo with her feelings.

"Bon, if you ever want to talk . . . about anything . . . I hope you'll call me."

He stared, the ice blue of his eyes boring into her. Triana could tell that his mind was racing, but he didn't release the grip with her hand. Finally, he said softly, "I'll call you."

She waited for a moment, then realized that she should be satisfied with this small step. She gave his hand a squeeze, let it drop, then turned and walked out.

Left alone, Bon watched through the glass as she hurried to the Dome exit. Then slowly he turned back to his work on the lab table, picked up the beaker, and swirled the mixture again. A few seconds later he raised his hand, the one that Triana had grasped, and inhaled her scent.

30

On his way down the corridor to the Spider bay, Gap stopped by an observation window. He leaned against the wall and peered out, his arms crossed. The inky blackness of space, punctuated with countless pinpoints of starlight, was almost hypnotic. He was pretty sure that this view would never grow old.

His mind drifted to thoughts of ancient civilizations on Earth and their tendency to create pictures in the night sky by assembling groups of stars into constellations. Orion, Ursa Minor, Virgo, Libra, Cassiopeia, the familiar characters who had kept sailors and shepherds company, inspired heroic tales, and had become the inspiration for both religious and superstitious beliefs.

His mother had taught him to recognize many of them. On one of his last nights at home before the launch, Gap had wept as he pointed out to her the constellation that housed his future home. He choked as he described the similarity of Eos to the sun, and the twin planets that each held the best chance for water and a breathable atmosphere. His mother had gripped his hand firmly, refusing to cry in front of him, trying to remain strong for him. But later, as he climbed into bed, he could hear her softly sobbing behind her bedroom door.

Now, not for the first time, he wondered about the star patterns they would see when they arrived at Eos. Would some of them look the same as they had on Earth? Would there be a mixture of old and new? And would the star travelers of *Galahad* become star artists themselves, and create their own zodiac images?

A more frightening question forced its way into his thoughts: would they even make it to Eos? Only four months into the trip and they were already dealing with a second crisis, this one more perplexing than the first because of the eerie, unknown factor. At least with the mystery of the stowaway, as life-threatening as it was, they knew they were dealing with a person. Exactly what were they dealing with from Titan? How could they combat it when they still didn't even know what it was? And could they solve the mystery before it was too late? They had five hours until the energy beam began its relentless assault yet again.

Gap turned his head and looked at his surroundings. This part of the ship, just down the hall from the Spider bay, was where they had originally confronted the madman determined to murder them. And it was where Gap's heart had taken a direct hit.

It was one of the reasons he had stopped at the window just now. His assignment was in the Spider bay, but he was obviously stalling. Besides, Hannah had burst into the picture now, a complication Gap had never expected. But then, he thought, you never do, right? At least that's what all the songs said. Was this moment of hesitation finally his chance to float all of his feelings to the surface, to figure out exactly how he felt?

That was the problem. He wasn't exactly sure what he felt.

"All right, enough of this," he finally said to himself, and pushed away from the window.

He swept into the Spider bay, which hosted *Galahad*'s eight remaining Spiders—one of which was unfinished and unable to support life in space—as well as the gleaming gray metal pod from Titan Research Station SAT33. Gap's job was to give the pod another once-over to see if they had missed something, anything that could shed some light on how to deal with this deadly energy beam. In particular, he hunted for data discs. None had turned up in the original search, but their desperation called for another try. Hannah had suggested that a data disc on the pod, with direct recordings from Nina or other station members, would have been spared the scrambled code.

A couple of long tables sat near the pod, covered with many of the items already pulled out during the initial search. Gap walked past these, his footsteps echoing in the large hangar, pausing long enough to pick through the scattered collection, until the pod's open hatch beckoned. He pulled himself up into the small craft, mindful to use his right arm primarily, still a little hesitant to put too much weight on his newly mended left collarbone. The pod's lights were on, as were a couple of additional work lights that had been assembled by the original search team. These bathed the interior with a soft glow and reduced the number of shadowy corners and crevices that might hold secrets.

For a moment Gap just stood there, swiveling his head to look around the cramped compartment, taking in the scene, imagining what it would be like to be locked inside, asleep for months or years as the pod sliced through space.

But the cryo tube intended for an adult had been empty, which meant that the person who could answer their questions and solve the mystery of SAT33 had missed the trip. Had it been an accident? Or had they missed the launch intentionally? Was it possible that *Galahad* was the last place they wanted to be?

Why?

"Yeah, why?" Gap said to no one. He walked past the coffin-like tube, running his hand along the clear glass top. The storage bins along the wall had been searched, more than once actually, and yet he felt obliged to check every crack and dark corner again. He stood on tiptoes and felt along the top, unsure of why anyone would stash a data disc in such a remote location in the first place but determined to cover every square inch, if necessary.

He moved over to the pilot's seat and gazed at the stitching along the back. No pouches, no hidden compartments. Crouching and climbing, he slipped into the padded chair with a grunt. The array of instruments that surrounded him would have been daunting without the extensive training he had received from Dr. Zimmer and the other *Galahad* instructors. His natural curiosity and love of anything technical kept him from being intimidated.

But there was nothing that looked out of the ordinary. Without having flown in this particular model, he could still recognize the gauges for rocket control, for internal life-support systems, for communication, for . . .

Wait. The communication system. He understood this switch, and this one. Even this one. But what was this? It looked like an extension to the communication panel, one that Gap wasn't familiar with. A small set of buttons, and one additional toggle switch, sitting there by itself, calling to him, daring him to push it.

So, without hesitating, he did.

For a split second nothing happened. Then, two green lights around the switch blinked, went dark, blinked again, and then became solid points of light. Gap heard a mechanical whirring, and watched, fascinated, as a small panel slid open, ejecting a small disc, small enough to fit into the palm of his hand. It sat there, gleaming in the soft glow of the cockpit and reflecting the emerald flecks of light from the console.

This time, Gap did hesitate. He blinked a couple of times and put his hand up to his face, rubbing his chin. Even without knowing the contents of the disc, he somehow knew that this could be exactly what they were looking for.

He finally reached out, extracted the tiny disc from the slot, then held it up to the light. There were no markings. The shiny gray surface had all of the features one would expect from a generic data recording disc. The space usually reserved for writing an identifying description was blank. Sloppy work, Gap thought, something you wouldn't expect from seasoned researchers assigned to such an important task.

Sloppy, unless the person recording the data was in a hurry. Or expected to be around to fill in the details later.

Maybe even expected to be on the pod when it launched, tucked soundly asleep in the cryogenics tube.

Gap slipped the disc into his shirt pocket and quickly scanned the rest of the control panel. Then, unfolding himself from the seat, he scrambled to the pod's hatch and dropped to the floor of the Spider bay.

This time the idea of protecting his mended shoulder never crossed his mind.

31

Triana had known for two years the faces that stared back at her now from around the table in the Conference Room. She had lived with them, trained with them, grieved with them, and, in rare moments, celebrated with them. She felt that she could read their expressions with a high degree of accuracy by now, whether it was fear, anger, doubt, joy, or dismay. Her dad had told her that faces might lie, but eyes never did, and until this extraordinary voyage she had never quite grasped the concept.

Today the eyes of her fellow Council members, and Hannah Ross, cried out for hope.

"I have some good news," she said, "and some . . . not so good news."

"Uh, but not bad news?" Channy said.

"No. Maybe another mystery to toss on top of the pile, but not bad. Yet."

The countdown until Titan roared from behind Saturn and resumed its assault on *Galahad* had dwindled to two hours. Triana figured that was the only bad thing, but it didn't count as news.

"I'll get straight to the point," she said. "Hannah and I have spent the past couple of hours opening the files on the data disc that Gap pulled out of the pod. The information is overwhelming, to say the least. At the end you'll see that we have yet another question to answer. But at least we have turned over a few more cards on the table. And, considering the boat we're in right now, every single bit of data is critical."

Grim, but silent, nods greeted this.

"I'm going to let Hannah tell you what we've turned up. She has spent so much time on this project, including the transmitted data stream, that she can probably best fill you in."

Hannah, who had lined up her work pad so that its base was even with the edge of the table, cleared her throat. "Triana's right, there's a ton of information on this disc, so bear with me. It's not everything we're looking for, but it has filled in a lot of the gaps." She glanced down at her work pad. "For one thing, the disc itself is almost a personal diary, of sorts, from Nina Volkov. It has several complete reports from her, including a few video reports. We . . . we actually have seen her telling us some of the stories."

As she listened to Hannah, Triana recalled the many faces of Nina Volkov captured by the video and audio recording files on the disc: curious in some, animated in many of them, and flat-out terrified in the last one.

"In a way," Hannah said, "this disc was meant as a ship's log. Nina had every intention of being on the pod when it left SAT33, but she knew the dangers involved, and the risks she was taking. She was prepared to go into cryogenic freeze, but for all she knew we would never make the rendezvous. Or any of a thousand other things could go wrong. She wanted a record, even an elementary one, to survive her. She threw as much stuff onto the disc as possible.

"Including a brief description of . . ." Hannah stopped and looked at Triana, who responded with a solitary nod of her head. "A description of the Cassini."

All of the Council members had the same question on their lips: Who are the Cassini? But each one instantly figured it out for themselves.

"So, those are our little friends on Titan, I suppose," Gap said. "They call themselves Cassini?"

"No," Hannah said. "That's the name Nina gave them. She had

no idea what to call them, so she just picked the name of the early space probe that explored Saturn and its moons years ago. Once she used the name she never bothered to go back and think of something else."

Lita spoke up. "You said she gave a brief description of them. I'm dying to know what she said."

This brought a half-smile to Hannah's face. Triana knew that they had touched on her passion, evident in her after-hours dedication, her studies, her conversation. Even in her artwork. Hannah would, no doubt, be the most excited crew member to talk about life outside of Earth's protective cocoon. The fact that this particular branch of life was very close to extinguishing *Galahad* and all of its passengers had apparently taken a backseat to the historic discovery.

"Here's the most important thing about the Cassini," Hannah said. "It seems that all of us, everyone on Earth, has always imagined that the first extraterrestrial life we found would be very primitive, maybe microscopic cells bumping into each other. Plants, if we were lucky. The first explorations for life on Mars concentrated on finding bacteria-sized life buried under the surface. Very few people thought beyond that.

"Then there were people who wondered about intelligent life. Would we ever talk to 'someone else?' Would we pick up radio signals from outer space? The whole SETI program was all about that: the Search for Extra-Terrestrial Intelligence. Giant antennas, or even groups of several, all searching the sky for alien broadcasts."

Gap interrupted her. "But the distances are incredible. Even if some intelligent beings, five hundred light-years away, picked up our own early radio shows, it would be a thousand years before we ever got a return call. They might be out there listening, all right, but that's a long time to wait."

"That's exactly right," Hannah said. "Hollywood didn't help matters, by making it seem like Earth is simply an easy exit from some alien superhighway. They've created an image in peoples' minds that when we find intelligent life, it's going to either look like us, or very similar. You know, two arms, two legs, a head. But . . . that's just not the way it is."

Triana smiled, now just as excited as Hannah. Yes, the threat still lingered, but somehow the exhilaration of this discussion—maybe it was Hannah's contagious enthusiasm—outweighed the doom. Triana found herself leaning forward on the conference table.

"Some people have claimed that we humans are arrogant," Hannah said. "That we think we're the most advanced creatures in the universe, therefore every other intelligent being will look like us. But I don't think that's the reason. I think it's just because . . . well, because we don't have any other template to go by. Since the earliest days of our civilization we've only known our kind. That's not arrogance. We're just naïve."

She squirmed a bit in her chair and made eye contact with each Council member. "The Cassini are obviously intelligent. In fact, Nina Volkov suggested that we're like toddlers who barely come up to their knees. Which is a pretty good analogy. We have barely started to grow, and the Cassini are well into old age."

"How old?" Channy said.

Hannah shrugged. "I have a couple of video clips on the disc from Nina herself. In one of them she tries to answer that question." She looked around the table. "Would you like to meet her?"

"Are you kidding?" Lita shouted. "Let's see it."

"Roc will play it for you," Triana said to Hannah. "Which file?"

"Number three seven seven, two oh oh, Roc, please."

Each Council member turned to one of the handful of vidscreens around the table. When the screens came to life, their eyes were suddenly transfixed on the image of a young woman, maybe late twenties, with short, dark hair that fell straight to her collar. A slender, pointed nose was set above thin lips that had been covered with a light shade of red. Nina Volkov appeared fit and strong, and the initial impression was that of a rebel. Wild hoop earrings dangled against fair skin, which also displayed a touch of makeup. Her standard-issue jumpsuit seemed to be her only concession to the rules, and even then she turned up the collar and added a brightly colored chain around her neck. From the chain dangled what appeared to be a man's ring, with a brilliant blue stone. She absentmindedly fingered the ring as she worked.

For the first thirty seconds of the video file she didn't pay much attention to the filming, instead focusing on getting her notes together and pushing at something just off the screen, as if to move it out of the way. She finally spoke, keeping her head tilted down to her notes.

"File number . . ." She seemed to search her work pad. "Number three seven seven, two oh oh. Nina Volkov, research station S-A-T three three." Her accent was distinctly Russian, and Triana liked the way she emphasized each letter and number. Another part of her rebelliousness?

She pushed again at something just off camera, then continued her report. "The Cassini study is breaking down again. The energy stream that has been bombarding us off and on has finally taken its toll. But from what Kel and I can make of the enormous amount of data . . . that's Kelvin Pernice, for the record. From what we can tell, it would appear that the Cassini are beyond ancient. Kel's guess—and this is only an educated, scientific speculation—would date their civilization at around a billion years."

There were gasps around the conference table. The thought was staggering. Nina put it into context with her next statement.

"That's so much older than any known plant or animal life-forms on Earth. We were still just cellular soup ingredients back then. But the Cassini had already begun a complicated life process."

"Hold the file there, please, Roc," Triana said. The image of Nina froze on the vidscreens. Triana looked around at the assembled group. "Now we know just exactly what we're dealing with.

This is not some parallel life-form. The Cassini have had a billion year head start on us."

Gap whistled. "I guess that explains why their power is so incredible. Why they can track us millions of miles away, even as a moving target. And why they seem to be able to play with our ship like a toy."

"I hate to be impatient," Lita said. "But . . . what are they?"

Hannah looked at Triana. "I'd like to try to explain that myself, if that's okay. But quickly, can we play just a few more seconds of this file? If you were like me you wondered what Nina was messing around with off the screen. Watch this. Roc?"

The image picked up again. Nina referenced another file for information about the power equations she and Kelvin Pernice had worked out. Then suddenly, an orange and black tail swished in front of Nina's face, and she shooed it away.

Channy blurted out a laugh. "It's Iris."

A moment later the cat walked completely into the picture, and Nina took the drastic measure of lifting her off the table and setting her on the floor. "Go play," she said.

Channy's face changed to an expression of sorrow. "Ohhhh. That makes me sad to watch. Iris was her little friend." She turned to Lita. "That hurts my heart." Lita put her hand on the shoulder of *Galahad*'s Activities Director.

Hannah paused the video playback again and wrinkled her brow. "It's hard to say exactly what the Cassini are. In fact, I think it's more accurate to say what the Cassini *is*."

Gap studied her face, trying to puzzle out the distinction in what she was telling them. "So," he said, "the Cassini are not . . . alive? They're . . . a machine, or something?"

Hannah shook her head. "No, we're definitely dealing with a life-form. But . . ." She squinted, trying to find the right words. "Nina and this guy, Kel, believed that the Cassini pretty much cover the entire surface of Titan. Like a net, or web. But all of the parts make up just one incredibly large being. The Cassini might be made up of trillions and trillions of pieces, but they all come together to form just one entity." She looked back at Gap, then Triana. "Does that make sense?"

Gap sat back in his chair. "That's . . . amazing."

"Yeah. Here's another way to think about it. Remember watching a huge flock of birds, hundreds of them in a pack, flying through the sky, and they all seem to turn sharply at exactly the same time? Or . . ." She glanced up quickly, then back at Gap. "Or a school of fish, a big school, all swimming in the same direction, then somehow the whole school darts another direction, almost like they're connected somehow? That's kinda what the Cassini are like. Connected."

"But not necessarily physically," Triana interjected. "You mean they're tied together through, what, thought waves?"

"Yeah, something like that. Like a trillion parts of one giant brain."

There was silence for a minute, then Lita finally spoke up.

"Wow. I guess that helps clear up a couple of things. One, the power that an entire moon-sized brain could muster would obviously explain what we've been dealing with. And, two, remember that message we got from Titan through Bon?"

Bon, who had been sitting quietly during the entire meeting, nodded. "The voices that came out of my mouth. They said 'I wait. I wait so long.' Not we. I."

"I'm getting creeped out again," Channy said.

"Yeah, well, if you like that, check this out," Hannah said. The vidscreen resumed its playback after Nina had deposited Iris on the floor. She made a notation on her work pad, unconsciously touched the ring hanging from the chain around her neck, then, for the first time during the recording, looked up, directly into the camera.

Her eyes glowed with a shade of orange.

32

Nina Volkov's bizarre eyes stared from the vidscreens in *Galahad*'s Conference Room. All five members of the Council, along with Hannah Ross, met the gaze across time and space, each of them holding their breath. It was Bon who finally broke the trance.

"Cool," he said.

Hannah stopped the video playback. She straightened her work pad, which had become slightly tilted, then looked at Bon. "I thought you might appreciate that."

Triana bit her lip. "So Nina is—or was—one of the few people in tune with the Cassini's mental frequency." She thought about this for a second. "That tells us a lot."

"Yeah," Lita said. "It tells us why she was able to gather so much information on the Cassini so quickly. Nina was already a scientific genius, or she wouldn't have been on SAT33 in the first place. Then, with that energy beam's 'improvement,' she leapt ahead like crazy. Just like Bon's training in agriculture, how he instantly started imagining new ways to improve our crops. The tweak from the Cassini seems to take a person's natural skills and amp them up a few notches, doesn't it?"

"I think so," Hannah said. "It probably enhances all of a person's abilities over time, but the earliest signs will come from their own instinctive talent."

"Wait a minute, though," Channy said. "Nina was obviously a smart girl. She had to know that this . . . this beam was . . . I mean, didn't it hurt them like it's hurting us?"

"We can't get in touch with them, so I'm assuming the worst," Triana said. She felt the same frustration that had blanketed her before, and took a deep breath, remembering her dad's comments about too much on her plate. One thing at a time. One thing at a time.

"We can't worry about what happened to them," she said. "We have our own issues right now." She turned to Hannah. "Does Nina tell us anything about stopping the energy beam from Titan?"

"She makes a reference to something that *has* to be about the beam. She called it 'the translator.'"

This caught Lita's attention immediately. "Of course," she said, spreading her hands. "We already know that the Cassini tries to communicate. They—or it, I guess; it's weird thinking about this as one being—channeled those voices through Bon."

"And," Gap broke in, "it altered the data stream from SAT33. We've already talked about trying to shut it down. A translating device makes total sense."

Hannah said, "Let me play the file from her that mentions it. Roc, I'm going to need number three seven seven, three oh four, please." Before hitting the play button, she explained what they were going to hear.

"Most of Nina's work, unfortunately, was loaded into the data stream. She put very little on this personal disc, probably because she expected to be on the pod and didn't know it would be her final report. As far as she was concerned, she would be there to explain everything. So a few of the files, like the one we just saw, were video records, but most of them are quick audio files, like this one. And this one," she said, looking around the table, "is her final entry. This is the last thing she recorded before the pod launched. It's the first time that it occurs to her that she . . . that she might not make it."

The gravity of what they were about to hear did not seem to be lost on the Council members' faces. Hannah pushed the button, and Nina's voice filled the room. She sounded anxious, out of breath.

"File number . . . oh, I don't know the file, and it's not—" A warning siren sounded in the background, and a low rumble could be heard beneath the sound. A pause occurred in Nina's account, and Triana could visualize the young scientist scrambling, trying to get the situation under control. A situation that very likely was deadly.

"Overload again on the main reactor," Nina dictated, "and this time I don't think there's any way to slow it down." There was a mishmash of sounds again, a worried sigh from the scientist, and the sounds of the siren cutting off. "Enough of that," Nina muttered.

After another minute of unintelligible noise, she picked up again, a tinge of terror in her voice. "Iris is aboard and asleep, the translator is aboard, along with a few of my notes. If I don't make it back, at least the data stream has the raw information." It was, as Hannah had indicated, the first sign that Nina wondered about her security. "I know it's foolish for me to go back, but there's almost six minutes until launch. That's plenty of time to go get Kel's ring and make it back. In any event, the automatic launch sequence is running smoothly." A muffled roar in the background sounded ominous. "I'll be right back," Nina added, which in other circumstances might have sounded funny in a personal recording.

Except *Galahad*'s Council members realized that she hadn't made it back.

"I don't believe it," Channy said, her eyes watering. "She actually went back into the station to get . . . to get her boyfriend's ring. That has to be the ring that we saw earlier on the video."

Lita was respectfully quiet, then said softly. "I guess we have to assume that Kel was her boyfriend, the same guy who worked with her on the Cassini data, and he . . ." She looked up at Triana. "He must have died."

Triana nodded. "And she didn't want to leave SAT33 without his ring. She lost her own life just by going back for it."

"Something happened in those six minutes," Gap said. "The situation must have gone from bad to worse quickly. I don't think she would have gone back if she thought—" He broke off the sentence, aware of every eye on him. "I mean, would she?"

Channy wiped away a tear and fixed him with a stare. "I don't know, Gap. Have you ever been in love?"

The awkward silence lingered until Triana spoke up. "Listen, we have to get back to business. No matter what happened back on the research station, Nina distinctly said that the translator—whatever it is—made it onto the pod. It's somewhere on this ship right now." She glanced at the clock in the corner of the vidscreen. "And we have one hour, fifty-two minutes to find it."

"I hate to throw negative vibes into this," Gap said, "but is it possible that the translator *was* on the pod, but Nina accidentally took it back into the station with her? Like, in a pocket or something?"

The sound of the room's ventilation system filled the silence as this question sank in. Lita finally shook her head.

"There's no way. She said, 'the translator is aboard.' That means stowed somewhere, not bouncing around in her pocket. The only problem is that she fully expected to hand it over to us when we picked up the pod, so I'm sure it's not labeled. We might have even seen it and didn't know it."

"What in the world does a translator look like, anyway?" Channy said. "Is it a box? Is it big? Is it a computer disc?"

Hannah shrugged. "Who knows?"

Triana bit her lip, listening to this exchange. She said, "I know this sounds crazy, but, Roc, what are the chances of us building one of these translators?"

When the computer answered her, the usual jovial tone was gone. "I think it's entirely possible to build a translator. We have the garbled data stream, and the beam itself, to study. But the problem is time, Tree. If we haven't been able to crack their code by now, an hour and a half won't be enough time."

Lita began silently tapping her stylus against her cheek, her eyes focused on a spot on the vidscreen in front of her. She suddenly put the stylus on the table and asked Triana, "If this translator, whatever it is, is really the answer, then why—"

"Why didn't the scientists on SAT33 use it to save themselves?" finished Hannah.

Lita nodded.

"They did, actually," Hannah said. "But not before it was too late. From what I can piece together from Nina's recordings, a series of explosions took out most of the crew. A couple more seemed to have taken their own lives, when it seemed hopeless. This . . . friend of Nina's, Kel, finally was able to build a prototype translator, which from all indications seems to have stopped their own power surges.

"But," she added, "even though he had stopped it, the damage was done to most of their reactors. A major malfunction released critical amounts of radiation in the lab portion of the station, killing the remaining scientists, including Kel. The only reason Nina was spared was because she was in a protective suit, preparing to leave the station and make repairs on the outside. It saved her life."

"Temporarily," Triana said.

"And she kept his ring around her neck after that," mused Channy. "I can't imagine how she must have felt."

"Yeah," Lita said, "the last person left alive out of thirty."

Bon slapped his hand on the table, making the other Council members jump.

"This is ridiculous," he said, his eyes now entirely back to their original ice blue, flashing. "I'm not coming this far to give up. The pod is just not that big. We *must* have missed it somehow." He looked down the table at Triana. "I say we go back right now and tear it apart."

A look of irritation crossed Gap's face. You weren't even there in the first place, he thought, and almost said exactly that when he remembered what Bon had been experiencing at the time. Instead, he said, "I don't even think that's necessary. I say we zero in on those tables full of stuff that we already unloaded. Nina wouldn't have hidden the translator in some secret compartment. She *wanted* us to have it."

Triana looked around the table. "Okay. Let's meet there in fifteen minutes. And we're not leaving the Spider bay until we have that translator."

33

On her way to the lower level, Lita made a quick stop into Sick House. She was relieved to find Alexa sitting at the desk, inputting data from the creepy incident with Bon and the other Cassini patients. Alexa looked up and pushed a lock of blond hair out of her eyes.

"So, what's the word?" she said.

"We've had a scavenger hunt dumped into our laps," Lita said, waving her hand when Alexa offered the chair, instead choosing to sit on the edge of the desk. "Not much of a challenge, though. We're only looking for something we've never seen before, we don't know what it looks like, and we have no idea where it might be. Other than that, no problem."

"Ugh," Alexa said. "Listen, I don't want to be mean or anything, but you don't look so good. When's the last time you got any sleep?"

Lita chuckled. "What's sleep?"

"That's what I thought. What can I do to help?"

"I guess just keep an eye on the shop here. In a little over an hour that orange moon is going to pop out the other side of Saturn, and we might have another round of patients spilling into the hospital. I appreciate your help more than you know." She stood up. "I'm heading down to the Spider bay. If anything comes up, you can reach me there."

Alexa climbed out of the chair and gave Lita a hug. "I'll be here if you need anything else," she said.

Lita walked out into the corridor and turned toward the lift. She knew that Alexa was right, that fatigue was becoming an issue, not just with her but with the entire Council. And tired minds didn't function nearly as well. She wondered if they would even be able to see clearly to find whatever they were looking for.

The door to the lift opened and Lita stepped inside. Think, she told herself, think. What would this translator look like? Think. And how would it be used? Where would you install it? Into a radio transmitter? Would it be something that Roc could use to intercept the energy beam and tweak it?

As the lift descended to the level that housed the Spider bay, she forced her exhausted brain to work harder than ever. How does the beam function? What effects did it have on the ship and the crew? For one thing it was taking over the power source of the ship. It also had linked up telepathically with Bon and several other crew members, channeling their thoughts and voices through the Swedish Council member. But what was its goal when it did that?

The door to the lift opened on the dim lower level, and Lita began the roundabout walk to the Spider bay, her mind still racing. Hannah had said that the power beam was a two-way transmission from Titan, delivering its "improvements" while taking back information about the ship. So that meant the beam was . . .

Lita froze in her tracks. Her face went slack, her eyes blinking slowly as the puzzle pieces began to slip into place. Of course, she thought. A two-way transmission from Titan.

"Why didn't I think about that in the first place?" she said, a smile spreading across her face.

Fifty-four minutes. Fifty-four minutes until the Cassini, embedded throughout the mysterious moon of Titan, reconnected with its target, its latest fix-up project: *Galahad*.

With all of the pressure bearing down, with a countdown that was a virtual death clock sealing their fate, Triana wondered how she could worry about anything else. And yet, she hadn't counted on this arrangement. All of the Council members, along with Hannah Ross, had agreed to meet at the pod to launch an all-out search for the SAT33 translator. Yet Lita had taken a quick detour to Sick House, Channy had gone to pick up Iris before joining them, and Hannah had not yet arrived. Which left Triana in the hangarlike Spider bay.

With Gap and Bon.

She felt an extra layer of tension wrap itself around her. Somehow it always came back to these two guys, one who had harbored obvious feelings for her, and another whom she had personally connected with for a brief instant. And now the love triangle—a corny expression, she admitted, but the only one that seemed to fit the circumstances—was exposed in a way that prevented her from escaping. She *had* to be here, there was crucial work to do, and somehow her feelings—and those of Bon, if he had any, and Gap, if they still existed—would have to wait.

Easier said than done, she thought.

At least there was activity to distract all of them. Triana sifted through the piles of objects that had been unloaded from the metal pod, three large tables' worth. Gap stood to her left, leafing through a stack of papers from a folder. The frown on his face was evidence enough for Triana that he had found nothing. Or did the frown represent something else?

Bon, kneeling to her right, peered into several boxes that had been stacked under the table. His organizational system entailed tossing a finished box into a corner, accompanied by a silent curse. So far his search had turned up spare parts, another first-aid kit, and some more emergency food rations. As Triana watched, he threw another box into the corner, then wiped his brow.

"Where is it?" he said. "I'm sick of this."

It dawned on Triana that Bon had an additional concern that she hadn't taken into consideration. His unwillingness to submit as a pawn to the powers on Titan was obviously fueling his intensity at the moment. She realized that the countdown was more than just a threat to the ship for the temperamental Swede; for him it marked the end of his independence, a concept more alien to Bon than any life force they would find on a distant world.

She resisted the urge to reach out to him. That would only make things worse, especially in front of Gap. Thankfully the moment was broken by the sound of footsteps approaching. She looked up to see Hannah.

"What do you need me to do?" Hannah said.

"Just dive in, anywhere."

Hannah hesitated, then walked slowly over to the table where Gap was hard at work. Triana thought she saw a flicker of a smile dart across Gap's face as he waved hello, the first smile she had seen from him in a long time. A moment later the two had teamed up to sort through the mound of paperwork and folders on the table before them.

Triana let out an exasperated sigh. Time was running out, and this didn't seem to be getting them anywhere. It wouldn't matter if a hundred people were helping right now; the translator was not going to turn up in this pile of junk, at least not in the next—she glanced at her watch—forty-nine minutes. For the first time, she felt her spirits begin to sink.

Yet she refused to let these feelings show. Instead, she tried to puzzle the situation out again.

"Okay," she said to the others, "here's the deal. All of this stuff had to have been stored on the pod for a while, long before Nina launched from the research station." Gap, Hannah, and Bon stopped what they were doing and turned to face her. "But, as far as we know, the only things Nina brought on board were the bag full of gear and rations, the data disc that Gap found, and . . ." She paused before finishing. "And Iris."

Gap looked puzzled. "What are you saying? That the cat is the translator?"

"No, but as far as I can tell, she didn't pack anything else."

Bon stood up and brushed the knees of his pants. "I agree. I think we're wasting our time."

Gap snorted. "So, what, we just give up?"

Triana was about to answer when the door to the corridor opened and Lita hurried in, smiling.

"Any luck?" she asked Triana.

"No. What are you so happy about?"

Lita didn't answer at first. She grabbed a sturdy box that had been stashed under one of the tables and sat down on it. Then she said, "We better find that translator, that's all I have to say. Because I think I've figured out how it works."

Hannah tossed a handful of papers onto the table. "What? What do you mean?" She and the others closed in around Lita.

Again the door opened, this time admitting Channy, who held Iris up over her shoulder like a baby being burped. The Activities Director took one look at the scene before her and said, "What did I miss?"

"Nothing yet," Lita said. "But I might have figured out how the translator works."

Triana crossed her arms. "All right, let's hear it."

Lita leaned forward, her elbows on her knees, and clasped her hands in front of her. "Okay. It finally dawned on me that this . . . this force, or whatever you call it, is all about communication. It doesn't have any feelings that we know of. It just relays information on how to improve the ship, how to improve the primitive life-forms on the ship, how to make everything more efficient.

"The ship has its own data banks and internal communications system, so when the Cassini retracts that information the ship is just basically acknowledging the changes. The ship has no feelings, either. It can't say, 'no, thank you.' It just takes its orders and implements them. So our ion drive will increase power to the point of blowing itself up. It doesn't have a rational mind of its own to tell the Cassini to stop. Like . . . like some aquarium fish; if you feed them too much, they'll just keep eating until they eat themselves to death."

Gap said, "I still don't see how the translator works, then."

Lita smiled at him. "Well, think about what happened with Bon and the others in Sick House. They went into a trance, right? Their eyes went crazy and a powerful energy beam started rattling around inside their brains because they're on the same wavelength. The Cassini started tinkering with them. But—"

"But," Hannah burst in, "it's trying to take *back* some information at the same time!"

Lita nodded. "That's right. Just like the information it took back from the ship." She looked at Bon. "When you started in with your creepy little chant, with all of those voices, that was Titan's way of acknowledging that they had accessed your brain. You were like a human blueprint that they were trying to read. They learned our languages pretty quickly, then went to work on 'repairing' you. Since then it's been a one-way conversation. Notice that your headache went away, and so did the voices."

Bon remained still, looking uncomfortable as the center of attention.

Triana bit her lip, then said, "Okay, that all makes sense. But I still don't understand how the translator fits into all of this."

Lita stood up and began walking in a tight circle around the group. "This power force, or beam, has locked on to Bon's brain, and the others', because they have frequencies that . . . fit, I guess you could say. Bon didn't have to do anything. With his mental frequency, the door to his brain was open, so the Cassini just walked right in.

"Now," she continued, her pace around the group increasing, "the translator should be nothing more than an object that he holds in his hands. It makes contact with Bon, and when the beam connects with him, his brain waves should be able to communicate with it. Turn it back into a two-way conversation. Then you can politely ask them to turn the beam off." She came to a stop and spread her hands. "In theory, anyway."

Triana stood still, biting her lip and staring at *Galahad*'s Health Director. The Spider bay was deadly silent. It seemed that everyone's brain was spinning, each trying to make the leap that would solve the mystery of the missing device. Iris began to squirm, so Channy put her on the floor, where she began to sniff the objects taken from the pod.

Finally, Triana said to Lita, "Does this help us figure out what the translator would look like?"

Lita shrugged. "Well, for one thing it wouldn't be very big. It would have to fit into the palm of your hand."

"Right," Gap said. "That eliminates some of this mess." He tossed a handful of papers onto the table nearest him. "This would be almost like a small piece of electronics."

"Has anyone seen something like that?" Triana said, looking around. Silent stares greeted her. Iris lost interest in the pod materials and began to purr and rub up against Hannah's leg.

Suddenly Channy jumped, as if jolted by an electric shock. "Oh! Oh! Oh!" she exclaimed, her hands coming up to the sides of her face.

"What?" Triana said, growing alarmed.

Channy, her eyes huge, seemed to be in her own trance. Then she turned to Triana and said, "The translator. I know where it is."

34

This might not be the best time to talk about this, but if Channy really knows where the translator is located, then I'd like to reserve some time to speak with the Cassini myself. There are a handful of questions that are begging to be asked.

Like, how long did it take for your web to spread over the surface of Titan? And what is the source of your power? Is it the internal core heat of the moon itself? Is it the radiation from Saturn?

And what about that power beam? If it's such a force for good, why hasn't Bon done something about that hair of his?

Without another sound Channy turned and sprinted toward the door that led out of the Spider bay and into the corridor. She yelled back over her shoulder, "C'mon!"

The other Council members, and Hannah, exchanged confused looks, watching Channy's bright yellow T-shirt streak toward the door. Triana looked at the others and said, "Well, let's go." She pointed a finger at Bon. "Especially you. If she really does know where it is, we have no time to waste." That time had dwindled to thirty-nine minutes.

By the time the group reached the door, they could hear Channy's pounding steps up around the curve of the corridor, closing in on the lift door. Gap yelled ahead to her, "Hold up!" He looked over at Hannah. "You know, I'm fast, but I don't think I could catch her in a race. That girl is a blur." Hannah only smiled in return as they raced toward the lift.

Rounding the corner, they found Channy leaning out of the open lift door, a look of urgency on her face. "C'mon," she said. The group, huffing and puffing, piled in with her. As soon as the doors sealed, Triana exhaled loudly and put her hand on Channy's shoulder. "Okay, detective, wanna clue us in?"

Channy's face broke into a wide smile. "Of course, I could be wrong—"

"Oh, great," Gap said, leaning his good arm against the side of the lift.

"But I don't think so," Channy finished. "It makes sense. As soon as you said it's something that you could hold in your hand. I've already held it several times."

Hannah seemed beside herself. "So tell us. What is it?"

But Channy was enjoying the attention. She beamed at Hannah, then playfully raised her eyebrows and flexed her bicep like a bodybuilder. "See, just because you have muscles doesn't mean you can't be brainy, too."

Lita turned to Triana. "I'm going to deck her before we ever get off the lift." Then to Channy she said, "And just where are we getting off this thing?"

"The Domes."

"The Domes?" the group said in chorus.

Channy was just about to answer as the lift came to a stop and the door opened to reveal the lush vegetation sprawled before them. "This way," Channy said, turning to her left and heading toward the short passage that led from the first dome to the second.

"Listen, we have—" Triana consulted her watch again. "We have a little more than thirty-five minutes. Is it okay if we walk and talk?"

The group clustered around Channy as she walked briskly toward the second of *Galahad*'s domes. In a moment they left the sterile confines of the passageway and found themselves under the glistening starlight of Dome 2. Not for the first time, Triana relished the scent that accompanied the flourishing plant life: smells of rich soil, flowering plants, fruits and vegetables coming into their prime. She inhaled deeply; the scents automatically triggered thoughts of home.

"You know what made me think of it?" Channy said. "Iris."

"How come?" Lita said, right on her heels.

"Because I've been trying like crazy to get her to play with it. She won't, of course, because she's a cat, and it has to be her idea."

It suddenly clicked with Triana. "That ball," she said. "It was a small, metal ball."

"Uh-huh." Channy pushed a large, leafy branch out of the way as she hurried down the path. "It was in the bag with Iris's stuff, and I just thought it was one of her toys. She kinda likes the stuffed mouse, but this ball did nothing for her."

"And since Nina was in a hurry and had to pack light, she just threw it in the bag with the cat's collar and stuff," Gap said.

"And, since she thought she would be here with us," Lita reminded them, "it was no big deal to her. She probably didn't give it a second thought to just toss it in with the other things."

Channy slowed to a stop. She looked back and forth, then dropped to one knee and scanned beneath a row of tomato plants. Gap squatted next to her.

"Well?" he said.

"I know it's around here somewhere. This is where I was when I tossed it to her. Right there," Channy said, pointing to a spot about ten feet off the trail.

The group fanned out and began pushing leaves and vines out of the way. Hannah fell to her hands and knees and crawled in a semicircle between two rows of plants. Bon moved off to one side, using his foot to push plant life aside, a scowl of frustration back on his face.

After almost two minutes of searching, Channy looked exasperated. "Listen, I know it was right here. I brought Iris up here a few hours ago, and I kicked the ball right over there."

"Well, it's not here now," Gap said. "Maybe the cat picked it up and carried it somewhere."

"No, I'm telling you she doesn't like it," Channy said. She squatted again and peered under the same set of leaves she had already examined twice. "It has to be here."

Triana peered behind a row of dirt that had been overturned recently, then looked to her right. A small gray metal box with plastic tubes sprouting from one side sat quietly by itself, a bright blue tag attached to it. She dropped to one knee and read the hastily scrawled information on the tag.

"Bon, come take a look at this," she said.

Bon and the others gathered next to Triana, looking down at the water recycling pump. She pointed to the blue tag.

"Correct me if I'm wrong, but this is a record of the pump's service history, right?"

Bon nodded. "With all the trouble they've had recently, we've doubled the inspection schedule. Even though Gap's department worked out the chip problem in them, I still want to keep a pretty close watch." He nodded a quick thanks to Gap, then read the date and time on the tag. "This was about two hours ago."

Triana straightened up. "Well, there you go. One of the farm techs must have come through here, inspected the pump, and seen the ball. It would be so out of place here that they'd be bound to pick it up."

Bon didn't say a word. He immediately took off, back up the path they had just traveled, headed toward his office. Channy looked ready to cry.

"I'm so sorry," she said. "I shouldn't have left it here."

Lita patted her on the shoulder. "C'mon, how could you have known? Besides, the tech might have just taken it to the office. Let's go."

Triana took a stealthy glance at her watch, not wanting the others to think about their deadline.

Twenty-nine minutes.

She quickly caught up with the group as they scurried along the path. By the time they reached Bon's office, they found him on the intercom.

"Well, where is he?" he yelled.

The voice on the speaker was tentative. "He went on dinner break about fifteen minutes ago. He should be back in less than an hour. Do you want me to—"

Bon snapped off the connection and punched in the ship-wide intercom. "Javier Serati. Javier Serati. Emergency. Please connect. Javier Serati."

Channy wrung her fingers, shifting her weight from one foot to the other. Gap looked out the window into Dome 1, running a hand through his hair. Lita stood by the door, her arms folded, staring at the floor. Hannah, her eyes wide, sat down in one of the chairs across from Bon's desk.

Triana walked a few feet out of the office and looked up through the clear dome into the star field above. In twenty-six minutes Titan would come roaring back, and the Cassini would continue its repair project. She wondered if this was her last chance to witness the beauty of the cosmos. She steadied her breathing and felt a sense of calm flow back through her body. Scanning the broad expanse of flickering stars, she slowly smiled and closed her eyes.

She felt the presence next to her before she heard the voice.

"Uh, Tree?" Gap said. She looked into his face and felt an odd sensation.

"I should probably head down to Engineering," he said. "Not that there's anything I can do, I guess, but . . ."

"No, you're right," she said. "We'll need to know that it's working. I mean, when Bon uses the translator, we'll need to know."

Gap just stared at her, shifting his gaze from one of her green eyes to the other. He finally nodded, his voice sounding resigned. "Yeah."

For a split second Triana had a flashback to a moment when they were alone in the Conference Room, months ago, during the crisis that had nearly destroyed them. She had been sure that Gap was on the brink of kissing her then. But now, the look he gave her was different, an almost melancholy air, as if there were still things that he wanted to say to her. His feelings had changed, she realized.

"Hannah's going to come with me," he said softly. "Unless you need her here."

Triana was startled. Through all of the months of their tension, it had never dawned on her that Gap might begin to look elsewhere. She had noticed the smiles and the glances he had shared with Hannah, but had somehow failed to make the connection.

And how did she feel about that? How *should* she feel?

She realized that the silence between them was growing longer and longer. She snapped out of her spell. "Uh, sure. I mean, no, she should go with you. Absolutely."

Why "absolutely?" Now she just sounded flustered. She smiled at Gap and reached out to touch his face. Before she knew what was happening, he leaned in and kissed her on the cheek.

"I'll see you in a little bit," he said with the sound of a final good-bye.

He turned and walked away. Hannah came out of the office, and together they disappeared down the path toward the lift.

35

How much time had passed? She didn't know. It could have been two minutes, it could have been twenty-two minutes, and their countdown might have evaporated. Her feet had taken root, along with the host of plant life scattered around *Galahad*'s Domes, and her mind had refused to process any incoming data, like a satellite dish nudged a degree or two from its signal.

Common sense told her that this was no time for an internal emotional conflict, but at the moment all rational thought was being overridden. And, for the second time since she'd walked out of the Agricultural office, a voice broke through the fog.

"Tree, are you okay?"

She snapped her head to the side and found Lita and Bon looking at her with concern. Before answering Lita, she checked her watch and did the mental arithmetic.

Fifteen minutes.

"Yeah, I'm fine. What's the story?"

"Well, I found Javier," Bon said. "He's the tech who made the service call on that recycling pump."

"And?"

"And he did pick up the ball, or translator, I guess. Anyway, he took it down to the Dining Hall with him, and actually gave it to a group of guys who walked out as he walked in."

Triana sagged. "Oh, no. Any idea—"

"Yes," Lita broke in. "That's what we've been running down for the last few minutes. The translator ended up with Elijah down in Engineering." She offered Triana a much-needed smile. "You'll be very happy to know that he's on his way up here right now with the translator."

Triana exhaled, pushing the air out through pursed lips. She shook her head and put a hand on Lita's shoulder. "We need a vacation."

The comment sank in for a moment before the two girls broke out in a fit of laughter. Another face-to-face appointment with death, the second in four months, had officially caught up with them, and the release felt good. They shook with their laughter while Bon stood by, the faint trace of a smile flickering across his face. For the time being Triana didn't care whether he smiled or not. Something had finally clicked inside, something that seemed to open a door to her feelings. If they survived this latest crisis, she knew that in a fundamental way she would never be the same again, at least emotionally.

If they survived . . .

Out of nervous habit she glanced again at her watch. Thirteen minutes.

Gap felt a curious sense of pride as he walked briskly into the Engineering Section with Hannah. Pride at having a beautiful girl at his side, witnessed by the several crew members on duty at the time, each of whom followed the progression of the couple as they hurried across the room. And pride at escorting Hannah into his domain, the zone inside the ship where he ruled. Whenever Hannah had joined the Council for meetings, Triana had been in charge; here, it was his responsibility, and an odd sense of satisfaction swelled within him. In a way, he realized that it was his chance to show off.

But maybe not for much longer.

That thought had crowded in on him while the two descended in the lift. It figures, he thought, that he would finally make a proactive move with his social life just as the timer ran out. And yet, was it that looming sense of finality that had ultimately pushed him to action? No matter, he decided. Desperate circumstances often brought out the very best in people, or awakened a resolve they never knew they possessed. Why should he be any different?

He also had felt a touch of impatience, for they never had the lift to themselves. Two other crew members had ridden with them as they left the Domes, and then, when those two had exited, another jumped on as the doors began to close. It seemed he was not destined to be alone with Hannah right now.

The atmosphere in the room was charged with a nervous energy that made his skin tingle. A cloak of fear settled over the crew as the clock ticked, and he knew he had to set a positive example. As he approached the power grid near the ion drive, Gap was glad to see his top two assistants, Ramasha and Esteban, already on the scene. "Hey, guys," he said with a smile. They both acknowledged him with a quick wave, their gaze flickering briefly on Hannah before returning to their work. Gap realized he would be the main topic of Gossip Central before the day was out.

Which seemed a fair trade to him; it would mean that at least they were around to gossip about.

"Roll your sleeves up," he said to the assembled crew. "It could start to get a little crazy here pretty soon." Anxious smiles greeted the comment, about the best he had hoped for.

"Roc," he called out. "I've been thinking."

"And I thought it couldn't get any worse," the computer said. Gap heard Hannah stifle a giggle beside him.

"Very funny," he said. "Listen, how long would it take to rewrite the code that controls the ion drive reactor?"

"The entire program?" Roc said. "You're talking about one of the most complicated systems ever developed, you understand."

"Right. How long?"

There was a pause as *Galahad's* computer brain sorted through the data. "I'd say . . . about two days. That's assuming I worked through lunch."

"Okay," Gap said. "So, that's out. What if we adjusted random parts of it?"

"I think I see what you're getting at," Roc said, "but you realize that's like stopping a flood with a paper towel, right?"

Hannah touched Gap's arm. "Could you tell *me* what you're getting at?"

Gap pointed to the power grid. "The Cassini has already done its homework on the ship's power system. It learned everything it could about how the ion drive works. But it had to take a break while it was behind Saturn."

Ramasha was standing to one side and suddenly exclaimed, "Oh, I get it. When it makes contact again, the code will have changed. It will have to relearn the program before it can start adjusting things again."

Hannah looked skeptical. "But . . . but that won't take it very long. Maybe a minute, if we're lucky?"

Gap shrugged. "Hey, right now I think we could use every break we get. If this buys us thirty seconds it might make all the difference in the world."

"Consider it done," Roc said. "I'm starting work on it right now. I might even throw in a bogus line of code here and there to trip it up."

Gap said, "Let me know if there's anything I can do to—"

"Sshhh," the computer hissed. "Quiet. I'm trying to work here."

Triana, Lita, Channy, and Bon waited nervously in Bon's office. As the ten-minute mark came and went, Triana bit her lip and stared out the large window into Dome 1. Lita stepped up and put an arm around her shoulder.

"You know what I miss the most about home?"

Triana looked into her friend's eyes. "No, tell me."

Lita pointed at the crops that gently swayed in the Dome's circulated air. "I look at those rows of food and it makes me really miss my mother's cooking." She gave Triana an amused look. "Not that the food on this ship is bad, but I'd give anything to have one of my mother's tortillas right now."

Triana smiled and leaned her head against Lita's. "My dad used to make us lasagna every Sunday. It was my favorite." Her eyes grew moist, and she blinked them quickly. "He used to tell me that I was going to get sick of it, but I never did." She pulled back and looked at Lita. "I haven't had lasagna once since the day he died."

Lita hugged Triana's shoulder. "Tell you what. When this is over we'll get together and cook. My mother's tortillas, and your dad's lasagna."

"Do we have the stuff on this ship to make those?"

Lita shrugged. "Who cares? We'll improvise. Or we'll combine the two and make lasagna using the tortillas. A Mexican lasagna."

Triana laughed. "It's a deal."

They heard the sound of running and saw two boys dashing down the path toward the office. All four Council members hurried to the door and met the boys as they drew close. Elijah, a popular fifteen-year-old from Poland, was red-faced from running. He stretched out his hand to Triana and dropped a small metal ball into her palm.

"Sorry, we got here as fast as we could," he said, catching his breath.

"Thanks, Elijah," she said. Then, turning to the others, she raised her eyebrows. "Uh . . . now what?"

Lita took the ball from her and examined it. "This has to be it," she said, eyeing the rounded spikes and vents. "It looks relatively new."

Channy said, "It better be it, because as a cat toy it stinks."

"And Bon just . . . what, holds it?" Triana said.

"Well, that's my best guess," Lita said. "Here." She handed the metallic ball to Bon, who shifted it back and forth between his hands.

Triana checked her watch. "Six minutes."

Bon looked up at her. "I don't want to sound stupid, but exactly how is this supposed to work? Am I supposed to think certain thoughts, or try to talk to them, or it, or whatever? I have no idea what I'm doing."

Triana managed a slight smile. "And we don't know any more than you. But if Lita's theory is right, then the Cassini will reconnect with you in just a few minutes and start sifting through your brain again. This little device will hopefully allow you to speak its language."

"Yeah," Channy added, "so start thinking 'stop, stop, stop.' Maybe it will get the message."

How's it coming, Roc?" Gap said.

"I think I've done about all the damage I can right now," the computer answered. "I must say, I feel a bit like a hooligan, just randomly vandalizing the computer program that drives the ship."

"Yeah, you're quite the delinquent. I just hope you remember how to put it back together again later."

"Oh," Roc said, "so I'm supposed to put it back the way it was? You should have told me that."

Gap saw the horrified look that crossed Hannah's face. "Don't listen to him," he whispered to her. "That's just his sense of humor. You have to learn how to filter out about half of what he says." He hoped that it sounded reassuring, but Hannah merely turned her gaze to the power grid and pressed her lips together tightly. Without giving himself a chance to second-guess things, Gap reached out and took her hand.

36

One minute," Lita said.

Channy paced around the office, a trickle of sweat dribbling down her forehead. Bon took another look at the translator, and inhaled a deep breath. He turned to Triana and said, "I want to be outside when I do this." Then, without waiting for a reply, he marched out of the office door, into the lush vegetation of Dome 1.

It didn't surprise Triana. Bon felt the most comfortable here, the most at home. He had grown up immersed in the dirt of his father's farm. After hesitating a moment, she followed him. Lita and Channy exchanged looks, then did the same.

They caught up to the Swede as he stood under the twinkling stars of the dome, his face extended upward, his hands at his sides, and his eyes closed. Triana wanted to speak to him, to say something to allay his fears, to let him know that she was there for him. But he seemed to have fallen into a state of deep meditation, all focus now on the emergency at hand, and she couldn't bring herself to reach out. Instead, she stood to his side, arms crossed, and waited. She wondered if she would know when—

Bon shook with a tremor. His neck stiffened, and a sudden spasm of pain creased his face. The connection with Titan had been restored, almost violently. Apparently the Cassini wasted no time.

A subtle groan slipped from Bon's lips. His head turned to one side, his eyelids clenched tightly, and he ground his teeth. No doubt the intense pain he had suffered earlier was back. Triana felt a hand grasp her arm, and she looked around to find Channy clutching her. Channy's face contorted with a look of sympathy, as if she felt the searing pain that Bon experienced. Tears welled in her eyes, and she peered at Triana with a look that suggested they do something. Triana placed a hand on Channy's and shook her head.

Another spasm racked Bon, and he almost stumbled. This time a small cry escaped from his mouth, and his head jerked back the other direction. Lita knelt in the dirt in front of him, watching his face, and now tears began to track down her cheeks as well.

A third tremor shook him, and Bon sank to his knees, his head still back. But now his eyes popped open, and Lita stifled a shriek. His eyes had begun to glow with an orange tint again, and they stared off into space. His lips trembled.

And then the voices returned. The chaotic jumble of languages spilled from his mouth, louder this time, almost as if they were demanding something. The words flowed out of him in a frenzy of sound, a chorus of terror that sent shivers through Triana. Her impulse to grab his shoulders became even stronger, and she fought the urge with all of the discipline she could muster. She glanced down to his right hand and saw him gripping the translator.

She blinked. A dull red glow leaked from the tiny vents in the side.

Here we go," Gap said, letting go of Hannah's hand and stepping up to the power grid. The lights had suddenly jumped, and an alarm began to sound, echoing through the entire Engineering Section. With a quick gesture he signaled to Ramasha to cut it off.

"I hope your tinkering works," Gap said to Roc's sensor. "I have a funny feeling that we have just really annoyed the Cassini." He scanned the grid, watching the readouts spike, then drop, then peak again.

"Is the power increasing yet?" Hannah said.

"No. But something is going on."

"I don't care how long the Cassini has been around," Roc said. "It has no idea who it's messing with here."

"Go get 'em, Roc," Gap said, forcing a smile.

The voices coming out of Bon's mouth slowed, and his head now tilted forward. The glowing eyes rolled back and forth, seeing nothing, or seeing something that Triana could never imagine. What he must be going through, she thought.

The hand grasping the translator continued to flex, but now there wasn't any doubt that the device had come alive. A flickering red light burned inside, increasing in brightness temporarily before fading back to a dull gleam, then becoming vivid once again. Triana wondered if it tracked an exchange between Bon and the mystical force blanketing Titan. She hoped that was the case. She felt Channy's grip on her arm tighten.

Lita shifted her gaze to Triana. "Should I try to give him a shot for the pain?"

Triana considered the idea, then rejected it. "Right now he needs to have full concentration on this." She gave a sigh of despair. "I know the pain has to be almost more than he can stand, but we can't take a chance right now with any medication. Who knows how it would affect him?"

Lita nodded, then wiped away a tear that had lingered on her face.

The alarm in Engineering sounded again before Ramasha turned it off. Gap watched the power grid light up like a fireworks display, with every gauge dancing back and forth.

"Did you feel that?" Hannah said quietly. "I mean, am I—"

Gap nodded. He had indeed felt a delicate shudder ripple through the ship. He turned to Hannah and murmured, "We'll be okay."

But he wasn't sure himself. The grid told him exactly what he didn't want to see. Power was increasing again. After almost a minute and a half of puzzling through Roc's code scramble, the Cassini had apparently worked things out and resumed its inevitable improvement in *Galahad*'s engines.

And if ten percent was the magic number, Gap had a sinking feeling that the end had arrived.

The grid showed power surging past the seven-percent mark and accelerating.

Just try to get them here," Alexa said into the intercom before snapping it off and sitting down at Lita's desk in Sick House. The connection with Titan had obviously been reestablished, and now desperate calls from around the ship had poured in. The original patients from the first encounter were once again doubled over in pain, and in some cases it appeared to be even more intense. It was enough to keep them from walking on their own to Sick House, leaving frightened friends and roommates to call and ask what they should do. Scattered as they were throughout *Galahad,* it was up to these friends to get them in somehow, even if it meant carrying them.

Alexa had barely had time to breathe when the first patient staggered through the door, supported by a grim-faced friend.

In an instant, the voices pouring from Bon's mouth stopped, as if a power switch had been thrown. His eyes flickered, then clamped shut as another cry erupted from his mouth, this one louder and more agonizing. Still on his knees, he seemed to lose his balance and appeared ready to topple. Triana dropped down beside Bon and grabbed his shoulders, steadying him. She felt tremors running through his muscles, a shudder that seemed to come from deep inside him.

"It's okay," she said softly into his ear. "It's going to be all right." She had no idea if her voice registered with him or not.

How much time had elapsed since Titan had unleashed its power again? She had lost all perception of time. Were *Galahad*'s engines beginning their overload march again? Had Gap or Roc found a way to buy them some time before the inevitable explosion? All of these thoughts fought their way into her mind as she knelt in the dirt, her arms encircling Bon, propping him up, feeling the shivers of pain that coursed through his body. It took a moment for her to realize that she was crying.

Nine percent. Nine point five. Gap watched the meters and once again marveled at the power that the Cassini was able to command at this distance. Yet he himself was, at the moment, completely powerless. I'm just standing here, he thought, watching. Watching and waiting. Waiting for the end.

He felt Hannah's grip on his hand intensify. She looked into his face, her eyes shifting back and forth between his. Strong eyes, he realized. There was fear in there, sure. But strength, too, an inner strength that mesmerized him. The ends of her mouth curled up into a faint smile and, once again acting on impulse, he lowered his face and brushed her lips with a light kiss. When he pulled away, her eyes were closed, and she tilted her head to rest on his shoulder.

Although pretty sure he didn't want to know, he threw a quick glance at the power meter, afraid that the dreaded ten-percent mark had been breached.

The red digits spit out the news: ten point five.

37

Triana recognized that her contact with Bon might somehow do more harm than good, but she knew that on at least one level it was the right thing to do. This was the moment she had searched for, the time for her to step up and give Bon the support he needed. Regardless of her feelings over the past several months, regardless of the hurt and confusion between them . . . he needed her now. With her arms firmly around his chest, she placed her mouth against his ear again. "Please, stop," she said softly. "Thank you for your help, but please stop now. Please stop."

Would this help Bon communicate with the Cassini? Maybe, maybe not.

"Your touch is killing us," she whispered into Bon's ear. "Please, do not help us anymore. Please, stop now."

Her gaze skated down to his lips. The voices were silent, but Bon's lips were definitely moving. No sound came from his mouth, but his lips appeared to be carrying on a spirited conversation.

"We appreciate your help," she said softly, "we are thankful. But we cannot survive if you do not stop. To help us, please stop what you're doing."

Bon's lips continued to flutter, and now his eyelids slipped open a fraction of an inch, emitting the brilliant orange sheen. Triana felt another shudder, and it took a moment to register with her that it wasn't coming from Bon. *Galahad* had trembled.

She heard the sound of sobs behind her, coming from Channy. From the corner of her eye she watched Lita climb to her feet and walk around to comfort their fellow Council member. Was there anyone with a better heart than Lita?

A memory of her dad suddenly burst into her mind, his smiling face, his gentle eyes. There was no sound with the memory; it was a silent montage, a jerky collection of images flipping past one another like a personal slide show. As usual, any recollection of her dad brought a tinge of sadness but a warmth that still permeated her soul. She felt her own muscles around Bon tighten. Her eyes closed again, and she breathed deeply, letting a sense of calm settle within her.

Again, she had no sensation of time. She had drifted away, her arms around Bon, the two of them leaning against each other, supporting each other. The sounds around her had melted away, merging into a blend of background white noise. At some point she finally became aware of a new sensation: a hand resting on one of hers. She slowly opened her eyes, with her head against the side of Bon's, and looked down where her hands were clasped in front of his chest.

It was one of Bon's hands. It took a minute for the image to make sense, for her mind to register that something was different. Then she heard his voice.

"Tree."

Her breath came out in a start. She pulled her head back and leaned to one side. Bon turned to look into her face. His eyes were almost back to their normal ice blue.

"Bon?" she said, a tentative shake in her voice. "Are you okay?"

His head tilted forward, his forehead coming to rest against hers. "Yeah," he said. "I'm okay."

Triana bit her lip. "What . . . what happened?"

"I don't know." He paused, then added, "I think it's over."

The casual way he said it startled her. She let go of him and fell into a sitting position in the dirt, staring up at him. "What? You mean . . . ?"

He shrugged. "Yeah."

Triana shot a look toward Lita and Channy, who were staring, wide-eyed, listening to the exchange. Channy finally broke the silence with a nervous giggle, her eyes gleaming with the residue of tears.

"So . . . that means we're okay?" she said, still holding on to Lita.

Bon said, "I think so."

Lita tilted her head back and laughed. She pulled Channy into a bear hug and let out a whoop of joy. "I can't believe it!"

Triana still sat in the dirt. Her feeling of disbelief lingered, and it was obviously apparent in her expression because Bon shrugged again, as if to say "Don't ask me." It finally dawned on her that there was an important call to make. She scrambled to her feet and sprinted out of the field, scattering plumes of dirt from her shoes.

She rushed into Bon's office and quickly punched the intercom, connecting with Engineering. "Gap," she called out. "Gap!"

The sounds that came back to her brought a wave of relief and joy and caused her to drop into Bon's chair. The screams that cascaded across the levels of *Galahad* could only be sheer happiness. A celebration was under way, and in her mind's eye she could see the hugs, the backslapping, the tears. She leaned back in the chair and brought her hands up to her face, wiping the tension out with a heavy stroke. The cheering was relentless, and she found herself in no hurry to interrupt.

She looked up to see Bon, Lita, and Channy standing across the desk from her, smiles on their faces. Did Bon's smile contain something more?

"Tree," came Gap's voice through the intercom. "I guess I don't have to tell you the news, do I? I'm assuming you can figure it out from—" Another roar blocked the rest of the sentence, and Triana grinned.

"You've told us everything we wanted to know," she yelled back, trying to cut through the noise. "Why don't we . . ." She waited for the cheering to subside, then decided upon an easier way to retrieve information. Smiling, she cut off the intercom and looked at the others. "Oh, let them celebrate. They've been on the front line through most of this." Lita and Channy nodded, smiles stitched across their own faces.

"Roc," Triana said. "I'm pretty sure you can give us the details."

"Do you want the good news or the bad news?" the computer said.

Triana repressed a laugh. "Whichever you prefer, Roc."

"Well, the good news is that the Cassini cut off its repair project after running up our ion drive system to about eleven percent above normal."

"Eleven?" Lita said. "Wow, we shouldn't even be here."

"And that's the bad news," Roc said. "My code rewriting not only bought us the extra time that saved our lives, but it allowed us to exceed all of the plateaus that the experts claimed was possible. That means I'm going to be expected to provide miracle after miracle the rest of this trip, and I just don't know if my poor circuits can keep it up. You're a very demanding group of humans, you know."

Triana chuckled and stood up to embrace Lita and Channy. "I love you both," she murmured in their ears. "Thank you for being here."

Lita's only response was a smile as she squeezed the Council Leader's shoulder. Channy wiped her eyes and exclaimed, "We need a party, and quickly." With that, she turned and trotted out of the office and down the path toward the lift.

Lita looked after her, and then turned to Triana. "You know, I couldn't adore that girl more than I do." With a quick glance at Bon, she added, "Well, I guess I better get back to Sick House. Who knows what Alexa is having to deal with?"

She strolled out of the office, and Triana knew her friend well enough to know that Lita was giving her privacy with Bon.

Triana just didn't know if that was a good thing right now or not. In the past twenty-four hours her emotions had taken a wild ride, and at the moment she couldn't tell what she was feeling. Her instincts, however, told her that Bon had warmed again.

She decided to keep it all business for the moment. "Well, you did it."

"I couldn't have done it without you," he said, taking one step toward her. "Not that I didn't know what to say, but your encouragement back there really helped. I . . . I have to admit I was pretty scared."

"We all were."

"But not all of us were dialed in to the Cassini."

That stopped Triana cold. She had forgotten that Bon not only attempted to communicate with the alien force, but that it had enjoyed total access to his brain, a concept that made her skin crawl.

"I'm sorry," she said. "That must have been . . . pretty frightening."

He shrugged, a gesture that she recognized as one of his primary forms of conversation. It often seemed to mean that he was uncomfortable with the discussion.

"Why don't you go get some rest," she said, placing her hand on his forearm. "We'll all get together later. I think we have a lot to talk about."

He gazed at her green eyes. "Okay," he finally said, and she wondered if he had picked up on her sudden distance.

She squeezed his arm once, then let go before he could say more, and walked past him, out the door.

It was an exit strategy that she realized she had utilized far too often.

38

It had become one of his favorite spots. Gap stood against the window on the lower level, the one just down the corridor from the Spider bay. It was, he had decided, one of the quietest locations on the ship. Rarely would someone trek to the bay that housed the Spiders and the SAT33 pod, and it was slightly out of the way for anyone who wanted to visit the gym or Airboard track.

Just the secluded setting he was looking for. Hannah stood beside him, her eyes skimming across the brilliant star field before her. The scene usually transfixed Gap as well, but now he found that he couldn't take his eyes off Hannah.

What a change, he decided. A week earlier he hadn't been able to think of anything except Triana and Bon. Had his feelings been able to shift so suddenly? Did he really have feelings for this impressive girl from Alaska? And, more important, had his feelings for Triana dissolved completely? Was this a distraction, or was this new infatuation legitimate? And how did one know for sure?

He decided that, for now at least, it didn't matter. He felt a sense of happiness, and that was an emotion that was alien to him just days ago. Who knew where these feelings would lead? But that was the beauty of exploring them, wasn't it? Suddenly, all of the weight that had been resting on his shoulders—and his soul—evaporated. And, he concluded, he deserved to feel good for a while.

Without another thought, he put his arm around Hannah and pulled her close. She leaned her head against his shoulder and slowly laced her fingers through his.

I appreciate your honesty with the crew," Roc said. Triana sat alone at her desk, her journal open before her. The crisis had ended almost six hours earlier, and, although she had tried to sleep, she had tossed and turned until finally she conceded defeat. Sleep was not going to happen for a while.

"If you mean about how close we were to blowing up, there wasn't much choice," she said. "The word would have spread eventually."

"True, but you showed a lot of leadership in letting them know right up front."

"I just hope I wasn't overly dramatic. It almost feels unreal to say that we were seconds away from death."

"But it's a fact," Roc said. "If I'm correct—and I'm always correct, by the way—we were down to our last ten seconds."

Triana slowly shook her head. "It's too much to think about. I don't know how many more close calls we can have before our luck runs out. First the stowaway, now the Cassini. We always seem to skate right along the edge, don't we?"

"It's why I signed up for this job," Roc said. "Of course, it was either this assignment, or take that job measuring variables in water pressure in San Diego's sewer system. Very tough decision, obviously, but I broke down and chose you over San Diego's toilets."

Triana put a feigned expression of gratitude on her face. "Oh, Roc, that's the nicest thing you've ever said to me."

She picked up her pen and glanced at what she had contributed to her journal so far: a recap as the crisis unfolded at the end, along with the final gift that the Cassini had bestowed upon the crew of *Galahad*. That stubborn one percent of power increase held on after all was said and done, pushing the ship along its path that much more quickly. Roc would have to recalculate their course, but that was a challenge he enjoyed.

What had the Cassini left inside the dozen crew members it had linked with? What tweaking had stayed behind in their minds and bodies? Lita had already promised a long, arduous examination, and wouldn't be satisfied until she knew that all was well. Triana knew one crew member who would grumble throughout the testing.

She looked ahead to the upcoming Council meeting. As a leader, she recognized the importance of lessons learned from any conflict. What had they learned from their first contact with another life-form beyond Earth? How would it serve them should they encounter intelligent life among the planetary system at Eos?

In her own mind, the primary lesson had been one of assumption. She, along with all of the other members of the crew, had experienced what could only be described as the default emotion when faced with something new: fear. Their initial reaction to the power beam had been fear that an alien being was attempting to destroy them. But why? And how ashamed should they be that, all along, the Cassini had only been trying to help? In the end, it came down to communication. We should never forget, she resolved, that understanding one another should be the first step. We assumed an enemy. How long would it take that instinct to wash from the human program?

And during their darkest hours, she had been convinced that things always went wrong. Wasn't there a personal lesson in there for her, as well?

She reflected on her description of the final connection between Bon and the Cassini. She hadn't yet received all of the details from him, and so didn't know exactly how the exchange had played out. The Council meeting was scheduled in about an hour, and she would wait to get the story along with the others.

And isn't it ironic that, after desperately wanting to know the contents of his mind for so long, suddenly I'm not so sure. It seems to have taken another life-threatening jolt to shake me from my obsession. I still feel something for Bon. At least I think I do. But now it has become an element of my life, not the overriding fixation that it was for months. Of course, this is happening just as Bon seems to have decided to explore his feelings for me. That figures. Will we ever be on the same page at the same time?

She set down the pen, then quickly picked it back up and added one additional line.

I'm not giving up on us yet.

Triana stood, walked over to her bed, and fell onto it. Rolling onto her back, she threw an arm over her eyes and didn't move for a long time. The sleep that had eluded her began to creep in.

And her final thoughts before drifting away were natural for her.

What adventure awaited them at the mysterious edge of the solar system, the mystifying region known as the Kuiper Belt?

I think a quick recap is in order right now. The ship narrowly averted disaster for the second time in four months, and the Council found a powerful helper in Hannah Ross. That's all good.

The whirlwind of romance has taken a couple of twists and turns that I just can't keep up with anymore, so I'm checking out of that scene for a while. Those crazy kids are just going to have to figure it all out for themselves. Or not.

Here's an interesting thought for you to chew on, however: If the translator truly provided an exchange of thoughts and feelings between Bon and the Cassini, wouldn't the powerful life force on Titan now be aware of the deadly assault on Earth by Bhaktul Disease? And isn't the Cassini all about helping? Hmm. Could that mean something down the road?

Galahad *will soon be streaking out of the solar system. Knifing through the Kuiper Belt should be a fascinating experience, and since it is most likely the birthplace of Comet Bhaktul, I would expect some frayed emotions to rise. Let's just keep our fingers crossed that there's not another entity like the Cassini lingering out there in the cold vacuum of deep space. Or, if there is, couldn't they just ignore us as we shoot by?*

I'll be busy over the next few days reprogramming the ion drive system and doing basic maintenance on the ship. Chores, really. Although I pretty much saved the ship and everyone aboard yesterday—okay, with a little of their help—I still have my chores.

But I think I also need to keep a close watch on the crew. When it comes to getting along with one another, things have been very good. Much too good, if you think about it. How much longer can that last before something—or somebody—pushes the boundaries? Is it fair to expect that 251 teens will all agree on everything all the time?

I would say that's a no. And I expect that The Cassini Code *will be just about the time that things get out of control, with the mystery of the Kuiper Belt as the backdrop.*

Read on, my friend.

Excerpt from

THE GALAHAD ARCHIVES BOOK TWO

Into Deep Space

including

The Cassini Code and *The Dark Zone*

by Dom Testa

Available June 2016 from Tor Teen

The warning siren blared through the halls, running through its customary sequence of three shorts bursts, a five-second delay, then one longer burst, followed by ten heavenly seconds of silence before starting all over again. There could be no doubt that each crew member aboard *Galahad* was aware—painfully aware—that there was a problem.

Gap Lee found it annoying.

He stood, hands on hips and a scowl etched across his face, staring at the digital readout before him. One of his assistants, Ramasha, waited at his side, glancing back and forth between the control panel and Gap.

"Please shut that alarm off again, will you?" he said to her. "Thanks."

Moments later a soft tone sounded from the intercom on the panel, followed by the voice of Lita Marques calling from *Galahad*'s clinic.

"Oh, Gap, darling." He sensed the laughter bubbling behind her words, and chose to ignore her for as long as possible.

"Gap, dear," she said. "We've looked everywhere for gloves and parkas, but just can't seem to turn any up. Know where we could find some?" This time he distinctly heard the pitter of laughter in the background.

"Are you ignoring me, Gap?" Lita said through the intercom. "Listen, it's about sixty-two degrees here in Sick House. If you're trying to give me the cold shoulder, it's too late." There was no hiding the laughs after this, and Gap was sure that it was Lita's assistant, Alexa, carrying most of the load.

"Yes, you're very funny," Gap said, nodding his head. "Listen, if you're finished with the jokes for now I'll get back to work."

This time it was definitely Alexa who called out from the background. "Okay. If it gets any colder we'll just open a window." Lita snickered across the speaker before Alexa continued. "Outside it's only a couple hundred degrees below zero. That might feel pretty good after this."

Gap could tell that the girls weren't finished with their teasing, so he reached over and clicked off the intercom. Then, turning to Ramasha, he found her suppressing her own laughter, the corners of her mouth twitching with the effort. Finally, she spread her hands and said, "Well, you have to admit, it *is* a little funny."

He ignored this and looked back at the control panel. What was wrong with this thing? Even though his better judgment warned him not to, he decided to bring the ship's computer into the discussion.

"Roc, what if we changed out the Balsom clips for the whole level? I know they show on the monitors as undamaged, but what have we got to lose?"

The very humanlike voice replied, "Time, for one thing. Besides, wouldn't you know it, the warranty on Balsom clips expires after only thirty days. Sorry, Gap, but I think you're grasping now. My recommendation stands: shut down the system for the entire level and let it reset."

Gap closed his eyes and sighed. Some days it just didn't pay to be the Head of Engineering on history's most incredible spacecraft. He opened his eyes again when he felt the presence of someone else standing beside him.

It was Triana Martell. At least *Galahad*'s Council Leader seemed relatively serious about the problem. "I don't suppose I need to tell you," she said calmly, "that it's getting a little frosty on Level Six."

"So I've heard," Gap said. "About a hundred times today, at least." He turned back to the panel. "Contrary to what some of your Council members think, I *am* working on it. Trying to, anyway."

Triana smiled. "*My* Council members? I'm just the Council Leader, Gap, not queen. Besides, you're on the team, too, remember?"

Gap muttered something under his breath, which caused Triana's smile to widen. She reached out and placed a hand on his shoulder. "You'll figure it out. Has Roc been any help?"

Her subtle touch was enough to jar him from his bleak mood. He felt the ghost of his old emotions flicker briefly, especially when their gazes met, his dark eyes connecting with her dazzling green. A year's worth of emotional turbulence replayed in his mind, from his early infatuation with Triana, to the heartache of discovering she had feelings for someone else, to his unexpected relationship with Hannah Ross.

Even now, months later, he had to admit that contact with Triana still caused old feelings to stir, feelings that seemed reluctant to disappear completely. Maybe they never would.

"Well?" Triana said. He realized that he had responded to her question with a blank stare.

"Oh. Uh, no. Well, yes and no."

Triana removed her hand from his shoulder and crossed her arms, a look Gap recognized as "please explain." He internally shook off the cobwebs and turned back to the panel.

"I'm thinking it might be the Balsom clips for Level Six. That would explain the on-again, off-again heating problems."

"But?"

"But Roc disagrees. He says he has run tests on every clip on Level Six, and they check out fine. He wants to shut down the system and restart."

Triana looked at the panel, then back to Gap. "And you don't want to try that?"

Gap shrugged. "I'm just a little nervous about shutting down the heating system for the whole ship when a section has been giving us problems. What happens if the malfunction spreads to the entire system?"

"Well, we would freeze to death, for one thing," Triana said.

"Yeah. So, maybe I'm being a little overly cautious, but I'd like to try everything else before we resort to that."

The intercom tone sounded softly, and then the unmistakable voice of Channy Oakland, another *Galahad* Council member, broke through the speaker. "Hey, Gap, did you know it's snowing up here on Level Six?"

Triana barely suppressed a laugh while Gap snapped off the intercom.

"I'll quit bothering you," she said, turning to leave. Over her shoulder she called out, "Check back in with me in about an hour. I'll be ice-skating in the Conference Room."

"Very funny," Gap said as she walked out the door. He looked over at Ramasha, who had remained silently standing a few feet away. A cautious grin was stitched across her face. "What are you laughing at?" he said with a scowl.

They were only chunks of ice and rock. But there were trillions of them, and they tumbled blindly through the outermost regions of the solar system, circling a sun that appeared only as one of the brighter stars, lost among the dazzling backdrop of the Milky Way. Named after the astronomer who had first predicted its existence, the Kuiper Belt was a virtual ring of debris, a minefield of rubble ranging from the size of grains of sand up to moon-sized behemoths, orbiting at a mind-numbing distance beyond even the gas giants of Jupiter, Saturn, Uranus, and Neptune.

Arguments had raged for decades over whether lonely Pluto should be considered a planet or a hefty member of the Kuiper Belt. And once larger Kuiper objects were detected and cataloged, similar debates began all over again. One thing, however, remained certain: The Kuiper Belt posed a challenge for the ship called *Galahad*.

Maneuvering through a region barely understood and woefully mapped, the shopping mall–sized spacecraft would be playing a game of dodgeball in the stream of galactic junk. Mission organizers could only manage a guess at how long it would take for the ship to scamper through the maze. Taking into account the blazing speed that *Galahad* now possessed—including a slight nudge from an unexpected encounter around Saturn—Roc told Triana to be on high alert for about sixty days.

Now, as they rocketed toward the initial fragments of the Kuiper Belt, both Roc and the ship's Council were consumed with solving the heating malfunction aboard the ship, unaware of the dark, mountainous boulders that were camouflaged against the jet-black background of space.

Boulders that were on a collision course with *Galahad*.

Tor Teen
Reader's Guide

About This Guide

The information, activities, and discussion questions that follow are intended to enhance your reading of *The Web of Titan*. Please feel free to adapt these materials to suit your needs and interests.

Writing and Research Activities

I. Into the Great Unknown

A. What does the word "unknown" mean to you? Write a definition, article, poem, or story or create a painting, model, or other visual artwork depicting your sense of the unknown. Go to the library or go online to find several definitions of "unknown" and related words, such as "uncertainty" and "knowledge." Compile your creative works and research into a collage or diorama presentation. If desired, make an illustrated list of famous quotations about the unknown.

B. As a *Galahad* crew member, you have mixed feelings about capturing the Titan pod. Write an e-mail to Triana citing your reasons for or against capturing the pod and what you suspect it may hold. Or, with classmates or friends, role-play a conversation in which you and other crew members discuss your uncertainties and questions regarding the pod's capture and possible contents.

C. After four months aboard *Galahad,* you have begun to have some routine in your life. Write at least three journal entries describing your daily activities, high points, challenges, your thoughts as you anticipate four-plus more years aboard the ship, and your deepest concerns about your unknown future. As you write your journal entries, consider whether having a routine makes dealing with the great unknowns in your life harder or easier.

D. In the character of Lita, write a series of medical reports describing the headache ailment of the crew, your treatment choices, and your reaction to Bon's strange eyes and speech. As a medical professional, what do you make of this unknown "disease"?

E. On January 29, 1984, the following quotation from the late Librarian of Congress, author and scholar Daniel J. Boorstin, appeared in *The Washington Post*: "The greatest obstacle to discovery is not ignorance—it is the illusion of knowledge." Write a short essay explaining how this quote applies to Triana's reflections at the end of the novel, and to the greater ambitions of the *Galahad* project.

II. A Moon Called Titan

A. Go to the library or go online to learn more about Saturn and its moons, particularly Titan. Use your research to create an informative poster, including details on why Titan might be capable of supporting some type of extraterrestrial life.

B. Visit http://www.nasa.gov/mission_pages/cassini/main/index.html to learn more about the real Cassini-Huygens Mission to Saturn. Make a list of at least five important facts confirmed, or discoveries made, during this mission.

Write an article for your school newspaper describing the Cassini-Huygens Mission and explaining why it is exciting and important. With friends or classmates, discuss the connections between your research facts and the plot and themes explored in *The Web of Titan*.

C. Learn more about the Titans of Greek mythology and their relationship to the Olympians, particularly the Twelve Olympians, during the War of the Titans. Write a short essay detailing your discoveries and relating them to your understanding of the novel. Conclude the essay with your thoughts on how the story of the Greek Titans might offer hints or insights into the events of the next installment of the *Galahad* story, *The Cassini Code*.

III. Reason and Romance

A. Can a computer feel? Go to the library or go online to learn more about cutting-edge research on artificial intelligence. Use your research to create an informative poster or pamphlet addressing this question. Include a short paragraph describing your understanding of Roc's "relationship" with the leaders of *Galahad*.

B. Had it not been for her relationship with Kelvin Pernice, Nina Volkov might have made it aboard the Titan pod, possibly dramatically changing the fate of *Galahad*. Write a prologue chapter to *The Web of Titan* in which you imagine the relationship between Nina and Kelvin and give more detailed reasons for her missing the pod launch.

C. With a friend or a classmate, role-play a conversation in which Gap decides to seek Channy's advice about his feelings for Hannah, Ariel, and Triana. Invite other pairs of friends or classmates to role-play the same situation. Afterward, compare and contrast the outcomes of each role-play.

D. Lita's song describes her complicated feelings about being a part of the *Galahad* mission. Think of a time when you had to make a choice or sacrifice in your life, considering what your "logical mind" felt was right versus what your heart told you. Write song lyrics describing the situation. If desired, compose music to accompany your lyrics or set them to the melody of a favorite song.

E. The *Galahad* crew begins to get a sense of the Cassini as a being with some sort of collective intelligence. In the character of the Cassini, describe yourself and your thoughts about *Galahad,* its crew, and your efforts to "improve" them.

F. Using colored pencils, modeling clay, or other craft materials, create an illustration or model of the Cassini. Compare your creation with the works of friends or classmates. What colors, shapes, or other elements are common to some or all of the Cassini representations? Which representations are most unique and most satisfying?

G. In the character of Bon, write an extended journal entry describing the connection/relationship you had with the Cassini. What made it painful? Was there anything good about it? Why do you think your connection with the Cassini was the strongest among the *Galahad* crew? Do you hope or fear future connections? How has your connection to the Cassini affected your relationships with members of the *Galahad* crew?

Questions for Discussion

1. In the prologue to *The Web of Titan,* Roc cites "fear of the unknown" as a critical human trait. Describe the ways in which this fear plays out on different levels in the course of the novel. How does Roc provide a bridge between the unknown and the

known for both the *Galahad* crew and the reader? What makes a computer the ideal character for this role in the story?

2. The opening paragraphs of chapter one describe a storm around Saturn and Titan. How does this visual description foreshadow the actual troubles that befall the crew and the discoveries they will make about Saturn's largest moon?

3. What relationship troubles in the novel's early chapters threaten to distract the crew from the critical job of capturing the pod? How does Gap respond to the attention he receives from Ariel and Hannah? Why does he react this way? Does his injured arm have any effect on his actions and choices? Explain.

4. How might you explain Triana's attraction to Bon? Is she ready for a real relationship, or is grief at the loss of her father still too powerful an emotion to make this possible? How has the death of Dr. Zimmer also affected Triana's emotional state?

5. Who discovers the beam focused on *Galahad*? What do the Council members make of this discovery? How does Roc help them deal with this challenge?

6. What do the crew members find aboard the pod? What, or who, is suspiciously absent from the vessel? Had you been aboard *Galahad*, what actions might you have suggested Triana take after opening the pod?

7. In chapter ten, Hannah begins to suspect that another life force is responsible for the energy beam. How does she react to this possibility? How do the other crew members react?

8. Throughout the novel, various crew members experience flashbacks and memories of loved ones on Earth. Are these

experiences helpful or hurtful? How have four months in space begun to alter the teens' thoughts about the past and the future?

9. What, if any, relationships do you see between Lita's frustration with the headache patients in Sick House and Gap's difficulties with the ion drive power plants? How does their sense of powerlessness affect their actions and decisions? Compare the concerns for the well-being of the sick crew members to those for the safe operation of the ship.

10. What is important about Lita's friendship with Triana? In what ways do they support each other? Do you enjoy a friendship with anyone similar to that of Lita and Triana? Or do you think the pressure of the *Galahad* mission makes their friendship different from friendships in your life? Explain your answer.

11. In the beginning of chapter twenty-eight, Triana contemplates the evolution of life on Earth from dinosaurs to Homo sapiens. Do you agree with her that another life-form will succeed humans in an unbreakable cycle? Or are humans smart enough to find a way to carry on?

12. What is Lita's reaction to the headache patients' orange eyes and Bon's strange speech? Had you been a Council member aboard *Galahad,* do you think your reaction would have been similar or different? Would you have left Bon in Sick House or moved him to some sort of containment cell? Would you have tried more aggressive treatment for the headaches?

13. How does the crew finally learn about and find the translator? How does Bon make use of the device? Do you think he could have controlled it without Triana's support? Is Bon done with the Cassini now? What evidence suggests that the alien life-form's presence remains entangled with *Galahad*?

14. Do you think that *Galahad,* having endured the attack of a madman in *The Comet's Curse* and the encounter with the Cassini in *The Web of Titan*, stands a chance at completing its mission? Should the crew consider a return to Earth? Do they really have any choice but to continue? If you were aboard *Galahad,* what would be your hopes for the future at this point?

15. At the end of the novel, Triana writes in her journal, "After desperately wanting to know the contents of [Bon's] mind for so long, suddenly I'm not so sure." Do the Cassini know the contents of Bon's mind? How might this mind link compare to or contrast with the connection Triana wants, or wanted, to make? Can *The Web of Titan* be read as an exploration of connections, intellectual and emotional, and their risks and rewards? Explain your answer.

About the Author

Dom Testa is an author, speaker, and the top-rated morning radio show host in Denver, Colorado. His nonprofit foundation, The Big Brain Club, empowers students to take charge of their education. Visit him online at DomTesta.com.